BLOOD
DEBT

BLOOD DEBT

TOM WOOD

SPHERE

SPHERE

First published in Great Britain in 2023 by Sphere

1 3 5 7 9 10 8 6 4 2

A CIP catalogue record for this book
is available from the British Library.

Hardback ISBN 978-0-7515-8486-8
Trade Paperback ISBN 978-0-7515-8487-5

Typeset in Sabon by M Rules
Printed and bound in Great Britain by
Clays Ltd, Elcograf S.p.A.

Papers used by Sphere are from well-managed forests
and other responsible sources.

MIX
Supporting
responsible forestry
FSC® C104740

For Andrei & Ema

ONE

Victor tried not to cause excessive damage. In part because he never liked making a mess. In part because killing someone was impolite enough without leaving their body in an untoward manner.

Sometimes this could not be avoided.

Fahim Akram lay as an island in a lake of blood. Maybe eighty per cent of the body's total volume had exited through the gaping wound to the neck that had severed both carotids, both jugulars and multiple smaller vessels. First, as a powerful spray that had coloured the sandstone walls of the chamber. Then, as blood pressure dropped rapidly and Akram fell to his knees, it had spread in an almost perfect circle around him, soaking into the dusty floor and expanding evenly through capillary action until the last neurons had finished firing inside his brain. As the corpse tipped over into the lake, the perfect circle was broken and the blood that Victor had been so careful to avoid splashed up onto his khaki trousers.

Such incidents were one of the primary reasons a knife

had never been his first choice of weapon. The most effective, efficient wounds were rarely neat, and to deliver those wounds required the kind of close proximity to the target that exponentially increased the chance the inevitable mess would not limit itself to the victim. Given the exactitude of forensic science, which was improving all the time, the odds of walking away from such a killing without carrying, or leaving behind, evidence was negligible.

Plus, why ruin good clothes in the process?

Hence firearms had been his preferred means of execution since the beginning of his career – almost two decades now, if Victor included his military service. Which he did, because, after all, the only notable difference between what he did now and what he did then was as a soldier he had received a regular monthly pay cheque. It had been all the money in the world to him and yet a month's cheque back then would not cover a day's expenses now.

Such as the knife, which had a black, high-carbon steel blade for increased hardness of the edge, meaning increased sharpness and cleaner cuts. That hardness resulted in inevitable brittleness, so it was a single-edged blade only. Which meant the false edge could be thicker for improved strength and rigidity. Because of that thicker false edge, the blade had a significant distal taper to narrow the blade as it reached its point. A fine weapon overall. Excellent at both cutting and thrusting.

Victor's target would not disagree.

Given that Akram had armed guards nearby, a noiseless kill was sensible. As Victor had been unable to procure an appropriate suppressed weapon in Kabul, a knife had to do instead.

There was a certain irony to this given the Afghan had been an arms dealer and Victor was here in his compound on behalf of another arms dealer. An irony made more pronounced by the fact Akram had just secured several crates of US-made suppressors as part of his latest major deal. A deal that was also the reason for his assassination.

Victor listened to the trickle of blood now leaking from the corpse by way of gravity alone. Outside the small building that served as a storeroom for the crates of suppressors, the compound was quiet at this hour as the sun dipped low towards the horizon. During the rest of the day it had been busy with activity. Which, of course, was why Victor had timed his visit for when the compound would be as empty as possible. From dawn to dusk there were numerous employees stripping down incoming merchandise and repackaging it for future sales. Akram had been keen to show off the impressive range of suppressors to the buyer Victor had played.

With the US withdrawing from Afghanistan, a considerable amount of arms and equipment was being left behind in abandoned bases and outposts. Some disabled, although not all irreparable for enterprising engineers. Not only were these arms abandoned by withdrawing forces, but large amounts of additional arms were also sent into the country at the same time to bolster the Afghan military who would be left on their own. Much of this brand-new weaponry, vehicles and ammunition in the hands of the Afghan forces was being handed over to the Taliban as part of ceasefire negotiations between the two sides. The remainder was up for sale.

Such diversion of American arms created a gold rush for dealers in the region. Everything from infantry rifles to Black

Hawk helicopters had entered the market. Victor's target was part of a cartel of local arms dealers rapidly establishing themselves as major players procuring the surplus munitions and selling them on to buyers across the Middle East.

Which was the kind of competition Vladimir Kasakov could do without. This local cartel had done such a good job collecting up American weapon systems the Ukrainian was impressed with the speed of their arrival onto the global arms black market and the initiative they had used to usurp more established players. Sadly for the cartel, an impressive competitor was one that could not be left alive.

And though Kasakov was not Victor's client, Maxim Borisyuk was providing the prolific arms merchant with a Victor-shaped favour.

He used the dead Afghan's satellite phone to make a call.

When the line connected, Borisyuk said, 'The job is off.'

'The second part of the contract has already been fulfilled. Only one remaining.'

'When?'

Victor made a quick calculation. 'Twenty-six, twenty-seven seconds since his heart stopped. Brain death is going to take a little longer, so perhaps I should have said the second part of the contract will be fulfilled imminently.'

Borisyuk responded with, 'Get out. Get out now. I have a plane waiting to take you to Turkey the moment you can get to the airport.'

'Then you're taking an unnecessary risk given NATO assets are cataloguing all incoming and outgoing aircraft.'

'I know and I don't care,' the Russian stated. 'Our man on the ground sold you out to the cartel. They know who you are.'

He did not mean it in a literal sense because not even Borisyuk *knew* Victor, but Victor understood the point: the arms cartel knew he was not the buyer he had been making out to be in order to get time alone with Fahim Akram.

'They'll be coming,' Borisyuk urged.

Listening to the roar of approaching vehicles, Victor said, 'They're already here.'

TWO

The compound consisted of several squat buildings surrounded by a stone wall clad in the pale pink of a desert sunset. Victor imagined it had belonged to a wealthy silk merchant or such in another life. Maybe the home of an extended family, affluent and cosmopolitan. Such times were now but a memory. And though the main building was still used as a home, the other buildings inside the wall were the storerooms, workshops and offices of a successful arms dealer.

Previously successful, at least.

Not only had Fahim Akram been part of an arms dealing cartel that had been snapping up all the leftover US weaponry, he had been the number one guy in the cartel hierarchy. Victor had already killed the cartel's number three guy during the previous week, the assassination looking like an accidental but fatal fall down the stairs – a professional first for Victor – that had left Fahim Akram and his number two, Najid Maqsoodi, with considerably more wealth and power as they inherited the leftover stake in the cartel. More importantly, the fall meant they did not change their routines or increase their security. They had not known a killer was hunting them down one by one.

With Fahim Akram dead at Victor's feet, the incoming vehicles had to be Najid Maqsoodi and his entourage.

Our guy on the ground sold you out.

That particular guy had been on the payroll of the Bratva, hired to provide Victor with the intelligence he needed to do his job in unfamiliar territory. Victor operated under the assumption everyone betrayed, so this was no huge surprise. The timing of that betrayal, however, was far from ideal.

Easing open the storeroom's only door a little, he peered through the slim gap to see two Toyota Land Cruisers stopping in the dusty courtyard between the buildings. With their windows down, the armed men inside were plain to see.

They spanned a range of ethnicities, although Maqsoodi was the only Afghan. He was either cautious of external threats or paranoid his cartel partners would turn on him because he liked to surround himself with foreign mercenaries. Such hired guns were the reason Victor had been leaving Maqsoodi for last.

Competence varied massively among private military contractors: from truck drivers who liked guns a little too much, to former special operators who had lost none of their finely honed skills. Exiting the vehicles ahead of Maqsoodi, they bristled with tactical gear and weaponry. Sweat darkened their T-shirts and glistened on their faces. Counting six, Victor noted each one wore the wraparound sunglasses that seemed so prevalent among such mercenaries he wondered if they were a stipulation of their contracts.

7

Najid Maqsoodi climbed out of the second vehicle to stop. He was a tall, slim man of about forty. Like his mercenaries, he was well armed: a pistol in a thigh holster and an expensive rifle held in one hand. He conferred with his contractors. They were alert and yet were not immediately primed for battle. Some held their weapons but others had them on slings down their flanks or strapped over one shoulder. Which meant they didn't know Victor was already here. The Bratva contact had supplied him with information only. He could not know when Victor had planned to make his move.

It didn't seem as though Maqsoodi had spoken with the two guards at the gate who had obediently let the vehicles through unchallenged. Without the Russian mafia's local asset accompanying Maqsoodi, he had no way to identify Victor on sight alone. He was no Afghan, sure, but neither were the contractors and neither were the many foreign nationals in the country in an effort to exploit the instability in one way or another.

Had it been in the middle of the day, with the compound full of employees working hard, Victor might have been able to simply walk out without being stopped. Now, there was no escape, with the only exit blocked by an arms dealer, six contractors and two guards, all armed.

The storeroom had plenty of crates but all were full of suppressors or other munitions. He might be able to avoid a casual sweep of the room by staying low and out of sight if not for the corpse of Fahim Akram lying on the floor in huge pool of his own blood.

Victor had managed to sneak his pistol along with his fighting knife past the compound's two guards, but neither weapon was going to be much help if this went loud.

Technically, he had enough bullets to kill every guy in the courtyard plus the two guards at the gate. Given the two vehicles providing easily accessible cover, there was no way of doing so, however, without receiving fire in return. There were too many of them, even if they had never opened fire on anything other than paper targets. They all had rifles and sidearms, and plenty of spare magazines. Some had knives. A few had grenades.

The building from which Akram had shown off his new wares to Victor was no kind of bunker. The only door was cracked wood incapable of withstanding a solid kick, let alone bullets. If he remained inside to fight this, he would only live as long as it took one of the contractors to realise they could drop one of those grenades through the gap in the wall that served as both window and air vent – far too small to climb through, otherwise Victor would already be halfway out by now.

He couldn't walk out, he couldn't hide and he wasn't going to fight his way out of this, that was clear. Not against nine in a firefight stacked in their favour.

He drew his gun from the back of his waistband and reached up a hand to position the pistol on the top bar of the thick doorframe. The FN Five-seveN was only just slim enough to balance against the wall without falling. Victor placed his second magazine with it.

The knife . . . he didn't relish giving it up too, but it wasn't going to do him much good if things went bad, and it was hard to present a non-threatening persona with such a killing weapon on one's person. It was too hard to balance alongside the gun and the magazine, so he jabbed the tip into the frame itself and left it protruding from the wood.

With that, he pushed open the door and stepped out into the courtyard.

If he couldn't run or hide or fight, perhaps he could talk his way out instead.

THREE

Heads turned and eyes behind sunglasses swivelled his way. Victor maintained a relaxed, confident manner, telling himself he belonged here as he met those gazes, searching for signs of recognition in the faces of the contractors and finding none. So far, so good.

Najid Maqsoodi had swept-back hair, dark brown and shimmering with pomade or wax. His beard was dense and jutted out from just below his cheekbones all the way to his Adam's apple. He was last to turn Victor's way, and when he did, there was undisguised suspicion in his eyes.

With no way to counter that suspicion, Victor met it head on.

Passing the six heavily armed contractors with guns, he approached Maqsoodi and presented his best, most welcoming smile as he went to extend his hand.

'I'm Boulanger,' he said, 'an associate of Fahim Akram.'

'*Whoawhoawhoa*,' one of the mercenaries barked, rushing to intercept him before he could reach Najid Maqsoodi. 'Hold your horses, squire.'

A Brit. A big guy, at least one hundred kilos. Face red in the heat and bright-sun crinkles around his eyes. On wide, dense shoulders, his head seemed small and round. Hair buzzed down to millimetres meant the redness of his skin was as visible across his scalp as it was on his face and neck. His long-sleeved tee was stretched taut across both a massive back and the bulges at his waist where projecting love handles spilled over his tactical belt.

He gestured to Victor's hands.

'Keep them where I can see them.'

'As you wish.'

The Brit performed a quick pat down around Victor's torso, under his arms, and down the front and back of both legs.

To Najid Maqsoodi, the contractor said, 'He's clean.'

Victor nodded. 'I've had two showers already today.'

The Brit was not amused. Maqsoodi showed a hint of a smile.

'Where is Fahim?' he asked in a polite, almost regal, voice.

Victor knew that his eloquence reflected his time at English boarding schools and tenure in the German aviation industry before the return home to put his business skills to use in a wholly different field. He had sharp, angular features, made more pronounced by a low body fat percentage. His eyes were bright and energetic. His teeth white and even.

Victor gestured to the main building of the compound. 'He's taking a nap. Perhaps I can help instead?'

'No, you cannot. This requires his immediate attention.' He gestured to the Brit. 'Go and wake him up. Tell him I'm here.'

Victor raised a palm to the Brit, 'He will be most cross if anyone interrupts his sleep.'

Fixing him with a stare of pure ice, Najid Maqsoodi said, 'And yet he will not be as cross as I will be with you if you attempt to hinder me.'

The two guards at the gate were not paying attention to the interaction and were too far away to overhear while they chatted to one another. Had Maqsoodi elected to question either then Victor's ruse would be over. Which was why he stood with his back to the house so the two guards were out of sight behind Maqsoodi in return.

'I work for Mister Akram, not you,' Victor said. 'And he, not you, is in charge of this operation.'

A risk to pull rank, sure, but a calculated one. Victor was already in a position of weakness without a weapon and facing multiple heavily armed gunmen. The last thing he wanted was for Najid Maqsoodi to see him as weak.

The Afghan controlled his annoyance and said, 'Fine, you will go and ... very, *very* gently wake Fahim from his nap. And then politely inform him that I wish to discuss a threat to us both that requires his immediate attention.'

'As you wish.'

'I do,' he said. 'I most certainly do wish.'

Victor nodded to show a little capitulation, to soothe Maqsoodi's bruised ego, which turned out to be a mistake because by declining his head he broke eye contact with the man. When Victor inclined his head back he saw Maqsoodi's gaze had become exploratory, passing over him from head to toe to get a better understanding of the man with whom he was talking. Victor realised his error a second before he was asked:

'Why is there blood on your trousers?'

The Brit, who had grown bored during the exchange, eyes drifting anywhere else, snapped back to attention.

'Why is there blood on your trousers?' Najid Maqsoodi asked again.

Victor looked down as if seeing the blood for the first time. 'Ah, that's annoying.' He made a self-deprecating sigh. 'Should have been more careful when I slaughtered that goat earlier.'

Maqsoodi looked at the Brit, who looked at him in return. A short, silent exchange during which Victor ran through the odds of disarming the contractor of his weapon, shooting him and then shooting the others before any of them could react.

Not impossible ... but as close to zero chance as any plan could realistically be right now.

'We're not taking chances.' The Brit reached for cable ties bunched on his webbing. 'Hold still.'

The odds of successfully disarming the contractor while cuffed with cable ties were even closer to zero than the previous plan, but now Najid Maqsoodi and the six contractors were looking at him like he might be a threat Victor had no plan at all.

'What is this?' he asked, feigning ignorance and apprehension as a confused, scared civilian would.

'You will need to humour me,' Maqsoodi said. 'We have concerns about security at the moment and you are a face I do not know. As soon as your master confirms you are who you say you are you shall be released.'

Victor allowed the Brit to loop the plastic cable around his wrists, resisting the impulse to headbutt the man now they were close, to go for his weapons while he was dazed, to shoot and keep shooting before a returning round struck his heart or brain.

'Don't take it personally, chief,' the Brit said in a quiet voice as he tightened the plastic straps until Victor's wrists were pressed together. 'Tensions are high right now.'

The cable ties were black plastic instead of clear or white, but otherwise were the typical kind used in securing goods and packages all over the world. Not easy to escape from, although far from difficult as there weren't many forms of restraint Victor had failed to escape. He knew that when met with enough force the locking mechanism of cable ties could be popped open. The problem was escaping from them without anyone shooting him before he had finished the process.

They held his wrists together in a tight, vice-like grip, so each palm faced the other. Different people tied them in different ways, he had found over his career. Some preferred one wrist crossed over the other. Some secured the hands behind the back. This guy had Victor's hands in front of him.

Maqsoodi said, 'You don't need hands to wake up Fahim, do you?'

He expected no answer and Victor provided none.

'Know that if you have done nothing wrong then there is nothing for you to fear. However,' Najid Maqsoodi said with an expanding smile, 'if you have lied to me in even the tiniest of ways I shall take great delight in peeling away your skin, centimetre by centimetre.'

FOUR

'Go with him,' Najid Maqsoodi said to the British contractor. 'Be quick.'

As they approached the main building, the contractor muttered under his breath in a mocking tone, '*Yes sir, thank you, sir ... whatever you say, sir.*'

Victor led the Brit through the arched entranceway into the cool air of the house. On the other side of the front door, a large hall had been converted into a makeshift workshop. There were benches and tooling for modifying weaponry. The floor was littered with metal shavings and offcuts.

The contractor muttered something else that Victor failed to catch, although he watched as the man looked over his shoulder and extended his middle finger back the way they had come, in his employer's direction.

Maqsoodi would not be able to see, which Victor guessed was the point. The contractor seemed to take a great deal of pride in the gesture, keeping the finger raised for several seconds.

He noticed Victor looking his way. 'It's all good, chief. He's a prize prick to work for.' He sucked in air between his teeth. 'You know how it is as a foreigner here in Afghan. They think we're scum. But beggars and choosers, eh?'

Victor knew the layout of the compound from his preparatory work as well as his initial conversation with Fahim Akram, although it was obvious from the curving staircase leading up that any bedroom would be on the first floor. The Brit headed straight for the stairs, ushering Victor in an effort to get the menial task finished as fast as possible.

'Mister Akram does not allow any visitors upstairs,' Victor told him.

'Like I give a shit?'

'He tolerates no bad language.'

'Eh?'

'And I agree. There's really never a need to swear. When there are so many beautiful words in the English language, why resort to using the ugliest of them?'

'Either this is a wind-up, or you have a seriously screwed up sense of priorities given the line of work you're in.'

'You have no idea.'

The contractor said, 'People who swear are cleverer than those who don't.' He sounded sure of himself. 'I read it once.'

'Where did you read that?'

'I can't remember where but it doesn't—'

'What methodology did the scientists use?' Victor asked as they headed up the stairs. 'I take it this was a double-blind study with stringent controls?'

'Yeah.' The man smirked. 'N=1, *dipshit*.'

'I'm not sure that means what you think it means.'

'Keep trying my patience, chief. Please, *please*, keep testing me. See what happens.'

Victor remained silent.

'Good boy,' he said as they reached the top of the staircase. He paused to look at the long landing and the many doors leading off from it. 'How the other half live, eh? Which way to his bedroom?'

'This way,' Victor said. 'And if the choice is between blasphemy and swearing, I'd prefer you swore.'

The man responded by giving Victor the finger, then added, 'Swivel on this, yeah?'

'Putting vulgarity to one side,' Victor began, 'I can't help but feel it's a shame the English seem to have abandoned tradition so quickly when it comes to swearing.'

'You what, mate?'

'The bird,' Victor answered. 'That finger of yours.'

'What about it exactly?' He rose it higher in emphasis.

'It's an Americanism, a bastardisation of the English V-sign. An insulting gesture that goes back centuries to the Hundred Years' War,' Victor explained. 'Most commonly attributed to Agincourt but probably goes back to Crécy.'

'You're just making up words now.'

'They're famous battles between the English and the French in the Middle Ages, the Battle of Agincourt being the second, most well-known, of the two. It's the backdrop to Shakespeare's *Henry V*.'

'I don't know about any battles but I always hated Shakespeare at school.'

'I'd agree that asking children to appreciate the Bard is counterproductive to the extreme, although he's really worth revisiting as an adult. I'm not exactly – *moved* – by much

18

in this world, shall we say. The Saint Crispin's Day speech, however. Goosebumps.'

Deep grooves of confusion had appeared between the man's thick eyebrows. 'I'm completely lost.'

'That's my fault,' Victor admitted. 'I veered off on a tangent. Anyway, before the battle began in earnest at Agincourt the French crossbowmen taunted the English longbowmen, promising to cut off their index and middle fingers, the fingers that are used to draw back an arrow nocked in the bowstring. You see, the English bowmen were as renowned as they were feared. A good proportion of them would have been Welsh, but I'm trying not to veer off on another tangent. Most of the continent used the crossbow since it was simple to use effectively, whereas the longbow – more correctly known as a war bow – took years of constant practice to develop the strength to shoot. The pay-off to all that training, however, was a weapon that could send many arrows at the enemy in the same time it took the crossbow to reload a single bolt.'

'I think I'm more lost now than when you started.'

'The English won the battle,' Victor said as they reached the end of the landing and the door to the master bedroom. 'By some margin. And in response to the pre-battle taunts of the French crossbowmen, the English archers raised their index and middle fingers in a V-sign to mock their fleeing enemies. This way,' he said, opening up the door.

It was a huge, impressive room with an ornate four-poster bed on a raised dais. Persian rugs covered the floors. Tapestries and animal pelts hung from the walls.

'Where is he?' the contractor asked, following Victor inside and looking at the bed.

'Must be in the bathroom,' Victor answered, gesturing with his chin to the closed door leading to the en-suite bathroom at the far end of the bedroom. 'I think the goat disagreed with him.'

The contractor shrugged. He didn't care.

Victor said, 'Going back to what we were saying before, I find it quite sad that now, after so many years of tradition, the English more commonly use the Americanised version, the single finger, instead.'

'So what about history? Who gives a damn about what happened thousands of years ago.'

'Hundreds of years ago,' Victor corrected.

'I don't care if it was five years ago. This is cooler.' He raised the middle finger in Victor's face. 'See?'

'I disagree.' He glanced down at his cuffed hands, inner wrists almost touching and hands unable to rotate, and tried to form a V-sign with the fingers of his right hand. 'Unfortunately, my current predicament is preventing me from illustrating the point.'

The contractor removed his wraparound sunglasses and hooked them on the collar of his T-shirt. 'Either this is a wind-up or you are in fact an utter psychopath.'

'That's an overused label,' Victor said. 'And you're way off, I'm afraid. I absolutely can't be a psychopath because I get terribly sad if I ever think about the lion cub's father killed in that stampede.'

'Anyway, you don't need to show me how to flick the Vs,' his captor said, shaking his head in equal parts amusement and frustration. 'I know what it looks like.' He glanced towards the bathroom door, now impatient. 'How long does it take to take a dump?'

Stepping closer, Victor said, 'Are you sure you know how to do a V-sign?'

'What? Of course I'm bloody sure.'

'Most people don't actually know how to do it correctly.'

'Are you joking? It's the V-sign, not sign language.' For emphasis, the man extended his index and middle fingers towards Victor. '*See?*'

Victor's bound hands snapped forward to close the distance, left hand grabbing hold of the man's index finger while the right hand wrapped the man's middle finger.

With a savage motion, Victor used the considerable pulling strength of his back to wrench in his arms as he flared his elbows, slamming his forearms into his own braced core, the force of impact popping open the cable ties.

That sudden release meant his elbows continued to flare open past either side of his torso until his shoulder blades almost touched in the centre of his upper back, his fists moving in opposite directions as they followed the trajectory of his elbows.

He kept hold of each of the man's fingers the entire time, one in each fist.

In doing so, he tore apart the contractor's hand all the way down to the wrist.

FIVE

Flesh is generally pretty resistant to tearing. Skin has a lot more durability than it is given credit for by most people. The strength of Victor's back was honed by a lifetime of climbing, by innumerable pull-ups. When he could raise his entire body weight multiple times with only a single hand, ripping the skin and soft tissues of the hand required little true effort. Breaking the cable ties had necessitated the full application of his strength. Ripping the hand apart had been easy in comparison. As a side effect of escaping the cable ties, it had been as good as effortless.

When experiencing sudden extreme physical trauma, no two people responded in the same way. Some passed out in seconds. Others wailed. A few barely seemed to notice until loss of blood or the debilitating nature of the injury otherwise impeded them. Having already lost three extremities by way of a wood-chopping axe, a captive of Victor's had still stubbornly refused to talk even when he lost the fourth too, wordlessly crawling on knees and elbows to cauterise the latest wound against a cast-iron log burner.

That had been a long night.

This contractor went white. The blood drained away from his face, leaching the colour from the skin, replacing the redness of his cheeks with the hue of fresh bone, and darkening the hollows beneath his eyes almost to black.

He collapsed to his knees, falling straight down as Victor released the two fingers.

The disjoined parts of the hand flopped in different directions.

Blood seeped out of the wound and soaked the man's long-sleeved T-shirt. It was far from fatal, however, as the common digital arteries run in parallel to the metacarpals, and so remained intact either side of the tear, whereas the superficial and deep palmar arches were merely pushed and pulled as the soft tissues tore around them.

Seeing his hand in splaying parts, fingers still moving yet the part with his thumb and index finger flexing independently from the part with the other three fingers, the Brit let out a single keening exhale.

'Do you happen to have a pair of scissors amongst your gear?' Victor asked as he closed the bedroom door to dampen the travel of any imminent cries or screams. 'I don't see a knife on your webbing.'

The horror became too much and the man lost balance, falling backwards from his weakening knees to lie prone on the floor. He didn't scream, however, because his stress hormones were doing an excellent job dampening the pain. A temporary respite only. The pain would come soon enough. For now, he was in shock.

'Maybe just a pocket knife?' Victor rubbed at the loops of cable tie around each wrist. 'These are really annoying.'

Lying on his back, the man tried and failed with his left hand to squeeze the two halves of his right hand back together. Blood bubbled.

Squatting down to open pockets and pouches of the man's gear, Victor said, 'Anything sharp will do.'

The Brit managed to cup the injured hand against his belly, where he could use that extra support to keep the two halves somewhat as one piece.

'How about nail clippers?' Victor asked when he failed to find either scissors or a knife.

In the cool air of the bedroom, steam rose from the wound. With wide, unblinking eyes the contractor watched the snaking plume as though it were the soul escaping from his body.

The Brit had two guns, ammunition, but nothing sharp that Victor could use to cut the ties.

'I have to make a confession,' he said, standing up to search the room. 'When I was talking about the origins of the V-sign earlier, I may have placed too much emphasis on the story of the French crossbowmen and the English archers. In truth, there's no actual historical evidence for the theory despite it often being told. Which is a real shame because I very much like it. It appeals to me in a way I can't quite articulate. I don't like cursing, swearing, as a general rule, although this doesn't seem to apply here. Maybe that's because of the story, where it is no simple vulgarity meant to cause offence but a symbol of defiance. Sadly, that idea falls apart when you remember the English were the invaders at the time and the French were defending their land against the attackers. So, I hope you will forgive the deception.'

Victor looked down at the Brit, who trembled and whimpered on the floor. The man made no answer. Shock made his eyes blink so fast, so continuously, Victor guessed the man's vision had a strobed effect. If he happened to be epileptic, the contractor might induce a seizure.

'Ah ha,' Victor said, then squatted down to remove the man's sunglasses from where they were still hooked to his T-shirt. 'You don't mind, do you?'

He took the lack of response as permission, then bent and twisted the frames until a lens popped free.

Positioning a little of the lens beneath one heel, he applied pressure until he heard the glass crack. With the resulting sharp edge, Victor set about running it in careful, sawing motions against the plastic of the cable ties until he had cut himself free. First the right hand, then the left.

'That's .better,' Victor said, rising to his feet as he massaged his wrists. 'You have no idea how good this feels.'

The Brit, still white, made eye contact. He managed to make a croaking sound that seemed like an attempt to speak or a prelude to a scream.

'If you're quiet,' Victor told him. 'You'll live through this. If you don't make any noise then there's no need for me to kill you. Maybe there's something in the air, but I'm feeling uncommonly charitable today. Who drives the Land Cruisers? Who has the keys? I didn't see when you arrived.'

The man trembled: shock and pain and fear overwhelmed his central nervous system.

'Try to control your breathing,' Victor suggested. 'Block out the pain. It's just a message you can ignore for a few minutes if you really force yourself. Like hitting snooze. Send your mind away to your happy place: an ice cave with a penguin or whatever works for you. Who has the keys? Charitable mood or not, I don't have time for this.'

There was no answer and no change in the contractor. No alteration of his breathing. No eyes closed to suggest a mental effort to overcome the pain.

'You need to pull yourself together,' Victor said, then looking at the two halves of wounded hand, added, 'no pun intended.'

A yell from outside echoed through the building. And although Victor could not make out what was said, he understood the message clear enough.

Fahim Akram's corpse had been found.

SIX

Victor collected up the contractor's carbine, tucked spare magazines into his waistband and slung the weapon over one shoulder. It had a single-point sling that attached to the housing so the gun hung muzzle-down along the right side of Victor's torso and hip. Comfortable enough, though more trouble than it was worth if he had to break into a sprint. Still, he wanted the additional firepower on his person for when he needed it. Until then, he kept the Brit's pistol in his right hand.

More shouts and yells from outside.

This time words and phrases were decipherable: '... he's inside ... kill on sight ... no way he leaves here alive ...'

The contractor on the floor heard them too.

He looked up at Victor, who looked back down at him.

The Brit knew what was coming.

'You being quiet doesn't help me any longer, I'm afraid,' Victor explained, then executed him with his own handgun.

Leaving the bedroom, Victor crossed the hallway to the

bedroom opposite, which had a window that overlooked the courtyard.

Swapping to the carbine, he opened fire on the first gunmen he could see from the elevated position: the two guards at the gate, who were looking surprised and confused by the sudden commotion.

Five squeezes of the trigger to drop them both and Victor was backing away from the window before the contractors in the courtyard could respond.

Glass cracked and shattered behind him as Victor headed to the staircase.

In the close confines of the house, he preferred to use the Brit's pistol, keeping his elbows tight against his torso so his arms stretched out as little as possible. He didn't want any enemies seeing his weapon appear around a corner ahead of him, giving them a split-second warning before he had even identified the threat.

Which the first two contractors to enter the house helpfully did, their rifles giving them away before Victor had even seen the gunmen themselves emerging from the top of the staircase.

They must have already been inside, perhaps idly wandering in before the first pistol shot, to have ascended so fast.

A double-tap for each and those rushing to follow were yelling and screaming for caution. Their echoes said they were still downstairs in the entrance hallway.

Victor appreciated the heads-up, tucking away the pistol and switching back to the carbine.

A quick peek revealed the other contractors were not covering the stairwell, which was a mistake in Victor's opinion. It made sense they did not want to engage him while he had the higher ground, shooting down at them in an open vestibule without cover, but unless he planned on jumping out of a window – he did not – then the stairwell was a perfect choke point.

Still, panic led people to make poor choices, and for that Victor was always grateful.

He crept down the stairs, staying close to the wall. Moving away from it to improve his field of view as he approached the bottom and the corner where it joined the entrance hallway.

No one.

He pictured them in the courtyard, having backed out with haste when the two had dropped dead at the top of the stairwell. The front door was ajar, lines of bright sunlight framed it on three sides. Maybe they had wanted it that way or more likely they had withdrawn so fast no one had considered whether it was better to have it closed or open.

Keeping to the shadowed side, Victor approached with caution but at speed. There was no point trying to be silent. They knew he was coming, however little noise he made in the process. He didn't want to give them too much time to prepare for his assault and more importantly time to control their fear. He wanted their heart rates as high as possible, their fine motor skills impeded as a result.

Leaving another way and circling the house would take too much time. It would give that time to them to work out exactly what he was doing and prepare accordingly. He didn't want them to start thinking clearly and tactically.

Better to rush them while they were still in a panic and prone to poor choices.

Even so, they would be covering the door with four automatic weapons.

A grenade would have been perfect in this situation, but the three already dead had none on their webbing unlike some of the other contractors. Victor glanced around the makeshift workshop that was the hallway. The tooling equipment was all far too big and heavy, and he didn't have time to search through drawers and toolboxes. He glanced down at the floor. A dense retaining bolt was nearby; too heavy. A crushed soft drink can was too light. A bent section of copper piping about ten centimetres in length, however, would do the trick.

He scooped it from the floor into his left hand, stood with his back to the wall and his shoulder against the doorframe, and tossed the pipe through the opening at about hip height.

A hard throw, so it went in fast. Too fast to immediately identify, and low to make sure it skipped and clattered on the paving of the courtyard.

A grenade would have been perfect, but for a few brief seconds the section of pipe sounded just like one.

Victor charged flung open the door as the pipe was still skipping along the paving and the eyes of the closest two contractors in the courtyard were following it, while a third and fourth man were already backing away as fast as they could.

Two double-taps from the carbine punched bloody holes in the shirt of the nearest contractor crouched down to the side of one of the Land Cruisers, then two more double-taps did the same with the second as Victor switched his aim laterally. Before each had time to do much more than flinch in response, headshots followed.

The third took three shots in the spine as he ran.

The fourth gunman – Maqsoodi – made it through the

door into one of the smaller buildings before Victor had him fully in his sights. It was the storeroom containing the US suppressors and Akram's corpse.

Victor resisted the instinct to squeeze the trigger and waste a bullet that an amateur might hope could hit and yet Victor knew would take a fraction of a second too long to cover the distance. There were few things Victor disliked more than wasting ammunition.

The copper pipe came to a stop against a tyre of the second Toyota as the three corpses collapsed to the ground one after the other.

They had had good positioning, each covering the doorway from a different angle with no risk of getting in one another's line of fire. No matter how fast Victor could move, how accurately he could shoot, there would have been no way to enter that room and live with them all looking his way.

He pursued Maqsoodi, moving at a quick pace but not hurrying because his quarry was going nowhere.

Victor heard an interior door slam shut before he had reached the storeroom. When he entered, he saw Maqsoodi had slipped in Akram's blood, then left a trail of it that led to one of the two interior doors leading off from the main room.

Now within a restricted space, Victor ditched the carbine and took his Five-seveN from where he had left it on top of the doorframe. It felt good in his hand.

As he circled the now-disturbed lake of blood and approached the door with bloody footprints leading up to it, bullets came through it in six neat holes. No splintering. Only little puffs of wood dust glowing as they drifted through the swathes of sunlight.

They struck the wall to Victor's right. Pretty close too, Maqsoodi good enough to read Victor's approximate location from the sound of his quiet footsteps alone. Not good enough to realise that if he didn't hit his target he would give away his exact location in return, however.

The holes in the door were at chest height and the holes in the wall almost in line with Victor's eyes, so he knew the Afghan was crouched or kneeling down in the room beyond.

He made a quick calculation and put three bullets of his own through the door.

The resulting holes were much larger and rougher because, while the 5.7mm pistol rounds were only a little greater in diameter, they had about a quarter the velocity.

More effective nonetheless.

A sharp grunt sounded from the other side of the door.

No death wail, Victor knew, so he dropped straight down prone to the floor before Maqsoodi unleashed a spray of rounds in return.

A useless gesture, but like panic, pain tended to encourage such ineffective responses.

Bullets ripped through the door – maybe two dozen total rounds – in a wild pattern, the Afghan's recoil control impeded by the wounds he had taken, or perhaps the pattern was reflective of his current state of mind: desperate, enraged.

When the shooting stopped, Victor was fast to his feet and kicking down the door. Hard to be accurate counting rounds when the firing was automatic, but if his estimate was correct Maqsoodi would be –

Reloading his weapon.

He was on the floor, back against a crate of the pristine

suppressors Fahim had been so keen to show off, legs splayed out before him having fallen from his previous crouching position. With one hand, he was hurriedly trying to insert a fresh magazine. The carbine was lying across his lap, an empty magazine discarded nearby, and, unable to use his other hand to stabilise the weapon thanks to bullet holes in his shoulder and arm, he was fumbling to fit the fresh one into the receiver.

With Victor now in the room, Maqsoodi froze. There was no way he was getting the rifle loaded and ready to fire in time with anything short of divine intervention.

'Should have gone for the pistol,' Victor told him.

At first, Maqsoodi looked back in utter confusion before realisation dawned and he glanced down at the handgun holstered on his right thigh as if seeing it for the first time. The weapon was centimetres away from his good hand but as with poor choices and ineffective responses, pain and panic also had a habit of making otherwise smart people forget the absolute basics.

For a brief moment, his head and shoulders sagged in self-disgust.

Looking back up at Victor, he said, '*Wait*—'

A single headshot proved the most efficient way of explaining to the Afghan there was no point in further discourse.

Victor disliked wasting words even more than he did wasting ammunition.

ONE WEEK LATER

SEVEN

The head of the Bratva preferred to travel with as little fanfare as possible. Given his stature secrecy was impossible, so the best that could be managed was discretion. An armoured limousine took Maxim Borisyuk from his dacha outside Moscow, shadowed by a modest security detail of four. His personal bodyguard travelled with him inside the limousine, along with Luda Zakharova, who ran the day-to-day operations of the Brotherhood with such efficiency his input was rarely necessary.

Though excessive for a relatively short flight, a long-range jet awaited Borisyuk at a private airfield. The jet was the newest addition to the fleet of aircraft owned by Bratva shell companies, purchased for a single task now complete, and Borisyuk, though rich beyond all reasonable measure, could feel the disapproving look of his mother who had always hated waste. Given the aircraft could fly non-stop from Russia to North America, had she been alive, his mother would not only have scolded him with her eyes but given him a clip round the ear as well.

Because discretion mattered, the four-man security detail remained on the tarmac as Borisyuk ascended the steps with his bodyguard and Zakharova following. The flight crew knew enough about him by now to forgo fawning greetings and insincere small talk, and so welcomed him aboard in a polite yet businesslike manner.

The cold breeze ruffled the wisps of hair stubbornly hanging onto his scalp when the rest had long departed. He smoothed them down once he was inside the aircraft.

He did not so much sit down into the chair, as fall. The day you stopped lowering yourself and let gravity do the work instead was the day you became old, Borisyuk knew. In his seat, he was served black tea with lemon and Zakharova, sitting opposite, received her preferred Japanese whisky with ice.

Take-off was smooth. Borisyuk was looking forward to a relaxing flight, drinking tea and watching a spaghetti western or two. Smuggling in pirated tapes of American TV and cinema had been one of his most profitable business activities in the late '80s. New media was hard to come by in Soviet Russia and so many of the tapes he could obtain were of shows and movies from prior decades. Borisyuk had fallen in love with the Old West back then, with the freedom of all that space to live without the shadow of an overbearing autocracy. He loved the gunfights too: so unrealistic to someone who had known many, and yet that was an undeniable charm to them. Stylistic and fun, without the stench of viscera and the stomach cramping terror.

Zakharova wanted to talk, however.

Any other employee of his would take the hint to leave him alone. Which was exactly why he valued her input so much. She had never been afraid of him. She never courted his favour. It had been he who tried so hard to bring her into the organisation and she never let him forget it.

'Would you like your itinerary now or when we arrive?' she asked him after they had both taken their first sips.

'Is never an option?'

She set her tumbler down and waited for a more grown-up answer.

The tea was too hot to properly enjoy, so Borisyuk blew onto the surface in preparation for a second sip.

'When we arrive,' he said at last. 'With the highlights now, if you please.'

Zakharova had a tablet in her bag, which she would have handed to him had he requested the full itinerary. Naturally, it was all committed to memory and so she listed the names of the various people he was to meet.

'Sounds tiring.'

'There are fewer meetings than you are used to.'

'I am a lot older than I am used to.'

She brought the tumbler back to her lips. 'You will get no sympathy from me.'

He always thought of her as young, since she had been when she entered his employment, and as they both aged she had never lost that vital spark that had made him so determined to hire her in the first place. Given he was in his seventies now, she must be fifty at least. He had felt old at fifty. He did not expect to still be alive when Zakharova reached the age he was now, though he imagined she would be as energetic as ever.

'You have that look about you,' she said, not lifting her gaze from her tablet.

'What look is that?'

'Lost in a moment, nostalgic yet bittersweet.'

'I thought I might marry you at one point.'

Japanese whisky older than the stewards sputtered everywhere.

Zakharova growled in frustration and annoyance as she dabbed her thousand-dollar trouser suit with a hastily grabbed napkin. 'You don't have to look quite so pleased with yourself.'

'I'm trying very hard not to, I assure you.'

She had never married, though he had been introduced to many suitors over the years at social functions to which they were both invited. She did not tell him why he rarely met any of them a second time, and he would not ask. It was not his place.

'Obviously,' she began, drying her hands, 'you were making some ridiculous joke I don't understand.'

'No joke,' he assured. 'It would have been for my daughter's sake. Mostly.'

'I'll pretend I didn't notice the pause before mostly.'

'We spend almost every day together as it is.'

'Which might be the worst justification for marriage I've ever heard.'

Her hands dry and as much whisky dabbed out of her suit as possible, she gestured to the steward for another.

'What would you have said?'

'You can't be serious.'

'I am serious. I'd like to know.'

She fixed him with a steely look of disapproval. 'I refuse to respond to a purely hypothetical proposal.'

'That's a no then.'

'It is,' she said, nodding. 'If you weren't brave enough to actually ask me to marry you then by default my answer is an automatic, *emphatic*, no. Cowardice is unrepentantly unattractive.'

'You'll recall that I said I had thought about it. Once.'

'You're old enough to be my father.'

'I assure you that I had no untoward intentions.'

'You're making it worse, not better.'

Borisyuk laughed. 'Women are impossible.'

'This attitude goes some way to explain why you remain a bachelor.'

'Perhaps,' he conceded, then returned to business. 'When in all this excitement will I be meeting with Vasili?'

'If I had my way you would not be meeting him at all.'

'I wonder what it is about him that you do not like.'

'I dislike the fact you like him,' she said.

'Jealousy does not suit you, my dear.'

She snorted. 'And deflection is beneath you, Maxim.'

'Tell me.'

'He is a hired killer.'

'We employ many killers.'

'He is not one of us.'

'Neither are half the people you have arranged I meet in London.'

She held his gaze for a long moment and as ever he found it impossible to read anything in her expression she did not want him to see. 'Loaning him out was unwise.'

'Kasakov is delighted with his effectiveness. But that's not why you do not like him, is it?'

'Your fondness for him makes you look weak.'

'I see. Is that it?'

'It makes you seem old.'

'I am old.'

'Older.'

'You didn't say that you think I look weak, that you think I seem older. What has been said about me?'

'Nothing,' Zakharova answered. 'No one would dare.'

'Except you.'

'It's a feeling,' she explained after a moment. 'The way they act around you.'

'Because of Vasili?'

'Not wholly, though in part. It's another sign of you going soft.'

'Business has never been better.'

'Maybe that's the problem. Maybe we are too much like a business for some and not enough like criminals.'

'Anyone who prefers fighting turf wars for a pittance can go back to the old ways.'

'I'm not arguing the merits of your leadership,' she said, sitting forward. 'I'm telling you how I perceive the mood of the table.'

'Noted.'

'You should not have arranged for your plane to take him out of Kabul.'

'At last, we get to the truth,' Borisyuk began with a hint of a smile. 'You do not like this jet as much.'

'I don't appreciate the attempt at humour.'

'Whereas I don't care that we had to scrap a plane.'

'And the entire company it was registered with.'

'We will not even notice it on the bottom line.'

'But others noticed. Not limited to the intelligence agencies tracking the comings and goings out of Afghanistan.'

'Go on.'

'Like any king,' she began, 'you rule because your nobles want you to rule. And such nobles only desire to be in the servitude of a king when that rule benefits them. When they see you take needless risks they see you putting them at risk.'

Borisyuk gathered his thoughts. He rarely felt the need to explain anything to anyone and yet he kept almost no secrets from Zakharova. 'The contact, our man, almost got him killed.'

'That does not explain why you care.'

'I never need concern myself with what he is thinking. At no point do I wonder about his inner thoughts because he hides nothing from me. He has no ambition. At least, how you or I would measure it. He has a debt to pay to me and all he desires is to pay it off.'

'You cannot possibly trust an assassin.'

'Who said anything about trust? I don't need to trust him. I tell him what he must do and he does it. I like the simplicity of my arrangement with him. When I speak to him I can be as honest with him as anyone and yet I know with him that he is as honest in return. I can't say that about a single other person.' He could not read her expression, but he understood her silence. 'I have offended you, I see. And yet this is my point because my honesty offends you when it has no need. I am not accusing you of deception.'

'Then I'm glad of that, at least.'

'Please, let's not pretend you tell me every thought you have, that you hold nothing back, that you share everything about you and your life with me, freely and openly?'

'And this killer does?'

'No, of course not. I tell him who to kill, he kills them.

That's the extent of it. The level of honesty he conveys is perfectly commensurate to the nature of the relationship I have with him.'

'Unless he's fooled you the whole time.'

'I don't think of myself as anyone's fool, though if I am mistaken then we will soon know of my foolishness.'

'What does that mean?'

'In London we shall put this killer's loyalty to the final test.'

EIGHT

In the five years preceding the ignition of civil war in Libya, European Union nations sent almost one billion dollars' worth of weaponry to the country. These stockpiles were raided soon after the fall of the regime and the arms were claimed by numerous, often disparate, groups of rebels, militia and mercenaries. Although spread out across the country, Vladimir Kasakov's vast network was quick to buy, steal and trade much of this weaponry before routing it to warlords in Mali. With constant fighting between government forces and those seeking to overthrow them, buyers there were delighted to pay over the odds for modern guns and heavy weapons that the Ukrainian had acquired for cents on the dollar.

With NATO munitions once more available in abundance, this time in Afghanistan, Kasakov was delighted to have the opportunity to repeat this successful business model. Even if he could obtain every single piece of weaponry entering the market he would not be able to fulfil the appetites of the many regimes and their opponents throughout the Middle East.

'The problem is you're too good at what you do,' Sergei explained, as his boss listened nearby, to the man on the other end of the phone line 'Which means you have come to the attention Vladimir Kasakov. You've probably never heard the name before and yet Mister Kasakov is easily the most prolific arms dealer in the world. He didn't get to that position overnight, and he's not held onto his crown without defending it from every competitor that bubbles up out of the cracks of warzones and failed states.'

He was perhaps laying it on too thickly and yet Kasakov was not about to intervene. He employed Sergei so he had time for more important things.

'Stay on your toes,' he instructed from the other side of the office space in his Sochi dacha. 'Never stand still.'

Little Illarion shuffled from side to side as his father had demonstrated, though the boy was flat-footed, more sliding than shuffling.

'On your toes,' Kasakov said. 'On your tiptoes.'

If his son understood the coaching, such delicacies of balance were beyond him. He had a big smile too. All glee as he threw pitty-patty punches without malice. The boy almost never threw a tantrum. He was pure sunshine and Kasakov prayed Illarion stayed that way for ever.

'He doesn't need your guns,' Sergei continued, 'but he doesn't want his customers buying your guns instead of his. He made you a generous offer for your cache of American arms and you beheaded his spokesperson and sent the head back to him in Moscow ... Oh, you now regret that ... I see you've heard what happened in Kabul last week. Yes, that emerging cartel there is no more so they will be unable to fulfil their promise to purchase your cache ... Ah, you would like to make a counter-offer now? Excellent news. And a far more civilised way of conducting business.' He presented a thumbs up to Kasakov, stretching out his arm so the gesture crossed into the Ukrainian's eyeline. 'We look forward to receiving the appropriate paperwork. And may I suggest you think very carefully about your asking price.'

Kasakov was down on one knee, his elbows tucked into his flanks and the pads held about sternum height so Illarion could reach them. He wore oversized boxing gloves far too big for his tiny hands. They were the closest fit Kasakov could obtain. If the boy showed promise, if he showed determination, Kasakov would order some gloves custom-made to fit the boy. He didn't want to do so if his son grew bored of boxing – or *playing with Daddy* as he thought of it now – and then have to throw the gloves away. Despite his obscene level of wealth, Kasakov was still a poor farmer's boy inside.

'Turn your weight into the punches,' he said. 'Twist your hips as you throw.'

Still smiling, his mother's fair hair flopping from side to side, Illarion did no such thing. He was having too much fun to care about technique.

'You're strong,' Kasakov told him, pretending to wince from the impact of the punches. 'You could be a champion someday. Would you like that?'

No answer.

It was hard to know if the boy was indeed strong or not. As Illarion was his first child – the first time he had ever really interacted with a child – Kasakov had no frame of reference. The boy was not big, he knew enough to know that, and all could see that too when the boy stood alongside his schoolmates for the class photograph.

'Okay,' Kasakov said, rising and removing the pads. 'Go and wash up before dinner. Tell Mummy that Daddy is very proud of you.'

Illarion did as he was told, removing the oversized gloves and shuffling away. As he neared Sergei, he squealed and ran as Sergei roared and darted from the chair to tickle him.

After his son had left, Sergei said, 'The returns on these guns will be positively nauseating.'

A young man, he had thick, dark hair that swept back and up from his forehead and flared out at the sides of his head. A beard added the same kind of breadth to his face, giving him the appearance of strength and yet Kasakov noted the thin neck that couldn't quite fill the collar of his shirt. He wore smart, tight chinos and a pale grey shirt with the collar open. His shoes were brown moccasins with shiny, brass lace holes. The bright blue-and-red chequer pattern added a little colour to the otherwise muted, though carefully composed, palette of his clothes. Kasakov, in joggers and a hoodie – both with holes – felt more peasant than oligarch in comparison.

'Tonight we shall raise a glass to American foreign policy.'

Beyond the huge amount of money to be made reselling US weaponry, Kasakov took much personal satisfaction in benefiting from those who made him a prisoner in Russia. The last time he had taken such pleasure in a business deal was when he had managed to acquire the contents of three separate supply drops meant for Western-backed militias in Syria that ended up in the hands of Daesh. According to the detailed manifests, he bought almost nineteen million dollars' worth of anti-tank missile launchers for seventy thousand and change. A fine profit margin even for a man worth billions, although it had not been the primary reason for buying the missiles. He made far more money shipping armoured personnel carriers, infantry fighting vehicles and main battle tanks to various regimes and militaries across the Middle East, and he did not want his regular customers getting angry and going elsewhere when their expensive vehicles were blown to pieces.

At least, not until their enemies were spending more money buying anti-tank weapons from him instead.

Sergei grinned. 'It's almost funny how quickly word spreads in this industry.'

Kasakov nodded, although it was not funny but predictable. Trafficking arms was huge business on a global scale, and yet the world of successful independent dealers was a small and dangerous one. When the entire leadership of a fast-growing cartel was wiped out, everyone noticed.

'Please arrange a suitable gift for Maxim Borisyuk.'

'Something opera related?'

'Good idea.'

'How about a Fabergé Swan Lake Imperial Egg? If I'm not mistaken there is an auction at Sotheby's at the end of this week. Fortuitous timing too, given Maxim will be in London.'

'Perfect.'

'And something of a bargain considering the profits you're likely to make this quarter given we already have purchase orders for almost eighty per cent of the Kabul cartel's stock.'

Sergei's tone suggested he thought the loan of Borisyuk's newest killer was nothing more than a favour and the gift he would arrange on behalf of Kasakov was the sum total of his gratitude.

Of course, the head of the Russian mafia did no one favours. They both knew Kasakov had paid for the killer's services in other ways.

'He's a good friend to have,' Sergei noted.

Kasakov agreed, except long experience had taught him that there could be no upside to anything in life without a corresponding downside.

He told the younger man, 'You must never forget that good friends make the deadliest of enemies.'

NINE

Meeting a client was something that Victor had once avoided at all costs. As a freelance contract killer, the less anyone knew about him the better, a principle that was even truer when dealing with those who employed him. By nature of hiring him they already knew more about him than almost anyone else, and given they were amoral enough to hire an assassin in the first place, providing them with even more information about their employee was a bad idea by default.

Maxim Borisyuk was different.

'When you came to me to confess your sins,' he said, pouring Victor a drink, 'I did not so much become your employer as your priest.'

The drawing room of Borisyuk's Pimlico townhouse had an old-world aesthetic that Victor found comforting. Where the walls were free of bookshelves, oil paintings hung squared within Georgian panelling. The mouldings were decorative, painted white, with the walls behind sage green. The ceiling was high, centred by a glittering chandelier. Columns rose to form an arch over the door. Somewhere on the other side was Borisyuk's bodyguard, who had greeted Victor at the townhouse's entrance before escorting him upstairs.

He took a seat in one of the two oriental-themed armchairs set before a disused fireplace. A huge vase of dried flowers sat where coal would have burned a century beforehand. Though he had no reason to believe the bodyguard was any threat, Victor chose the chair that backed the fireplace so he faced the room and arched doorway. It meant the room's tall window was behind him. An almost identical townhouse sat on the opposite side of the narrow street, making a fine nest for a marksman. At such short range any shooter would need only rudimentary skill to hit a target in this drawing room. The window's heavy drapes were drawn, and a glance as he had entered the room informed him there was no exploitable gap between them, so Victor felt no need to adjust the chair's position.

He doubted Borisyuk would have been so diligent – he left his security to other people – which meant the bodyguard was thorough. While Victor never relied on another for his own precautions, it was good to know he did not need to also concern himself with Borisyuk's safety.

The old Russian seemed out of place in the grandeur of the townhouse. He dressed himself in no finery, preferring comfortable loungewear, plain glasses and rubber sandals. He wore no jewellery. Only the watch betrayed his wealth, and even that was understated, with a leather strap and steel face surround. Victor imagined it was a gift.

'You seem tired.'

Victor only nodded in response. 'Thank you for the jet.'

'You're welcome.'

'But you should not have done that with all the attention it will have brought you.'

Borisyuk handed him vodka over ice in a cut-crystal tumbler. He had one himself, though Victor noticed his own glass had a far more generous serving.

'Vladimir Kasakov is very pleased those potential rivals are no more, so I too am pleased. My people let you down in Kabul so that means I let you down since I sent you there, no?' He did not wait for a confirmation. 'So there is no need to thank me, Vasili. I did only that for you which you would do for me.'

'I have no jet.'

'That's not what I meant.'

'I know. You shouldn't have so much faith in people.'

'Not in people.'

The townhouse had seven bedrooms, four bathrooms and two reception rooms over five floors. As far as Victor knew, it was only Borisyuk and his bodyguard staying in the property. It was owned by one of the many shell companies that made up the legitimate front of the Brotherhood, and left unused when Borisyuk was not in London. Over the past twelve months the Russian had previously visited the city a single time. Although it had a state-of-the-art infrared-based alarm system, there were no armoured windows or reinforced doors.

Given the enormous wealth of Borisyuk and his organisation, improving the house's security with the best money could buy would not have been a significant expense.

'I can provide a simple plan to improve the security of this building. There are several weaknesses that should be addressed.'

'Unnecessary,' Borisyuk said with a single shake of his

head. 'The only people interested in my demise are those that sit with me at the head table. Few outside the Brotherhood even know who I am right now. If I turn everywhere I reside into a fortress then I will inform the others at the table waiting to sit in my chair that I am afraid and I am weak. And at the same time I will tell all those out there who do not know me that I am someone of value.'

Victor understood. Anonymity was perhaps his own best defence against any threat.

A knock on the drawing room door interrupted Borisyuk, who said, 'Yes?'

The door opened and his bodyguard stepped over the threshold. He was a large man, though his bulk did not stray into detrimental territory. Excess muscle mass was useful on the stage only, though Victor had encountered plenty of security personnel hired by virtue of the width of their shoulders. Taken to the extreme, too much size slowed someone down and weakened their cardiovascular system. Sometimes to a lethal degree, as Victor had recently witnessed in a derelict seafood restaurant. This guy was light on his feet, and more importantly, he never once let Victor be in his blind spot. The instant the door was open enough to see inside, the bodyguard's gaze found Victor, ignoring Borisyuk until it had been established exactly where Victor was and exactly what he was doing. A tiny action, almost indistinguishable from a casual glance. The bodyguard knew Victor was dangerous, whatever Borisyuk's trust in him, and the bodyguard knew Victor was aware of that opinion. Although not an opinion because it was true.

The bodyguard said to Borisyuk, 'The canapés prepared by the chef have been sitting out for a while. I'm going to cover them and put them in the refrigerator unless you would like me to keep them out?'

Borisyuk gestured Victor's way. 'Hungry?'

'I'm good,' Victor said, looking at the bodyguard as the bodyguard looked at him.

Borisyuk told the man, 'Eat as many as you can stomach and do whatever you would like with the remainder.'

'As you wish, sir.'

He backed out of the door, his gaze remained fixed Victor's way until the door was closed.

Borisyuk then said, 'I have a feeling he doesn't like you very much, does he?'

The Russian's tone suggested that this was both a rhetorical question and a fact that intrigued him.

'He's right not to,' Victor said in return. 'Which makes him a good man to have at your side.'

'I've known him for many years now,' Borisyuk began. 'He never comments on the company I keep unless responding to a direct question of mine. That said, he is not a man who understands how to hide what he is feeling. So, over time I have come to know without effort who he respects and who he cannot stand. I believe you are the first to be both.'

Victor raised an eyebrow. 'I do prefer to be the exception instead of the rule.'

'Fortunately, you don't strike me as the kind of man who is too concerned how others feel about him. However, there is a price to pay for such a lack of popularity. When people like you then they will do for you that which neither money nor power could persuade them to do instead.'

'I'm happy to make friends with targets instead of killing them if that's what you'd prefer?'

Borisyuk laughed. Still smiling, he finished his vodka and set the empty glass down next to the bottle. When he looked at Victor again, the Russian's face was serious once more.

'Perhaps I should have made friends with those who wronged me instead of having them murdered,' he mused. 'How might things have turned out that way? It's too late to know. Life's ultimate irony is we can only understand ourselves in retrospect. Meaning we come to know who we are when we're no longer that person any more. So, when we die, we don't really die. Another version of us dies, a person we'll never get to know.'

'I know who I am.'

'You see yourself as a killer and nothing more.'

It was not a question, but Victor nodded regardless.

Borisyuk said, 'You must have performed a dozen such jobs for me by now.'

'The Afghan cartel makes eleven contracts,' Victor corrected.

'Eleven or twelve, the specific number hardly matters. What does matter is that you have done these jobs for me without complaint, without any blowback for myself or the organisation. For that, I am grateful.'

Victor sipped some vodka.

'I will admit that when you entered my service I was wary. Not that you would shoot me in the back, but whether you would truly honour your debt. It's no small thing to commit to such a task without knowing how long it will take or what it will ultimately entail. Especially when you in return had absolutely no way of knowing if I would honour it on my part. I could have brought you here to have you killed as I could have done many times before. In truth, I have thought a lot about this, at times feeling that whatever my respect for your sense of honour, keeping you alive is too much of a betrayal to my daughter.' He paused in thought. 'But, ultimately, you are the man who pulls the trigger, not the man that decides who dies. If you are held to account for your actions then I must be condemned.'

Borisyuk set his drink down on a round coffee table. He used the arms of the chair for support and pushed himself up as he stood. Victor saw it was not easy for him. He knew, however, any attempt to assist him would be greeted with scorn, if not rage.

'Your debt to me is now paid and you are free to go back to your life.'

'Thank you.'

'Alternatively,' the Russian continued, 'you could remain in my service as a trusted soldier. Paid handsomely, of course.'

Victor said, 'I'm not sure what to say.'

'Speak whatever is on your mind.'

'It's been a long time since I had any such similar arrangement with a single client. In my experience such relationships inevitably break down. I don't trust anyone, I never have, which means no one can truly trust me in return. That's not a productive dynamic in this line of work and. I would prefer it when I leave your service there are no hard feelings.'

'I understand,' Borisyuk replied, 'and I respect any decision you make on the matter, though I shall be sad to see you go. But before you do depart in finality, I have only one request.'

'Name it.'

'Take a day to think it through first. I will still be in London tomorrow night, so perhaps you could wait until then before providing me with your answer.'

'Sure,' Victor said. 'However, given I had intended to leave tonight I'm not sure what I will do in the meantime.'

'Where lies the indecision?' Borisyuk asked, bemused. 'You're in one of the largest and most interesting cities in the world. Do what anyone else would do?'

The Russian saw that Victor was equally bemused.

'Behave like a normal person,' Borisyuk said, laughing. 'Have a little fun for once.'

TEN

It was rare Victor had time to kill, and even rarer for such an opportunity to present itself so unexpectedly. Much of his existence was meticulously planned, whether via protocols he had established over many years, specific preparations to his current contract, or simply to survive the day. After remaining awake in his hotel room until almost dawn he had slept through the morning, giving him an entire afternoon free of obligations before he was due to meet Borisyuk in the evening.

After eating breakfast, he bought a fresh burner phone from a kiosk inside a convenience store, connected it to the Wi-Fi inside a coffee shop to download appropriate apps from a private server hosted in Bahrain to secure the handset, and sent a coded message via an encrypted communications app to a contact he had in the city.

Though someone peering over his shoulder would see only a seemingly random series of alphanumeric characters and symbols, his contact would read it as:

Champagne bar St. Pancras Station 1600.

With a few hours to spare, and thinking of Borisyuk's suggestion for him to have some fun, Victor headed to one of his favourite locations in the world: the British Library.

Though the library was free to use, the reading rooms were only available to those with a pass. He made sure to renew the pass connected to one of his British legends so he was always able to take full advantage of the library's resources whenever the opportunity presented itself. Books could not be taken away, though they were accessible in one of the eleven reading rooms. He knew from past visits that some books were not stored in the main library itself and could take a day or more to arrive from one of the other storage locations. Which meant that some books he would never get to read. Even when he knew he would have adequate time in London, protocol dictated he could never potentially provide enemies with such an insight to his movements.

It was often a lottery as to how busy any one reading room might be, although all seemed busy during the summer and before Easter, when undergraduate students swelled the visitor pool.

With a vast wealth of knowledge available, it was hard to know where to start. Spoilt for choice when it came to books, Victor decided to go a different route and headed to the third floor where the Maps Reading Room was located. After perusing the catalogue, he settled on a railway map of Ireland drawn by the War Office in 1940. He made a request, then made his way back downstairs to check out the exhibits while he waited.

He bought two tickets to an exhibition about Buddhism and spent an hour wandering through the rooms, learning about the teachings of Buddha across many panels. He took his time admiring scriptures written on tree bark, beautiful illustrations, scrolls and palm leaf manuscripts. Exhibitions like this were always a good way of drawing out shadows, though he didn't want to insult the curator's efforts, or the religion as a whole, by not paying an appropriately respectful amount of attention. He had the entire library in which to take proper precautionary countersurveillance measures, so protocol could wait for a little while.

Maybe that was why he paid attention to a different kind of interested glance that could otherwise have gone unnoticed.

She was about forty, with long glossy hair wrapped up in a bun. Wearing an ankle-length flowing dress beneath a bulbous oversized sweater and brown leather jacket. The soles of her boots were so thick, almost platforms, she was almost his height.

'Forgive me for asking,' she began with an accent he couldn't quite place, 'but are you actually enjoying the exhibit?'

'Very much so.'

'Oh good,' she said, relieved. 'Sorry to bother you.'

'Not at all.'

She had a little rectangular badge pinned to the sweater denoting her employment at the library.

He said, 'You're the curator of the exhibition.'

'Not quite. I mean, I did help put it together, though very much an assistant more than a curator. I like to take a peek every now and again to see how people find it. I really couldn't tell with you.'

'My face isn't very expressive.'

She smiled, assuming light-hearted self-deprecation. 'Meanwhile I couldn't hide what I'm feeling to save my life. You should see me playing poker ... Or, perhaps I should say, *not* playing poker.'

He responded with a small smile of his own to humour her.

Even bunched up, some loose tendrils of hair hung down way past her shoulders. Fully down, he imagined it reached her lower back. Wet, it might meet the point where her spinal erectors met the hips. He expected she bunched it up for work, for convenience. It was rare to see hair so long, and a welcome feature. No killer of any talent would have hair like that, leaving long obvious strands of DNA wherever they went, providing enemies or targets with something so easy to grab. Victor could identify a threat by what they wore, by how they stood, by any number of factors.

The hair was almost a badge, almost a sign for him to read that said No Threat.

He asked, 'What time do you finish work?'

ELEVEN

The champagne bar was located on the grand terrace of the upper concourse in St Pancras International Station. The railway station was a short walk from the British Library that took Victor almost an hour to complete after leaving Penelope. He chose his route at random, taking lefts and rights that appeared if and when a pedestrian in front of him reached into a pocket. He went left if they used their right hand and right if they used their left hand. He cut through plazas between office buildings and passed ramshackle housing minutes away. He snaked between shops, cut down side streets and crossed roads at the whim of strangers. He didn't imagine Borisyuk had sent anyone to shadow him, but he could never rule out the possibility of enemies tracking him down, whether they intended to kill him, arrest him or merely find out what he was doing. And for every enemy he knew to have reason to follow him, he had to assume there was that same number again in those he had no idea he had crossed. When he had killed so many people who were

63

ignorant to their fate, it would be foolish to ever pretend he could relax.

At one time he had imagined a future in which he had hid himself so far from anyone that he might sleep beneath the sheets for once.

The arrogance of youth.

'I trust I didn't put too much strain on your schedule?'

Marcus Lambert smiled a little at that. 'You gave me just enough warning for my PA to reshuffle my meetings.' He smiled wider. 'But not enough to gather a protective detail. Which I guess was the point.'

'Something like that,' Victor said, pretending he believed Lambert was alone and there were no contractors elsewhere in the station.

He had spotted four potentials already on the nearby platforms and walkways, and was still deciding whether the couple at a nearby table were letting their champagne go flat in their flutes for a reason other than each other's rapturous company.

'Thankfully,' Lambert continued, 'I'm only on the Rock a few days a month. The company might be based in Gibraltar, but business is conducted in London.' He glanced at their surroundings. 'Which has its benefits, although I'm sure you chose to meet here for reasons I don't quite understand.'

Victor nodded as if there were such reasons. In fact, he simply liked the location. He liked the deco surroundings and the lofty height of the station ceiling providing the feeling of dining al fresco indoors.

Lambert was a heavyset man. Victor would have placed him in his late forties, though via his research into the man he knew he had just turned fifty. He also knew that his parents had emigrated to the UK in the '70s from Nigeria and Lambert had served twelve years in the Parachute Regiment before working for British Intelligence as a private security contractor. Exactly when he had begun supplying mercenaries to the highest bidder was unclear, though Victor knew that business had begun in Afghanistan and Iraq, and now Lambert's clients included African states, Middle Eastern corporations and organised crime networks.

Most recently the latter included the Bratva, though indirectly.

His hair was shaved down so that just a few hints of stubble remained on the otherwise smooth scalp. He wore an expensive navy pinstripe suit, no doubt bespoke, a bright white shirt with cutaway collar, and a salmon pink woven silk tie. His cufflinks were black opals set within a ring of white gold. He wore a titanium wedding band and gold bracelets on the same wrist as his Rolex Explorer.

There was no obvious sign of a weapon, which made sense given the UK's strict firearms laws, though Victor expected that anyone who knew even a little about him would never meet him unarmed.

Lambert ordered oysters and caviar. 'I'm not hungry and I don't really like either, but when in Rome ...' He was quick browsing the champagne list before ordering a bottle of Dom Pérignon 2012.

'Between you and me,' he said in a quiet, conspiratorial tone once the waiter had left, 'I always used to pick the most expensive bottle of whatever was on a restaurant's menu. But it's not a very classy move, is it?'

'I wouldn't know.'

'Someone once told me that the funny thing about class is

the more you try to buy it, the cheaper you look. Or words to that effect.'

'They sound like someone worth knowing.'

Lambert shrugged. 'Past tense. Anyway, given the number of operators I'm down thanks to you, I think the very least you can do is come and work for me. How many is it now?'

Victor preferred not to share the numerical specifics of who he had killed in the same way many people didn't like talking about money. But in the same way those people still knew what they earned, Victor couldn't help but keep count.

'You don't seem especially sad to lose employees.'

'Contractors,' Lambert corrected. 'They're all freelance. The only employees we have sit behind desks. And I value every single one of both. However, when the central tenet to your business practices is pointing guns and having them pointing back at you then losses are inevitable. Every contractor knows the risks, which is exactly why they are paid so very well.'

The couple on the table nearby were both young, both vibrant and animated. On appearances, in love, or on their way. Victor could not hear what they were saying over the noise of his own conversation with Lambert and the ambient chatter of the bar, though he read the word 'Christmas' on the young man's lips as the young woman was leaning forward across the table, eyes wide yet with a sadness in them Victor could never understand.

'Your firm operates all over the world,' Victor said. 'You're careful not to advertise how many mercenaries are on your books, though your literature uses phrases like "substantial resources" and "unequalled combat capabilities".'

'That's correct.'

'Tax returns show tens of millions in revenue every year.'

'We don't like to brag. But where are you going with this?'

'So you have hundreds of mercenaries.'

'We really do prefer to call them private security contractors.'

'You have hundreds of mercenaries working at any one time, which means thousands on the books.'

'You'll understand if I can't go into exactitudes, though you're in the right area. I still don't get why you're telling me about my own business.'

'Because you have no need for another freelancer.'

'Ah, now I see,' Lambert said. 'Need and want are two very different things. And I made it in this industry by working with talented people, by recognising talent and using it to its full potential.'

'It takes a lot more than flattery to recruit me.'

'You wouldn't have arranged this meeting if you weren't interested. You wouldn't have bothered responding to my initial requests to begin a dialogue.'

'I was not in active employment then,' Victor continued. 'Though I had other commitments.'

'Which are now fulfilled?'

Victor nodded. 'Except I find myself with an unexpected offer of work.'

'Then I'm not the only one who recognises talent when he sees it.' He thought for a moment. 'You're obviously considering this other offer so it must be an attractive alternative. Listen, I'll see what I can work out with HR to sweeten our package. But I'm going to urge you not to play too hard to get as neither you nor I know for sure how long it will be before we're at crossed swords again.'

He paused because his oysters had arrived.

Though the young couple nearby would pick intermittently at their sharing platters of charcuterie and cheese, they were ignoring their champagne.

'Before I tuck in, I'm curious to know why you wanted to meet in person at all.' Lambert's tone was curious and also careful. Maybe he thought he might be pressing too hard or was concerned about the potential answer. 'I mean, I already figured you're just like me and accept that this is a business whether you're fulfilling the contract or it's your name printed on it. You don't take it personally.'

'Life is too short to hold grudges.'

'Exactly. Our prior interactions have been ugly and unfortunate, let's not pretend otherwise. Only that's the world we work in. It's an ugly place. We don't have to make what we do worse by bringing vendettas into it. The way I see it is that there is no such thing as an enemy, only a target. But everything I knew about you suggested a face-to-face would be a non-starter.'

'At one time that was true,' Victor admitted. 'It's far more prudent to handle everything remotely and electronically, for the obvious anonymity benefits. However, what I found was that by keeping my clients and brokers at arm's length they also had the benefit of keeping me at arm's length.'

'You're saying it gave them too much protection in case of any – for want of a better word – negligence?'

'In part, although invariably it is easier for me to get to them than they me. What I mean is, in dealing with me remotely they did truly not understand with whom they were dealing.'

Lambert listened as Victor's tone slowly lost its neutral cadence and became more deliberate and telling.

'So,' he continued, 'now I prefer to meet the people who will be dealing with me.' He held Lambert's gaze with a blinkless one of his own. 'That way there can be no doubt of who I am and what I will do to them in instances of such … negligence.'

Lambert swallowed.

TWELVE

Marcus Lambert did not finish his oysters or his caviar. He did not finish his champagne. He remained in his seat after the killer departed, for the sake of appearances. He played on his phone, reading and sending emails, checking on the sports news until he decided the killer was long gone. Then, when Lambert left his seat, he did not go far.

Six short steps and he took a seat at a nearby table.

'You bloody idiots,' he hissed between clenched teeth.

The young man and the young woman were taken aback in surprise, in confusion.

Lambert flicked the champagne flute of the young woman and the flute in front of the young man. 'He made you.'

'We were very convincing, trust me,' the young man said with a shake of his head. 'We did the entire job in character, even before he arrived. Honestly, it was so good my guy developed actual feelings for her.'

'Ah, really?' the young woman said, beaming.

'My guy is head over heels, no word of a lie.'

She put both palms to her heart. 'Thank you. Thank you so much. I'm so pleased she was a credible character. And just so you know, I was really moved by your story about Christmas. Teared up for real, swear to God. If I heard it off-job I would still be crying my eyes out right now.'

The young man shook his head and clapped his hands in excitement, pleased and proud.

Lambert was incensed. 'Is this some kind of bad joke? I'm telling you he made you both and you're too busy having a love-off to actually understand that you dropped the ball.' He slammed a palm on the table. 'I told you. I mean ... I *really* told you that this was a Code Blue priority. All you had to do was sit there and look like you belonged.'

Still, they were confused.

'You ordered a two-hundred-pound bottle of fizz.'

The young woman said, 'That's way sub norm for operational expenses, even considering the short time in character and the locale. First thing I would look for in a place like this is someone drinking the cheapest item on the menu.'

Lambert flicked the man's flute and the glass rang a sharp note. 'You barely took three sips of it.'

'Consumption of intoxicants on-site is bad SOP.'

The young man added, 'I won't even touch coffee in character.'

'And you know what's worse for standard operating procedure?' He flicked her flute too. 'Poor background integration.'

'I'm not following.'

'Look,' Lambert said, flicking her glass a second time. 'No ...' Then a third. 'Sodding ...' And a fourth. 'Bubbles.'

Both of them saw the champagne in a new light.

'There's no way he would have noticed that,' she said, looking to her partner for support.

He shrugged.

Lambert said, 'If I noticed you weren't drinking your champagne then he noticed. In fact, I guarantee he noticed before I did and I'm your bloody boss.'

'What do we do?' the young woman asked.

Lambert exhaled. 'Good question, but far too late. If I were you, I'd start praying he's not waiting for you both to leave so he can murder you in your sleep.'

The young man released a nervous laugh.

'Oh, I didn't realise I said something funny because I'm being stone-cold serious here. Assuming you survive the night, do you two really want to go back to guarding diamond mines in Zimbabwe?'

'No,' he said.

She added, 'Of course we don't.'

'Then next time you're in character at a bloody champagne bar you might want to consider drinking the bloody champagne.'

THIRTEEN

A limousine was far too impractical for London's narrow, twisting streets, so Zakharova had arranged for a Bentley Bentayga to ferry her and Borisyuk around the city. The old man had little interest in the mode of transportation so long as he had a comfortable ride, whereas Zakharova was more particular. She had been specific in choosing viridian for the paintwork for its blue undertones and nod to traditional British racing green. She chose to forgo a colour split for the interior leather, opting for magnolia for the main hide, to contrast the dark exterior, and imperial blue for the console leather, to complement the viridian's undertones. Finally, she went for a more contemporary look for the fascia and door waist rails, with diamond-patterned brushed aluminium. The bodyguard offered a nod of approval her way when he first took his seat behind the wheel, which she appreciated.

For a long day going from one meeting to the next, the Bentley was a smooth, almost tranquil ride. The traffic was hellish and without the detailed guide of the satnav, the bodyguard would have taken the wrong turning at least a dozen times. The chaotic maze of roads in the city was a source of continued amazement. No doubt it would have been quicker to use the Tube, but the bodyguard would never allow Borisyuk to be put in such an uncontrollable environment, and the old man would have complained incessantly about all the walking and escalators. And though she had had a modest upbringing, many years of service to the Bratva had given her a taste for luxury and a mindset that often the most time-efficient way to do something did not make for the most pleasurable way.

She took her shoes off when inside the Bentayga so she could make the most of the lambswool of the floor mats against her toes while she briefed Borisyuk on the details of their next appointment. Unnecessary to an extent, since his role was more about giving important associates face time with the boss while she handled the minutiae. She could tell Borisyuk anything she liked, in fact. He was never going to ask to see her tablet to check for himself. She wasn't sure he really understood how to use the device. It had taken forever to convince him to use a touchscreen phone because he didn't trust something that had no buttons, no tactile feedback.

He still read a physical newspaper.

'Why do you want to know what happens a day after it happens?' she would ask.

He would respond by licking his thumb to turn a page.

'You haven't told me about your meeting with Vasili.'

Without looking at her, he said, 'Why don't you tell me what you really want to tell me?'

'Fine,' she adjusted how she sat to face him easier. 'The man is a liability, one you were unwise to bring into your inner circle and one you are borderline insane to keep there. He's a threat to you and to the wider organisation, both due to his past associations and indiscretions and because of the way he is perceived by the rest of the table. Oh, and lest we forget, he is an extremely dangerous contract killer without loyalty who absolutely cannot be trusted by default. Did you know he killed the last person he worked for?'

'Yes.'

'What about the person before that? Do you know? Because I don't.'

'I have not asked because it's none of my business. As for you, I know you've been looking into him. Who he is, who he was.'

'Do you know how many bodies he left strewn around the French Riviera before he came to work for you?'

'I remember glancing at the headlines.'

'Are you aware that he used to work for us?'

'Indirectly,' Borisyuk said with a nod. 'Via that scoundrel Norimov, if I recall. Whatever happened to him, anyway?'

'I believe he's retired, although not my immediate concern,' was Zakharova's curt answer. 'Then you are also aware that the reason Vasili ceased taking our contracts is because he made enemies in the FSB and SVR?'

'What do I care what he did or who he angered when he was a mere pup?'

Zakharova fixed him with one of her impenetrable gazes. 'His enemies become our own. Did he tell you what happened in Tanzania? Did he tell you about Minsk? Did he tell you—'

'Enough,' Borisyuk interrupted in a voice louder than he would have liked.

'Do I also need to remind you that he killed your son-in-law?'

'I'm unlikely to forget while my daughter is still grieving. What of it?'

'While no one beyond you and I are aware of this fact, many at the table know of the turmoil that took place in Marseille and the disruption to the heroin trade in North America. It is not a challenge to wonder how Kirill's demise in the US might be connected, and how your new employee joins those dots.'

'He came to me to admit his culpability in Kirill's death. He did not need to do this. By doing so he showed more bravery and integrity than I have ever demonstrated myself.'

'He came to you because he knew there was no escaping the ramifications of his actions. He was perfectly aware of the length of your reach, of the Brotherhood's influence, and decided to roll the dice with you face to face. That's all. You're mistaking pragmatism for bravery.'

'You can say that now since we know how I responded, yet he had no idea. Had he run, he might have made it a year before our people caught up to him. Or maybe he hid himself in the remotest corner of this planet and by the time we had managed to track him down I might be long dead.'

'You give too much credit to saying sorry.'

'And you do not give enough. Every job he has performed for me he has done so quickly, efficiently and without complaint.'

'You already have an executioner.'

'For internal problems, yes, but the Boatman is no chameleon. He cannot drift around Europe unnoticed in the same way as Vasili.'

'Promise me one thing,' Zakharova said, sitting back in defeat.

'Name it.'

'If he causes even half of the mess he created in Minsk, you cut off all ties with him, whatever remains of his debt.'

Borisyuk considered his answer for a long moment, then said, 'If it makes you feel better, brief the Boatman to be ready. Where is he now?'

'Negotiating a peace between our people in Marseille. The city has yet to recover from Vasili's actions there.'

Coming from south of the river, his townhouse was geographically the next port of call, except he said to the bodyguard, 'Drop Luda off first.'

'Of course, sir,' was the prompt reply.

Borisyuk's townhouse was in Pimlico, whereas Zakharova preferred to be closer to greenery and so stayed a few minutes north in Belgravia, a short stroll from both Hyde Park and Green Park. The Bratva owned almost two dozen residential properties in west London alone, from Georgian townhouses to contemporary condominiums. All kept empty when not in use by one of the hierarchy and all available for Zakharova to stay in whatever her particular whim, Borisyuk's favoured residence aside.

She said, 'You have no further meetings scheduled for today.'

He did not look up from his newspaper. 'I have something to do before I retire for the night.'

'I assume you're referring to your pet hitman.'

'He doesn't like that term.'

'Does he prefer to be called a domesticated hitman?'

Borisyuk licked a thumb to turn a page. 'He's coming to meet me later this evening, if you must know.'

'I see,' she said, not seeing why she was to be dropped off first then, but also understanding his tone well enough to know it would be a waste of time to question him further. 'Get some rest.'

'I do not need mothering.'

'Good, because I'm not your mother.'

The Bentayga pulled up outside the Belgravia townhouse. A beautiful building of yellow brick above a white rusticated base storey. She would have liked to stay on a street lined with trees, and such properties were available, but not of this townhouse's luxury, of which the elevator was her favourite feature after a long day. Given the master bedroom was on the third floor, it was a lifesaver for her tired legs.

Inside the elevator, she thought about Maxim and his pet hitman, and the fact he was keeping things from her. With so much at stake, it was a concern to be kept out of the loop.

Dangerous times were coming.

FOURTEEN

First, Victor slotted in the plates, in a neat row from largest to smallest, from right to left. Then he added the forks, then the knives and finally the spoons. The cooking utensils had already been fed into the dishwasher during the meal's preparation as and when they were no longer required. Penelope did not eat meat or fish, so he had prepared a meal with the ingredients that she had on hand, utilising butternut squash and spinach to make a mild curry. She had wanted to cook for him given it was her kitchen and he her guest but had succumbed to his insistence.

Although he didn't take her for an assassin who killed her targets by bringing them home and poisoning them, it was just easier for him to do the cooking and take a break from his professional's paranoia. And it had the added benefit of letting him snoop around her possessions on the off-chance an inconsistency gave her away.

Victor finished loading the dishwasher, gently slid in the two racks, inserted a tablet and quietly closed the machine after selecting the most appropriate program for the crockery inside.

He traced his movements from the bedroom to the hallway, to the living area, retrieving the rest of his clothes from the floor and his shirt from the shade of a floor lamp where it had ended up after Penelope tossed it away. Cushions from the sofa were either on the carpet or had been squashed and scrunched. He set them back in their right places, plumping those that needed it back into shape.

The flat had a single bedroom and the distance between it and the kitchen was minimal, so Victor eased the door shut after him to dampen the rumble of the dishwasher's cycle.

Penelope was still asleep when he checked on her, strewn diagonally across the mattress, the bedclothes bunched up around her in a chrysalis of penguin-themed duvet cover. He heard her breathing; a quiet contented rumble.

He had declined her offer for him to stay over, thankful to have a genuine excuse instead of adding yet another lie onto the growing mountain of them. She knew his time in London was limited, at least. There was no deception in the temporary nature of their association.

The front door needed some force for the locking mechanism to catch so he could not avoid making a noise. He hoped Penelope was used to the ambient sounds of inner-city living and the little slam went unnoticed in her sleep.

He hailed a passing taxi to take him out of the immediate area, figuring even expert surveillance could not have known the exact moment he would exit onto the street and synchronise a vehicle in motion to be driving by at the same time. The black cab's licence plate began with an H so he asked to be taken to Holborn, then seemingly realising mid-journey he had to be somewhere else, had the driver go to Westminster instead. He paid in cash and told the driver to keep the change, which equated to what Victor considered a modest tip that was around the sweet spot of being enough to avoid provoking a negative reaction from the driver without being so much as to risk a positive response. He wanted the man to have forgotten him by the time he picked up his next fare.

In case he had picked up shadows in the taxi, Victor headed to the first pub he saw, which was on the corner of the main road where the taxi had pulled over and a narrow two-lane side street.

On his way to the bar, he overheard conversations about the fit of sports jackets and the punctuality of buses. A woman hurried from her seat to the bar to inform her husband she did want a rosé after all.

He ordered a gin and tonic so he had something to sip while he took a seat on a stool at the bar, positioning himself to see the entrance at the same time as he kept the mouth of the hallway leading to the toilets in his peripheral vision. His drink came in a goblet glass with an overly bulbous bowl and a thin stem, which was more awkward to hold than a regular highball that could be set down quicker should he need the sudden use of the hand holding it. The flip side was the goblet's disproportions meant it would require almost no effort to break off the bowl – quickly knocking it against the bar or snapping it off himself – leaving the stem as a decent improvised stabbing weapon, especially if he had time to secure the base in his grip so the stem protruded between his closed fingers.

When no one entered the pub after him, Victor allowed

himself a moment to consider the offers of work from Lambert and Borisyuk. He could not keep either man waiting much longer – especially the latter, who would expect an answer when Victor arrived at the townhouse in Pimlico.

Lambert and his private security firm would act as a broker for Victor should he take that offer. Borisyuk, however, would be his sole client. In the past, he had used several brokers. He would not have dreamed of relying on a single broker or client to provide him work. That created enormous risk. The reverse had proved just as a dangerous. By using a number of unconnected brokers, he had created multiple possible enemies.

With either a broker or a client providing work, it was always a question of balance. Both would acquire more information about him than any exterior enemy could ever hope to compile. They knew his targets, his movements, even his modus operandi. If they turned on him then his level of exposure was considerable. Unless he turned on them first, of course.

Either scenario was less of an *if* than a *when* in Victor's experience. It was impossible to know which way around the ultimate betrayal would come from, although it was never his intention to betray. A sad reality of the profession was that no one trusted him, whatever his level of loyalty, and to many clients and brokers it was simpler to have him killed than to believe he was no threat to them.

At least, it often seemed simpler to those who knew no better.

Hence, he sometimes needed to pre-empt such betrayals to avoid the inevitable inconvenience of neutralising a kill team and then hunting down a client who knew he was coming for them.

On paper, neither Lambert nor Borisyuk was a harder or easier client to kill should it come to that. The Russian had a global organised crime network at his beck and call, whereas Lambert had an army of mercenaries on his payroll, and many intelligence agencies and governments who owed him favours.

Victor did not relish either as a foe, albeit in a scenario he expected a long way off into the future, although he accepted he could be wrong. The risk was worth it, of course, in either case. Without someone to find him contracts or provide them directly, Victor was less a professional killer and more unemployed freelancer.

Besides the obvious monetary benefit, a well-connected broker or client was a necessity in Victor's line of work. Both men knew people everywhere and in every field. Private security, banking, finance, technology, arms and more. Lambert's network of connections extended into the intelligence agencies of many countries. Borisyuk had the personal numbers of many lobbyists and politicians. As his relationship with either grew so did the number of resources he could access.

Victor had acquaintances from his past dotted across the globe. Some were useful contacts who had procured him goods beyond his reach or provided services he could not perform himself. There was usually a limited shelf life to such contacts. He used them only a handful of times each for both of their benefits. It was better for him that they never knew him too well, and it was even better for them. Sometimes, they expedited a premature end to their usefulness. He remembered a forger in Amsterdam who had been of rare talent and resourceful. Alas, he had only used her services on one occasion as she let her greed overcome her good sense. Another forger in Italy had, for reasons Victor had never been able to determine, been quite fond of him. Until enemies hunting Victor had tortured the man for information on their target.

Even though he made a continued effort not to, he thought about the last broker he had worked for before his tenure with Borisyuk.

The only people who entered the pub within the next half an hour were a couple of late teens or early twenty-somethings, with multiple bags each that suggested they were, or had been, travelling. Either way, far too young and far too laden down with luggage to be professionals.

He checked his watch a couple of times to seem as if he were waiting for someone, and when they failed to show he left with his drink unfinished.

With no more time left in which to think, Victor made his decision.

FIFTEEN

Borisyuk was not one for airs and graces, so his bodyguard knew to let the old man open his own door to exit the vehicle, and to offer no help as his employer climbed out, however tortuous it was to witness as Borisyuk shuffled and swivelled in the seat to dangle one leg down to the pavement, clutching the bodywork and the door before pushing and pulling himself out of the car with slow, awkward movements. He had always been old. He had had white eyebrows and almost no hair ever since the bodyguard had first been employed, though he had seemed energetic back then. He had needed no help getting around. Now he needed help and would not accept it. Only a single time had the bodyguard made the mistake of offering a hand to steady him. The rage that had lit up Borisyuk's face had been intense and terrifying even for a man a head taller and twice the weight.

Still, he was quick to be out of the driver's seat and round the Bentley just in case Borisyuk lost his footing. He had fallen once in recent times and had a hip replacement as a result.

The bodyguard had been nowhere near and yet the old man's daughter had been livid, showing the same fiery temper as her father in blaming the bodyguard for not being there to help. He had apologised to Oksana over and over again and she still had not forgiven him for something that was not his fault.

When he had both feet steady on the pavement, the head of the Bratva pushed the door closed behind him, only it failed to make the telltale clunk of closure. Borisyuk did not notice he had not used enough force and so the bodyguard needed to correct the mistake. He would go with his employer inside the townhouse, make sure he had gone upstairs or was otherwise far enough away so the bodyguard could claim he had left something inside the Bentley without Borisyuk understanding the ruse.

He saw a ripple of curtains at a window of the house opposite. No doubt a curious neighbour spying on the visitors to their quiet street. Given Borisyuk was in London only a couple of times a year, such infrequent visits would be a curiosity to the permanent residents.

The bodyguard had been hired because he had been in the military, was battle-hardened, had worked with the FSB and SVR as well as many private clients in the years following. He had a stellar CV and flawless recommendations highlighting his awareness to threats and his diligence in mitigating them, his reliability, his integrity and, most important of all, his utter devotion to securing the safety of his clients in the face of imminent threats.

In becoming the personal protection of an organised crime lord, the bodyguard could not have predicted the threat he spent most of his time protecting Borisyuk from was the old man himself.

It had been a long day driving Borisyuk and Zakharova around the city and waiting for them while they had their meetings. Sometimes that meant sitting in the car and other times it meant standing nearby or outside a door. He was used to long hours driving and waiting, though the time difference meant he was a little sleep deprived.

The day was made even longer when Borisyuk surprised him with a request for an evening stroll, so by the time they returned to the townhouse the bodyguard was ravenous. He tried not to eat or drink too much when he was working, to limit the number of bathroom breaks he needed to take. He was looking forward to digging into all the food that had been brought in by caterers to cover Borisyuk's stay. There was always too much and it was always delicious. The old man never ate very much, so after Borisyuk had retired for the night the bodyguard could help himself.

As soon as Borisyuk was done with that no-good assassin, Vasili, the bodyguard intended to eat so much food he would have to take off his belt just to finish it all. There was always a variety of cuisines. The refrigerator was full to capacity with pots of fresh beet borscht, fermented cabbage shchi, solyanka with bacon and sausage, chopped pickles and extra lemon, cheese-stuffed puff pastry pirozhki, pelmeni dumplings to go with the borscht and solyanka soups, shashlik kebabs, beef stroganoff with extra tomatoes and served with noodles as Borisyuk preferred it, blini pancakes filled with dark chocolate syrup, buckwheat porridge with condensed milk, and vast quantities of sour cream to accompany many of the different dishes. Borisyuk was no fan of seafood so there was never any ukha, which the bodyguard often missed on such trips.

No alcohol, however, because the bodyguard did not count the honeyed kvass. It was so weak he used to drink it as a child.

'Vasili will be here soon,' Borisyuk said.

The bodyguard nodded – he knew the old man's scheduled appointments and did not trust himself to speak without betraying his true feelings.

Borisyuk detected them nonetheless.

'You do not need to worry about him,' he told the bodyguard. 'I do not.'

'That is exactly why I do.'

He patted the bodyguard on the arm in a welcome touch of affection and headed up the stairs. It was hard to see Borisyuk struggle because of pride. The bodyguard would think no less of the man for accepting help. In fact, he would consider it a strength because to suffer unnecessarily was never noble. How could pain be prideful? He knew it was not his place to question such a distinguished man, so he remained baffled and hoped when he reached that age he would have the humility to accept assistance when it was offered and ask for it when it was not.

Unlike the townhouse where Zakharova stayed, this one had no lift. One could be installed here, he presumed, if it could be installed there. Borisyuk's ascent was predictable in its slowness.

The bodyguard took a long time removing his jacket and hanging it on one of the hooks by the front door, close enough to spring into action if Borisyuk slipped and fell. Whatever his lack of speed, the old man did seem sure of foot, making good use of the banister, which he held in a strong grip.

He looked back over his shoulder. 'If Vasili meant me harm he could have exacted it many times before now.'

'All hounds are friendly until the day they bite you.'

'With you at my side this particular one would be foolish to ever bare teeth, no?'

The bodyguard nodded again. 'However sharp his fangs, mine are sharper.'

Borisyuk chuckled. 'Oh, to be young again and feel the need for such bravado.'

When he was sure his boss could no longer see him, the bodyguard snarled into the mirror.

SIXTEEN

Victor used the bathroom before leaving the pub. In part because he needed to, but it also gave the other patrons a chance to react to his absence. If they were civilians as he expected, there would be no change in the atmosphere when he returned. If anyone was paying him more attention than they should then they would need to hold their nerve while they could not see him. When he dawdled longer than he needed, those nerves would be pushed to their limit. Upon his return, they might not be able to hide their relief.

The bathroom was a horrid space. They always seemed to be filthiest when the door came with a piece of paper attached to it on which a schedule attempted to prove the strict regularity of the cleaning.

Privacy screens made of thick white porcelain separated the urinals. Victor's first thought was not of privacy but that they were solid enough to crack an assailant's skull against and their edges smooth enough so as not to split the scalp in the process. No mess. No damage to the screens.

It was almost a shame he was not under attack at this moment so he could test the theory.

Everything is a weapon if you're creative enough, his mentor had once told him.

No one seemed relieved when he left the bathroom, so he headed for the exit.

The temperature had dropped a few degrees, he found. Red buses passed by, crammed with passengers and absent of smiles. One still had advertising for a film that had flopped years before.

On the opposite side of the street, a small electric car vomited out a gaggle of laughing women wearing pink sashes across their coordinated cocktail dresses. Tall heels clacked and dragged on the pavement as they headed to a club's entrance, joking in loud voices with one another about how red their young taxi driver had gone by the end of their journey, then immediately assuring the doorman that they were not, in fact, too drunk to be let inside. Talking at an un-inebriated volume, the doorman's words were not audible to Victor on the other side of the street, though his lips were simple to read as he over-enunciated to ensure he was understood.

Your ... IDs ... please ...

Borisyuk's townhouse was a fifteen-minute walk away, which Victor stretched to almost an hour as he took a circuitous route, interspacing it with random left or right turns depending on whether the next bus that passed him did so on the near or far side of the road. London was ever changing, seeming a different city depending on which street he walked. Buildings of steel and glass constructed in the previous century looked like a glimpse into the future standing next to those built of stone before the invention of the light bulb.

An old man in a tan raincoat and wide-brimmed hat, walking at a sprightly pace, came to a sudden stop as they reached each other, 'Have a good evening,' he said, in a powerful, almost regal voice that made the words sound more like a command than a salutation.

'I'll do my best,' Victor assured him.

On the way, he detoured into a Tube station, descending underground to catch the train and staying on for a single stop before crossing to the line's other platform to take the next train straight back.

Outside the station, a cyclist almost collided with a pedestrian as they stepped off the kerb having looked both ways for motor vehicles only. Not a Londoner. The cyclist's finely honed reflexes saved the pedestrian.

'You're an idiot,' the cyclist yelled.

The pedestrian was too startled by the narrow escape to respond in a timely manner, and when they did, they shouted back, 'You're the idiot,' immediately scowling at themselves for their lack of creativity.

No one pinged Victor's threat radar and he arrived at the Pimlico townhouse a little earlier than arranged. He preferred arriving anywhere much earlier than anyone anticipated, although it wasn't always possible or practical. Turning up an hour early here would mean standing on a residential street with nowhere to justify his lingering. Borisyuk's diligent bodyguard would never let him inside before he was due.

Victor knew something was wrong within seconds of ascending the short set of stone steps leading to the entrance.

The bodyguard, aware of Victor's penchant for early arrivals and not shy about showing his distrust, was always ready and waiting to greet him whatever the venue. Last time, the bodyguard had been watching for Victor's approach and opened the door while he was still on the pavement. At other times, the bodyguard would be standing vigilant outside a restaurant or bar. There had never been an incident when Victor entered anywhere unchallenged or had to knock on a door.

When he reached the townhouse's wide and tall door and saw his own reflection on the weighty brass knocker without the bodyguard already in the process of opening it, he stopped. No pedestrians on the street. No cars passing.

Not even the sound of the bodyguard approaching from the other side of the door.

But no ambush.

Had this been a trap, nothing would have changed. Victor would have been greeted by the bodyguard in the usual manner so as to encourage him to lower his guard. He would be well inside the house, perhaps even sitting upstairs with Borisyuk, before he realised anything was wrong.

Victor took a single step back – all the room available on the top slab of stone – and kicked open the door.

SEVENTEEN

The lack of space restricting the full application of force, Victor needed three kicks to break the door's high-end locking mechanism. The solid hinges resisted the impacts and the door itself showed only minor indentations from Victor's heel. Until the strike plate tore away from the door jamb, ripping free screws and cracking the wood.

To stave off the January weather, Victor wore a black peacoat over his charcoal suit. It was already open, so his gun was in his hand in an instant, held tight to his chest with his elbow pushed back as he charged in, trusting to speed and aggression because there was now no opportunity for stealth.

He darted to the left as the door swung inwards and struck the hallway wall – denting the plaster – to provide a laterally moving target to anyone covering the entranceway from further down the hallway or from the top of the first staircase, and at the same time to give himself a better field of fire by bringing his gun into the centre of the space and away from the opposite wall.

No shots came his way. No gunman waiting for him.

Five fast steps brought Victor out of the narrow entrance hall and into the wider space at the bottom of the stairway. Closed doors led to a sitting room, a dining room and a music room, which he ignored for the moment because at the far end of the hallway, past the staircase, he could see into the kitchen and a dark shape sprawled on the floor tiles.

Which glistened with blood as Victor hurried closer and his viewing angle improved.

The bodyguard, dead from multiple bullet holes and surrounded by spilled soup and pastries. No gun in his hand or nearby meant he had had no chance to defend himself, the attacker or attackers too fast or sneaking up behind him.

The pool of blood surrounding the body was still glossy so he hadn't been dead long. Coagulation began in less than a minute, although that amount of blood would still look wet at room temperature for maybe an hour.

Wet droplets of spatter on a countertop, however, told Victor this had happened within minutes of his arrival.

He rushed out of the kitchen and approached the stairs with caution, ascending backwards so he wouldn't be shot in the spine by an enemy waiting on the far side of the landing.

No one in that ambush spot, so he spun around and crept up the final few steps before darting onto the landing in a burst of speed in case a threat was positioned in one of the doorways that overlooked the head of the staircase.

When he found no target and saw no open doors, he repeated the process for the next flight of stairs that led to the top floor.

Again, no ambusher, but the door to the master bedroom was ajar.

Because it was an old building, the door opened inwards to the room instead of against the adjoining wall. Which would provide Victor with a degree of cover as he entered but also obscure any occupants at the same time, while giving them a split-second heads-up, reducing any advantage he had in surprise.

So Victor charged in, kicking open the door to both cause a fast-moving visual distraction for anyone inside and to make sure the door slammed into someone waiting perpendicular to the doorway.

The door met no resistance and struck the wall with a loud bang.

The entrance was positioned in the corner of the room with the shortest wall to Victor's immediate left so he switched the gun to his left hand to give him a more beneficial angle as he swept in to the right, practised gaze ignoring the furniture and fixtures, seeking any shapes that were organic and alive.

Borisyuk was in the centre of the room in front of the four-poster bed, sitting on an armchair that had been pulled away from a desk in the corner. Duct tape secured around his ankles and wrists kept him locked to the legs and arms of the chair.

Nowhere for an enemy to hide except under the bed itself – and someone competent enough to catch the diligent bodyguard unawares would never trap themselves in such an indefensible position.

Borisyuk's head was slumped forwards. The white shirt he wore was red with blood as was the carpet beneath the chair. Coming closer, Victor saw bullet holes in the shirt.

Victor wasn't sure if he heard the Russian take his final breath or if he only imagined it.

He did not imagine seeing a drop of blood drip to the carpet, telling him however recently the bodyguard had been killed, Borisyuk was even more recent. Maybe mere moments ago.

Maybe encouraged by the second or third kick it had taken to get through the front door.

Victor hurried back out of the room, picturing the layout of the house, its acoustics, knowing he would have heard someone on the first floor had they descended while he was investigating the ground floor. Even if they had made next to no noise, with careful steps, all the doors were closed and they could not have shut one without making a detectable sound in the minuscule window of time there had been before he had ascended.

The diligent bodyguard had been caught by surprise, which had been no small feat. There was a door in the kitchen that led to a small garden out back, as well as French doors in the dining room that did the same. Maybe the kitchen door had been left unlocked, but could someone have entered it unnoticed while the bodyguard was eating in the same room? Possible, though the far more likely explanation to catching the man off guard was by attacking from inside the house.

Invited in, or they broke in on a floor above.

Not the first floor, because they would have sought to exit the same way and Victor would have heard.

Which meant they had entered on the third floor.

The windows were closed and the drapes drawn in Borisyuk's room, which overlooked the front of the townhouse. Had both been open Victor would still have ignored that window as a point of entry. A competent assassin wouldn't risk being seen by neighbours or passers-by any more than they would risk being seen by the target.

Other townhouses stood to either side with no gaps in between, so Victor headed straight for the bedroom at the rear of the building, picturing a terrace or at least a ledge to provide the best point of entry for the intruder.

If they had killed Borisyuk as soon as Victor was kicking down the door, then they could have reached that terrace or ledge while he was still in the kitchen. He wouldn't have heard with two floors in between. They could already be on the roof or part way through scaling the wall down to the garden by now.

As he reached the door to the bedroom, he heard the wind hissing through an opening on the other side and rushed in, eager to catch the assassin while they were vulnerable mid-escape ...

... unless that competent professional chose not to rush to leave themselves in such a compromising position and would prefer instead to end an incoming threat.

It was exactly what Victor would do, he realised as he entered the room, rushing straight into the assassin's ambush.

EIGHTEEN

That assassin had hidden against the wall onto which the door opened, obscuring both his own line of sight and Victor's for a brief moment, planning to shoot him in the back or push him out of the open window as Victor had done to a foe not too long ago.

Realising his enemy was using the same ruse, Victor was already turning to face the threat as he cleared the door, his gun sweeping into line at the same time as the assassin's own – both within arm's reach, both blocked and pushed to one side by the other's free hand before the muzzles were on target.

The assassin – a man of similar size, dressed in dark cargo trousers, black long-sleeved T-shirt, and rolled down balaclava – squeezed the trigger of his suppressed pistol anyway. Maybe in hope or delusion, or in desperation.

The report was loud in the close confines.

Glass shattered from a cabinet somewhere behind Victor as they turned on the spot, wrestling for position as each tried to disarm the other's weapon while resisting the attempt on their own.

Victor saw first that the stalemate wasn't going to break without intervention, so heel-stamped the left shin of his enemy, who was already moving inside his reach to change the dynamic his own way.

The stamp broke his balance, his forward momentum uncontrollable, so he fell into Victor, who fell back against the force, striking the cabinet with his shoulder blades and sending more broken glass to the floor.

Victor lost hold of his gun with the impact, but whipped an elbow against the man's skull before he could recover his balance and pull back.

Instead, he swept Victor's load-bearing leg out from under him while his stability was already compromised by the broken glass on the floor.

The assassin let go of his grip on Victor's arm so he fell straight down. Glass crunched beneath him, though he felt none of it pierce his clothes to slice the skin beneath. The assassin had the edge in mobility, his attire chosen for its practical advantages. Victor's peacoat reduced the speed at which he could move his arms and restricted their range of motion. A minuscule impediment to a civilian's daily life, yet a potentially lethal problem when grappling a professional without that disadvantage. Still, it shielded him from the broken glass on the floor.

He was already rolling away before the assassin could line up the shot, scooping up a glass shard and tossing it at his enemy's face as the gun fired.

A bullet singed a hole in the carpet and the floorboards beneath as the assassin let out a grunt as he flinched in pain or alarm. It didn't matter if the glass had hit its mark because the flinch gave Victor enough time to be on his feet and charging into his foe before he could recover and shoot again.

Victor batted the gun-holding hand away, threw punches to the assassin's body and elbows to his head, the former striking ribs but the latter were slipped and blocked from finding their mark. The assassin intercepted the next attack, trapping Victor's right arm under his own as he whipped the gun at Victor's skull.

He dodged the attacks with darting head movements, taking glancing hits to his shoulder and defending arm he brought as a shield.

Powering forward while they were locked together, Victor positioned his lead foot between his opponent's legs to trip him at the ankle.

They fell down as one, the assassin releasing Victor's right arm as they rolled and grappled on the carpet. He felt impacts from knees and fists as he fought to wrench and twist the gun from his enemy's hand, which fought back to line up a deadly shot.

The assassin knew his groundwork, knew to stay in motion, to never present any part of his body as a static target to strikes or Victor's attempts to snare and break limbs. Keeping the gun in hand reduced his options, but it reduced Victor's equally. To ignore it would be a lethal mistake. Concentrating on taking it and preventing its use meant Victor could not gain a mount or otherwise trap his enemy in one place.

Their constant motion gave the assassin the opportunity to roll on top of Victor, to try to fix his knees either side of his opponent's hips, a catastrophic situation Victor saw coming and used his whole body to throw the man over his head.

For a second, Victor lost control of the gun, losing his grip on the assassin's arm so the throw's momentum didn't rip Victor's arm out of the socket, but he used that same momentum to half-roll, half-flip backwards, crashing into the assassin before he could recover from being thrown.

Using both hands, Victor grabbed the gun and the assassin's forearm, locking the wrist and twisting the weapon against the joint to force it free.

The pain must have been excruciating, but still the man kept hold.

Before Victor could position himself to apply more strength, the assassin used his free fist to pummel short hooks into the side of his skull until he let go of the assassin's wrist to block them before one found his temple and ended his ability to fight back.

He felt the burning build-up of fatigue too, his opponent as strong and fast and relentless as himself, doggedly resisting Victor's attempts to disarm him and exploiting those attempts to counter-attack with stinging strikes that sapped even more of his stamina. Had the assassin not been wearing a balaclava, Victor would be biting chunks from his face or neck by now.

Victor's gun was in sight and nearby on the floor amid the glass shards and debris from the broken cabinet. Almost within arm's reach, though any attempt to go for it would mean first giving the assassin full control of his own weapon.

The whine of sirens in the distance could be coincidental,

only to Victor a potential threat was a certain threat until proven otherwise. The sound told him he had no time left either way.

The assassin heard it too and he heeded the same warning, because he thumbed the safety catch on his pistol in as obvious, if wordless, a sign of diplomacy as Victor had ever witnessed.

However much Victor did not want to be inside the scene of a double murder when the police arrived, the actual murderer wanted to be here even less.

Victor relaxed his right arm, which had been drawn back to deliver a downward elbow strike, lowering that elbow to his side, answering the assassin's opening offer of truce with a concession of his own.

In response, the masked man released his grip on the gun so only his index finger kept hold by way of looping through the trigger guard.

Instinct compelled Victor to attack, to exploit the sudden weakness in his enemy's offensive capabilities. He resisted because for now the police were the biggest threat, and for a moment he wondered why he was even fighting this man at all, and then let go of the assassin's wrist.

At that point, they parted, the assassin rising to his feet as Victor did the same, both gazes locked on the other, keenly aware of the danger posed even in parley and ready to initiate violence at the merest hint the other might do the same.

Victor retrieved his handgun in slow, deliberate motions, reaching down with his index finger extended to loop through the trigger guard, the whole time primed to explode into action at any indication the assassin was going to renege on their silent deal.

With the gun held loosely down at his side, the assassin backed away to where the French doors opened to the terrace.

Stopping briefly on the other side, he nodded a single time.

Maybe in gratitude for being allowed to leave, or in recognition of a rare display of honour between previously mortal enemies. Or, as someone had done to Victor years before, as a mark of respect to a worthy foe.

Then he was gone, and Victor dashed back through the building, descending so fast he cleared half of each staircase by leaping the remaining steps.

The sirens were loud now, but not so loud that Victor would rush out straight into police officers. Through the front door, he glanced in the direction of the wail, seeing the flash of blue in the distance, and walked away in the opposite direction at a relaxed pace.

He turned off the residential street as soon as an intersection gave him the opportunity, looking back to see a police car stopping outside Borisyuk's townhouse and two officers climbing out. Neither so much as glanced his way.

Average response time in London was about eleven minutes so this vehicle must have been nearby when the emergency call came in. Almost certainly a neighbour in one of the adjoining houses reacting to him kicking in the door.

Moments later, he flagged down a passing cab, feeling a tenderness in his ribs as he extended his arm. The assassin had caught him with a few good shots.

'Where to, mate?' the driver asked as Victor climbed into the back.

'Soho.'

After he was dropped off, Victor entered the seediest

massage parlour he came across, paying cash for an hour's service to the woman who welcomed him inside, and then when he was in a private room with its warm red glow, to the masseuse's confusion he told her he only wanted to rest.

NINETEEN

At a certain point in life what mattered most was not sex or money or power, it was comfort. That came in many forms, from the comfort of food and warmth to a loved one's embrace, but most of all it was the absence from worry, from stress. As the aide to the head of the world's most powerful crime syndicate, Luda Zakharova was rarely free of either. Her entire life never ceased being stressful; she never stopped worrying.

She could, at least, gain respite by way of a long, near-scorching soak. Her head had not been submerged beneath the water's surface and yet her face was as glistening as her arms or her knees protruding from the bubbles. Maybe it was because of the relentless stresses of her work that relief only came when the bathwater was so hot she had to stifle a yelp when she climbed in. Her legs were the colour of radishes. Steam rose in wisps from the water, clouding the bathroom's many mirrors and turning the glass of the floor-to-ceiling shower cubicle an impenetrable grey. Bath oils and foam infused with coconut, aloe and sweet almond oil caressed her skin as the soothing aromas of lavender, jasmine and rosewood filled the air.

Wall-mounted speakers bellowed Wagner's *Tannhäuser* Overture. One hand swayed and lilted to the music, while the other held a crystal tumbler containing a generous measure of Karuizawa Ghost Series whisky. She had a single stainless-steel sphere inside the glass, which had been chilled in the freezer, cooling and smoothing the liquid as the small amount of moisture from its icy coating diluted the alcohol content just enough to allow the depth of flavour to shine through. While not the rarest of Japanese whiskies – many were overrated in her opinion – the set of seven bottles she had ordered through one of the Bratva's many companies had cost over one hundred thousand pounds.

An extravagance, perhaps, though she only drank from them when visiting London. After all she had done, all she had achieved, it was less a luxury and more a right. And at a reserved half-a-bottle per visit, it was costing the Brotherhood a mere seven thousand pounds and change.

Which meant the contents of the tumbler gripped between thumb and index finger were worth over one thousand pounds.

So, when she heard a noise that startled her and caused a little to spill, a hundred pounds worth of whisky fell to the floor as a single drop.

At first, she dismissed the intrusion on her comfort. London was a city that never quietened. The streets were too narrow and many buildings built long before the invention of motor vehicles, or even the idea of television, radios or home music systems. Such a city was never quiet. It knew no calm, no harmony. To expect quiet solitude was only to know incessant frustration.

The British were tiresome enough to deal with without allowing their capital's guttural ambience to bother her as well.

With her free hand she swiped the sheen of sweat from her face and smoothed back her hair. The heat from the bath caused her pulse to soar and she breathed slowly and deliberately to force her body to be as calm as her mind. It was not a pain thing – she had no sadomasochistic bone in her body – it was the utter sensory overload of the heat that trumped any other feeling, any thought, any worry or stress.

In that excruciating heat, she found true peace.

Alone in the house, she had the bathroom door ajar. In part because she had no need of privacy and yet also because whatever the implicit security of her position in the Bratva hierarchy she was still a woman by herself.

She closed her eyes and set the back of her head against the folded towel cushioning the rim of the bathtub.

This was true comfort.

Until she became aware she was not alone.

In the doorway stood a murderer with a gun.

TWENTY

'Put on some clothes,' Victor said from the bathroom door-way. 'We need to talk. Right now.'

Zakharova's initial surprise and alarm turned to rage at the sight of him. 'Get out of here immediately. How dare you break into this house? Get. Out.'

'Borisyuk's dead.'

'Wh ... what?'

'He was murdered. I'll wait for you in the next room.'

She stared at him with huge eyes, no words emanating from her mouth. She managed to keep hold of her whisky, however.

Victor closed the door to respect her modesty and waited in the master bedroom. He had already done a sweep of the house to make sure no assassin was hiding anywhere, so he put away his gun and stood where he could see the door to the en suite and through open bedroom doorway.

He expected her to be fast, and she was, still tightening the belt of her robe as she entered the room. There was no point waiting for the inevitable questions so he told her what he knew, emphasising what he considered were the most important details.

'The killer is a professional, and a good one. Well briefed. Careful. I think he secured Maxim first, quietly, then killed the bodyguard. He broke in from an upper floor so he was as far away from the bodyguard as possible. He must have known the man wasn't simply muscle and that he wouldn't be taken by surprise easily. That Borisyuk was tied to a chair and wasn't simply executed suggests part of the contract included the retrieval of some information or something only Borisyuk knew where to find.'

She had taken a seat on the end of the bed partway through his summary of what he had found. By the time he had finished, her head was in her hands. Trails of wet hair hung loose over her face.

'This is a dangerous business,' she said in a quiet voice. 'We all know that. We have enough people executed to know a bullet is only ever a phone call away. And yet ... I never really thought this day would come. Whatever his age and increasing frailty I almost expected him to live for ever.'

Victor remained silent.

'How did the murderer get away?'

'Because he's good. When he heard me kick in the door he must have shot Maxim and then waited to see what I would do next instead of making a hasty and sloppy escape that I might have interrupted.'

'He got the best of you then.'

'He'll have as many bruises as me come sunrise.'

'Why didn't you come here straight away? What have you been doing all this time.'

110

'If there was a contract on you as well, it would have been executed at the same time and you would have been long dead by the time I arrived. Rushing from one crime scene to another would have done no one any good.'

She lifted her head and pushed back her hair so she could look at him. There was suspicion in her gaze. 'You were meant to meet with Borisyuk, yes?'

He nodded.

'The bodyguard would have let you in. You were expected. His guard would have been down.'

'His guard was never down around me,' Victor said. 'Because he knew exactly what I am.'

She waited for him to continue.

'I'm going to say this a single time: I did not kill Borisyuk. If I had wanted to, I could have done it at the ballet in Moscow when I first met him. I could have killed him inside the private box or on the street outside. I could have done it many times since in many less surveyed places than the centre of London. And had I killed him, I would kill you too because you know a little about me, don't you? Even if Borisyuk didn't care who I was or what I had done before, you do. It's not your style to be ignorant of the facts. That's not how you ended up in such a powerful position. Which means I would have come here to shoot you three times in the head for pure pragmatism, and then I would have changed my mind given the opportunity you presented me with. I would have saved the bullets and I would have drowned you in your bath a moment ago. I would have crept up behind you while your eyes were closed and you would only have known I was there when I took hold of your hair and thrust your head beneath the water. There wouldn't even have been time to scream or fill your lungs with air. You would have thrashed and fought and it would have made no difference. You could have had a bodyguard downstairs and he wouldn't have heard a thing. It would have happened so fast it would only have occurred to you to claw at my hand with your nails when it was already too late to make a difference. I would have held you like that for the two minutes it would have taken you to lose consciousness and then I would have continued to hold your head beneath the water for another three to make sure every last neuron inside your brain ceased firing.'

She exhaled to release the building sense of dread inside her, and nodded. 'Okay,' she said. 'Okay. You didn't kill him.'

She stood up, the initial shock wearing off and her mind turning to practicalities. 'We have a lot of work to do. Whoever had him killed already knows about it by now and it's only a matter of time until the rest of the hierarchy finds out. It's going to be chaos when that happens and we need to be ready. We need to be organised and prepared for what follows because the Brotherhood has not been in this situation for decades. There's going to be a succession crisis of unprecedented proportions. I need to get dressed and I need to start making phone calls. While I'm doing that, I need you to—'

'I'm going to stop you right there,' Victor said. 'Even had Maxim not told me yesterday that he considered my debt paid he's no longer alive. I don't you owe a thing. I came here in case you were still alive so I could tell you I'm done.'

She handled her surprise fast. 'Are you joking? You think it's that easy to walk away? That this is a nine-to-five you think you can quit when you've had enough?'

'Nine-to-fives pay a salary,' he answered, 'but otherwise, yes.'

'Without Borisyuk, I'm the one calling the shots for the time being. So you work for me. You're my man now and you had better start acting like it.'

'You don't want to go down that route, Ms Zakharova. I don't respond well to assumptions of ownership over me. It would be a very big mistake to see my willing servitude to Borisyuk as something that you can inherit without my consent.'

'You can't simply walk away from the Brotherhood and expect to be forgotten.' He watched her confidence rise. 'You are not quite as anonymous as you think you are, Vasili. Maxim may have been happy to have you in his service without knowing who you are, but that wasn't the case for me.'

'I'm sure you've done your homework, Ms Zakharova. I can tell you feel quite smug by what you have learned about me. It wasn't easy, was it? What little you know you had to really work for, didn't you? That's why you feel smug about what you managed to dig up. But by nature of this conversation you failed to learn the absolute, single most important thing to know about me.'

She refused to ask what that was, but he could tell she was desperate to know.

He didn't keep her waiting long. 'I'm not someone you want as an enemy.'

She steeled her gaze. No shifting of weight. No shuffle backwards. No folding of arms.

He had to respect her guts.

'So be smug,' he told her. 'Maybe tell Dmitri all about how you put me in my place on your next date. Assuming you're still seeing him by then. You enjoy the company of powerful businessmen and yet you tend to grow bored of them before too long. Grigori still sends you messages, doesn't he? Poor man is smitten and can't take the hint. He doesn't know about Dmitri yet. I wonder why you didn't tell him that time you met him for coffee. That was a nice thing for you to do given all the worry he was going through with his mother's illness.' He paused. 'Never forget that while you might know a little of my past, I know which side of the bed you sleep on and the colour of your eye mask.'

'No you don't.'

'Because you have two,' Victor said. 'One is burgundy and the other is royal purple.'

Silence from Zakharova.

'You were smart to look into me, which makes me wonder why you were foolish enough not to expect I would do the same for you.'

'I think you're forgetting you prostrated yourself before Maxim because you knew very well that if he so chose there was nowhere on this planet you would be safe. Not from him personally but from the Brotherhood. That hasn't changed until I say so.'

'You're about to have an unprecedented crisis of succession,' Victor reminded her. 'Who's to say where that will leave you once the dust has settled? No one's coming after me for a long time, even if you do survive what's about to take place. But let's say you do and you remain in a position of influence ... Because whatever else happens, the last thing you want in this world is to ever see me again.'

'You think I'm the only one you need to worry about? By your own admission you're the last person to see Maxim alive. There are plenty of people who sat at his table who loved him like a father. Those people are going to wonder why the last person to see him alive, an assassin at that, has vanished into the wind.'

'Then you'll have to convince them of my good nature, won't you?' he said as he approached the exit. 'Because if I ever hear even a hint of Russian accent behind me then the next time you look into my eyes it will be through a filter of bubbles and bathwater.'

TWENTY-ONE

No one could say exactly when London had become the dirty money capital of the world. It had not been an overnight process, after all, with the city's once respectable financial heart blackening little by little across the early years of the twenty-first century. And though it was impossible to put a precise date on London's ascension to the throne, Shivika Chandi could name the very moment she became aware of the fact.

At first, when she overheard a couple of senior desk officers at the Park refer to an investigation into some of the bankers of 'the Laundromat', Chandi had figured this to be an inside joke. Still wet behind the ears then, she hadn't thought too much about the meaning of the term beyond the obvious Americanism. With a high proportion of the financial market dependent on the Dow Jones and the dollar, those desk officers had to be referring to bankers across the pond. Because even the most Americanised of Brits – who lived inside an apartment instead of a flat, who ate cookies with their tea instead of biscuits, who played soccer instead of football on a Sunday morning – would use a laund*rette* if their washing machine was in need of repair.

Only later in Chandi's career did she hear of the Laundromat again. Only when she understood how the real money was made inside the banking industry did she come to realise that the Laundromat was London.

Specifically, it was its financial heart – the City – with its numerous banks that were all too willing to take the dirty money of almost anyone in the world, no questions asked, and spin it through multiple accounts until it came out the other side squeaky clean. The same bloodstains that could not be removed from clothing even by the best dry cleaners in the world posed no problem for the bankers of the Laundromat, who could wash any amount of blood from the money deposited in the accounts they managed.

Not a simple process, of course, which was why those with dirty money brought it to London, where diligent bankers ensured every deposit, every transfer, every withdrawal, was done by the book, nice and legal. And that was the part that blew Chandi's mind when she dug deeper into how the system worked. It was all legal. No laws were broken when those bankers set up shell companies for their clients, the accounts of which received the money in the first place. Similarly, there was nothing illegal about splitting up those initial deposits between multiple bank accounts in the company's name across many banks. Nor was there anything wrong about the hundreds and thousands of transactions and transfers that were conducted, moving the money around so many times it automatically created a financial maze that was almost impossible to navigate for anyone else. Finally, it was not only perfectly legal to integrate that money into the economy by way of purchasing assets like property, cars and luxury goods, it was actively encouraged as it benefited the country's all-important GDP and nothing made politicians look better than a growing economy.

On those rare occasions a clients' personal or business activities attracted too much attention someone from the government might feel obliged to keep up appearances by asking some difficult questions. Almost never did it go any further than that, however, because the Laundromat's extensive network of lawyers and accountants were on standby, always ready and waiting to reply to those difficult questions with indecipherable answers.

Well over one hundred billion dollars were washed clean through the City of London every year and the only factor that kept that figure from growing exponentially higher and higher was the physical size of the city itself. There were only so many properties available to buy with dirty money and only so much land on which new properties could be constructed. Looking out of the conference room window at the numerous tower blocks that had sprung up higher and higher over the preceding decade, and the many more in varying stages of construction, Chandi knew the Laundromat was always working on solutions to that particular problem.

It was a depressing thought that almost nothing could be done without the political will to make it happen. There was plenty of that will on display now, however, for a different reason. Given the gravitas of the situation, it was standing room only with representatives of the various police and intelligence divisions all brought together, which was unusual in itself. Chandi had sat through more Marvel movies than cross-department task force briefings, and yet here she was listening to the Deputy Chief Commissioner of the Metropolitan Police saying:

'The Home Secretary wants a speedy resolution to this, which is no surprise. We all know how heavily the Russian mafia is involved in the London crime scene so the expectation of reprisals and turf wars is very real. She absolutely doesn't want headlines. Frankly, neither do I. So, let's nip this one in the bud sharpish, okay? To that end the Metropolitan Police will be working in tandem with the National Crime Agency and MI5.'

She stood on a small, raised platform at the front of the conference room, which was on one of the uppermost floors of Scotland Yard headquarters.

'Now,' the Met's number two continued, 'that means we have a lot of resources to make use of, but it also means we have more egos in the paddling pool who will want to make the biggest splash. Don't go down that route. We're all on the same team here. We're all going to get a pat on the back if we wrap this up and we're all going to get the same bollocking if we don't. Even a single whiff that any one of you is holding anything back for personal, or departmental, glory and you're out. Is that clear?' She gave it a few seconds and continued. 'Steve Penk here is our rock star from the NCA who will be leading things on the ground. Hold your hand up, Steve, for those of us who have yet to have the pleasure of seeing your beautiful face.'

After rolling his eyes, a grinning Penk raised a palm. A few heads turned his way to follow where others were already looking.

'MI5 have graced us with their fiercest superspy, Shivika Chandi, whose glories put everyone else in this room to shame.' She called out to her, standing at the back of the room. 'Just how many foiled terrorist attacks have been credited to you personally at this point?'

She waited until everyone's gaze was on her before counting on her fingers until she ran out. With a little shrug, she said, 'One or two.'

Smiles and chuckles rippled through those present.

The Deputy Chief Commissioner said, 'I forgot to add that Shivika is frightfully modest about her achievements. She also happens to be the Park's resident expert on Russian organised crime in the UK.'

A colleague nudged her with his elbow. A little too forcefully, but it felt good, like a standing ovation.

The DCC gestured to an aide, who worked a laptop nearby. On the screen behind the Deputy Chief Commissioner a series of images appeared. A little fuzzy blown up so large, though all the details were still clear.

'These were taken last night by a door camera across the street from where Maxim Borisyuk was murdered. What you're looking at is an as yet unidentified male approaching the house ... drawing a firearm and kicking in the front door ... then emerging a few minutes later. I don't want to prejudice the investigation but I'm going to go out on a limb and say this fellow is our prime suspect.'

A few muted chuckles.

'As it happens, one of our cars was nearby and responded to the scene soon afterwards. By which point this man was gone, naturally. Thanks to facial recognition we have already identified the suspect as James Lexington.' She gestured to her aide, who promptly brought up an image of a passport. 'Australian national, thirty-seven years old, entered the country two days ago. We're currently in the process of liaising with Interpol and the Australians to find out as much as possible about Mister Lexington, but while we're waiting for those details, we can be reassured by the fact he has not yet departed these fair shores. At this point, we don't know who he is or why he is here, beyond the murder of Borisyuk. What his connection is to the man, to the Bratva, is currently a mystery. Which is why you're all here. The Met is obviously on the lookout for Lexington, and so far we have nothing to go on besides keeping our eyes peeled.'

'Hotels? Car rentals?' someone asked.

'He might be paying cash or he has associates putting him up.'

Cooper said, 'Or he's using different ID.'

'We're hopeful that's not the case.'

'CCTV?'

'So far, the door camera is all we have.'

'That seems unlikely.'

'It's Pimlico,' Chandi said. 'Not Brixton. Besides, just because he left the scene on foot doesn't mean he stayed on foot. By the time he ended up somewhere with cameras he could be in a car.'

'Or a bus, or a cab, or the Tube,' Cooper commented.

The DCC nodded. 'Which is why you'll be wanting to sweet-talk TfL and every ride-hailing app out there, isn't it?'

'Probably had a getaway driver parked around the corner. We'll have to check every licence plate within a quarter of a mile.'

'Within half a mile,' she said.

Cooper whistled at the amount of work that would involve.

'Like I said,' she continued, 'the Home Secretary wants

this solved before either the press get wind of it or before the Bratva turn London into Aleppo. And lest we forget: Borisyuk is not the only victim. His bodyguard was also killed and we can presume by the same shooter. The only fly in the ointment is there are signs of a struggle in a separate room upstairs.' Photographs were shown on the screen behind her as she spoke. 'We have broken glass from a cabinet and even a few bullet holes. But no blood. Remember: Borisyuk died in a separate room, tied to a chair, and the bodyguard was found shot in the kitchen. Our current theory is the latter was killed first by the intruder, who proceeded up the stairs to find Borisyuk in his back room. They struggled briefly, before he was taken to the bedroom and executed.'

Chandi asked, 'Why would the killer take the time to take him to a separate room and tie him up, only to then execute him? After securing him to the chair there could only have been thirty or so seconds left on the clock, right?'

'I'll repeat, that it's the fly in the ointment.'

She said, 'Maybe the killer was sending a message. Not only to kill the head of the Bratva but to humiliate him, to have him found tied up and powerless?'

'Ask him when you catch him,' the DCC answered, 'which I'm sure you'll do in no time at all.'

TWENTY-TWO

Zakharova had wanted to keep the news quiet for as long as possible, with only those who absolutely had to know informed. For as long as possible turned out to be just a few hours. The Russian ambassador to the UK had phoned four times already to pass on condolences from himself, the Kremlin, and the entire-Russian speaking world. Flowers were being delivered in a constant stream from every corner of the globe. Most had to be thrown away as soon as they arrived. There was only so much room, after all.

The house in which Borisyuk had been murdered was sealed off and it might be several days before anyone was allowed inside, so it was to her own townhouse that all the bouquets were delivered, where the succession talks would begin. Where they would end, she had no idea, although she was sure not every person gathered to take part in those talks would still be alive by the end.

Without Maxim's influence, it was only a matter of time before they began tearing one another apart.

'Whatever happens next,' she said. 'We must remain calm.'

London was no one's first choice for a meeting of the uppermost echelons of the Bratva hierarchy. It meant most of those attending had to fly in from Russia or further afield. Zakharova had to corral them to her because she could not leave when Maxim's body was cold in a local mortuary, nor when she had to assist the police and answer their multitude of questions without incriminating herself or any part of the organisation in the process.

'Calm? We should already be tearing this city apart.'

Igor Rakmilevich paced around the large dining room that had become their makeshift conference room. He had a narrow face and a small, pointed chin. The only hue in his skin came from his lips, and the dark, purplish tones beneath his eyes. Thinning hair had been positioned with utmost care and precision to cover as much scalp as possible. Under the harsh downlighting, the illusion disappeared.

'We should be out there now telling every gangster, every pimp, every dealer that either they give us a name or we give them a bullet.'

'We cannot act on emotion either.'

Rakmilevich did not seem to hear. A dark red shirt was the only colour he wore. His shoes and suit were both black, and his tie a pale grey.

'Sooner or later, someone will talk. They always do.'

'You think some stupid teenager selling coke to yuppies will know who called such a hit?' another said.

Seven of the most senior members of the Brotherhood were spread out around the dining room. Some were sitting at the table, others stood. With them were their most trusted advisors and lieutenants.

124

'We won't know for sure until we start cracking open skulls and seeing what spills out.'

Andrei Linnekin had been quiet until now. He had brown hair swept back, shiny with product, straight until it curled at the nape of his neck. His sideburns were greying, as was a goatee beard. He wore a dark suit and white shirt, open at the collar and the next two buttons unfastened as well. Gold chains glittered amid the curls of his chest hair. He cradled a tumbler in his palm, making a circling motion with his hand so the whisky inside swirled around and around until it formed a little whirlpool. A small smile suggested this pleased him.

Looking up from his glass, he asked, 'What do the police know?'

She shook her head. 'Nothing more than we do.'

'Is what they're telling you.'

'This is your city,' she countered. 'What are they telling *you*?'

Rakmilevich turned Linnekin's way. 'How could you have let this happen on your territory? Maxim should have been untouchable here.'

'Yes,' Linnekin said with a nod. 'The old man was famously so welcoming of protection he didn't ask for, and so very forgiving of those who did not respect his wishes.'

Rakmilevich threw up his hands in frustration.

Zakharova added, 'He's right and we all know it. Maxim was never one for fanfare and he never wanted to be seen as any kind of warlord surrounded by soldiers. It does no one any favours, him least of all, to lie to ourselves, to pretend he was someone he was not. He's dead now. We cannot change it, however much we would like to. All we can do is deal with the fallout.'

'We should name a temporary successor,' Linnekin said. 'To show the rest of the Brotherhood stability has been re-established, that there is no need for anyone to panic.'

'I agree,' Zakharova said. 'I suggest that I keep the ship steady for the time being.'

'Oh, I'm sure you do.' Linnekin laughed. 'He's not even in the ground and you're already trying on his shoes.' He looked at her feet. 'They're not going to fit quite that easily.'

'I've been steering this organisation for years at this point. Nothing has to change with me making the decisions, so there's no need to restore stability.'

'Nothing has to change,' he said in a mocking tone.

'We can all grieve, we can bury Maxim, and then at an appropriate time all of us can sit down around a table and work out what we do next.'

'The wealth of this organisation is embedded here, in my city. From all over the world, our little brothers' hard work only pays off because of what I have built here with these snobs. Maxim was the last tie to the motherland. London should be the capital of our enterprises going forward.'

'That's a dangerous position to take so soon after his death,' Zakharova told him. 'Especially since none of us yet knows who killed him or why.'

Linnekin chuckled at the insinuation. 'Was it not you who arranged this particular trip?'

'I arranged all such trips.'

'I note that you don't seem particularly upset at his passing. In fact, you seem to be quite enjoying the fact that you are no longer cold in his great shadow.'

Now it was Zakharova's turn to laugh.

Rakmilevich said to Linnekin, 'We cannot avenge Maxim

if we are fighting among ourselves. We need some unity. We need a show of strength.'

With a growling exhalation, Linnekin nodded. 'For now only. Then, the day after he's buried, we sit down and we work this out.'

She nodded too. Looking around the room she saw the others nodding along.

'Then we are in agreement.'

'And what of this Vasili I've heard so much about?' Linnekin said. 'Where is he now? Why is he not here to tell us himself what he found?'

Rakmilevich, quiet and thoughtful for a moment while looking his phone, added, 'I've just received word from a source inside the Metropolitan Police. They have a suspect.'

All attention turned his way. He held up his phone and the images it showed of a man with dark hair, wearing a pea-coat, kicking in the door to Borisyuk's townhouse and then leaving afterwards.

'Isn't this the hitman, Vasili?'

'He was due to meet, Maxim,' Zakharova answered. 'As we have already discussed.'

'So he kicked down the front door?'

'When he knew something was wrong.'

'From outside?' Linnekin scoffed. 'That's quite a feat. Does he have X-ray vision?'

'I want him dead by the end of the week,' Rakmilevich growled. 'I want to drain all the blood from his body myself.'

'It's not looking good for your hitman, Luda,' Linnekin said. 'If I recall correctly, wasn't it you he came to see first after discovering the crime?'

'He's not *my* hitman,' she corrected.

'Where is he now?'

'He didn't tell me where he was going, only that he was going.'

Rakmilevich said, 'We put out the word to everyone, to everyone. We find him, we drag him back here by his eyeballs, and then we do whatever it takes to find out what really happened last night, even if we need to bring in a blood bank to keep him alive.'

From the entranceway, a voice said, 'There's really no need for anything so drastic.'

TWENTY-THREE

Victor watched all eyes turn his way. There were seventeen men and women spread throughout the space, with a concentrated cluster in the centre consisting of Zakharova and two men: one short, in designer sportswear; the other larger, in a dark suit and overcoat. Victor recognised him: a man named Linnekin who he had crossed paths with some time ago.

The shorter man, Rakmilevich, stepped towards Victor. At first, with hesitant, confused steps as though he was acting on instinct alone while his consciousness was unaware of his movements. He had an expression of disbelief that became rage.

Then he charged.

A crazed, reckless attack without anything close to finesse.

The Russian was no warrior. He rushed Victor's way with so much uncontrolled fury that it was impossible to predict what he would do when he entered into range because the man had no idea himself.

With a longer reach, faster reflexes, greater strength, better positioning, incomparable skill and experience, and not impeded by unhelpful emotions, it was no effort to slip Rakmilevich's clumsy charge and redirect his momentum into spinning him around and into a chokehold.

Victor applied just enough force to the man's carotids to divert his focus from attacking to staying alive.

'I didn't come here to hurt anyone,' Victor told Rakmilevich as well as the others.

Though the sudden application of intense pressure on his neck had indeed doused any violent ideas of Rakmilevich himself, he could still speak in a croaking wheeze to instruct others to do that which he could not.

'Kill ... him.'

Zakharova was about to call for calm, but no one was listening.

Victor released his hold on Rakmilevich and swept his legs out from under him because at least three guys on the periphery of the room were responding to the man's croaking instruction.

No guns were drawn, at least. No one was about to start shooting in such a confined space.

The first Russian who came at Victor did a better job than Rakmilevich just by default. There was no rage in this guy's approach and, although it was equally lacking in skill, on account of the Russian's size and self-assurance his greater mass could do the job alone.

Victor ducked the looping haymaker as he darted forwards and to the flank of his attacker, sending a short side kick to the outside of the man's lead knee.

He wasn't trying to put the guy on crutches for the rest of

his life, just disable him, only the big Russian's balance was atrocious and all his weight was on that leg.

When he collapsed to the floor, clutching at his knee, his shin and foot flopped side-to-side as if still attached by nothing except skin.

The next two reached him at more or less the same time, the first going low for a takedown while the second hung back a moment to see the result and how best he could assist.

Victor shot his legs back so when the guy reached for them he found nothing but air, with Victor now above and driving down the Russian's face into the floor.

Zakharova winced at the *crunch* the impact made.

Before Victor could recover his stance, the Russian who had held back darted a step forward to swing a punting kick at Victor's head, which was the obvious move for a target in a seemingly vulnerable position and so Victor knew it was coming long before the kicker had decided to commit.

Still on his knees, Victor caught the leg in both hands by the ankle and wrenched it closer, pulling the guy off his single grounded foot.

His coccyx took the hit, the sudden jolt of pain overriding any thoughts of reacting, giving Victor all the time he could ever need to throw himself at the downed man, scrambling on top of his foe's chest and using his knees to trap his arms to his sides before throwing elbows at the unprotected face and skull until Zakharova yelled, '*Enough.*'

The Russian at his mercy made an incoherent sound. It could have been an attempt at words or maybe just the sound of exhalation struggling to get through a flattened nose and mouth full of blood and broken teeth.

Victor rose to his feet.

The three Russians who had rushed to attack him remained on the floor.

There were four others who looked like they might have intervened had proceedings continued a little longer. In Victor's experience, in such crowds there always seemed to be those suddenly getting ready to fight at the exact moment the fighting was already over.

Linnekin was holding back Rakmilevich and had been since he had scrambled back up to his feet, although what the man really hoped to achieve if he broke free of the grip was a mystery to Victor.

Zakharova issued orders to some of the other men nearby. 'Get them out of here and get them medical assistance.' She clicked her fingers when those orders were not carried out fast enough. 'Now.'

Groaning and semi-conscious, the three injured men were dragged or lifted out of the room.

'Was that really necessary?' she asked Victor.

'I only do what is necessary.'

Linnekin said, 'Why is it that you seem familiar to me?'

Victor remembered threatening him and Linnekin's subsequent sending of professionals to get revenge, but the Russian evidently did not. 'I just have one of those faces.'

Almost true. Surgeries between then and now had altered his features. There had been many such surgeries over the years. Never anything drastic: mostly fillers and implants that could be swapped or removed, widening or narrowing his jaw, extending or reducing his chin, adding a cleft; thickening or slimming his nose, sometimes adding a bridge, other times extending the nasal tip; softening the prominence of his cheekbones; he was no longer sure if he had natural dimples or if they had been added once. It had been many years since he had undergone anything more drastic, incapable at the time of providing a good explanation to the surgeon as to why he wanted a 'more ordinary face'. He had paid enough to overcome that doctor's ethical reluctance.

He wondered if Linnekin knew his assassins had failed. Perhaps there had been no agreed confirmation and he simply assumed they had been successful. One of them had been very pretty, Victor recalled. A Finnish woman.

'We have heard much about you,' Linnekin said, stepping closer. 'Vasili, yes?'

'That's what they call me.'

'You're not Russian?'

'Are you sure?'

'You're either incredibly brave or incredibly stupid to come back here after what you've done.'

'I assure you I'm neither,' Victor told him. 'I said this once to Zakharova and I'll say it a single time to everyone here: I did not kill Borisyuk.'

Linnekin looked neither convinced nor unconvinced. Rakmilevich's expression was too full of anger to discern what he thought beyond the obvious.

Victor added, 'But I'm going to find out who did.'

TWENTY-FOUR

It was common knowledge that many of the peers who turned up to sit in the House of Lords did so only to pick up the generous attendance allowance. Given that the only stipulation to claim the allowance was to – quite literally – sit, you had to be rich beyond measure or dim beyond reasoning to snub what amounted to money for nothing. The official literature noted that members may choose to forgo the allowance, and a few show-offs did, as show-offs were wont to do, though these were strictly of the nouveau riche variety. Which meant they were not hereditary peers because many of the landed gentry were filthy rich in assets and yet needed the daily allowance to afford to heat their sixteen-bedroom stately home through the winter. Lord James Milburn was neither. He had no estate, no gifted title by birth, and neither was he flush with enough cash to have bought his peerage by way of donations and favours to the current or former governments.

He had been made a peer as reward for countless years of loyal service to his country. He liked to refer to himself as a humble servant of the crown. That much of said servitude consisted of wearing frightfully old-fashioned gowns and napping through tediously boring speeches was immaterial. He had earned this quiet retirement. Yes, he had to actually vote now and again to justify the allowance and the additional expenses he charged for, but he never took the piss like many of the other peers. Mentioning no names, he knew of at least three lords who had arrangements with minicab drivers that meant they would be dropped off at chambers and the drivers would leave the meters running all day long. Said peers were perfectly entitled to claim travel expenses, however ludicrous the sum, and naturally, the driver and the peer would split the profit. Tens of thousands of pounds could be claimed per peer per year with little to no actual work done to justify it. Only last year one of Milburn's chums managed to squeeze over forty thousand pounds of expenses while voting only a single time.

Milburn would never be so bold. He was happy to do his duty. Plus, he took a healthy measure of satisfaction from ruffling the feathers of the traitors, hacks and chancers of Downing Street whenever he could. Too many times had political roadblocks made his life needlessly more difficult as a civil servant, so he was owed a little revenge every so often.

Leaving chambers could be a slow, tiring process. There was always someone who wanted your ear. Milburn only wished to get out of the place as efficiently as possible and hop on the train home to Hampshire. First class, obviously, though Milburn had the good manners to have a season ticket to save the taxpayer a little on his expenses.

One of the Lords spiritual was talking inanities at Milburn as they filed out of chambers and through the various hallways of the House. Bless him, an honourable Bishop of London, he had assumed Milburn was actually interested in the discussion of the day. When he took out his phone to switch it off silent mode, Milburn stopped so suddenly the bishop carried on walking unawares.

There were various messages and email notifications from his wife, his children, his lover and his accountant, most of which did not require his immediate attention and could wait until he was relaxing on the train before responding.

Another message focused all of his attention.

From a number that was not saved in his contacts.

It read: *You're a Winn3r!*

Followed by a suspicious link to follow and claim the prize.

'Everything okay, Jimmy?' the bishop asked, backtracking to where Milburn stood.

He should be better prepared, he knew, but he was out of practice.

'Oh, yeah, I . . . ' came his stumbling reply. He held up his phone as a prop. 'One of those blasted phishing scams.'

The bishop squinted to get the screen in focus. 'Bloody nuisance things. I struggle to believe there is anyone left alive who falls for them at this point. I barely give my number out to anyone these days and they still get hold of it somehow.'

'Once it's out there, it's out there for ever.'

'Joining us for a tipple?' the bishop asked as he held up a hand to say 'one moment' to some other peers motioning for him to join them.

'I'll sit this one out,' Milburn said.

'Your choice.' Then, as Milburn slipped away his phone, 'Bet you wish now you had spent more time at MI5 going after fraudsters and less time chasing terrorists.'

Milburn forced a smile. 'Skewed priorities, I know.'

The bishop winked before he walked away. 'That's karma for you.'

At any other time, without the distraction of the message, Milburn would have joked about a Christian clergyman referencing a Buddhist philosophy, maybe recognising that the bishop had done so with a healthy dose of irony.

You're out of practice, old boy, he told himself.

That self-awareness did not extend to noticing he left the House at an unusually swift pace, that his manner drew a few curious glances from peers who knew him to be quite sloth-like.

Out on the streets in Westminster, he was lost. He was forced to pace about in ignorance, chastising himself for being so out of practice he didn't even know where to find the nearest cashpoint. Then, when he had stuffed the money into his wallet, he further added to his indignity with even more blind walking.

By the time he had walked into a phone shop, he was red faced and floundering, amusing the slip of a girl who served him when he asked to buy a phone.

'Erm ... what kind of phone?'

Too flustered to be embarrassed by the derision in her manner as she talked him through the options, he paid in cash for a handset, left the packaging in the shop, and spent an age working out how to get the bloody SIM card inside the ludicrously tiny slot.

He flopped down on a bench so he could balance his regular phone on his thigh after opening up the message with the link so he could see the sending number. He thumbed that number into the new phone and called it.

A few seconds of dial tone before the call was answered.

'You know who this is?'

'Yes,' Milburn said.

'You know why we're having this call?'

'Yes,' Milburn said again, voice strained with rising anxiety. 'Cleric is back.'

TWENTY-FIVE

Zakharova poured both of them a drink. There was a tiny moment of hesitation as she moved the mouth of the decanter over the second glass, which Victor read as resentment. She didn't want to waste the fine Japanese liquor on him even if etiquette dictated she pour Victor a whisky as well. It was nice enough, although not remotely worth the staggering price tag. He had sipped plenty of better bourbons that cost less for a bottle than a single measure of this.

He made sure to drink his measure fast and ask for another.

'After our last conversation,' she began, trying not to frown as she poured his second, 'I didn't expect to see you again. I thought you'd be on the other side of the world by now.'

'I expected the same,' he replied. 'Yet here we are anyway.'

'I have managed to convince the others to back off for the time being. It would have been a lot easier had you not put three of Rakmilevich's men in the hospital.'

'A lot of things are easier without violence,' Victor said.

'Sadly, violence is sometimes the only way to get that point across.'

'You said you're going to find out who killed Maxim.'

'I am.'

She studied his expression. 'And why exactly do you care if they do? You told me before that you've paid off your debt so you're out of the Brotherhood. What's changed?'

'I was never in the Brotherhood in the first place,' he corrected. 'And yes, I have paid off my debt. But Borisyuk asked me to stay regardless.'

'That doesn't explain why you care who killed him.'

'Had the situation been different and it had been me shot dead in that townhouse, would Maxim have found my murderer?'

She thought for a second and nodded. 'Whatever my reservations about you, he felt differently. Yes, he would have tried. He would have tried hard to find out who killed you.'

'That's why,' Victor answered.

'An honourable hitman,' she said. 'I almost can't believe it.'

'I'm not a hitman, Ms Zakharova. I don't perform *hits*. I kill people for money. That's it. I'm a killer.'

'As you wish, Vasili the killer. But know that this is also how those in line to succeed Maxim see you. They will only withhold judgement for so long.'

'Your tone suggests you know exactly how long.'

She nodded. 'Three days.'

'And once those three days are up?'

'You know exactly what I'm saying. After three days have passed, if you have not discovered who killed Maxim, they will settle for you.'

'Hardly vengeance if they have to settle.'

She gave him a look of both contempt and pity. 'Maxim held this organisation together through force of personality. Those in that room might hate and fear one another but they would never make any serious moves with Maxim still alive. Now he's dead they're just waiting to tear each other apart for the chance to sit in his place. Whoever makes the first move will look the most guilty, and will risk uniting the others against him.'

'But only while I'm still alive,' Victor added.

'Exactly. When you're dead they will have free rein. You still breathing is all that stands in the way of Maxim's successor. So don't be surprised they are counting down the hours.'

Seventy-two hours to be exact, he thought. Which was not long before the full wrath of the Bratva was turned his way. Their reach was as long as any intelligence agency and they were utterly unbound by the law.

'I need to work fast,' he told her, 'so I want to know Borisyuk's exact movements the day he died. The day before too, and for the next day. I need his schedule, I need the details of everyone he met, why he met them and who he intended to meet had he not been killed. I need to know who knew he was coming to London, who knew where he was staying. I need—'

She showed a palm. 'I'll stop you right there. That information is confidential for all sorts of reasons. Most of those Maxim met are associates of the Brotherhood and its many business practices. I cannot give out their names just because you want to satisfy your bizarre killer's sense of honour.'

'You appreciate, of course, that if the others continue to question my involvement in Borisyuk's death then they're going to start to wonder if I killed him for my own reasons or whether someone instructed me to do so. Should they decide it was the latter, who do you think they will believe gave me the order?'

She set down her tumbler. 'What do you intend to do if I should give you what you request?'

'Ask questions. Listen to the answers.'

'Why do you think you'll find who killed him by talking to those with whom he met? Do you have reason to believe any of those people had him killed?'

'Not yet.'

She hesitated for a moment, then gave him a slow nod of acquiescence. 'In return, however, I want to know your movements and I want you to report your findings to me.'

'No, and no.'

'Then you're on your own.'

The prospect of finding any clue as to who killed Borisyuk would be next to impossible without her assistance, so Victor said, 'Give me your number before I leave and I'll report to you. But you don't get to know my movements.'

'Fine,' she agreed. 'Know that it will be harder to keep the Brotherhood calm if I can't tell them where you are.'

'I'll be in London.'

She sighed, then nodded. After manipulating the screen for a few seconds, she handed him a tablet computer.

'This is a schedule of the meetings he took prior to his death and the additional one he will no longer be able to attend. Business meetings, mostly,' she explained. 'Maxim had many investments, many legitimate interests outside of the Brotherhood's activities.'

Victor scrolled through a list of names, times and addresses. 'What about for today? There's nothing listed.'

'A day off. Maxim would have stayed inside his townhouse and watched westerns, one after the next, until he fell asleep.'

'What about the names in italics?'

'Only a few of such people would have any idea who he really was beyond a Russian oligarch. Those names in italics know the truth.'

'Then I'll start there. What does King John mean? Because I'm guessing there hasn't been a change of monarch and line of succession since I last turned on the television.'

'It means lunch,' she answered. Then, when she detected his confusion, added, 'He's an old acquaintance of Maxim, a criminal, but a man he was fond of, nonetheless. He owns a pub. We ate there, but John himself sadly could not join us. As such, I don't see how he could help.'

'I'll be the judge of that,' Victor said. 'I note there is only one such meeting scheduled for after Borisyuk died.'

'Maxim prefers to get business out of the way as soon as possible on such trips so he can then relax before heading home. Sadly, it was not possible to organise all appointments for the same day.'

'The Nightingale Foundation,' Victor read. 'What is that?'

'A charity of which Maxim is a patron. They have seasonal mixers.'

'It's tomorrow.'

'Like I said, it couldn't be helped.'

'They're not in italics,' Victor said.

'It's a charity mixer.'

'That Maxim was staying in London explicitly to attend?'

'I think you're reading too much into that. And you can't possibly think a mixer he did not attend has anything to do with his murder?'

'I already know every single person in that meeting in your dining room had a motive so there's no point starting with them.' He gestured to the tablet and the schedule displayed on the screen. 'Before I look internally, I want to know if anyone else had a reason to murder him.'

'Every person in that meeting?' she asked him in a careful tone.

Holding her gaze, he answered, 'Every single one.'

TWENTY-SIX

Beyond the necessity of cleaning dirty money there was another reason so many oligarchs set up shop in London. Not only did that wealth gain legitimacy, so did the possessor of that wealth. In London, one's monetary value was the only personality trait that mattered. As such, it did not matter if the rich man was a former KGB spy who had murdered his way to oligarch status, the doormen still tipped their hats. The sommeliers still smiled as they poured dessert wine.

The Laundromat washed away all sins.

Zakharova thought about her own sins as she fixed herself another drink. A larger one this time, since she had poured herself a smaller measure before so that she could pour him a similarly small amount. Of course, he had been ill mannered enough to ask for another after not taking the time to appreciate the first. Some men were simply not house-trained.

Sipping her fresh whisky, she paced about the room for a few minutes to give herself a moment to think. Thinking about what he had said and what he intended to do, thinking about Maxim, thinking about the vacant throne of the Bratva that could be her own if she played things just right over the next few days and weeks.

She knew Linnekin and Rakmilevich well enough to know the instant they found out about Borisyuk's death they would have been plotting to take that throne for himself. What would they do next, she wondered?

There was a precious window of opportunity that was shrinking by the hour. She might be able to squeeze through it to the other side and reap the rewards if everything went her way.

Assuming she survived it all.

There was so much to do, so many people with whom to speak.

It was only a matter of time before someone made the first move into violent ambition whether they waited the full three days or not. After that first blood had been drawn, the succession crisis would descend to all-out war. Even those who had no intention of fighting to be the new head of the Brotherhood would quickly realise that they could still be perceived as a threat to the ambition of others. And all would need to pick a side eventually. Choose to back the wrong candidate and it was as good as signing your own death warrant.

She went to take another sip and found her glass empty of anything but the stainless steel ball.

Instead of pouring yet another, she picked up her phone and dialled a number.

When it was answered, she said, 'I need your help.'

TWENTY-SEVEN

The muffin had all sorts of seeds and things stuck to the top to give it the appearance of health and nutrition and not seven hundred calories of flour and sugar. Brian would go ape if he knew she was eating something like that, reminding her about the danger of diabetes as he lectured her about the fragility of her microbiome. Before the divorce, he had sent her off to work each morning with a travel mug full of viscous green sludge that he called a smoothie, which had been lovingly prepared to include a complete balance of vitamins, minerals, antioxidants, phytonutrients and fibre. So much fibre. The only missing ingredient was a little something Chandi liked to call drinkability.

She had never been able to escape the house unless Brian first witnessed her take a big gulp. Given the breakup of her marriage, it still annoyed her she had made so much effort to make the resulting *mmmm* convincing.

She sat overlooking the park's small lake – or was it a pond? – which glittered in the rare spell of uninterrupted sunshine. Still freezing, naturally. Chandi wore a beanie hat, scarf and mittens in addition to her winter coat to protect herself from the chill afternoon air.

With no trace of wind, the lake's surface was a mirror to the grey sky above, cracking apart only when the ducks passed. Chandi watched the mirror ripple and calm back to a perfect, glassy sheen. There was something relaxing about watching the lake and the birds upon it. She liked being close to nature. At least, nature contained in an organised, cultivated manner. Left to its own devices, nature was pure chaos. It needed the steadying hand of civilisation to be at its best.

Lord Milburn approached, wearing a long coat and yet no hat. His ears were red in the cold.

Milburn took a seat on the far end of the bench after swiping away some dew with a leather-gloved hand.

Chandi held up the muffin. 'You should get one. They're really good.'

The café she'd purchased it from stood nearby.

'I figured you'd been taught better than to do this somewhere so public. Why aren't we doing this in your car?'

'Because I take the DLR into town.' Chandi sipped some coffee, which was now a little too cooled by the outside air to be at its best. 'Besides, this is close to headquarters.'

'You're making this worse, not better.'

'I'm on a task force. I can't disappear for two sodding hours to meet in a place that would make you less twitchy.'

Milburn scoffed. 'I'm no such thing. Can we please make this as brief as possible?'

Chandi nodded. She slid the remains of her muffin into the paper bag it came in and swiped her hands to get rid of the crumbs. '*Shoo*,' she hissed, kicking out a foot at the pigeon that immediately swooped in to capitalise.

To Milburn, she said, 'You've heard about the murder of Maxim Borisyuk by now, I'm sure.'

'I have.'

'I'm helping Scotland Yard and the NCA, who are hoping to wrap it up sharpish before these fair streets are running with Russian blood from the fallout.'

'How is Cleric involved?'

'Prime suspect,' Chandi said, drawing forth a phone. She unlocked the screen and opened up images to show Milburn. 'Here's the stills from some old busybody's door camera.'

Milburn swiped through the photographs. 'They're not very clear. Are you absolutely certain this is the same man?'

'Of course I'm not certain,' Chandi answered. 'You didn't tell me to only let you know when he resurfaces if I'm absolutely certain, did you?'

'I suppose not.' Milburn exhaled as he handed back the phone. He gazed out over the water. Ducks and geese drifted along, content. 'Bloody hell, this is the last thing I need right now.'

'Skeletons in closets aren't known for their considerate timing.'

'One mess was more than enough to deal with,' Milburn said, drumming his fingers on the bench's armrest. 'It was nothing short of a miracle we managed to keep it so contained. All those dead bodies ... God, what a shitshow.'

'Perhaps the single best clean-up I've ever known, or even heard of,' Chandi said. 'A privilege to be a part of it.'

'You're too kind, Shivy.'

'Should be in the textbook.'

'And thank goodness it isn't,' Milburn chuckled. 'We would have to be behind bars first.'

When he smiled, his teeth were more grey than white and more crooked than straight. He was part of that old breed, happy to pay for black cabs to avoid the peasants on the Tube, happy to shop for groceries in Fortnum's, happy to drop a couple of grand on a suit, yet wouldn't dream of visiting an orthodontist's office. He would consider it frightfully plebeian to waste money on such extravagances.

'The file's technically still open, you know?'

'For no good purpose. I swear that's down to nothing but spite from my replacement.'

'The Park's gone to hell without you at the helm.'

'I can believe it. I really can. It's all politics now. It's little more than a PR department for Downing Street. We all know where to look for the bad guys, but we have to tread so very carefully.' He shot a sudden, awkward glance Chandi's way. 'No offence.'

She didn't glance back. 'Why would I be offended?'

Milburn hesitated. 'Oh, no reason. But you know what I mean.'

'Yeah,' she said in a certain tone. 'I know *exactly* what you mean.'

Milburn did not seem to hear.

A squirrel edged closer in testing, nervous advances. Little scuttles that brought him from a tree to the path, to the bare earth that surrounded the bench.

'I saw a red squirrel once,' Milburn said. 'Just one time in my entire life. Can you believe it?'

'Why wouldn't I?'

Her former boss shook his head to say it wasn't important. His expression changed, becoming pensive. Maybe sad.

'I do so miss it, Shivika. The game. The stakes.'

'Lordship isn't all it's cracked up to be?'

'A bloody monkey could do it,' he said with a huff. 'Still, it beats tending rose bushes or whatever else one's supposed to do in retirement. Tell me, is there anything more pointless than growing flowers?'

'They look pretty.'

'Don't go mushy on me. It doesn't suit you. I've seen into your soul, remember.' He paused to collect his thoughts. 'So, what does your gut tell you about Borisyuk's murder?'

Chandi answered, 'Head of Russian organised crime is assassinated. Our boy is a renowned contract killer. I'm getting a distinct two-plus-two feeling here.'

'That's not what I mean. He's not still working for Six, is he? Bumping off the Bratva's leader doesn't feel like their style and yet I wouldn't put it past them.'

'As far as I can tell he hasn't been on the payroll of MI6 for a long time. In fact, I heard a rumour he was dead.'

'People like Cleric are only dead if you see their corpse with your own two eyes. I take it no one at Six knows he's back from the dead?'

'I can't know for sure but if they did, they would have people all over him, wouldn't they?'

Milburn chewed on the thought. Nodded. 'The Yanks?'

'Are quiet. Nothing suggests they know he's alive, or even care if they do.'

'Suggests? That doesn't reassure me.'

'I can ask them if you like.'

Milburn huffed. 'That's really not very amusing, Shivy.'

'I generally prefer to go by Shivika these days.'

'Oh, is that right? Bully for you.' Milburn watched the ducks for a moment. 'Is there anything you can do?'

'What are you asking me to do exactly?'

'Oh, I don't know, do I? I want to know for sure if this really is Cleric or some lookie-likie. That would be a good start.'

'I doubt that will be possible unless he's taken into custody.'

'That's a little bloody late for me.'

Chandi shrugged. 'Then what do you suggest?'

'Can't you throw a spanner in the works? Make sure he doesn't get caught?'

'At this point? A resounding no. The scrutiny on this one is ridiculous because the Home Secretary is shitting a brick. She wants this sorted pronto.'

'Of course she does,' Milburn said, shaking his head in disgust. 'I imagine there's so much Russian money in that place it might as well be a wing of the Kremlin. The only question is, does she want it solved quickly because the longer this goes on the more it shines an unflattering light on this fair Londongrad, or is she worried the oligarchs might take their money elsewhere?'

'The end result is the same.'

'You can tell me, only it's not your reputation on the line.'

'You're worrying too much,' Chandi said, rising from the bench. 'Don't forget who we're talking about here. If it really is Cleric in those photographs then he's been a tad unlucky, but he's no fool.' She tossed away the dregs of her coffee, aiming for the pigeons but they were far too quick. 'The man knows he has a colourful history in this city, so trust me on this one, okay? Cleric is long gone by now.'

TWENTY-EIGHT

At one point, London had been a city with a low ceiling. Compared to lofty giants like New York City, the capital of the UK had been positively dwarfish. The number of buildings with twenty or more storeys had been rare at the beginning of the twenty-first century. Within a couple of decades, planning permission for almost one hundred such towers was being applied for every single year. Not all were approved, of course, though Sarah Zhou's property development company never seemed to be denied. She would joke about friends in high places and being naturally lucky when asked at functions and parties about her undefeated record. She knew her industry rivals whispered behind her back about corruption, about bribes, and she didn't care one bit. It just meant they were weak. They didn't know how to play the game that she had perfected.

There were so many stages to receiving planning permission in London it was amazing all those buildings were approved every year. Getting a winning vote from a local borough council was hard enough. Throw in the mayor's office as well, with one eye ever on public perception and the next election, and the whole business was more like a magic show with illusions and misdirection than it was a series of negotiations and compromises.

Checking the trade news on her phone, she had to laugh at the reasoning behind a recent rejection. The City of London had approved the proposed three-hundred-plus metre skyscraper, only for the mayor to overturn the decision. The reasoning mentioned the building's harmful impact to the skyline, which was laughable given how that skyline had been obliterated within the last twenty years by dozens of similar constructions. The mayor also noted the resistance to the project from heritage associations, that the building's design was not harmonious with its neighbours, and that it failed to provide a positive social contribution to the city.

Which all sounded fair enough in theory.

However, everyone in the industry knew the real reason for the overturning of planning permission: once someone pointed out that the bulbous top of the skyscraper made it look a little like a three-hundred-metre-tall penis, it was impossible to see it as anything else.

Such a schoolboy error.

Zhou never allowed any design out of the conference room if it even so much as dared to be bold. A building had to look just interesting enough so it wasn't ignored by the councillors who had to vote on it, and that was it. She had fired architects on the spot for beginning their pitches with talk of 'wow factor' or 'contemporary edge'.

They were designing buildings, not creating art.

Four walls and a roof were plenty.

Her latest baby was still in its first trimester, with construction having begun within the last six months. It was her most ambitious project yet, with a price tag to match, and formed the second stage to a development completed five years beforehand. This second phase comprised over half a million square feet, on which would be more than three hundred homes, a five-star hotel, office and retail space, new transport links and recreation space. Zhou hated that last part but it was an unavoidable hit she had to take. Every tree they had to plant, every bench built, every stretch of bloody grass laid down, meant a smaller footprint of actual, profitable construction.

She hated the idea of some smiling carefree couple sipping lattes in the sunshine on one of her green spaces, utterly unaware that to provide a place for their arses to park had cost her millions.

'Is this some kind of a sick joke?' she asked the foreman of the site, shouting to be heard over the jungle of different noises that made up a modern construction site.

'I'm afraid not, Mrs Zhou,' Otis answered, scratching at the back of a thick neck. 'We're looking at two inches of water in basement floor one, three inches of water in basement floor five, and about four inch—'

'Yeah, yeah, I can work out the punchline for myself, thanks.' She growled. 'How did they get on-site in the first place? There have to be a hundred signs up boasting of our twenty-four-hour security.'

'Forgive me for being blunt, but they're just signs.'

'Signs? You are not seriously telling me that we have hundreds upon hundreds of millions of pounds guarded by nothing except signs?'

'The Excelar boys pop off at five,' Otis explained. 'In winter, we're not through the gates until six a.m.'

'Let me guess,' she responded, taking a calming breath in. 'If they stayed an extra hour that pushes them into double time . . . which no one's allowed to take while we're over budget.'

He nodded. 'Them's the rules.'

'Shitshitshitshit.' No amount of inhalation was going to calm her down. 'How long until the water's cleared?'

'A week at least.'

'Then why is everyone standing around doing nothing?'

'The pumps won't arrive until this afternoon. Not much we can do until then.'

'You haven't heard of buckets?'

Otis released a chuckle of nervous energy. 'There must be ten thousand gallons down there.'

'Which is why you should already have started, isn't it?' Her site radio crackled and she stepped away to answer it. 'Don't you dare give me more bad news.'

It was one of the Excelar security personnel. 'You have a visitor. He—'

'This literally could not be at a worse time. Even if it's the mayor, I'm too busy. In fact, unless it's Jesus himself come to turn all this water into Pinot Noir then tell them they can piss off.' She realised Otis was still nearby, waiting for her to finish. To him she said, 'What are you waiting for? Get bailing,' and into the radio, she said, 'Do not bother me again.'

'Wait,' the security guy urged. 'The visitor says he's a representative here on behalf of Maxim Borisyuk.'

She released the SEND button and exchanged looks with Otis, whose face became grave.

'Did you not speak with Borisyuk only yesterday?'

Zhou nodded, her own expression showing a similarly increasing amount of concern. 'What do you think "a representative" means?'

Scratching the back of his neck, Otis said, 'Do you want me to—?'

'Yeah,' she answered. 'Stay close. Please.' Into the radio, she told the security guard to, 'Tell him to head up.'

TWENTY-NINE

Victor met Zhou on the twelfth storey of the building. It was a cold, windy floor without walls. Orange safety netting swayed and rippled. Zhou had her hands in her pockets and her shoulders hunched as she paced about the concrete, waiting for him near the single working elevator. The moment she saw him emerge from the stairwell, she strode his way and passed him to check no one had followed him up.

She gestured. 'They didn't tell you the lift works?'

'They did, but I need the steps.'

'There must be two hundred of the things.'

'Closer to three,' he said.

She went to say something else, then shook her head to dismiss the thought. She didn't care why he had taken the stairs. She wore a set of coveralls over what he presumed to be a suit, and over the coveralls was a dark puffa jacket to shield her from the weather. Maybe forty or maybe fifty, with great skin and some Botox. Despite many procedures, there had never been any need to paralyse his facial muscles. He had no desire to appear younger, only different, and he made so few expressions there would have been little need for such injections even if he wanted them for vanity purposes.

The floor was almost all bare cement and exposed steel superstructure. The outer walls, the curtain wall, would seal it off from the elements much later in the construction. Such feats of engineering were eminently impressive to Victor, who recognised his only talent lay not in creating but destroying.

Grey sky surrounded them in every direction, the monotone broken up only by other skyscrapers. Some nearby bright, despite what little sun reached their glass façades, others dulled or disappearing into the clouds. Up here, the air was fresh and felt lighter to breathe without the weight of pollutants saturating every inhalation.

Zhou read his appreciative gaze as the distance closed between them. 'Gives me chills,' she told him. 'When it begins to take shape, when I see it for the first time not as a drawing or a model ... '. She spread out her hands. 'When I'm standing here inside the beast I built ... There's no better feeling in this world.' She brought her hands back down and then extended one in greeting. 'I'm Sarah Zhou.'

Victor shook the hand. Her fingers were cold.

She asked, 'Is Maxim not joining us?'

'If he were, that would be an impressive feat given he's dead.' He was quick to deliver the salient facts. 'He died last night.'

'Jesu—'

'Don't blaspheme.'

She withdrew her hands from the pockets of her jacket so she could stroke her chin and jaw. A self-soothing gesture as she processed the news. 'How did he—?'

159

'That's really not important for you to know right now,' he interrupted. 'I'm retracing Maxim's steps, speaking to those with whom he met during his visit. You had a meeting with him in the afternoon, yes?'

She seemed to struggle to remember. 'I ... I guess I did. In the site office.' She began to point and then stopped when realising it was an unnecessary specific. 'Why do you want to know?'

'Because someone murdered him,' Victor answered.

'Murdered?'

'Shot dead a few hours after meeting you.'

'You can't possibly think that I had anything to do with it?'

'Why would I not think that?'

'Now hold on one second ...' She had a look of disbelief, then disgust. 'I believe our conversation is over.'

'I'm not done yet.'

'You're not the police, I don't have to talk to you.'

'Only one part of that statement is accurate,' he explained. 'Especially when Maxim was considering pulling out of further investment.'

'Wait ... what? He told you he was—? He really said he was going to pull out?'

Victor nodded to roll with the lie, to see where it would go. 'What did you discuss in your site office?'

'Discuss? The usual. Nothing worth killing over. Mister Borisyuk likes to pop in every now again on these projects,' she told him, looking off into space as if picturing the meeting. 'He doesn't just like to see the end result, he wants to see how the sausage is made. I mean, he knows – knew – the development is over budget. That's not new and it's happened before, so why the change of heart now?'

160

'I'm hoping you can enlighten me on that.'

'All investors have been asked to increase their stakes,' Zhou said. 'He was asked long before he came to the site. Why wouldn't he have brought it up with me? Or are you saying he changed his mind because I wanted him to help sway those who are still reluctant?'

'When you say "sway" do you mean you wanted him to threaten them?'

'Oh, no, I really wouldn't put it like that at all.' She forced a smile at the notion of intimidation. 'More persuade, I guess.'

'You understand that Maxim Borisyuk was the head of a brutal criminal organisation, yes?'

More hesitation.

'Let's not be coy,' Victor said. 'You know very well where Maxim's money came from and you didn't care as long as he invested in your developments, which he did as part of a complex money laundering operation. Trust me when I say I'm really not the kind of man who judges others on their business ethics or lack thereof.'

'What did you say was your association with Mister Borisyuk?'

'I didn't say, but when you're asked about this visit you can tell them I'm an accountant and that you don't remember the name I gave you.'

She said, 'You haven't actually given me your name.'

He nodded. 'Then it won't be any trouble to forget, will it?' He did not wait for an answer. 'Back to Maxim Borisyuk, your business partner and organised crime boss.'

'He can ... could be very persuasive,' Zhou conceded after a moment. 'And, yes, I may have asked him to direct that persuasiveness in one particular direction.'

Victor said, 'Give me a name. You must know who your investors are.'

'I can't ... Not exactly. Yes, I know my investors but many are just faceless companies or communicate via overseas brokers. I think I've only ever met one in person.'

'You'll have names of companies, payments, debts, addresses, emails, bank details and so on.'

'Yes, of course we do. Hold on, I'm sorry, are you asking to see confidential information? Because that's highly unethical, not to mention illegal.'

'I think you might have given up your right to morality when you agreed to work with the Russian mafia.'

She looked away, eyes closing in the wind for a moment, before she met his gaze once more. 'Okay,' she said. 'You can have everything we have but it'll be no use to you unless you know how to navigate that world.'

'That's my problem, not yours.'

She nodded. 'Then fine, I'll get it all to you as soon as we're down in the site office.' Then her expression changed as a thought occurred to her. 'Hold on a moment, when you told me to say I'd forgotten your name ... Who exactly is going to ask me about this visit?'

'Maybe other associates of Borisyuk,' Victor answered. 'And almost certainly the police.'

'The police?'

'They'll be conducting a murder inquiry, naturally. Which means, like me, they're going to want to get a better picture of his movements the day he died and they'll be keen to understand his business arrangements. Are you okay? You look a little pale.'

'I'm ... I ...'

'As a friendly suggestion,' Victor said, 'it might be worth finding an excuse for your lawyer to be on-site for the next few days.'

She nodded. The faraway look was back. 'That's a good idea.'

THIRTY

Working in a mortuary was not quite as morbid as it might first appear. Sure, there were bodies and viscera and the unrelenting scent of death and decay, but there were upsides too. For one, Julian Garanger was left to his own devices most of the time. As a mortician's assistant, he had plenty to do and so long as he kept the forms filled and floors clean, he had little stress. And since blood held no more horror for him than any other bodily fluid, it really wasn't a bad job at all. Garanger had worked in hospitality and he had worked in retail, so he knew how good he had it.

Dealing with live customers was infinitely more revolting than corpses.

The main problem with the job was other people. Specifically, telling other people about his job. And, more importantly, it was telling women what he did for a living. There was no way to dress up the reality of mopping up what was left behind after an autopsy, of bagging and organising limbs so they could be laid to rest with the rest of the body parts after a gas explosion had separated them all. Even if someone otherwise liked him they would start to look at him differently once they understood how he spent his shift. He could see the question starting to take shape in their eyes: did he enjoy what he did for a living? And, if so, what did that say about him?

So, it was only temporary.

By the time he was thirty he wanted to settle down, buy a house, start a family. All that good grown-up stuff. Given he only had a few years left before his twenties were a memory, he needed to find a partner first and for that he needed a career that didn't make potential wives worry he might be a serial killer.

'Just tell them you work in a hospital,' his friends would tell him.

'It's actually the coroner's office.'

'So?'

'So, it means I work for the courts, the legal system. Nothing to do with the NHS.'

'I'm trying to help you get laid here.'

At the weekends and a couple of times during the week, they would hit Shoreditch and sometimes Covent Garden if they were feeling flush, slamming tequilas and lagers as they moved from bar to bar. Most of the time the evening would end slumped in front of the TV, but sometimes – just sometimes Garanger might be struggling to remember if the flat was in a state or not as he took a member of the opposite sex home.

Tonight was not one of those nights.

'Slim pickings here.'

'Try another?' Garanger suggested, although neither one

of them had any real hope for meeting Miss Right on a wet Wednesday evening.

'Third week of the month,' was the reply. 'Everywhere's going to be dead now until payday.'

'I'm going for a slash,' Garanger told his drinking partner after finishing the last of his pint. 'Then let's hit the road.'

A nod of concession.

As he crossed the pub on his way to the toilets, his gaze was drawn to a group of women in a corner. He saw two bottles of rosé in aluminium coolers and wine glasses at various levels of capacity. They were in the right age bracket, which for Garanger meant anything from late teens to late twenties, and they had that loud, happy vibe. Almost certainly some singletons among them but guaranteed there would be at least one who would be in a long-term relationship, miserable, and would eviscerate him if he dared approach one of her available friends and ruin their girls' night. Even legless, with his decision-making capacity nothing more than a philosophical musing, Garanger would never make that kind of mistake again – he could still remember the cruel taunts about everything from his hairline to his fingernails. Not much he could do about the former. That said, he had kept the latter fastidiously neat ever since.

He still looked over, however. There was always the off-chance for eye contact and the off-chance of the off-chance of a smile.

Which he would count as a technical pull. Better than nothing.

Because his gaze was on the corner of the bar and the group of women, and because he was hoping that one of them would look up as he did, Garanger was blind to the other corner of the bar and the man who sat there by himself.

He had seen him earlier but there had been no reason to pay him any attention. The only men that you needed to look at twice on a night out were the kind of men you made sure *not* to look at twice. The man in the corner did not give off those danger signals. A middle management type. Divorced. Must be a loser of epic proportions if he's sitting on his own in a pub all evening.

Garanger had not noticed that this particular man had entered the bar a little after him, and neither did the mortician's assistant notice this man stand up from his seat a little after Garanger had stood up from his own.

The only thing Garanger *did* notice about the man was, when they passed each other, their shoulders almost brushing as the man headed to the exit, the man's eyes, and though he could not articulate why, he felt that perhaps this middle management divorcé might not be such a loser after all.

Bladder emptied, Garanger sent the women in the corner one last hopeful look before returning to his friend, who handed him his jacket.

At the bus stop, he realised he couldn't find his wallet when he boarded and went to tap in. Panic building, he jogged back to the last place he had taken it out – the pub – that panic immediately becoming sweet, joyful relief when the barmaid saw him and said:

'Looking for this?' In her hand, she held his wallet, explaining, 'Some guy found it and handed it in.'

'Must be my lucky day,' he said, so pleased to see it bulging with cards, notes, coins, receipts and breath mints that he didn't bother to check if every single item was present.

He would only realise in the morning that his work's magnetic pass card was not inside where it should be and was in fact by the front door, on the doormat next to where he kept his shoes in the hallway.

An odd place to find it. Either it had fallen out of his wallet as he hung up his coat, or someone had posted it through his letterbox. He couldn't understand how one single card had slipped free from his wallet and ended up on the floor by itself, but the other explanation made even less sense.

THIRTY-ONE

There were three levels of body cabinets that filled one wall, each cabinet accessible via a single stainless steel door. The upper two rows were uniform in dimensions, with the lowest row having fewer cabinets of larger storage dimensions to accommodate obese corpses. A nearby hydraulic stacking trolley with rollers was used to insert and remove bodies from the cabinets. On the wall adjacent to the cabinets was a digital gauge monitoring the temperature of the cabinets. It showed several numbers: the current temperature, 4 degrees Celsius, being the most prominent, with the set temperature and the maximum temperature above and below the larger number. A bulb of red glass jutted from the wall next to the gauge, no doubt flashing if the current temperature rose to the maximum, which was two degrees Celsius higher. An alarm would sound too, Victor imagined, loud and shrill if a cabinet were ever left improperly closed or a fault developed in the cooling system. At a glance, he saw thirty cabinets. Some were differentiated with yellow biohazard labels, others with clipboards to list their contents of individual body parts, and a few for unidentified or unclaimed corpses.

He opened the cabinet containing Borisyuk's corpse and slid out the tray before folding back the sheet.

The Y-incision ran from both shoulders and connected at the sternum to form a single straight line down the abdomen. The scalpel cuts were flawless, the pathologist a seasoned pro of countless autopsies, that was clear enough. The sutures, though almost certainly stitched by an assistant, were tight and neat. Victor appreciated the uniform distance between insertion points, both on the horizontal and vertical planes. He was reassured so much care and attention had been paid to Borisyuk's corpse. Though it was obvious how Borisyuk had died, the law required a post-mortem examination carried out by a coroner and performed by a forensic pathologist.

The bullet holes were ugly in comparison, though the grouping was tight. Point blank range, yes, although rushed. Hurried by Victor's intrusion.

The assassin was good. But he already knew that. Victor's bruises were more than enough evidence.

He pictured the fight in the townhouse, the strikes and parries, the attempts to disarm and choke. Fighting a life-and-death duel with an enemy he had no need to fight.

Ligature marks around Borisyuk's wrists and ankles showed he had been bound to his chair with inescapable force.

The lack of other cuts or bruises suggested he had freely answered his captor's questions or requests, or that Victor's arrival had spared his former client the inevitable price of resistance.

What questions was he asked?

What did the assassin need from him?

Not for himself. He would be a professional hired to extract ... something. Though such instructions had been part of the contract's terms, the assassin might have no idea what he was asking or why. If Victor had prevented the man fully completing the job to the client's requirements, what then?

Victor knew all too well that clients frequently considered professionals such as himself to be disposable assets. Borisyuk's murderer might already be dead, lured into an ambush to sever the link to the client, else killed for failing to obtain whatever it was that warranted Borisyuk tied to a chair.

Early evening, the mortuary was quiet. Victor heard only the sounds he made himself and the gentle hum of the cooling system that kept the corpses from rotting. He found it a peaceful place.

Using a burner phone, he called Zakharova.

'Yes?'

She answered on the fourth ring, her voice even, no hesitation despite the unfamiliar number calling. He imagined she knew it would be him.

'Borisyuk had a lot of money invested in property, in the latest skyscraper.'

'I told you he had many legitimate business interests. These days more than illicit ones, in fact.'

'You didn't tell me he was leaning on other investors on behalf of Sarah Zhou.'

After a pause, she asked, 'Which investors? That's news to me.'

'I don't know yet, but maybe someone didn't like the intimidation game he was playing. I have a lot of information on companies and no way to sift through it on my own. Who managed Borisyuk's money in the City?'

'A worm named Ritchie Forrester. He's a wizard with numbers but he steals from us. Maxim always tolerated it because Ritchie is the best at what he does. I'll send you his details.'

'Good. Did you find out anything about The Nightingale Foundation?'

'Why would I look into them?'

'It's in both our interests to find out who killed Maxim.'

He heard a sigh. 'Call me before the mixer. If I learn anything, I'll tell you then.'

He hung up.

Returning his gaze to Borisyuk's corpse, Victor considered the wounds, the ligature marks, the assassin he had fought to a stalemate.

They all told a story, only one that made no sense to him, alone in the mortuary. Security was terrible for such an important institution. Aside from a rudimentary alarm system, it was unguarded. With the pass card from a mortician's assistant, Victor had free rein. Most people who died and were brought here were not murdered, though Borisyuk could not be the only one, and the exactitudes of other deaths might be of incredible importance for all sorts of reasons. The ease with which someone could manipulate evidence came as a surprise to Victor. Not that he had any intention of interfering now, but it was good to know for the future.

Victor was not consciously aware of why he stopped

what he was doing. He trusted his instincts nonetheless. Something had changed. Maybe he felt the minuscule change in air pressure from an open door, or the rise in temperature as a result. Perhaps it was the softest of sounds out of sync with those he made himself. Whatever the cause, his brain knew before he did.

He was not alone.

No mortician would make so little noise as to be almost silent. No security guard either. No police officer.

Only a professional.

Though he himself was operating with as much care as possible, there were trade-offs when examining Borisyuk. He had no intention of being here all night. Did that mean whoever was here with him had heard?

Either they had followed him to the mortuary or they had been watching it before he arrived.

Victor reached beneath his jacket to draw his weapon.

The mortuary was a series of interconnected halls without doors, to facilitate the back-and-forth movement of bodies. Small rooms led off from the main mortuary for offices, lavatories, and for viewing of the deceased by families or other claimants.

The entrance to the examination hall was behind him, so Victor dropped low as he spun one hundred and eighty degrees, keeping the gun close to his chest to reduce the distance it had to travel before it was aimed at the entranceway and the dark figure stood against the backdrop of darkness.

THIRTY-TWO

A lean silhouette of a man. Practical shoes, trousers and jacket. All dark greys and blues. He wore black leather gloves. In his right hand, he held a small pistol with a suppressor. It was held down at his thigh, muzzle pointed at the floor. No immediate threat, though a threat by its very nature.

The Boatman.

So named by the Bratva because he ferried the souls of the dead across the River Styx.

Victor rose back to standing. He kept his own weapon exactly where it was: near his chest and pointed at the man before him.

Who walked forwards. A slow, deliberate pace. He moved out of the dark entranceway and into the light of the examination hall. The fluorescent bulbs washed out his pale skin so it seemed as white as wall and floor tiles, and sharpened the angles of his face into something starved and feral.

Though lean, a strong neck protruded from the collar

of his jacket. Victor saw the carotids just under the skin. In the efficient threat assessment he made of everyone he encountered, he searched for weaknesses as well as strengths. There was no point concluding a person was dangerous without also determining the fastest way to neuter that danger. Everyone had a throat, everyone had eyes, everyone had arteries. Alas, they were not always accessible. Subcutaneous fat made for excellent protection, so much so that Roman gladiators had been notoriously overweight. When drawing blood meant entertainment for the crowd, it was in the gladiator's interests that blood only ran from superficial sources. The Boatman had no such armour. What drew Victor's attention for longer than the cursory glance necessary for his assessment was how soft the carotids seemed. The Boatman's blood passed through them easily, smoothly. Victor pictured a heart beating at a sloth-like rate, with such efficiency there was no discernible pressure in those arteries even when a gun was pointing the Boatman's way.

He had such a sense of calmness, of control, Victor wondered if the man's adrenal system produced stress hormones at all.

As the Boatman neared Victor, the unblinking eyes shifted their focus to the corpse of Maxim Borisyuk.

'Father,' he said in a whisper, left hand reaching out as if to lay on the shoulder of Borisyuk and yet stopping millimetres from the skin to hover for a moment of absolute stillness.

He closed his eyes.

He had no scent. Victor detected no body odour, no fragrance. Not even coffee on his breath.

Victor backed off to create distance, though not too much.

He had the advantage with his weapon already aimed and had no desire to give the Boatman room in which to manoeuvre while making him a smaller target in the process. Victor wanted to keep his weapon hugged tight to his own body where it was harder to disarm. The downside was he lost accuracy by not being able to aim. At point-blank range he didn't need that accuracy.

When the Boatman opened his eyes, he released a long exhalation, then put away his gun. Without looking at Victor, he circled the trolley to examine the corpse. He had a deliberate, careful manner. No movement was rushed or sudden. Not slow, Victor observed. It was an efficiency of action. He reached only as far as necessary. He bent closer, enough to see every detail in sharp focus, and no further. When he stepped away from the corpse at last, he did not so much as glance at it again.

Instead, he approached an electric hoist that lay in one corner of the room. It had eight castors to move in any direction, with a battery-powered lifting system. On the handheld operating switch box a warning sticker proclaimed its maximum capacity to be three hundred kilograms. There were three sets of straps to loop around the ankles, hips and ribcage, with a hammock-like cradle for the head.

'Do you know what this is for?'

A practical device, was Victor's first thought, as he knew from long experience how difficult it could be to move the corpse of even a slender person. For morticians of lesser strength and mobility than he, the risk of strains and injuries must be massively reduced with such a machine, as well enabling the job to be done with fewer people.

'Beyond the obvious,' the Boatman continued.

It took Victor a moment to understand that using the hoist would, 'Preserve the dignity of the deceased.'

'Not usually a consideration in our line of work,' the Boatman said. 'Although I never like to show undue disrespect to the corpses of my targets.'

'Murdering them is enough of an affront,' Victor agreed. 'How long have you been in London?

'Not very long.'

'Hours?' Victor asked. 'Days?'

'I've just arrived.' He returned to Maxim's body and leaned closer to the bullet holes. 'No powder burns, but the grouping is extremely tight.'

'The assassin has a good aim.'

'From the doorway of the bedroom.'

'That's my conclusion.'

'You didn't hear the shots?'

'Not over the noise I made kicking in the front door.'

The Boatman nodded.

'You aren't curious to know how the assassin managed to take his shots at the exact same time?'

'Multiple kicks,' the Boatman answered. 'The first kick notified him of your presence and he reacted accordingly.'

'How do you know it took more than one kick?'

'Because of the short top step. Your long legs gave him plenty of time.'

'That's the third time you've said him.'

'The bullet holes indicate a downward trajectory. Not a very steep angle, but from the doorway that would equate to a height of approximately one point eight two metres, assuming the shooter's arm was partially extended. Not many women of that stature.'

'Your stature.'

'Or your own with your arm further extended.'

'Why would I extend my arm at such close range?'

The Boatman asked, 'Why do you still have your gun pointed at me when my hands are empty?'

'Perhaps because the assassin who killed Borisyuk is just like you.'

'I'm led to believe you had a violent interaction with him.'

'I did.'

The Boatman looked up from what he was doing to where Victor was standing nearby, alive and well. 'Then he's not like me at all.'

'If you killed Borisyuk,' Victor said. 'I will find out, and I'll find out who gave the order. Neither of you will survive what follows.'

'I say your words back to you.'

'Don't waste your time. There's only one truth.'

'Which is why you will fail.'

Victor waited.

'It does not matter what the truth is,' the Boatman explained in a tone that Victor almost took to be regretful. 'It only matters what those who sit at the head of the table believe.'

THIRTY-THREE

Watching a grown man shed tears was always an unpleasant experience. Even in the worst of grief, dignity should be maintained. Cry in private. Wail behind closed doors. How hard could it be?

'Here,' Linnekin said, removing a silk handkerchief from his trouser pocket. 'Take this.'

Rakmilevich didn't hear him at first, such was the volume of his sobbing. Only when Linnekin thrust the handkerchief in his face did the man understand and take it. He wiped his eyes. He blew his nose.

'Keep it,' Linnekin said as Rakmilevich went to hand back the sodden cloth.

Referring to the background din of machinery, Rakmilevich said, 'Is it always this noisy?'

Linnekin nodded. Each day, collection vehicles reversed into the tipping floor to deposit household recycling sacks into huge piles. Scooping trucks transferred sacks to the splitting machine, whose slow-turning blades pulled them open without causing excessive damage to the contents. A conveyer belt carried the loosened recycling on a steep incline out of the tipping floor and into the main facility housing the sorting and separating machinery.

That machinery could be heard everywhere on-site, even in Linnekin's office.

'Walk with me.' He motioned for Rakmilevich to follow him, handing him a spare pair of ear defenders that hung from the door. 'I'll give you the tour.'

Although commonly referred to as a recycling factory, its technical title was materials recovery facility. The facility primarily processed glass, plastic, metals, cardboard and paper that was the waste of almost six million people, equalling more than one hundred thousand tons every year. Linnekin's plan was to double this capacity within five years. With evolving technologies and increasing willingness to recycle from the public, the industry was growing continuously.

'Why does it matter?' Rakmilevich asked. 'Why do we even need to discuss who gets to sit in Maxim's seat before that seat is even cold? The only thing that matters now is justice, is revenge. Someone murdered our father. Someone took him from us. I never got to tell him how I loved him. But I will tell the person who killed him. I will explain exactly how much I loved him as I break every bone in his body, one by one.'

Upon reaching the main facility, the ballistic separator shook the mixed recycling, using paddles to separate it by size and shape so metal and plastic were deposited onto one conveyer belt while flatter papers and cardboards ended up on another that travelled to a dedicated cabin, wherein larger pieces of cardboard to be recycled elsewhere were removed by workers manning a series of smaller conveyer belts. Between three and five individuals worked each of these conveyer belts, depending on their experience and efficiency, separating the non-recyclable items such as food and nappies. They wore thick safety gloves and high-vis vests. The noise of the conveyer belts and nearby ballistic separators ensured no one could hold a conversation here, which pleased Linnekin. If workers talked, they joked. If they joked, they laughed. If they laughed, they couldn't concentrate on their jobs and their efficiency suffered. Any reduction in efficiency meant smaller margins. And while making money was not the primary goal of the facility, it needed to be profitable on paper to ensure governmental contracts were renewed.

'And that is precisely why you need to care, my friend. If Zakharova is allowed to make the decisions for now, she will always make the decisions from now on. If we do not change this then you can forget all about your revenge because she will see to it that it is always the wrong time. There will always be another priority. She will always plead for restraint. Eventually, it will only be us at the table who still care. What do you think will happen then? How long do you think she will let us sit at the table?'

'She would never dare try to remove us.'

'Not yet,' Linnekin explained as they reached a quiet corner of the facility. 'Not until she has cemented her position. We will need to sit quietly like good little boys or we will not be invited back. To avenge Maxim, we must first protect ourselves. She had him killed. She will do the same to us eventually.'

'Without proof I won't make any move against her,'

Rakmilevich said. 'For all I know right now you killed him and are trying to turn me against her for your own benefit.'

'Exactly,' Linnekin hissed, batting Rakmilevich on the shoulder with a palm. 'That is exactly the way you should be thinking. I don't trust you so why should you trust me?' He didn't wait for an answer. 'But above all else, neither of us should trust her or that assassin, Vasili.'

'Then what are you proposing? The leadership are in agreement that we do not make moves against one another. We must stay united. We have agreed. He has three days to prove himself.'

Linnekin said, 'Or three days in which to cover his tracks and find a scapegoat all the while Zakharova cements her power.'

'If we go back on our word, she will be able to turn the others against us. Whatever the truth, we will be pariahs.'

'I know,' Linnekin said again. 'We cannot do anything ourselves.'

Maybe it was grief and maybe it was not, but it took Rakmilevich far longer than it should for him to catch up.

'But someone else can?'

'Finally, you understand.'

'But who? No one in the Brotherhood.'

'Of course not,' Linnekin agreed. 'None of them would risk going against the leadership. At least, not anyone with any competence. And anyone so reckless as to agree would demonstrate they cannot be trusted in doing so.'

'Either you have an answer to your own questions or you are wasting my time with hypotheticals.'

'The Brotherhood are not the only criminals operating in this city,' Linnekin explained. 'And there are many who would help to earn our favour.'

'By doing what?'

'Kill Vasili before Zakharova is crowned and sends him after us.'

'Do you have a name?'

'Not merely a name, but a title,' Linnekin said with a smile. 'King John will do that which we cannot.'

THIRTY-FOUR

The visitor was over six feet tall and wearing a charcoal suit. The man had a lean, athletic build. The handshake was brief and neutral, neither strong nor limp. He had dark hair, maybe two inches in length in a formal side-parting kept neat by a matte wax or clay. He had a short, neat beard, equally dark. He wore simple glasses with burnished steel frames that surrounded eyes so brown they seemed pure black. He looked and acted exactly like a thousand identical business professionals Ritchie Forrester had dealt with over the years. Bland. Boring. The kind of guy that Forrester might say 'hey' too in the morning if he still worked in an office, but not the kind of guy he would invite to the casino on a Friday night. In fact, Forrester pictured the visitor as the kind of person who not only brought a packed lunch with them every day but labelled it too. Probably had a label maker dedicated to this task.

There were few cities on the planet as multicultural as London. And though the financial industry was overstocked with privately educated, to-the-manner-born Brits who had lucked out into six-figure salaries because their dad was on the board or their manager had also gone to Eton. Forrester's old firm alone had been forty per cent foreign nationals from every corner of the globe. He had developed an ear for accents. He could differentiate an Aussie from a Kiwi within minutes. He never offended a Canadian by mistaking them for an American or a Czech for a Slovak. The visitor, however, stumped him. This guy spoke with the kind of mid-Atlantic twang of someone for whom English was a second language. In Forrester's experience, if the native accent wasn't obvious then their English would be more American than British, so he was veering towards a European. The tan suggested a Mediterranean background, though he ruled out Spanish on appearances and Italian on personality. Perhaps the Balkans then, though it was rare he crossed paths with Croats and Albanians.

'You must be Swiss,' Forrester said, his thoughts spilling out into words.

'Must I?'

'I couldn't place your accent,' he admitted. 'Which is rare for me. Then I remembered how you guys are often trilingual by the time you leave school.'

'Well observed,' the visitor said.

'Meanwhile we Brits can barely speak our own language without butchering it. Pronouncing the letter "t" seems to be a lost art these days.'

Forrester worked from his six-bedroom home in Richmond. It was close enough to the City to make the once or twice a week trips for meetings with clients, and yet far enough away that he could own a luxurious mini-mansion instead of an overpriced apartment. He had the whole house

185

to himself for the week: the missus and the triplets were at the seaside. It was nice to get a break from all the screaming and nappy changing, and yet he missed them all already. His eldest child, his junkie lad, was probably off his face by now in a dosshouse somewhere in the East End. He missed Manny too, nonetheless.

'I don't usually take meetings this late,' Forrester reiterated to the visitor. 'But I appreciate you're pushed for time while you're in London.'

'My schedule is somewhat inflexible.'

Forrester knew desperation when it sat before him so he was absolutely one hundred per cent sure he already had this guy's business. Everything that followed would be perfunctory. People came to Forrester when they had money they shouldn't have and needed that money legitimised. Which was how Forrester preferred to think of himself. He wasn't a money launderer, he was a money legitimiser.

A millionaire at fifty, Forrester had to admit the chances of him making a billion before he was in the ground were non-existent. You could be a self-made millionaire, sure, as long as you had talent and ferocity and so much ambition it was bubbling out of every pore. But that was the glass ceiling. There wasn't a billionaire on the planet who had got there by himself. They all had help, no matter what they said. Forrester was in a tiny minority as it was; nearly every supposedly self-made millionaire had a leg up or three. Even those without an early investment from a generous uncle – who would never in a million years have invested in a stranger with the same idea – had the benefit of knowing that even if they lost everything they could still crash in dear Papa's pied-à-terre until they were back on their feet.

Forrester never had that safety net. He never had any doors opened to him by family connections or because he went to the right school. Every penny in his bank account he had earned himself. No one had given him a deposit to buy his first flat. If he hadn't worked night shifts in a warehouse, then he would have starved while studying for his degree. So, the billionaire dream was exactly that: a dream. Therefore, he decided, he would settle for a hundred million. He would have to break a few rules along the way to make it happen, naturally, but when the deck was stacked against the Forresters of this world, playing by the rules was as good as admitting defeat.

His only fear was the walls coming crashing down before he could make the most of the gold rush. Sadly, the Laundromat could not last for ever. Nothing ever did, and especially not such a profitable racket of money laundering on an industrial scale. However, Ritchie Forrester knew it would take a monumental change of not only policy but attitude too, to make any discernible dent in the Laundromat's efficiency. He could only imagine seeing such revolutions happening in light of an unprecedented global catastrophe. Only a war in Europe would do it, he reassured his clients, or perhaps a pandemic.

'Which is why I always drink to peace,' he explained, 'and modern medicine.'

A new year had just begun, and with it a new decade too. Forrester expected the twenties would be little different to the previous ten years, which meant it would be a very profitable one for him and his clients. He had read something about bats and China, but those in the know said it was nothing to worry about.

'Perhaps I could present a scenario to you,' the visitor began, 'and you could provide some insight for me.'

'Shoot.'

'Say a foreign national sets up multiple shell companies in the UK and with them multiple bank accounts, and transfers in huge quantities of money that, as you explained, ends up in assets like property and cars.'

'I'm with you so far.'

'And say the foreign national has someone here handle all those transactions over several years and it's always the same person taking care of the accounts.'

'Makes sense. These things are so complicated that it's madness to use a different banker once one has been established. You'll literally never be able to make sense of the data unless you've been balls deep inside the spreadsheet since day one.'

The visitor tensed in his seat and Forrester saw a prude sitting before him. It was sometimes easy to forget that the way bankers spoke to one another was not how all business people conversed. He made a mental note to be on his best behaviour around this one.

The visitor continued: 'What would you say if this foreign national decided to use a forensic accountant to sift through those spreadsheets with a fine-tooth comb and came to the conclusion that the value of the investments didn't exactly match the funds deposited?'

'That's inevitable,' Forrester said, trying not to grow frustrated answering such noob-level questions. 'There's always between point five and point seven difference after agreed fees when you're dealing with such large sums of money and numerous transactions. It's not so much in error, but the price of doing business. Terms of the various institutions and individuals involved change constantly and part of the value of someone like me is to keep the price of doing business as low as possible.'

'And if the forensic accountants found that disparity to be point eight three per cent, what would you think?'

'Well, I really don't like bad-mouthing anyone,' Forrester said in a careful tone, 'but I think the banker handling this foreign national's money is skimming off the top. You could argue seven, absolutely. When you start approaching eight then they're taking the proverbial.'

'This is exactly why I'm here, Ritchie,' the visitor said. 'Maxim Borisyuk understood the price of doing business. He even tolerated skimming off the top because he knew it is inevitable that everyone betrays ultimately. When you were only taking point six he thought you had no guts. When you took point seven you finally had his respect. When you pushed it to point eight you told him in no uncertain terms that you had forgotten with whom you were conducting business.'

'Tell Maxim that I have his money. I mean . . . I can get his money. I'll pay him back. I'll pay him double. He'll never lose even point two again.'

'It's too late for that, I'm afraid,' the visitor said as he withdrew a small pistol from underneath his jacket. 'Because Maxim Borisyuk is dead. He was dead before he could give me the order to kill you. But, as we discussed, he cared very much about loyalty. Which is why I'm going to kill you anyway.'

THIRTY-FIVE

Ritchie Forrester's home office was a small, neat space on the ground floor. It contained a plain desk and padded chair, computer, phone, filing cabinet and shelving unit with numerous box files, stationery and reams of paper for the printer beneath the desk. On one wall hung a framed portrait of Forrester who was a lot younger and a lot slimmer, his wife and a small child. A similar photograph showed the same family some years later. The small child was a teenage boy and he, Forrester, and Forrester's wife each held one third of what had to be triplets.

'Sorry, what?'

'Tell me when you decided to have Maxim killed,' Victor said. 'If you don't then your death won't be easy.'

He walked behind the desk to pull closed the curtains because the window looked out onto the street. Even though there was nowhere watchers could conceivably set up to observe them, and a marksman would need to climb onto the roof of the suburban house opposite to have any hope of a shot, there was never any reason to make the jobs of such people any easier.

'Did you fear he suspected you were stealing his money or was it that you knew he would eventually find out and decided to solve the problem before it materialised?'

Holding up both palms, Forrester pleaded, 'I swear to you I did not kill Maxim. I had nothing to do with it. I'm not a murderer. I'm a good person.'

'You took money from the Russian mafia, Ritchie, money that they made doing horrible things. You took it and you didn't care where it came from, which means you aren't innocent.'

'And you are?'

'No, I'm in no way innocent,' Victor answered. 'The difference is that I don't care, I don't pretend to be someone I am not. Trust me when I say you sleep better at night when you accept who you are. Take out a pen and a piece of paper.'

Forrester removed a notepad from a drawer and withdrew a fountain pen from a desk tidy. He looked at Victor for guidance.

'Write,' he told him.

'Write what?'

'You know what. Goodbye, cruel world . . . '

Forrester's fingers did not move with any speed or dexterity. He held the pen in an awkward grip between his fingers. Victor did not rush the man because he was in no hurry himself. It was no play on Forrester's part, no stalling for time, Victor knew. He had been in enough similar situations to understand that impending demise either made people act and move with speed beyond their normal capabilities or it slowed them down to a tragic crawl. It was almost impossible to predict which way a person would go: the usually meek might transform into a wild animal of adrenalin and instinct to survive, the bold and fearless could find that when It really mattered all that daring had only ever been a front fooling themselves their whole life.

Forrester was trembling. He had his eyes pinched shut and his shimmering face was now drenched with sweat, as were his clothes. When he heard Victor step around the desk, his eyelids trembled as he fought the instinct to open them and look. Whatever his fate, Forrester did not want to see it coming.

'Fear is good,' Victor began. 'It's designed to keep us alive, to tell us at a biological level that something can harm us before it does actually cause us harm. We should always listen to fear. When we're scared, we shouldn't ignore what makes us scared. But when we do more than simply listen to that fear, when we obey it without question, then it works against us. It paralyses us. We no longer have the option to fight or to run away.'

The man's eyes remained closed. He continued to cower.

'This is fear working against you. You didn't listen to it, you obeyed.'

Forrester shook so much the sweat dripping from his nose and chin never reached the floor but splashed on the wall next to him.

'And yet, it might just keep you alive anyway.'

The shaking did not relent, but there was a twitch in his eyelids as they almost opened.

'I'm told you are a financial wizard. Is that true?'

No answer.

'If it's true you should answer. If you don't answer, I'm on my way.'

Forrester understood what that meant and he managed to find his voice.

'Yes,' he said, quiet and afraid. 'It's true.'

'Then I'm not going to kill you.' He reached out a hand. 'Take it.'

Slowly, one by one, Forrester opened his eyes.

'Get up,' Victor said. 'This is the first day of the rest of your life.'

A sweaty hand gripped Victor's, and he hauled Forrester to his feet. He was unsteady, still jittery from the overload of stress hormones and the escalating feeling of euphoria. Whatever rushes of endorphins he had experienced in the past, this would trump them all, because seconds ago he was experiencing the worst moment of his entire existence.

'This is not mercy,' Victor told him. 'Now, you owe me your life. Now you work for me. I need someone to investigate Maxim's financial interests and given you laundered so much money for him you're obviously qualified for the job.'

Forrester, who could not keep still, watched him without comment. Overwhelmed by adrenalin and cortisol, the banker paced about as much as the close confines let him, his arms in constant motion, fingers closing and flexing. He swallowed. He licked his lips. The only parts of him that remained motionless were his eyelids. They remained wide open. He didn't blink once.

'Why don't you try sitting down?' Victor suggested.

Forrester didn't seem to hear. He paced about the room as if compelled, his stress hormones elevated to such an extent that being still was simply an impossibility. Victor noted the unblinking eyes were red and the blood vessels in his temples pushed out in relief beneath the skin. The rate at which he was breathing became faster and faster.

At fifty-something and overweight, with Forrester's blood pressure through the roof and beginning to hyperventilate, Victor could see a cardiac episode in the making.

He glanced around the room, gaze stopping when he saw envelopes stacked in neat piles on a shelving unit. He took an A4 manila one, scrunched the opening together in his fist to form a roughly circular hole, and held it out to Forrester.

'Breathe with this over your mouth and nose,' Victor explained. 'It'll help regulate the carbon dioxide-to-oxygen ratio in your bloodstream and calm you down.'

The man obeyed, taking the envelope from Victor's hand.

'Take a few breaths and you'll feel better.'

He watched Forrester do just that.

After a few seconds of inhaling expelled carbon dioxide back into his lungs, Forrester's breathing began to slow down. With that, his heartrate fell.

'Now remove the envelope and breathe normally.'

Forrester coughed and spluttered.

'Close enough,' Victor said, taking the envelope out of his hands and guiding him into the padded chair that he pulled out from beneath the desk.

'Relax,' Victor told him. 'I told you I needed your help. I need you to study some paperwork for me and find out who owns the companies that made these investments.' He laid printouts of the information Zhou gave him. 'Here and here.'

Forrester leaned over the desk to look. 'Why?'

'That's not important for you to know, and it's better for you the less you do actually know. But I want to know if there are any other irregularities with his money. Particularly if he ripped anyone off who might want revenge, or if his investments were stepping on anyone's toes. Is that possible?'

'For the money I handled, yes,' Forrester said. 'But ... I don't understand. You think I killed him.'

'Of course, I don't,' Victor said with a shake of his head. 'But I needed to see you at your worst to know whether I could use you and I can. Look for connections to these Russian nationals.' He gave him a list of names Zakharova supplied of Bratva bosses. 'If something called The Nightingale Foundation comes up, even if it's not related to the other investors, I want to know about it.'

'I recognise that name,' Forrester said. 'Maxim was a patron of theirs.'

'Do you know what they do?'

'I don't think it ever came up. Why?'

Victor said nothing because he had no answer. So far, The Nightingale Foundation was purely a name to him, nothing more. Except Borisyuk had intended to prolong his stay to attend their mixer tomorrow.

With something on which to focus his attention, Forrester's fear diminished, the blood vessels in his temples becoming less pronounced. He took hold of the pages one by one, adjusting his glasses as he looked over them.

'There's not enough information here on those companies to know who owns them. They're all registered overseas. You're talking about a week's worth of solid work to even scratch the surface.'

'Which is why you should start right now. You're not going to be able to go to sleep tonight anyway, so you may as well make use of the inevitable insomnia.'

'I have a job. I have clients. They rely on me.'

'Call in sick. You *are* looking a bit pale. When you phone them in the morning after working all night your voice will sound genuine, don't worry.'

'Not only my day job.' Forrester's tone carried shame. 'The other things too. I can't just call in sick with certain people. They're bad news. They run drugs. They'll ...'

He could not finish.

Victor said, 'Know that while you work for me you never need be afraid of anyone else ever again.'

Forrester was not convinced, however, which Victor found interesting.

After a moment's thought, he asked, 'What do they have on you?'

'Not me,' Forrester said, quiet and afraid again. 'My boy.'

He noticed again the framed family portraits photograph on the wall: A young Forrester, his wife and a small child. And Forrester, his wife, the triplets, and the son, now a teenager. Given the newer portrait showed a Forrester with less grey in his hair, Victor figured that teenager would be a young man now.

'What do they have on him?'

'They have him.' It took Forrester a moment to gather the strength to continue. Victor saw the man's shame and the will it took to admit it. 'Manny's an addict. He fell in with the wrong crowd at school. They did drugs. They sold drugs ... He's been in trouble ever since. The last time he came home to visit he actually stole some of my wife's jewellery – his own mother. We had a break-in last year. I'm sure it was him.'

'He's one of their crew?'

Forrester shook his head weakly. 'They give him the drugs so he thinks they're his friends. He lives with some, in one of their drug dens or whatever you call them. I mean, at least he's not on the streets, right?'

Victor waited.

'When I tried to stop working for them,' Forrester continued, speaking as though every single word required a considerable effort just to form, 'my boy ended up in hospital. An accidental overdose, the doctor's told me ... They didn't admit it was them, but I knew. I knew they did it. My wife doesn't know a thing about what happened. She can't know. She knows he's an addict but she can't know it's my fault he's the way he is.'

'Do you have a friend, or better yet a relative, who doesn't live in London? Someone they don't know about? Ideally, somewhere isolated.'

'My cousin lives in Birmingham. Why does it matter?'

'That doesn't sound isolated.'

'Why is that important? He lives in Solihull, but he has a caravan. They go to Wales a lot, where it's quiet. Why?'

'That can work.'

'If you're talking about my son, he'll never agree. Manny doesn't want to get clean. He won't answer my calls. He ... Listen, I told you: he thinks they're his friends. They won't even let me through the door to see him.' Forrester paused to control his escalating emotions. His eyes glistened. 'I haven't so much as heard his voice in months.'

Victor said, 'Where's the den?'

THIRTY-SIX

Of all the places he had called home it was his dacha on the Black Sea coast that Vladimir Kasakov held most dear. Situated just outside of the city of Sochi in southern Russia, the sprawling Italianate house had belonged to him long before his holidays had become limited to within the federation's border. With multiple international arrest warrants to his name, travelling outside of the country had become as good as impossible.

'I'm sorry, Illy,' he said. 'Daddy isn't allowed to go to Disneyland right now because bad people don't want him to go. What else would you like to do for your birthday? We can do anything you like except that.'

An arms dealer since the disastrous invasion of Afghanistan by the Soviet Army, Kasakov had made himself an enemy of many NATO countries by selling arms to their enemies, often their own. The industry of war had proven to be such a fantastically profitable business venture for the Ukrainian that he had the good sense to befriend the Kremlin once he felt the creeping hand of Interpol. By the time he could no longer get away with bribing, bargaining and battling to keep his freedom, he set up shop in Moscow from where he would never be extradited after becoming a citizen.

'I don't want anything else.'

Kasakov towered over the little boy. He refused to squat down like they did in the movies so they could look children in the eye at their level. It was no way to instil respect. A child should never feel that you are their equal.

'It's been years now, Vlad,' Izolda began. 'I can't believe anyone still cares enough to be waiting for you at the airport.'

'Of course they still care. They haven't forgotten me when they've been trying for decades. The longer they can't touch me the more it eats them alive. What was a passion then is now obsession.'

'Do you realise how incredibly arrogant you sound?'

'Don't pretend that you didn't find that attractive when we first met.'

'You're my husband now. I need you to be there for Illarion before anything else.'

'I would die for that boy.' He snapped his fingers. 'Like that.'

'Then come to Disneyland.'

'I can't protect him if I'm rotting in a cage in some American hellhole for the rest of my natural life.'

'If they still cared so much about bringing you to justice then we would know about it. They would ... Oh, I don't know. They would make it clear. We would read about it in the paper. Seriously, when was the last time a journalist even asked for an interview that wasn't about philanthropy?'

'They don't need to care for their systems to beep and tell

them who I am. I'd be in chains before you could collect your TUMI cases from the carousel.'

'I can take him. You can stay here.'

'No.'

'Just no? That's the argument? You're not even willing to talk about it?'

'Nothing has changed since our last conversation.'

'The lawyers say there's nothing they can do. No one wants to put me in chains and no one can. The greatest of all my sins is my only sin and that is my marriage to you.'

'That's enough to make them hate you.'

'They can't arrest me for that so let them hate as much as they want.'

'It's not about that. You don't understand what these people are like, the lengths they will go to in an attempt to lure me out of the country. They'll do whatever they can to make your life hell. They will make up something, they will lie, they will plant evidence in your luggage to keep you there, to force me to get you out of it.'

'I will take a lawyer with me. I'd be taking the nannies as it is, so what's another ticket going to matter? I can even arrange for American lawyers to be there at the airport waiting for me. I might have to spend an afternoon waiting in a grey little room for it all to be sorted out, but they'll never be able to try it again.'

'That's not the point,' Kasakov insisted.

'Then what is the point? What exactly is the problem of us going without you?'

Illarion was sullen and pouting, although there was no tantrum from the little bundle of sunshine. He was unable to understand why Daddy would not fly them to Disneyland when all the other students from the exclusive private school had been.

Even with an army of lawyers accompanying her – plus the nannies and the modest staff she couldn't live without, of course – Kasakov did not trust the vengeful Americans not to use Izolda against him. If they ran out of ways to ruin their trip or exhausted excuses to delay their departure, they would drip poison in her ear. They would tell her how much better Illarion's life would be out of his father's shadow, how they could ensure citizenship for the both of them. It wouldn't work initially because most poisons took their time to do damage. And once he had allowed one trip it would be harder and harder to disallow future holidays. Each time the only two people he cared about in this world would return to him with more and more resentment.

Then, at a point in the future, while they were shopping in New York City or attending movie premieres in LA, he would receive the call in which Izolda delivered the news they were not coming back.

It would break his heart to have her murdered.

He would do, however, without hesitation, despite his deep, unyielding adoration for her, his wife, with whom he had known the purest of happiness, the most exquisite of joy.

At least, until he had held his son for the first time and known that the love he had for Izolda was not really love at all because *this* was love.

If she took his son away from him, if she made that phone call, he would make another the second he had hung up. With tears in his eyes, he would ensure she was dead within days and his son back in his arms where he belonged.

'Well?' she asked when he gave no response.

He could not tell her the real reason, so he said, 'It reminds me that you both deserve better than me.' A man of his upbringing and generation did not hurry to show emotion, but he tried here. 'And I hate myself for that.'

She rushed to embrace him, to throw her slender arms around his thick shoulders, to reassure him he was good enough. She kissed him on the cheek, only stretching a little to reach thanks to her long legs. 'Don't talk like that. It's not true and it doesn't suit you. We can work through this, I promise.'

He nodded without agreeing. There was no solution to this particular problem.

A polite cough alerted them to the presence of another.

'I'm sorry to interrupt but this cannot wait.'

Sergei gave Izolda a tight, apologetic smile and she raised her arms in defeat.

'I know,' she said, 'I know. Even at the beach, we're still at the office.' She said to Kasakov, 'We will continue our conversation later.' She gestured for their son. 'Come with Mummy, Illy. Let these boys bore one another to death with talk of purchase orders and bills of lading.'

The child did as he was told without complaint. He always did because he was perfect in every conceivable way.

'Of course,' Kasakov said to her, thinking he should make arrangements now as by the time Izolda made that phone call he might no longer have the appropriate contacts to activate. 'I'll try and keep this brief.'

'I'll be by the pool,' she said, drifting past Sergei and trailing a hand to lightly brush his arm.

She might have whispered something too that Kasakov did not hear.

Once she and Illarion had gone, he beckoned his aide closer. From the serious expression on Sergei's face, Kasakov knew this was nothing to do with purchase orders.

'What is this?'

Sergei answered, 'Something's happened in London.'

THIRTY-SEVEN

Victor took Forrester's Lexus, despite the man's initial reluctance to hand over the keys. A ninety-minute drive east took him north of the Thames, to the borough of Newham. Here, the city wore a shroud of poverty and darkness. The rain was lashing down by the time he arrived in the right neighbourhood. If the city was a living entity, this estate was its bowels, congested and filthy.

Victor parked closer to his ultimate destination than protocol allowed, but he was accounting for a reluctant companion upon his return. In such a scenario, the less distance he had to drag or carry Forrester's son, the better.

On the west side of the street was a short line of commercial properties – takeaway, convenience store, off-licence – and then a long line of terraced housing with yards just big enough to store bins. On the opposite side of the street were four-storey tower blocks of sandy-coloured bricks. They were perpendicular to the road with space between each for communal parking.

Somewhere nearby fireworks were launched into the sky. He could hear the whining screech of their ascent before the inevitable concussive boom when they exploded. Those explosions were happening in parts of the sky Victor could not see, although a hint of coloured light brightened the upper floors of some buildings in pink, blue and green. He had no idea if this was a celebration like a birthday or a team winning an important game, or whether it was just for fun.

Maybe a signal, he thought. One crew signalling to another, or perhaps the signal was a kind of warning. A sudden alarm or call to action that all nearby heard and understood without the need for multiple phone calls that would inevitably be slower to make and with no guarantee all would pick up or notice. The whole neighbourhood heard the fireworks at the same time, barring a second or two for the sound to travel. Much faster than all those calls and it didn't matter whether the rest of the crew were in the shower or in a car playing loud music. Efficient, Victor thought, and safer. No records of the message on anyone's phone for the police or rivals to use against them at a later date. He was impressed with the simplicity of the system.

Before Victor had even engaged the handbrake, figures were approaching, huddled against the rain, hoods pulled down low and zippers all the way up, with strings tightened so all that was visible of their faces was a circle containing eyes, nose and upper lip. Some wore huge puffa jackets that would have made them seem twice as broad if not for the skinny legs poking out the bottom. Young guys, obviously. Maybe teens. London had high youth unemployment, especially in these deprived districts. And no one older than twenty-five partook in such street crime. Either they had gone legit by that point, or if they were still criminals they would have moved on to more profitable activities that came with less risk. Career street dealers and muggers went to prison or they ended up dead.

He ignored the knuckles rapping on the driver's window expecting him to lower it and purchase whatever street drugs these youths sold.

They backed away a step or two when he pushed open the door and climbed out into the rain.

Glances were shared between them. Whoever they were expecting to emerge from the car, Victor was not it.

'Narc,' he heard one whisper.

Another spat on the pavement in response, though the saliva disappeared into the downpour before it could reach the ground.

'Excuse me,' Victor said after he had closed the car door behind him.

No one moved.

Six of them in total, although three held back.

One laughed, mimicking Victor's words in a mocking tone, as if the simple request was somehow worthy of scorn.

The address Forrester had provided was nearby and it was far from prudent to provide any advance warning here, so Victor opted for the simplest, most peaceful solution and went to carry on his way.

'Whoawhoawhoa, whoa.' A tall youth, his jeans hanging so low on his hips that the stripes of his boxer shorts were visible, stepped in Victor's way. 'You buy or you go home.'

'Fine,' Victor said. 'How much?'

'For what?' came the response. 'Whaddaya want to buy?'

'I don't know what you're selling.'

'We got weed, hash, pills, blow and V. What tickles your fancy? You look like you could use a little of everything.'

A hint of a goatee beard ringed his mouth. Red acne scars added the only colour to his pale cheeks, which were drawn and hollow.

'Let's keep it simple and go for the first option,' Victor said. 'What do I get for fifty pounds?'

More glances were exchanged. Small eyes in round faces darted back and forth.

'Eighth of indica. Give you a quarter for seventy.'

'An eighth sounds plenty.'

'Show me the dollar bills.'

Victor took out his wallet, removed two twenty-pound notes and a ten. The tall youth attempted to snatch them right out of Victor's fingers.

The hand darted out and gripped the money to jerk it away again and nothing happened.

A thin hand with long, emaciated fingers held the notes between thumb and index finger. The skin was pale except along the knuckles, which were red in the cold air. The network of blood vessels formed a dark relief across the back of the hands. His nails were short and rough – bitten down or torn – and the cuticles were prominent and dry. Some had tears and tiny dark spots where blood had coagulated into scabs.

'The indica,' Victor said as the confused youth failed to pull the two notes from his grasp.

'Let go of the money.'

'We had a deal,' Victor explained. 'Trust me when I tell you it's the greatest bargain of your life so far.'

'Give him the bills,' another said in a strained pitch.

Though his gaze remained fixed on the tall youth trying to rip free the money, Victor was aware of the activities in his peripheral vision. The other five were becoming exponentially anxious.

No one would come running to their aid because such dealers operated in small groups in designated areas. But if this particular group was part of a larger gang then other members could be nearby. Smoking or drinking or selling drugs or looking for something else to do. When Victor had been a similar age, his own crew would break off into smaller groups. There had been no direction and no strategy. No hierarchy even. Everyone did as they desired, whether stealing cars or picking pockets or devising other crimes. It had been rare that everyone had ever been together in the same place at the same time for the same purpose. Whenever he was passing through the old stamping ground, Victor left cash or valuables in one of the various dead drop points they had used to ferry stolen tape decks and alloys. Two decades later, those drop points were stuffed with more wealth than all of them could have ever dreamed of, all uncollected. He continued to add to such stashes anyway, just as they had sworn to do, just in case. Maybe one of them was still alive and needed it. He knew they would do the same for him if they could.

Blood ties never died.

Victor did not expect this group of dealers had firearms. Knives, however, for certain. Impossible to keep them all in sight at the same time so he would need to drop each one fast, moving onto the next before that next youth could process what was happening. Dropping them fast meant brutal, disabling strikes. Broken bones at the very least. Screaming. An ambulance would be called.

Police following.

Victor let go of the money.

The tall youth had been pulling so hard that the sudden release of resistance sent him stumbling backwards to the point he would have fallen to the pavement had one of the others not been in the way to cushion his momentum.

'Bad news, blood,' he said as he recovered his balance. 'Indica ain't on the menu tonight.'

'I'll live,' Victor said.

'Maybe come back tomorrow, yeah?'

'Now get out of my way.'

One laughed. 'Calm down, bad man.'

Sliding the money into a hip pocket of his jeans, the tall youth kissed his teeth. 'Yo, you can't park here without a ticket, and I don't see a ticket. Which means you need to buy one from me.'

Thinking about broken bones and screaming and what would inevitably follow, Victor said, 'Better for all concerned if I park elsewhere.'

THIRTY-EIGHT

Victor had been expecting the address Forrester gave him to correspond with a residential property. He pictured a house with enough bedrooms and reception rooms to allow a dozen or so addicts to smoke or inject in relative peace and privacy. Maybe a dealer or two on-site to provide additional supply and to make sure the denizens kept a low profile.

He was wrong.

The address corresponded with a rundown manufacturing unit that lay as part of a cluster of industrial properties flanking the housing estate. The first problem was it was no isolated drug den. He saw clusters of silhouettes even at distance, lone figures with seemingly nothing to do, who kept their phones in their hands the entire time.

Sentries.

On the lookout for police or rival dealers, not someone like him. Although, when he was so obviously out of place, they could easily mistake him for a cop as the six youths had shown. And even if they decided otherwise, they would still use their phones to call ahead and to pass on the sighting. As he closed in on the den, whoever was there would be waiting for him.

Though not professionals, they still had numbers and the advantage of terrain: they knew their neighbourhood better than he could ever do. Any threats in the den would be ready for him by the time he arrived, and he would leave his back exposed to the sentries.

Even in the UK, some could have guns.

Amateurs, yes, but bullets didn't care who fired them. At close range, in territory he didn't know and with circumstances he couldn't control, it was conceivable that if things didn't work out then it could go loud.

There was no reason it couldn't go smoothly. He might walk into the den and leave with Forrester's son after nothing more than letting a dealer or two understand that stopping him was the last thing they wanted to do if they had any plans to walk at any point during the rest of their lives.

Amateurs, not professionals.

Almost certainly it would play out without going loud.

Victor did not operate like that, however.

If there was even a small chance of it going loud then he wanted to clear his exfiltration ahead of time.

He ran over the first sentry.

Simple enough to do. Victor turned onto the street at a conservative speed, only accelerating at the last moment when the youth was a few metres ahead.

He had his back to Victor, turning around when it was far too late, his low-hanging jogging bottoms restricting his mobility.

Victor jerked the wheel to hit the youth with the left

corner of the Lexus's bumper, taking his legs out from under him so he catapulted up and over the bonnet.

To control where he ended up, Victor slammed the brake and swerved back onto the road before the youth could roll up and onto the roof. He lay flattened to the windscreen for a moment before tumbling back the way he came and tumbling down to the tarmac.

Victor hit the release for the boot and was out of the car within three seconds, circling around to where the youth lay on his back, groaning, the mobile phone nearby but out of reach.

A stamping heel made sure it had no capacity to warn anyone and a kick to the skull silenced the groans.

He hoisted the unconscious youth up and over his shoulder before depositing him in the open boot.

All over inside thirty seconds.

Shutting it again, Victor glanced around.

No faces at windows. No curtains twitching. Not that kind of neighbourhood. Residents here would not peer out of their homes for anything short of a prolonged gun battle.

The second sentry required a little more elbow grease.

He had better awareness than the one in the low-hanging joggers. As soon as he saw Victor nearby, the phone came up to chest height in readiness. Thumb no doubt hovering over the only number saved in the phone's contacts.

As Victor approached, the phone began to lower, from chest height, to waist, and then down to his side.

'How many have you had?' he asked, watching Victor stagger and sway, walking more in a zig-zag than a straight line.

'I'm looking . . . for . . . '

'Yeah . . . ?'

'For . . . '

'For . . . ?'

Victor was now close enough that when he feigned a trip, he fell into the sentry, who began to laugh at the ridiculousness of it all until his nostrils flared, and he realised he could smell no alcohol on Victor's breath.

Which came far too late to make any meaningful difference to the outcome.

With a shove to one shoulder and a pull to the other, Victor spun the sentry one hundred and eighty degrees and snapped on a chokehold.

The sentry reacted well, turning into the choke to protect his carotids.

A good effort, although it only delayed the inevitable and extended his suffering. He fought for every single second until he passed out, attempting to land elbows to Victor's ribs, trying to kick back at his shins. Nothing of any effect got through Victor's defences, but the sentry didn't give up until his body gave up on him. Victor respected that kind of perseverance.

The second sentry went into the boot with the first one.

Who was somehow coming round despite the kick to the side of the head. Perhaps an abnormal thickness to his skull, although more likely he had the reinforcement of a titanium plate from a past injury.

'What's . . . going . . . on . . . ?'

There was no such plate in the sentry's chin, however, Victor discovered with an elbow.

Given the second was a lot larger than the first sentry and the Lexus was not a large car, so, after relieving him of his black puffa jacket, it took some effort to get the boot closed again with both of them inside. Should either wake up before Victor was done, they would be far too compacted together to have any hope of reaching and activating the internal release.

He checked the jacket pockets, finding nothing but a lighter, a packet of cigarettes that also had a hand-rolled joint inside, small change and gum. The latter was spearmint flavour, so he left it alone. He took the lighter and the joint, fighting the urge to take the cigarettes too for completion. He knew having them on his person, even for character, was the first decline of a slippery slope. The voice inside his head would tell him he would appear less threatening with a lit cigarette in his hand, that it was a reason to be outside, whether walking or loitering, that it was an easy way for threats to dismiss him until it was too late.

Holding a lit cigarette without inhaling looked suspicious after a while, of course.

Better to inhale to complete the part.

Ah, but a single inhalation wouldn't be enough, would it?

And he would need to practise for it to look natural.

He took a deep, slow, breath and let it out even slower.

The hardest battle was always fought against the self, he knew well.

He folded the black puffa jacket into a tight roll he secured under one arm, and walked the last distance to the den. A chain-link fence topped with coils of razor wire secured the perimeter. With such a dilapidated site there was a chance, although no certainty, he would find a section that had been cut to let degenerates through, but he found none in the areas that were not overlooked by passing traffic or nearby windows.

An inconvenience only, thanks to the sentry's puffa jacket.

He held onto one sleeve and threw up the jacket so it landed on the razor wire, where it caught on the blades and remained in place.

The fence was four metres tall and wet with rain, so it took Victor almost six seconds to clear it. The biggest hurdle was the puffa jacket, which although it did a fine job neutralising the blades, the bulbous nature of the garment meant Victor had fewer useful handholds at the top of the fence.

Dropping down the last two metres on the other side, he left the jacket in place. The black material meant it would be hard to see for anyone not in the immediate vicinity. Though he was not expecting to need to exit the same way unless Forrester's son was both surprisingly athletic and amenable to leaving with an utter stranger, it was protocol to have a back door from any scenario.

The area around the den was clean of drug paraphernalia. None among the litter, no glints of foil in the darkness, not even the little aluminium bottles that once housed nitrous oxide that he had seen in many gutters. Either the dealers here kept it this way as a precautionary measure – in which case he was impressed by their diligence – or the den itself in the vicinity meant there was just no need for anyone to get high in the cold.

A group huddled near the site gate noticed him and did nothing. They were there to look out for rivals or cops approaching from the outside. They were not concerned with anyone already inside the fence. At this distance he was nothing more than a dark silhouette. If they had any interest as to why he was outside of the den, they did not show it.

Amateurs, not professionals.

It made for a pleasant change.

The flip side was he could not think like them. He wouldn't instinctively know how they would react to his actions. He had no idea what their routines would be, how they would conduct themselves in normal circumstances or under pressure.

He lit up the joint, taking a long draw into his mouth only and keeping it there for a moment before directing the smoke at his chest as he blew it out again. He stubbed it out against the wall before dropping it back into a pocket in case he needed it a second time.

The guy at the entrance to the den had a bald head shaved to smooth skin that pooled the little ambient light and made his scalp seem polished and glossy. He wore a leather jacket that bulged at the shoulders, arms and stomach. He had the kind of size that made him look like a regular doorman keeping the peace outside a lively bar on a Friday night. His sense of spatial awareness was terrible, however, only noticing Victor when he was within arm's reach.

'Been here before?' the man asked, slipping away the phone he had been toying with, then looking Victor up and down in suspicion. He relaxed a little as he noticed the scent of marijuana.

'Not for a while.' Victor answered. 'Anything I need to know?'

'If you hit it too hard, no one's calling an ambulance. You get yourself out and get yourself some help, or you stay inside and die, yeah?'

'I wouldn't want it any other way.'

THIRTY-NINE

Inside, the den was a little warmer without the wind chill and the drizzle, although Victor could still see his breath clouding if the light caught it at the right angle. The air seemed more humid too. The entrance hallway's brick walls were painted an off-white so darkened by grime it was closer to a sickly yellow except where calcium deposits had built up from leaking water pipes. They criss-crossed the brickwork, muted brown in colour. Verdigris gave the occasional connection a bluish tinge and rusting screws stained the wall in intermittent, vertical lines.

As he delved deeper into the building he could smell the smoke of tobacco, marijuana, hash, opium, crack cocaine and other narcotics he did not recognise. The hallway soon opened up to what he supposed was once a factory floor, although now it was a warren of rooms, corridors and open spaces separated by temporary walls. Some were the kind of screens and dividers used in offices, others were constructed from stacked wooden pallets, blankets and throws suspended by washing lines, corrugated steel sheets, garden fencing, and anything else that could be used to carve out a degree of privacy.

The first occupied room was strewn with large beanbags and scattered with bare duvets and cushions. Everything was so filthy it was almost impossible to know the true colour of any material. At first, he thought it was empty of people until what he thought was a row of cushions began to snore. He took a step closer to gain a better angle on the sleeper, seeing a young woman with cracked and split lips.

Music emanated from the next room: some soft, electronic music that reminded him of waves lapping against the shore of a lake near to Guatemala City. He had fond memories of the time that followed, of mornings spent in the sunny valleys of Switzerland and afternoons on the ski slopes.

A group of four were sitting in a circle in the centre of the room, cross-legged and facing one another as they shared a glass pipe that bubbled when a naked flame was set beneath it.

Acrid smoke rose into the air.

'Manny?' he said, holding back the plastic sheeting that served as a doorway.

No one answered so he stepped inside, circling their circle to check their faces. In the dim light they seemed almost inanimate, showing little sign of life until the pipe came their way.

An emaciated woman propositioned him in explicit detail. Victor politely declined the offer, electing to refrain from criticising the vulgarity of the language used. She had more pressing problems to address than swearing.

He found no one else young enough to be Manny on the ground floor, so he ascended a set of stairs.

Graffiti was everywhere on the walls here. As he moved deeper into the floor he saw some had been sprayed with fluorescent paints, which glowed bright under ultraviolet lighting, providing the only other colours visible. He saw crudely drawn satanic symbols and pentagrams intermingled with verses of scripture.

Unlike the floor below, there seemed to be only a single main room without dividers, maybe twenty metres from the door to the other end. A hallway led off from each of the adjoining walls and a pair of doors stood together in the centre of the far wall.

Several sofas, chairs and mattresses littered the floor in a layout he could only describe as chaotic. Little of the floor was visible due to the layer of empty glass and plastic bottles, fast-food cartons, pizza boxes, crisp packets, biscuit wrappers and cigarette stubs.

Fourteen people in total.

Ten men. Four women.

Some young. Some old. Some so dirty and destitute they could be twenty or seventy for all he could tell.

As well as the scent of drugs and body odour, he could smell vomit too. No obvious mess to correspond with the odour so he guessed the doorman's warning was taken seriously by those who lingered here.

A few looked his way out of curiosity. Some were so inebriated they had no ability to discern his presence. Most had no interest in him.

One set of eyes, however, stared.

Those eyes were narrowed, but they were clear. The pupils were dilated because of the dim lighting only.

A young guy, long and stringy, stretched out on a sofa

without cushions, head against one armrest and legs dangling over the other. He smoked on a fat joint that seemed to have little effect on him beyond his lounged demeanour.

'Whaddaya need?'

'I'm good,' Victor said.

'Whatever you bought, I have better. For real.'

Under the ultraviolet light, the dandruff on his shoulders glowed white and bright.

'I believe you.' Victor made his way along the centre of the room, gaze sweeping back and forth to examine the other nine men. 'But I'm good.'

'Is it?' was all the man said in return.

Victor recognised Manny at the far end of the room, splayed out on his back, half-on half-off a bare mattress. His head and one side of his body lay on the bare floor as though he had passed out like that or rolled over in his sleep. His mouth hung open and his eyelids flickered in a deep, blissful rest.

A few years older than he looked in the most recent family portrait, he now had longer hair and a drawn, almost hollow face.

Victor lowered to his haunches in the space between the mattress and the far wall, letting him use a hand to give Manny a gentle nudge while he kept his gaze on the rest of the space.

'Manny,' Victor said. 'It's time to go.'

The kid did not respond to the physical attempt to rouse him, but his head moved a little at the sound of his name.

'I'm here to help you.'

'What ...?' a quiet voice asked.

'You need to wake up. We need to leave.'

'Go ... away ...'

'That's not going to happen,' Victor explained, 'unless you're coming with me. Your father misses you. Your mother too.'

Eyes still shut, he said, 'They hate me ... They're ashamed ...'

'You're probably half right, only that changes nothing. They're still your parents. They still love you. They want you to come home.'

Victor expected that was how people felt about their children, even those who like Manny acted in ways of which they did not approve. The tone was probably off since Victor could not relate to such feelings and could only pretend to understand.

'I'm going nowhere,' Manny said, voice a little clearer now he was more awake. He was more certain too, however, slithering back fully onto the mattress and rolling onto one side, facing away from Victor. 'Leave me alone.'

'You probably weigh all of seventy kilograms. I've hiked through the Hindu Kush with more than twice that in kit on my back, so don't think I won't simply sling you over my shoulder if that's what it takes.'

Manny pushed himself up onto one elbow as he stared at Victor. 'Who are you?'

'Maybe think of me as your guardian angel.'

'Then you'd better be carrying some gear.'

Victor took it that Manny was not referring to weapons and so removed the joint to present to him.

'Crack?' Manny had hopeful eyes.

'Marijuana.'

He kissed his teeth in disappointment. 'You're less angel and more like a demon.'

221

Victor raised an eyebrow. 'You have no idea.'

'Come back in the morning with something stronger and we can talk again.'

'Come with me and I'll get you whatever you want.'

'For real?'

He may have been off the mark with his tone in expressions of affection, but he never missed when it came to deception. 'Absolutely. Whatever you want. As much as you want. All you have to do is go home.'

'Okay,' Manny agreed with a nod. 'Let's go.'

Pleasantly surprised that he didn't have to knock him out and carry him, Victor helped Manny to his feet. Which took a few moments as the kid struggled to find his balance and coordinate his limbs.

By this point, the guy on the sofa had sat up.

He was off the sofa by the time they were crossing the room in line with him. Victor had one arm – the left – supporting Manny, who was either too weak, too high, too tired, or all three, to walk in a straight line without help.

'What's this?'

'We're friends,' Victor said, then to Manny, 'aren't we?'

'Best friends, Beanie,' he agreed with too much enthusiasm. 'We go way back, like all the way back. Best baby friends at nursery.'

The age difference meant the guy called Beanie didn't believe him, but he didn't care that much beyond Manny was leaving of his own volition. 'All right.'

He peered over Manny's shoulder to where he had been lying on the mattress, which Victor assumed was to make sure there was no evidence of messy bodily functions left behind.

222

'Seeya tomorrow,' Beanie said when he saw there was nothing.

'Nah,' Manny said with the same over-the-top enthusiasm. 'Matey here is going to get me whatever I like.' He grinned. 'So long as I say hi to the old dears, that is. Don't ask me why because I'm a massive disappointment to them and always have been. But whatever.'

Victor kept his expression neutral in case the guy didn't fully process what Manny had just said.

'Is that right?' Beanie asked, then to Victor, 'Anything he likes, right?'

'He's exaggerating.'

'You wouldn't be trying to steal a customer, would you?'

'Perish the thought.'

'What?'

'No,' Victor reiterated. 'I'm not a dealer, as I'm sure you can see.'

Manny's stress levels immediately spiked. 'But you told me you will get me whatever I want? As much as I want.'

Beanie eyed Victor. 'I know that game. It's the one we all play. Freebies at first, as much as they like, *more* than they like, and then when the freebies stop they can't give you money fast enough to get more.'

Beanie had a long, skinny physique. His loose clothing accentuated that leanness so he almost seemed underfed. Not starving, because there were no sunken cheeks or jutting clavicles. He ate enough, but Victor imagined he spent too much of his time burning calories hustling for his frame to ever fill out. Beanie was only hungry for money, for success in his chosen field.

'You're mistaken,' Victor said. 'I could take the time to

223

explain to you exactly why you're wrong, but I don't really want to spend one more minute in this place than I absolutely have to. When I say that even to someone like me this is a deplorable way to conduct business, you should really listen.'

'He's lying to you, Manny,' Beanie said. 'Either he's no dealer and can't get you what you need or he wants you to buy his supply and charge you more for it than we do. You know us. We're friends. He's staying and you're going. Right now. Or you're going to be in a world of hurt.'

'Who do you think I am?'

'What?'

Manny said, 'He's a demon.'

'Hyperbole,' Victor said, 'but in this case it might as well be gospel. I'm walking out of here with Manny and the single best decision you will ever make in your entire life is to simply let me.'

With new eyes, Beanie looked at Victor, and for a moment it seemed as though he was going to step aside.

Until the doorman entered the room.

He began to say, 'Hey, Beanie, do you know where the bleach is? Can't find it. Did Lester take it when he—' but then focused on Victor escorting Manny. 'What's all this about?'

Victor released Manny because he knew however much Beanie had paid attention to the voice inside his head, now he had backup. Alone, he had been willing to listen. Now, he no longer needed to hear.

'He's robbing us,' Beanie shouted to the doorman while moving away from Victor as he pointed in an accusatory manner. 'He's taking Manny away so he can sell to him instead.'

The doorman seemed surprised, although pleased as well.

He smirked, the tip of his tongue appearing between his teeth before he said, 'Then you've made an almighty mistake, haven't you?'

'The only error I made,' Victor said with a sigh, 'was deluding myself into believing I could do this without the nurses in the local emergency department having to work through their breaks tonight.'

Confusion creased the big man's face. 'You what, mate?'

Stepping closer, Victor said, 'Allow me to explain.'

FORTY

The creases of confusion remained on the doorman's face for the three seconds it took Victor to cover the distance. He walked at a casual pace, without any signs of coming aggression, so the doorman did none of the things he might have done to impede the coming attack.

He was so used to intimidating adversaries into submission with fear alone he didn't notice it wasn't working here. Almost every animal on the planet stood down to a larger creature, although only someone weak on the inside needed to appear strong to others. It was a rule Victor had learned in his youth, when poverty had stripped him down to thin, jutting ribs. He had won fights against larger boys who believed their advantage in size meant they didn't need to fight. And when they realised they did, they were unprepared for his ferocity. He would take two punches gladly if it meant he rushed close enough to bite a chunk from that boy's cheek.

When Victor was within reach, amusement took the

place of confusion as the doorman finally understood what was coming.

'You can't be serious. Do yourself a favour and back down before you get—'

Victor's stomp-kick turned his words into a scream as his lead knee collapsed backwards, the leg folding in on itself and the doorman collapsing straight down ...

... and into the palm-strike/elbow combination that Victor aimed to intercept the descending face.

The groan was silenced just as fast as it began, the doorman landing in a heap on the floor, unconscious before he came to a stop.

'Let's go,' Victor said to Manny.

Who hesitated at the sudden and horrific violence. He looked even paler. He seemed even less stable in his movements.

'Is this for real?'

'Unfortunately so,' Victor answered, ushering him forwards.

Beanie was already sprinting ahead, yelling, '*Quick, quick, it's kicking off.*'

If not for the subsequent necessity to murder everyone else in the building, Victor would have shot Beanie in the back on general principle. Some people just didn't have the good sense to be alive.

Manny stopped. Shook his head. 'I'm going nowhere. This is messed up.'

'There will be plenty of time to discuss the pros and cons on the ride home.'

Manny was still shaking his head, his gaze on the unmoving form of the prostrate doorman. 'Is he dead?'

'Not even close.'

'How can you be so sure?'

'Just trust that I know what I'm talking about.'

He used a palm to push Manny towards the stairs. The kid wasn't strong, and didn't physically fight, but he wasn't making it easy. He resisted. Getting him down the stairs took so long that by the time Victor had Manny on the ground floor, the group hanging around at the entrance to the site had arrived, drawn by a phone call or message. Beanie was at their head, brave now he was not alone.

Their huge numerical advantage meant those Victor would not consider threats as individuals became a serious problem. Even with instincts and skills honed over many years, he would never have eyes in the back of his head. There was always a limit to what one could do against many. Especially with Manny in tow.

The terrain, however, worked against them. The warren of small rooms and narrow passageways prevented them spreading out. Congregated together, they were boxed in, shoulder to shoulder, unable to use their numbers. There were ways of flanking him, of course – by navigating the warren to come at him from the rear – but they were not thinking tactically yet. They wanted a show of force. Victor had counted eight at the entrance and nine stood before him now, including Beanie.

The main problem was time. Going through nine enemies, one by one, could take minutes if none ran. In their territory, with money and reputations and loyalties at stake, he might have to beat them all until they were physically incapable of fighting back. In that kind of time, it gave others plenty of opportunities to find their courage to attack him from behind and with nine in front of him, he could not afford to take his gaze from them for a single second. The length of time also meant there was the chance reinforcements would arrive from elsewhere on the estate.

Manny was the priority, but he was also the liability.

All they had to do was convince him to stay. Victor could not drag him out and fight his way out at the same time.

Which left only one practical course of action.

He drew his Five-seveN.

With a swift and smooth action, he whipped it from his waistband in an upward arc, the muzzle coming to rest in line with Beanie's head. 'Back off.'

'You think you're the only one with a gat?'

'I just want the kid,' he told the others as well as Beanie. 'No one has to die here.'

A bluff, of course: he wasn't killing anyone here because if he killed just one person then he had to kill absolutely every single last human being in the building. Which might have been simpler, granted, only he didn't have enough bullets.

'I doubt you make a lot of wrong choices,' Victor said. 'Don't start now.'

'You're in our digs, not the other way around.'

'I'm leaving now. There's nothing you can do to change that fact. The manner in which I leave, however, is entirely up to you.'

'You don't know me at all if you think you hold all the power here.' Beanie spoke with utter confidence or a flawless act of it. 'What is SCO19?'

'The firearms unit of the Met.'

'They carry Glocks,' Beanie explained. 'In the boots of their armed response vehicles, they have MP5s.'

'Why are you telling me this?'

'Because it takes them four minutes to get to this estate when they're called. We know because we've had them here on three occasions in the last few years. The first of those, we didn't know they were coming. Someone reported seeing a gun. Luckily, no one was pinched. But we were worried. We don't like surprises. So the next two 999 calls we made ourselves. Now we know how long we've got.' Beanie smiled. 'We start blasting, the feds will be all over us long before we're finished.'

'It won't take me four minutes to get out of here.'

'I didn't hear you park up out front. You gotta get Manny all the way to your ride too. I don't know who you are, I don't know why you're here, but I know for sure you don't want to tangle with the cops any more than we do.'

Victor nodded. 'You know what? You're right, I'm not going to squeeze this trigger. I have to admit, I'm impressed with the way you think.'

Beanie grinned. 'If you ain't strong, you better be smart.'

'Let's not get carried away,' Victor said as he slid the gun back into his waistband. 'Because I'm still walking out of here.' He rocked his head from side to side to crack his neck. 'Only now we're going to have to do it the hard way.'

FORTY-ONE

Having witnessed what happened to the doorman, Beanie wasn't foolish enough to make the first move. Instead, one of the guys from the entrance did, stepping forwards. He had a squat, solid build. His torso had a barrel-like quality, suggesting plenty of effort in the gym and no less time spent in the pub afterwards. He made the classic brawler's mistake of hiking up his trousers in readiness. It advertised the coming punch, the dominant hand that would deliver it, and provided Victor with so much advance warning it didn't seem fair. Which was exactly how he preferred any altercation.

The guy did the work for him. He charged forwards, eager and reckless. All Victor had to do was slip the punch and direct the guy into the wall, where he broke his nose and cracked his teeth against the brickwork.

The squat man wasn't done, however. He spun around, fast, ready for more despite unsteady footing and a glazed look to his eyes. Victor only needed to push a palm against the guy's chin, forcing his head back and driving him back into the wall so his skull collided with the brickwork this time. The resulting shock and pain took away the last of his stability, making it easy for his legs to be swept out from under him.

For a moment, it seemed that the others would make the sensible decision to back off. Perhaps they would have done, without Beanie there to spur them on.

They had the numbers to surround Victor, to counter his skill and speed with sheer mass of bodies, only they did not have the space and attacked without any sense of coordination or tactics that might have slowed Victor down. Instead, they came at him one at a time, another arriving just as the previous was falling down, then joining them just as fast only for someone else to follow suit.

When the next was on the floor reeling, Beanie and the others hesitated, afraid to follow suit but too many for Victor to attack as one so he pulled down a wall made of pallets to block their path and dragged Manny another way.

The unfamiliar layout and the many interconnecting corridors and rooms meant even Victor's sense of direction was strained, and Beanie's guys might have taken Victor by surprise at several points if only they hadn't felt the need to announce their presence, yelling '*Oi you*', '*Hey*' and '*Let's have it.*'

Victor always appreciated enemies who went out of their way to make his day a little easier, so he repaid the favour by limiting the repercussions to casts and crutches instead of comas.

No one thanked him for this kindness, however.

'This is insane,' Manny said, wide-eyed, as he stepped over a writhing guy with neon green hair while Victor tore a weakened section of piping from one of the brick walls.

He used the pipe to break both arms of a dealer wielding a pair of machetes.

Victor discarded the pipe after the excruciating pain caused the dealer to vomit over it before he slid down the wall to join his neon-haired associate on the floor.

'I assure you this is entirely rational.'

Manny looked as though he could not discern whether Victor was being serious or making a joke. There was no time to explain because ...

The next charged out of the darkness of an unlit space, a shrill battle cry providing Victor with a welcome warning to what might otherwise have been a surprise attack he didn't see until it was too late.

A quick sidestep ensured the attacker's momentum found only empty space except—

The arm Victor left in his way at head height.

Charging his face into Victor's braced forearm took him from his feet but didn't knock him out.

The floor did that. The back of his head whipped against the cement.

'Ouch,' Manny said, then, 'Oh, shit.'

When Victor felt hands grab at his jacket from behind, he threw himself backwards, going with the resulting pull instead of fighting it, crashing into his enemy unprepared for sudden collision. The resulting impact sent them both into a table, the youth folding onto it with Victor on top, who used the momentum to roll over the man and come to his feet while his enemy was still prostrate on the table below him.

Victor's downward palm strikes were delivered with so much force that one of the brackets holding a table leg in place snapped and the table collapsed.

Skinny fingers snatched at Victor's shirt. He responded by grabbing the wrist in one hand while he used the other to snap every skinny finger, one by one.

His attacker dropped to the floor, crying.

The next guy knew what he was doing. He had a solid stance, feet apart and knees bent, so Victor snapped up his lead foot and stomped a heel down to the top of the guy's closest kneecap, ripping it free from its attachment to the femur. His victim screeched, then passed out when Victor kicked him where the kneecap had been, striking the unprotected joint with his heel.

When there was no one left with the will to step in Victor's way, Beanie had no choice but to do so himself. Whatever his fear of Victor, he couldn't lose face in front of his whole crew given most of them were unconscious or wishing they were instead of crying and suffering.

As expected, Beanie took out a weapon. He wasn't going to face Victor without one. But no firearm. As they had already discussed: neither of them wanted the police to respond.

Victor hadn't been sure what kind of weapon it would be, although he knew it would be no machete or the like. Something small and compact that could be carried without being noticeable and disposed of easily if the cops were coming.

In the dim light it was hard to make out at first. Then, with a strong flick of the wrist, the telescopic baton extended to its full length.

Victor would have preferred to go against a knife.

The baton was several times longer than a blade, giving a significant reach advantage. While a knife could open an artery it had to hit true, edge aligned. A baton could wound on any plane of attack. The knife had only one narrow edge and point.

Victor could block a knife with his arm if necessary, accepting a superficial cut to escape greater injury. Blocking a baton with his arm meant a shattered bone.

With distance still between them, Beanie made a flourish of deft wrist movements, causing the baton to dance and loop before him.

He was saying something about the price of arrogance, of stealing customers, of disrespect, but Victor wasn't listening. He shoved Manny into the closest sofa to make room and to reduce the odds of a wayward baton swing cracking his skull. He flopped backwards along its length, with legs splayed and one hand draping to the floor. He gave some moan of protest but made no move to get himself back up again.

Victor kept moving forwards, knowing Beanie would either thrust the baton out to keep him at a distance, or raise it high and ready to strike.

The second option.

Beanie came at him with an overhand attack, the baton held up overhead to bring it swinging down in a fast arc.

Victor ignored the weapon itself, darting forwards as soon as he was in range of the baton, coming inside of Beanie's looping downward swing, which sent the weapon over Victor's back.

With his leading shoulder slamming into Beanie's bony chest while his foot blocked the youth's inevitable backwards stumble, Victor barrelled Beanie to the floor.

He hit the cement hard but kept hold of the baton in a tight grip Victor exploited with a quick stamp.

Multiple bones broke beneath his heel.

The resulting screech was more than enough encouragement for anyone left of Beanie's crew to abandon any ideas of intervening.

One youth almost fell over in his rush to spin around and flee back the way he had come.

'You should thank me,' Victor said to Beanie as he whimpered on the ground.

Beanie's cheeks glistened.

Victor motioned for Manny to get up off the sofa. 'Let's take you home. You're about to go on a little trip.'

His eyes wide with a mix of amazement and disgust, Manny nodded. 'Whatever you say.'

Stepping over Beanie, Victor said, 'I'm sure by the time you can use a can opener again you'll be glad you spent all those months in a cast and went through all those long months of physical therapy because you'll never go back to doing this. Who knows, one day you might even be a productive member of society? Something to think about.'

FORTY-TWO

The best time of any day was the morning, naturally. When the sun was rising, new opportunities arose along with its ascent. The problem was that at this time of year, the day had long begun by the time the sun got off its arse. Shivika Chandi had been up at five, in the office by six thirty, and had been to three separate briefings before the first rays of light emerged in the east. Nipping out for breakfast was a convenient excuse to watch the sky brighten. The buildings blocking the view meant she missed the moment the sun appeared above the horizon, but she watched it rise over the skyline while she ate her muffin and sipped her coffee.

With the sheer amount of work the task force had to do, she would get a right royal rollicking if any of the higher-ups knew she was loitering in the park.

Sorry, there was a queue. What did I miss?

'We have to keep this brief,' Chandi said. 'Because I have a train to catch.'

Scrolling through the latest photographs on her burner

phone, Milburn said, 'Bloody hellfire, this really is Cleric, isn't it?'

'Certainly appears so.'

'You told me he was no fool, Shivika. You promised me he would be long gone by now. Long gone before now, in fact. Why isn't he? Why is he still here in London?'

'Just to clarify, in no way did I promise you he would be gone by now. I believe I suggested he would be clever enough to have left.'

'Spare me the semantics. What is he doing?'

'When we pick him up, it's the first thing I'll ask him.'

'Now is really not the time for making jokes.'

'I try to find humour wherever I can. You know what they say? Don't take life too seriously, you'll never get out of it alive.'

'You're taking a perverse pleasure in this, aren't you? It's really not very becoming. We're looking at life in prison if he starts singing.'

'Calm down, James. I'm just pulling your leg. When did you get so uptight?'

'The day that unscrupulous officer blackmailed me, that's when. When I had no choice but to clean up after her. I've been looking over my shoulder ever since. My sense of humour has never been the same.'

'And who did you turn to when you needed a cleaning job so sparkling you could eat your dinner off it?'

'Well,' Milburn began. 'You. Obviously.'

'Did I do a good job?'

The park was quiet so early in the morning. A few walkers with dogs, a few joggers. The odd harried bloke deciding to take a short cut through the park to his next appointment and realising he was now lost.

'Spare me the foreplay and tell me what it is you want.'

'Who says I want anything?'

'Because you're a manipulative little shit,' Milburn hissed. 'That's why. That's why I bought your you in the past. You helped me bury that mess and you got a lovely promotion out of it, didn't you?'

'And I've been promoted three times since then.'

'There's only so much of this merry-go-round I can take, Shivika. You didn't call me to warn me about Cleric out of the goodness of your heart and you haven't broken the law to show me confidential task force materials. What. Do. You. Want?'

'I think I'm winding down with Five. I've been there sixteen years now and there's only so high I can go without the gig turning into some boring, middle management role. It's already halfway there as it is. That's not what I signed up for. The Borisyuk task force is the most interesting thing I've done in the last twelve months and I'm nowhere near the action as an advisor. Who knows, when it's over, how long it will be until I get something else as juicy?'

'If you want to go back to wiretapping and kicking down doors, you can get a demotion all on your own, I'm sure.'

'That's not quite what I had in mind,' she said, glancing at her belly. 'When I move on from the Park completely, I want to go into politics. You can give me a leg up.'

'You think I can get you a peerage? Are you out of your mind?'

'Don't be ridiculous. I merely want you to put in a good word for me. You must know loads of politicians at this point. They all have assistants and aides and special advisors. That's what I want. I want to be on an MP's staff.

Which is the first step to becoming one myself one day, isn't it? I don't care what party. As long as I'm on the TV one day, it doesn't matter whose scandals and failures I'm spinning.'

'If you help me, if you keep helping me, I'll see what I can do. But first: how close is the task force to Cleric?'

A murmuring of quacks sounded as ducks glided by on the lake. Further out, two swans nuzzled. Near them, a pelican thrust its head beneath the surface.

'It's hard to say. We all know he's out there but he's a slippery sod.'

'At this point, I'd hide him in my spare room if I thought it would help.'

'They missed him by a matter of hours yesterday,' Chandi explained. 'But that's the only time there has been a hit on facial recognition worth organising a response. Either he knows we're onto him or he's very lucky. If it's the latter, then his luck will run out eventually. The longer he stays in town the closer to inevitability his capture gets.'

'You could at least have let my delusional sense of relief last a smidgen longer.'

'I'm here for a hug whenever you need one.'

'Charmed, I'm sure.' Milburn sighed. 'Even if Cleric keeps schtum in questioning, it's only a matter of time before they start putting his history together. They're going to realise he was in London back then, aren't they? They're going to link him to her, which is going to link him to me.'

'Exposure is not the same thing as culpability. You didn't put mercenaries on the streets of the capital.'

'No, that blackmailing MI5 officer did and I covered it up.' He sighed again. Tutted. 'I was never especially talented, Shivika. I freely admit that. But I had guile and I had

240

determination. I managed to carve out a respectable career in the intelligence business and while I had some missteps along the way, I'm proud of what I accomplished. I'm proud to sit in the House of Lords, whatever the pointlessness of such an institution. Even if you're right and nothing actually sticks to me, they're all going to smell it on me, nonetheless. Westminster is nothing but a palace of rumours and sniggering. I won't have them laugh at me behind my back because of one bloody mistake. I simply won't have it. We have to do something. We can't let it come to that.'

'If the task force corners him, there's nothing I can do. I want to help however I can, I do. My hands are tied. I don't have the clout to engineer an escape route for him. I just don't.'

'Say Cleric is apprehended, how do you imagine it will go down?'

'Overwhelming force,' Chandi said with confidence. 'No other option with such a volatile suspect. As many SCO19 units as is possible to round up. Encircle his location. Clear it of civilians first, probably. It will tip him off as to what's about to go down, but he should have nowhere to run at that point and the Home Secretary won't allow any action that leaves voters bleeding in the gutter.'

'Surveillance first?'

'Oh, absolutely. Multiple rotating teams to establish his movements and help identify the best time to go into action. We need to build up as much intel as possible before showtime.'

'You don't expect a rapid response takedown?'

'No way. This guy is armed and dangerous. It'll get people killed, guaranteed. And it's not like there's any risk of him blowing himself up on Tower Bridge, is there? He's a professional, not a terrorist.'

'You're saying this will be a carefully coordinated operation that will only take place in the optimal circumstances?'

'Is this a test? You know all this without needing me to answer.'

Milburn said, 'When I walk into a room, people stand up to greet me. They don't stay sitting down with their hand extended as if I should be grateful for their considerable efforts. They stand. Because of who I am, because of who I have been. I will not have that change for anything. Not for you, not for him. I will not have them stay seated.' He paused. 'How would you like a back door straight into Downing Street?'

'I'm listening.'

'The PM's top spin doctor is looking for aides.'

'You can get me the job?'

'Of course I bloody can't,' Milburn snapped. 'I can, however, make sure you get the interview and, more than that, I can make sure they like you before you even sit down in the chair. How does that sound?'

'Too good to be true,' was Chandi's careful answer. 'What do I need to do in return?'

'It occurs to me that I'm still connected to a lot of very useful people in the intelligence business, public and private sector. A lot of very capable individuals. You're going to know where Cleric is well before anyone makes a move on him, based on what you've just said and how we used to do things under my watch. Which will provide us with a small window of opportunity for a couple of capable people.'

'To do ... what?'

'Don't be coy,' Milburn said, losing patience. 'You know full well what I'm talking about. We cannot allow Cleric to be taken into custody.'

Chandi was silent.

'You'll be nowhere near the deed,' Milburn assured. 'You can be with the rest of the task force as they plan the take-down. All you'll need to do is pass on where he is. No one will ever so much as suspect you had anything to do with what transpires. It'll look like the Russians got to him. Some of them are obviously gunning for him as it is, so no one will see any other possible motive.'

'It's risky. For me, for whoever you call, and for you by proxy. It's really risky.'

'As is getting out of bed in the morning. And I don't hear you offering any alternative plans. Although, if you have a slice of tactical brilliance hidden up your sleeve, now's the time for the grand reveal.'

Chandi offered no such theatrics.

'So, *Shivy* my girl,' Milburn said, 'do you want that interview or not?'

FORTY-THREE

The fool of the Fool's Arms was no regular buffoon. He was that celebrated entertainer of the medieval court, the jester. Shown on the pub's sign in traditional motley costume of green and red, and with the iconic cap 'n bells hat, this particular fool had a wide, bright smile. With his colourful attire and welcoming grin, he was especially popular with patrons' children, who sipped cola or lemonade as they played in the beer garden on summer afternoons. They gave him names. Some years he was Timmy, other times he might be Percy. The painter, a prolific artist who had put his signature to many such signs the length and breadth of the country, had never so much as considered naming his subject. Likewise, the publican who had commissioned the sign had similarly not put that much thought into the character depicted, although he enjoyed the fact the little rascals who made use of his sandpit and slide paid attention to such details.

He would take the time to squat down to their level,

knees creaking and cracking as he did, and ask them who they thought the jester might be? Not only his name but his manner. Was he a nice man? Did they like him? Were his tricks fun or mean-spirited?

King John was happy to encourage them. He enjoyed listening to their opinions, he liked that his very own jester had a name. Given the Fool's Arms was King John's very own royal court it was only fitting.

This he still held in the basement level, in the function room accessible via a narrow hallway that ran past the gents and the ladies.

Here, every spare inch of wall was lined with nicely framed black and white photographs of famous Londoners and Jamaicans. Almost all were sportsmen and musicians from the '60s and '70s, from King John's youth.

After a big inhalation, he let it out as a bigger sigh. 'How are we going to sort this out then?'

Sitting across the circular table from him, as far away from one another as they could possibly be, were two lads. If their ages were doubled, King John would still think of them as young, and yet each ran his own squad.

'I was selling first,' Rollup insisted, directing his words to King John and happy to ignore his rival dealer.

Fred Head also made sure to address the king as he argued, 'I didn't see no sign. It's not finders keepers, is it? I move more product.'

'I don't need a summary.' King John alternated his focus between the two. 'I know the situation, right? I've been listening to you both whine about it for so long Terrance has almost finished his grub.'

At the far end of the room, near to the door, Terrance

nodded. He had better things to do than get involved, such as enjoying his breakfast, which was last night's leftover takeaway. The Fool's Arms served food only because the modern pub was expected to be a restaurant as much as a supplier of alcohol, and the menu was not to Terrance's tastes. If the dish didn't end in vindaloo or madras, the big lad didn't want to know.

'Do you want peace?' King John asked Rollup.

'When he packs up and goes, there will be.'

'It was a yes-or-no question.'

There was so much unbridled aggression and hatred in Rollup's curt 'No' that King John wondered if this particular generation was even human at all. He had never hated his rivals like this. Having competitors was part of doing business. It elevated both parties to greater heights. Even boxers hugged after beating the stuffing out of each other for twelve rounds.

To Fred Head, he asked the same question, adding, 'Yes or no?'

'Never.'

King John said to Terrance, 'What did you tell me before these two numpties arrived? When I asked you what you thought about this sit-down?'

Wiping his mouth with a napkin as he finished chewing, Terrance answered, 'Waste of time, boss man.'

'Hear that?' King John said to the two youths. 'Terrance can see into the future.'

Rollup and Fred Head waited.

'Talking is a waste of time these days,' King John continued. 'Which makes me feel really, really old.' He sighed again, then rose to his feet. 'If you won't work it out yourselves, I'll work it out for you.' He motioned with alternate palms, for the two young men to rise. 'Come on, up. We're through here.'

Rollup was first to rise, although he did so with slow, awkward movements as he had to hike up his trousers on the way. 'So who's getting the estate?'

'Neither of you wants peace, so what else is there? I'm calling it now. The estate belongs to neither of you.'

'Whoawhoawhoa, you can't do that,' Rollup protested.

'You're out of order,' Fred Head, still in his seat, added, and he was correct, but he made the mistake of also saying, 'You need to calm down, John.'

Screaming, *'It's KING John,'* he flipped the table over with a single hand.

It crashed to the floor, scattering and smashing glasses, spilling drinks. Glass shards and ice cubes glittering together in the mess.

Terrance did not stop eating.

Rollup was already out of his chair, so it was easy for him to dart backwards to be clear of spillage. Fred Head, sitting shocked, flicked a slice of lemon from his thigh before rising too and stepping away.

'No more bloodshed on the streets,' King John said, turning his head from side to side to alternate looking them in the eyes. 'You want to kill each other, fine. You can go ahead and kill each other and I'll even give you my blessing. But you do it here. You do it now.'

Fred Head forced a laugh. 'You cannot be serious.'

'I'm as serious as your massive cranium, son.'

The two young men exchanged glances. They both shifted their weight, then looked back at King John as though they were expecting him to burst out laughing, to tell them that he was pulling their legs. That this was all one big joke.

King John was as far from joking as they had ever seen him.

'I didn't bring a blade,' Rollup said.

'You took my gat at the door.'

'Then it's a fair fight, isn't it? You're both as pathetically weak as each other so no need to worry about one-punch knockouts.' He noted their nervous expressions and utter lack of appropriate fighting postures. 'Bet you wish you'd come down the gym to learn how to throw a punch when you had the chance instead of wasting your time playing video games, don't you?'

Both lads, previously so full of cocksure bravado, didn't know how to react to the sudden transformation before them. King John, the benign monarch they had always known, was now the tyrant he had always been and yet they had never borne witness.

'This is going to be good, I can tell. Ding, ding.'

He saw Rollup look down at the floor, at the pieces of broken glass.

'Forget it,' King John said. 'I don't want to go having to replace the floorboards.' He used the sides of his shoes to sweep the broken glass away from the two young men. 'You use your fists' – he mimed punching – 'you use your hands' – he mimed strangling – 'but you don't you use weapons in my gaff. Come on, get to it.'

Fred Head was first to back away in earnest, but it was Rollup who looked towards the door at the far end of the function room. The door Terrance was sitting adjacent to while he ate.

King John asked him, 'Have you finished your brekkie?'

'Just about.'

Terrance wiped the last remnants of curry from his plate with a corner of naan.

'Kindly make sure neither of these boys leaves before only one can.'

'Be my pleasure, boss man.'

King John had a head of height on either lad. In his prime, he had not been able to walk square on through most doorways because his back was so massive his arms could not hang straight down, leaving his elbows permanently flared. For every fight where he triumphed by way of his fists there were three more he won just by standing up from his chair.

Terrance, however, made King John seem like he'd had a calcium deficiency as a child. Like his pituitary gland had failed to secrete enough growth hormone.

Swallowing the last of the naan, Terrance used a napkin to wipe the corners of his mouth, then took the knife and fork from the plate and set them to one side of it before standing up to his full, towering height.

'He once auditioned to play the Incredible Hulk,' King John told them. 'Only they decided CGI would look more realistic. Now, he may be as old as your dads, but Terrance is still a young pup all things considered,' King John continued, 'which means he never got to hang out with most of the boys I used to work with way back. But Terrance has that thing – what do they call it? – when you're nostalgic for a time you never knew. He likes to hear about the characters from back in the day almost as much as he likes a plate of Delhi's finest. And, bless his cotton socks, he absolutely loves it when I introduce him to the few old geezers still luckily north side of the worms. Did I ever tell you about Lenny the Sieve, Terrance?'

'Can't say you have, boss man.'

'He's still around,' King John explained. 'Owns a huge waste disposal facility past Stratford. You see, Lenny is licensed to get rid of all sorts of horrible stuff. I mean, absolutely the worst, most harmful, dangerous materials you can find. Volatile compounds, industrial-grade solvents, asbestos, pesticides, petroleum by-products, even biological hazards. Stuff bad enough you need letters after your name just to pronounce it. Some of things Lenny disposes of are so unsafe, so unstable, you can't even break them down to other substances a little less awful. The only thing you can do is seal it up, store it somewhere secure, and never, ever, open it up again. Lenny's mostly legit these days except when he's getting rid of the odd body or two. Out back, I've got a barrel big enough for the both of you, for Terrance to stuff you into. Lenny can be here within the hour to collect it. By this time tomorrow the only parts of you that will still be solid will be the gold from your teeth. Which brings us neatly to the reason why they call him Lenny the Sieve. Because once you're nothing but liquid sloshing around in a bucket he's going to pour you slowly through a sieve so he can fish out anything of value.' In a quiet voice, he added, 'You're on the clock because I have a visitor arriving very shortly and he's not the kind of someone even the likes of me keeps waiting. You get to decide right now who goes in that barrel. But if you can't or if you won't beat the other to death in the next five minutes, you both go in. And it won't even be a tight squeeze given you're both so scrawny. I mean, seriously, look at the state of both of you. I've laid logs with more quality mass.'

Even terror wasn't going to make either back down, King

John could see. Voluntarily, at least. Bravado could only disguise cowardice, it could not overrule it, so he gave them the out they craved and yet for which they could never bring themselves to ask.

'Or,' King John said in a careful, pointed tone, 'perhaps you'd like to reconsider making peace, after all?'

FORTY-FOUR

After helping Forrester take Manny north the previous night, Victor took the train back into London. Which was comfortable enough, if dirty. The pattern of the seat coverings and carpet could no longer hide the accumulated grime of thousands, maybe tens of thousands, of passengers over many years of service. A certain acceptance of mess was necessary to a man of Victor's profession, he had learned, and his nun-enshrined philosophy of cleanliness had been one of the many early barriers to success he'd had to overcome. Despite the tolerance he had built up over the years to the inevitable mess of blood and viscera, he couldn't quite bring himself to rest the back of his skull against the headrest with its dark, oily stain.

The train stopped several times en route, giving Victor the opportunity to disembark and re-enter into a different carriage whenever he felt the need. He continued his countersurveillance once the train had reached its destination, circling the concourse of the expansive station, letting the crowd guide him. Overhead, pigeons cooed and flapped their wings, perched with impossible grace, despite the mine-field of thin spikes arranged to deter them or impale them, Victor was not sure which.

The crowd was a water-and-oil mix of commuters arriving into London and those heading elsewhere. It was a chaotic, unpredictable flow of movement divided between those who knew exactly where they were going and those staring up at electronic information boards or straining to see their plat-form number, exit or the person they were meeting. Half of the crowd would have collided with the other half had that proportion not been well practised in the fine art of avoiding those not looking where they were going.

Such a crowd, he thought, was a living organism made up of numerous cells working in harmony until one mutated. All it took was one person to disrupt the harmony, to destroy the unspoken synchronicity. In this case, a young man skirted around one flank instead of filing in behind the swell, attempting to cut in at the barriers and bypass the wait, hoping to be let in by someone too polite or too conflict-averse to stop him. Another, older man was in no such mood.

It began with insults, but Victor saw their body language, both in a rush and carrying the stress of that urgency now untapped by the other person's own. Blows would be exchanged before it was over and yet neither understood the inevitable path they were walking. Victor did, and so left the crowd before it happened and all eyes turned that way.

Outside the station, the clouds parted enough for a swathe of morning sunlight to reach the city streets, casting long shadows and glittering on wet paving. Somewhere overhead and hidden by the canopy of tall buildings, a helicopter hovered, the mechanical roar of its rotor blades as loud down here as the passing traffic. Could be a police vehicle or the personal transportation of a tycoon who refused to be burdened by traffic lights and speed limits.

After performing countersurveillance on foot, Victor headed to a multistorey parking garage near Waterloo Station. The traffic, noisy enough at the best of times, was now deafening with angry horns and insults exchanged through hastily buzzed down windows that formed an orchestra of tempers, a teenager on an e-scooter the impromptu conductor.

No one who drove in London climbed out of their car in a better mood than when they had first sat behind the wheel.

Victor watched various vehicles and people enter the garage and leave it too. He saw couples and families, young and old. He was looking for a person on their own, someone leaving the garage in a hurry or distracted manner.

Stealing cars was something Victor did so often it was perhaps the single crime of which he was most guilty. He could jimmy doors open and hot-wire starter motors with the best of them, but the best way to break into a car was not to break into it at all.

He had no desire to take a vulnerable person's lifeline, so he took the time to ignore an elderly man and then an infirm woman using a crutch. He dismissed a young man walking so fast he was almost breaking into a jog, because the man wore no jacket and jeans that looked so tight to Victor's eye that he feared for the man's future fertility.

In Victor's experience patience was always rewarded, and now was no different. When a man of about forty left the garage, Victor followed. The man had brown hair swept back, shiny with product, straight until it curled at the nape of his neck. His sideburns were greying, as was a goatee beard. He wore a nice suit beneath a long brown overcoat. A phone in one hand captured his entire focus to the extent he would have bumped into several pedestrians had they not moved out of his way.

The man walked at a relaxed pace so it was simple enough for Victor to overtake him and then make a sudden stop a few moments later.

Using the sound of the man's footsteps as a guide, Victor turned at exactly the right moment for them to collide face to face.

'Forgive me,' Victor was quick to say.

The man jolted in surprise, snapping out of his phone's hypnosis, and snarled, 'Watch where you're going, idiot.'

Victor stepped to one side and the man continued on his way, muttering insults, utterly unaware that practised fingers had slipped into the pockets of his overcoat. The man held his phone in his right hand and led with his left foot, so the odds were he would slip his keys into his right pocket.

Not the overcoat, however. Victor found only gum and lip balm.

He had taken the gum anyway as recompense for the man's poor manners.

Victor could wait for another mark, of course, but the man's muttered insults had veered into some especially ugly words.

'Excuse me,' Victor said as he caught up to the man, placing his right palm on the man's right shoulder so he turned around that way in response, the open overcoat swaying open further as he did, letting Victor's left hand reach into the right pocket of the suit trousers while the man's focus was firmly on the second intrusion.

'For God's sake,' the man hissed. 'What now?'

Victor's jaw tightened at the blasphemy. 'I forgot to say, have a lovely day.'

A heavy sigh in response. 'Drop dead, dickhead.'

'It's really not that easy.'

A moment of frowning confusion before he gave up and walked away.

Victor slipped the man's set of keys into his own pocket and examined the other item. He had never been a fan of gold even before he had realised it drew too much attention, and yet he appreciated the timelessness of the metal. Its appeal had outlasted its necessity.

For practicality, Victor had taken the man's car keys.

For the blasphemy and crude language, Victor had taken the man's watch too.

He donated the latter to the first homeless person he came across, then thumbed the key fob inside the multistorey garage until he had identified the man's car.

Heading out of the city, he called Zakharova from a fresh burner phone.

'I've put Forrester to work looking into the other investors,' he told her. 'And now I'm on my way to the Nightingale mixer. What have you found out?'

'They've been around for almost ten years and Maxim was a patron for almost the entire time. As far as I can see they're exactly as they appear.'

'Then they're hiding it well.'

'Hiding what?'

'Maxim was no humanitarian,' Victor told her. 'And no hypocrite either. They're dirty, of that I have no doubt. If he was due to attend their mixer then he had an angle.'

'What kind of angle are we talking about?'

'That's what I'm going to find out,' he answered. 'Because if Maxim had one so do they.'

FORTY-FIVE

The stately home hosting the Nightingale Foundation's function was a fifty-minute drive west of London into the heart of Buckinghamshire. Surrounded by fields and woodland, the entrance to the estate was flanked by towering oak trees centuries old. Black wrought-iron bars formed the gate itself, which was remotely operated. Two cameras looked down from both the left and right stone gateposts. A third camera looked out from the intercom panel to send a clear and unobstructed view of any visitor's face to the round-the-clock security personnel.

Victor did not have to press a button to announce his arrival.

As soon as he buzzed down the door window, a woman's voice projected through the intercom said, 'Name, please?'

'I'm here on behalf of Maxim Borisyuk.'

'Mister Borisyuk provided no indication he would not be attending himself.'

'That's because he's dead.'

A pause, then, 'Please, wait.'

He did, imagining the woman monitoring the gate was now phoning or radioing someone higher up the chain. Which meant this was a singular incident. Not surprising there would be no protocol already in place to handle such a thing.

After fifty or so seconds, the gate buzzed open.

The voice on the other end of the intercom was silent as Victor drove through onto the estate.

The driveway was a mile in length and formed an almost straight line to the house, smooth tarmac giving way to a circle of gravel with a fountain at its centre. A deer park surrounded the house and grounds, which featured a maze of yew trees. Poseidon himself was at the centre of the water feature as if emerging from cresting waves and flanked by dolphins. The fountain overlooked an expanse of lawn as large as a football pitch. The grass was a bright, even green despite the season. The huge windows of an orangery reflected the clouds and dazzled with the morning sunshine in intermittent bursts when those clouds parted.

A rogues' gallery of luxurious cars was parked outside the house itself. Mostly Bentleys, Rolls-Royces and Range Rovers in muted colours, intermixed with a few over-bright supercars that must have struggled with the long, gravel drive. Which suggested the drivers had not been here before today. Victor parked alongside a lemon-yellow Lamborghini.

Upon stepping into the entrance hall, a large man greeted him.

He was maybe sixty. Grey and white hair, thin and cut short. Tanned skin, beaten and weathered, covered a wide Neanderthal-like skull. A sharp, black suit jacket struggled to contain the torso within. Huge, gnarled hands that looked like they could wrestle sabre-toother tigers gestured to a stainless-steel bowl nearby.

'If you would like to place your phone inside, please.'

The polite tone was in stark contrast to his caveman appearance.

'I have no phone.'

'Very good,' the polite Neanderthal said, taking a step back.

His reaction showed nothing. Perhaps he was especially good at hiding his thoughts or Victor wasn't the first person without a phone. He could not imagine those others were professionals like him who preferred to avoid carrying a tracking device on their person. More likely any such invitees had been here before and knew that no phones were allowed inside.

He was armed, Victor saw. The black suit jacket that struggled to contain the man's chest and shoulders flared out a little at the narrow waist. On the right hip, however, it flared a little bit more. Victor pictured a small handgun holstered at the belt.

Taking a second step back, the polite Neanderthal gestured to another man, who proceeded to use a metal-detecting wand to check Victor, sweeping it up and down the length of his person, and from side to side, keeping the device about ten centimetres away at all times. It was a discreet, sleek wand that made a series of noises as it passed over his belt buckle, the metal-rimmed lace holes of his shoes, his watch and the non-prescription glasses tucked into the breast pocket of his suit jacket. Given the polite Neanderthal had requested his phone, Victor took it that this scan was to locate listening and recording devices more than weapons.

Whatever this was, privacy was as much of a priority as security.

Further into the entrance hallway, several displays showed the logo for The Nightingale Foundation without providing any information as to what the foundation was or did. Images of smiling people from the developing world appeared on a long banner with the words *Global initiatives for the betterment of all.*

The function was spread across several resplendent reception rooms, each lavish in decoration and ornaments and themed by a specific colour: the drawing room was gold, the library red, the music room violet. With no prior understanding of the occasion, Victor took a slow circle through the interconnecting rooms and hallways, overhearing small talk about stocks, golf, the weather and politics. No one seemed to be discussing the reason why they were here. The only surreptitious conversation, of which he read the lips of the participants huddled in a corner, regarded mistresses.

Waiters with stiff backs rotated around the rooms, carrying silver trays upon which rested sparkling crystal flutes bubbling with champagne mixed with orange juice. There seemed to be as many staff as guests. Every hallway had at least one stationary woman or man in a smart black suit, black shirt and maroon tie. Trays of drinks and canapés were circling every room, carried by waiting staff in black uniforms with white half-aprons. They spoke only if spoken to as they passed by, making themselves and their offerings obvious for any guest who wanted another glass or something to nibble, without interrupting conversations or intruding unnecessarily.

The canapés looked delicious and the reactions from the guests told Victor they were as good as they appeared. Almost no chance of knowing when or what he might reach for, but almost no chance was not the same thing as no chance.

A cellist played Beethoven with such effortlessness Victor found himself watching her longer than could ever be prudent. He remembered a music teacher helping him improve his skills as a pianist but only to a point. Regardless of his dexterity, of his understanding of the instrument, of his endless hours of practice, she told him he would never master the piano. He didn't appreciate her reasoning at the time and yet watching the cellist play with a passion he could never recreate himself, he understood at last.

She was lost in the music, swaying from side to side as she pushed and pulled the bow, not only playing but feeling. She was part of the melody.

For the few minutes he ignored protocol to watch the musician play, her eyes were closed. They had been closed before he had stood to watch. No doubt they would be closed long after he turned away.

He had not played the piano since that last lesson.

It's the only thing I've ever been good at, he once told someone in regard to something other than music. He should have listened to himself. He should never have pretended there could be anything else for him when he had devoted his existence to the singular mastery of an entirely different skill set.

'A big house like this needs a big man to fill it,' he heard someone comment in a superior, derisory tone. 'Otherwise, you might as well be playing dress up.'

Victor exchanged pleasantries with a few guests, who he soon learned were donors to the organisation or sat on the board of directors.

To blend in, Victor gestured to a nearby waiter ferrying a tray of drinks. He had a young, clean-shaven face. An elastic tie held back his long hair in a ponytail, pulling the hair tight to his scalp before it flared out at the base of his neck.

As he took a flute, the waiter said, 'Is there anything else I can help you with today?'

Victor raised the glass as if to sip, but the rim never touched his lips, 'Such as?'

'You seem a little lost.'

'It's my first time here.'

'I know.' The waiter nodded a little. 'If you would like any assistance, I'd be delighted to help.'

'Thank you.'

The waiter with the ponytail continued on his way around the room.

'They can smell it,' a guest said as he approached.

He wore an undyed linen shirt beneath a thin blazer, which was open. That fact, combined with the slight sheen of perspiration on his face, told Victor the man had an over-active thyroid or his testosterone-to-oestrogen ratio was out of balance. In the cool air of the house, he was too warm. His body would acclimatise eventually, but that process was slower than usual. It meant the man slipped way down as a physical threat. If it came to it, the man would tire fast as the exertion elevated his body temperature outside of a tolerable range. He would be doubled over and gasping for air long before Victor broke a sweat.

'Excuse me?'

'Money,' the man answered. 'To those who do not have it, we stink.' He wrinkled his nose and gestured with a hand as if wafting closer imaginary incense. 'They can smell it on us a mile away. Like sharks, they are. Our money is blood in the water to them.'

He leaned closer, in a conspiratorial manner. 'If you ever want to know if someone has money, arrange to meet them somewhere, see who arrives first ... You see where I'm going? Well, put it like this: when you're rich, people wait for you, not the other way around.'

'I shall bear that in mind,' Victor said without sincerity.

'Until next time.' The man gripped his shirt between finger and thumb and made a fanning motion. 'I need some air.'

Above a fireplace large enough to sleep within, a massive painting hung in a gold-painted frame. The scene depicted a shooting party with breached double-barrelled shotguns hung over their forearms. From a thicket, a hound emerged with a grouse in its jaws.

As Victor looked upon it, a voice said, 'Four men with guns to kill one bird and they think this feat impressive enough to display for all to witness? They advertise their inadequacy.'

'Yet they believe themselves triumphant,' Victor replied, rotating his head to look at the woman approaching. 'If you are able to quantify your achievements with whatever merit you choose then there can be no inadequacy, only glory.'

'In one's own perception.'

She had an oval face and a pronounced widow's peak, further enhanced by hair brushed back and held tight to her scalp by a clasp at the back of her head. Her hair was a dark brown but hints of copper and blonde where it shone in the sunlight from the window.

'Surely that is the only perception that truly matters.'

'I'd give you that one,' she said after a moment's thought. 'Except you're missing the obvious.'

'Which is?'

'If one's perception was the only perception that truly mattered,' she answered with a growing smile, 'then there is surely no need for such a public display.'

Looking up at the massive painting, he answered, 'I concede the point.'

The woman chuckled and offered her hand, 'I'm Shivika Chandi.'

FORTY-SIX

In its previous life, the Fool's Arms had been the Woodsman's Arms for almost a century. That name had not sat right with King John, who was a London boy born and bred. He had never much liked the countryside if he ever ventured outside of the M25. All those pasty yokels peering at him with suspicion from underneath their flat caps like they believed a little melanin meant an entirely different species. And woods were too old and too creepy by default. So, when he had taken over the pub, the original name had to get on its bike. First, he had called the pub the King's Arms as a fitting representation of his rising station, to proudly announce his royal rule. He had been young then, of course. He had needed to flex, as the kids today would call it if he told them the story.

That sign had hung for the several years it had taken him to understand how to be king. That the crown he wore sat there still because of the respect he had earned through old-fashioned elbow grease, not because he pointed to it with one of his massive, fat fingers.

Though many criminals still paid him homage, which he valued far more than the taxes they paid him, he no longer had the clout to stop them dealing drugs or mugging tourists. Not without pulling irons. Not without fighting pointless wars. They fought enough of those between themselves. King John spent too much of his time comforting wailing mothers without adding to their heartache himself.

There was a certain illogicality to the fact that today's gangs had replaced yesterday's gangsters.

Once Terrance had seen Rollup and Fred Head out of the Fool's Arms – only after King John had made them tidy up the function room – he returned to find King John straightening up one of the black and white photographs on the wall. A few more contemporary faces were sprinkled here and there among the other famous people from yesteryear, though they were hard to find unless you knew where to look. Such newcomers had needed to be squeezed in where they would fit, with smaller photographs and in faraway positions. The walls of the function room had been filled at least two decades ago, so now any new candidates had to be exceptional to warrant a place. Not only because it meant taking the spot of someone who had already earned their reverence but also because it meant tracking down the stepladder.

'Your visitor will be down in a jiffy,' Terrance announced. 'He's just finishing a phone call.'

King John nodded. 'Did you give those two idiots back their tools?'

Terrance said, 'Nah. Told them if the peace lasted they could have them back then and only then.'

'That's very wise of you, big fella. You're cleverer than you look.'

'Cheers, boss man. I appreciate that.'

Terrance seemed pensive and King John knew him well enough to ask why.

'What's on your mind?'

'How come I've never met your mate Lenny the Sieve?' Terrance asked with a pout so prominent he looked more tantrum toddler than terrifying titan. 'I thought you'd introduced me to all the old crew still alive.'

'You're feeling left out, ain't ya? I guess you're more sensitive than you look.'

Terrance shrugged his massive shoulders and nodded, a little embarrassed.

'Do you know why I haven't introduced you to him before now? Because you might say he was a useful, yet entirely ethereal tool created solely in the pursuit of diplomacy.'

Terrance was bemused.

King John tutted, then gave him a solid backhand to the chest. 'There is no Lenny the Sieve. I made him up, you absolute sausage.'

He would have spent longer taking the piss out of the younger man had it not been for door of the function room opening.

Once, only King John's own men had been allowed into the court itself as they took a well-deserved breather from a hard day's work on their liege's behalf, telling tall tales as they smoked and drank, or sometimes figuring out the details of their next big deal or heist. King John missed those days, when there was more gold on display down here than in a jeweller's window, when there was never any drama no matter how much booze was sunk because no one wanted to ruin their Savile Row suit.

Only gentlemen had been welcomed here. His men had never robbed from anyone who would miss it nor cracked the skulls of anyone who didn't deserve it.

'Not like today,' King John muttered under his breath as the visitor entered the function room, thinking about Rollup and Fred Head, but mostly about the new arrival.

He approached his guest as Terrance took up his post by the door.

'It's been a long time, Andrei,' he told the Russian. 'I'm taking it this is not a social call.'

'Even when we were more sociable men, were these visits ever so?'

'I'd like to think they were.'

'Then I'll keep this brief,' Linnekin said. 'I have a problem that I cannot solve myself and I cannot give to anyone in the Brotherhood.'

King John knew what kind of a problem Linnekin meant. 'Why me?'

'Because you owned this city once.'

'Before your lot took over.'

'We were always in charge, John. You were merely keeping the throne warm. Fortunately for both of us, however, most of the street thieves and hustlers still answer to you.'

'And yet here you are asking for a favour.'

'I'm not asking. You will do this for me and in return it is you who will have the favour of the Brotherhood, and when it is established, the friendship of its new leadership. Gifts befitting your station. That's why I'm here. Because you've been here the longest. You know this city inside out. The people, the streets ... No one is better connected, no one commands more respect. Those who work the underbelly of this town may fear the Brotherhood, but they love you. They do not call you "king" for no reason.'

'You don't call me king.'

'Emperors name no one "sire".'

King John took that on the chin. You had to when it came to the Russian mob. He used to joke with his crew that when the Bratva said jump you didn't say how high, you said sorry for not having jumped already. If the likes of Rollup and Fred Head were so full of unreasonable hatred for each other that King John doubted their humanity, then the Bratva heavies of Linnekin's ilk were capable of so much cruelty that they seemed like they were from another planet.

Still, taking it on the chin did not mean rolling over and showing his belly.

'I was assuming this wouldn't be a friendly chat about old times. But what I wasn't counting on was outright dis-respect in my own place of business. That doesn't give me that nice warm feeling inside me I like to have when a talk is productive. Instead, I've got this acidic tightness, this rising bile sensation that bubbles up when someone takes the piss. Don't really happen very often, so when it does it takes me by surprise, which only makes it worse.'

Terrance, quiet goliath by the door, took a few heavy steps closer.

Linnekin, alone and flanked by two men who might as well have been four given the size difference, showed no signs of distress.

He did, however, nod. 'Forgive my manners. Tempers are thin after Borisyuk's murder.'

'I understand,' King John replied. 'Water under the bridge.'

Terrance looked a little disappointed and King John felt bad for denying the big lad the one thing he was put on Earth do to: beating seven shades of shite out of anything with a pulse.

'I was sad to hear what happened to Maxim,' King John said. 'Even if we never saw eye to eye when it came to how to conduct business, I always liked the fella. Maybe that's a generational thing. Sod's law I was supposed to have lunch with him the day he died, but I had to cancel last minute because two numpties were threatening to go to war.'

'No one can know this comes from me,' the Russian said. 'Tell your people whatever it takes, but my name is never mentioned. The Brotherhood is never mentioned. If I find out someone knows I'm involved then I know it could only have come from you. Is that absolutely clear?'

'Sure thing,' King John assured. 'Going back to your problem, I don't want to ruffle anyone's feathers. I turn your problem into brown bread I don't want a load of Bratva psychopaths kicking down my door in retaliation.'

'That will not be a problem. This man doesn't answer to anyone any more. He's not one of us so he has no friends here or back in Russia. He worked exclusively for Maxim Borisyuk. With his passing, this man, who we know only as Vasili, should be considered someone disassociated from the Brotherhood.'

'Are you going to tell me why?'

'Why I want him dead and why you will kill him for me share the same reason,' Linnekin explained. 'Vasili is the one who murdered Maxim.'

Eyes narrowing, King John said, 'In which case it will be my pleasure.'

'Good,' Linnekin said. 'I'm glad to find you are agreeable, although it is my duty to warn you about Vasili.'

271

'I know you said he's dangerous but that's okay. I can round up some dialled-up-to-eleven bruisers to do a real job on him. Tell us where he is and we can be there within a couple of hours.'

'They're with you now?'

'Don't be soft. I'll drive around and pick them up.'

'One car's worth of men is nowhere near enough.'

'I told you, these are proper showmen I'm talking about. Two in front, two in the back is more than enough. And when I say two in the back I'm doing so because it would be physically impossible to fit another soul between them.'

'Forget it,' Linnekin said again. 'You do nothing until you have enough men to fill three cars. With weapons.'

King John was shaking his head before Linnekin had finished speaking. 'This lad is a proper character is what I'm hearing. He's some Spetsnaz SAS cyborg super soldier, yeah? I got it, loud and clear. That's okay. Terrance was in the military and I've hired former special forces myself, as have my competition. And I bet they're brilliant in a warzone, on an actual battlefield behind-enemy-lines search-and-destroy top-secret mission. Of that I have no doubts. But very little of that counts for a fat lot in this business. He gets cornered by half a dozen showmen with the combined weight of an Indian elephant and he's a mess on the pavement. That's just how these things work. It's basic science.'

'Not him.'

'You're bigging this boy up a lot. He's not a ghost, is he?'

'To you, he might as well be. Do you think Maxim Borisyuk kept him around without good reason? Borisyuk had an army of men who would have laid down their lives for him without hesitation and yet he still had Vasili do his murdering for him. He has eyes in the back of his head, so you need to understand that the moment you see him he's already seen you. Before you're out of the car he will be ready for you, so you will have to be fast. Ready to go the second you have him in your sights because he wIll vanish the very next second. If you want the favour and the friendship of the Brotherhood you put together the cars, you fill them with your people, and every single one of them has the tools for the job. Only then, at that point, when I know you are serious, will I tell you where you can find Vasili. You treat him like he's a bear. If you don't, he'll rip you all to tiny pieces.'

King John, who had never backed down from anyone, who had not so much as had a nightmare in decades, felt a little twist of unease in the pit of his something. Like the acidic bile of disrespect, he did not like this feeling one bit.

'Fine,' he said. 'We do it your way. We hunt a bear.'

FORTY-SEVEN

Chandi wore all black. Boots, jeans, turtleneck sweater and leather jacket. All different textures, some matt and others satin that focused the light into pools of white on the most prominent edges and ridges. A silver chain, almost lost in the folds of the turtleneck collar, glinted as she moved.

Victor gave a fake name and said, 'Pleasure to meet you.'

The music stopped as the cellist came to the end of her set.

The few polite claps went unheard beneath the enthusiastic applause Victor gave. For a few seconds he was content to trade his anonymity in this setting to show the cellist the appreciation she deserved.

'Do you know her?' Chandi asked.

'No,' he answered. 'But I admire her abilities.'

'Ten thousand hours and all that.'

'To master the skill,' he agreed. 'Which I imagine is probably only ninety per cent of it.'

'The other ten?'

'Will.'

'Explain, if you would be so kind.'

'Skill is mechanical. It's fatty acids insulating neural pathways to deliver faster signals. You do something often enough and you'll get better and better at it. Eventually, after ten thousand hours or so, you have mastered the task. The rest is will. Do you want it enough? Are you willing to dedicate your life to that skill?'

'It sounds like you're talking about passion, about love.'

He didn't tell what the music teacher had told him and said, 'Perhaps.'

'What are you passionate about?' she asked him. 'Besides music, I mean.'

'Small talk.'

'Excuse me?'

He said nothing.

'Oh,' she said, understanding. 'Point taken.'

He noted the subtle change in body language revealing her discomfort. She didn't take a step back or fold her arms in an effort to create distance or defend herself. She did, however, turn so she was no longer standing square to him. A defensive position moving her vital organs away from potential attacks, yes, but also a fighting stance. She kept him in range. This was someone who did not flee from threats. She stood her ground. Her instincts were to fight back.

She said, 'I accidentally crossed over into frank and personal conversation, didn't I? I promise to renege at once and stick purely to the most diminutive of talk.'

'Never make promises you can't keep.'

'Good advice, I'm sure. But perhaps it's more accurate to say we should not make promises that we ought not keep.'

'Perhaps.'

'What is it that you do for a living?'

'I'm a consultant.'

She smiled, pleased with herself. 'I didn't take you as a philanthropist. Which I mean as a compliment, I assure you.'

'I am assured.'

'I often think that philanthropy is the rich man's Prozac,' she mused, gaze passing over the other guests. 'After a lifetime of lying, cheating, stealing and ruining lives, of amassing obscene levels of wealth while avoiding taxes, the rich man gets to wash away all those sins by giving away wealth to those causes he deems worthy of it. For this, he is lauded, he is clapped by those who pay their taxes, he is honoured by the society he has impoverished. And the best part, he only puts himself forward to receive this adoration once he has bought his yachts, his planes, his mansions, and these excesses have ceased to bring him joy. Only when he has all the money in the world does he realise he never needed it in the first place. Only when he has spent his entire life taking all that he could take does it even occur to him to see how it feels to give a little back.'

'I try not to judge anyone's morality.' He paused. 'Or lack thereof.'

'Is that not a judgement in and of itself?'

'I'm not sure.'

She did not press the point. 'Would you like to know about my own work?'

'Certainly,' Victor said.

'I represent the interests of several different people and organisations in several different countries. My firm, Adeptus Global, acts as the front of house for those who prefer to conduct their business on home soil and yet need more agile assets overseas on whom they can rely upon to speak for them.'

'Including The Nightingale Foundation?'

She bowed her head in a small nod.

'And what does the organisation do? More specifically than global initiatives for the betterment of all, I mean.'

'Well, I did recommend they change the wording of that slogan. Evidently, my advice fell on deaf ears. However ... ' She regarded him with a curiosity that led him understand he had made his first mistake. 'I've never known an invitee to one of these functions do so without first understanding why he is attending.'

'I know why I'm here,' he said.

Her smooth skin creased a little. 'A contradiction if you don't know what this is, surely?'

He nodded. 'I'm present only because the invitee could not attend.'

'That's a highly unusual situation.'

'Not only unusual,' he agreed. 'Unique.'

She waited for elaboration.

'The man invited here is dead so I'm here instead.'

'Oh,' she breathed. 'Now it makes sense. But how very unfortunate. For the deceased, I mean.'

He noted that her posture did not change. She did not revert to standing square on to him. Either she didn't believe him – which he found hard to believe himself – or more likely she believed him while still being cautious of him. She didn't trust him even though he might have convinced her of the reason for his presence.

Which meant her instincts were good.

And given that when faced with a threat, she stood her

ground, Victor considered her someone he needed to behave very carefully around. These facts about her also meant he found himself wanting to be around her.

'Who is the deceased, if you don't mind me asking?'

'There's very little I mind,' Victor admitted, then, 'Maxim Borisyuk.'

'I see,' was her reply. 'Russian property tycoon.'

The way her tone shifted as she spoke those last three words told Victor she knew exactly who Borisyuk had been behind his public image. Which was not exactly a surprise. That it didn't seem to change her ongoing assessment of Victor, however, was something he had not expected.

'Had you been working for him for a long time?'

'Less than a year,' he answered. 'A temporary arrangement, although perhaps it might have continued on a longer basis if not for his passing.'

'How very sad,' she said without recognisable emotion. She raised her glass. 'To Maxim.'

He did the same. After sipping, asking, 'Did you know him personally?'

'Of course. I've chit-chatted with him at these gatherings over a glass or three of fizz many times. Maybe too many times. And, naturally, my firm has also played go-between for some of his companies over the years. A thoroughly pleasant man whom I shall miss enormously.'

Victor said nothing. There were many emotions he could imitate with ease but grief was not one of them. Better to appear cold than to fail at faking warmth.

'Aside from representing him in his absence, how else are ... were you involved with his businesses?'

'He brought me in to unravel the inevitable knots that

form in large operations like his. As an outsider, he felt I was better placed to both identify and solve the kind of problems that those internally might not be able to recognise.'

'Ah,' she said, nodding along. 'You're a troubleshooter.'

'Something like that.'

'Background?'

'Mostly freelance,' he answered.

'You get bored staying in one place for too long?'

'Maybe restless is a better way of saying it. I don't like to stand still.'

'I hear you.'

'And, invariably, if I work for one client for too long then it means both that I'm being underutilised and they're not getting their money's worth.'

'Because you're too efficient shooting all of those troubles.'

'You might say that the problems I solve stay solved.'

She used two fingers to mime a gun. '*Kapow.*'

He raised an eyebrow. 'You have no idea.'

She did the same. 'Maybe I do.'

FORTY-EIGHT

It was the ceilings that the waiter with the ponytail liked the most about these massive old houses. No need was served by light fixtures hanging from joists thirty feet up. It was sheer luxury. In fact, it was such brazen excess even all the money in the world couldn't convince him to live in such a home. He would feel small and insignificant, and worse, desperate to appear worthy of the grandeur. Undeserving of the respect he so obviously craved.

The waiter with the ponytail inhaled from his vaporiser and let out a plume of moisture that tasted of watermelon. A synthetic parody of watermelon, sure, but better than the rank taste of tobacco. Even as a teenager trying desperately to be cool, the waiter had hated smoking real cigarettes. They always made his mouth fill with water and that horrible feeling lingered on his tongue for days afterwards. Still, he had never stopped. The transition to vaping had been easy, although he was pretty sure he vaped twice as much as he ever smoked. He switched to get rid of the taste, not for his health, although that was a nice bonus. Assuming that whole popcorn lung issue was blown out of proportion.

The polite Neanderthal joined him. He still smoked old school out of habit. The waiter hadn't yet been born when the other man had been the same age.

'That went well,' he said as he lit up.

'Always does.'

'What did you make of the guy?'

'The uninvited guest?'

'Who else?'

The waiter shrugged as he exhaled. 'Vanilla. For Bratva, that is.'

The polite Neanderthal responded with a nod, although he did not seem to agree.

'What is it?' the waiter asked him.

Leaving the cigarette between his lips, the polite Neanderthal tapped his right hip.

'So?' the waiter asked.

'The uninvited guest clocked it.'

'You're joking me?'

'Why would I joke?' The polite Neanderthal took the cigarette from his lips. 'He knew I was carrying.'

'Then you screwed up, didn't you?'

'You looking for a slap?' he asked the much smaller man.

'Only if you're asking for a hiding,' the waiter told the much larger man.

Both smiled.

'Seriously, though,' the waiter said. 'Are you sure he saw the gun?'

'He could not have seen it, but I saw his eyes. He glanced down when he thought I wasn't looking. But I see everything, don't I? I've done this gig more times than you and him combined have had hot dinners. There's nothing interesting to see about my waistline beyond the fact I'm pushing single-digit body fat at sixty-one years of age. Except, if you know what you're looking for, my jacket hangs differently on this side.' He tapped again for emphasis. 'The uninvited guest noticed that.'

'Maybe you're reading too much into it.'

'I saw what I saw.'

'Fine, he's not as vanilla as I first thought. But why?'

'That's what we need to find out,' the older man said as he looked out over the Buckinghamshire countryside. 'Let Hawk know we may have a complication.'

FORTY-NINE

'I don't know when the golf course became the new conference room,' Lambert said as he lined up his putt. 'Because no one ever asked me if I wanted to play a sport at the same time I made deals.'

On a chilly January afternoon, there was only a scattering of golfers taking on the par 71 course. The green was damp beneath Victor's shoes. Blades of grass stuck to their soles. A little sun slipped through the clouds. Not enough to provide any discernible feeling of warmth on his face, however.

Victor watched without interest. 'An activity can only be a sport if performing it causes you to sweat. Otherwise, you might as well be playing tiddlywinks.'

Lambert chuckled as he made a gentle swing of his putter and the ball rolled less than two metres only to stop on the very brink of the hole. He groaned, took a few steps closer and toed the ball into the hole.

'Only suckers play by the rules,' he said, then winked. 'Even when it's only tiddlywinks.'

He scooped the ball out of the hole and placed the flag back inside.

The golf club was located in a leafy suburb of south-east London and had been in use for hundreds of years, dating back to 1608.

'Probably the first ever club of its kind,' Lambert explained. 'We can thank James IV of Scotland for gifting us the sport. Kind of funny that the upper crust of England are so partial to it when back then they wouldn't have been caught dead partaking in anything so Scottish.'

The club had a strict dress code and so Lambert had stressed that Victor should come dressed in recognised golfing clothes and shoes. No jeans, no tracksuit, no cap on backwards. Lambert wore tan slacks and a baggy polo shirt that was one of the few types of shirt allowed to be worn untucked. A down-filled body warmer covered most of it given the winter weather. Leather golfing gloves creaked when he rubbed his hands together to generate a little extra heat. They had a strange protrusion on the back of the hand that Victor eventually worked out was a magnetic ball marker.

Victor didn't think any of the other golfers were watchers, for any of Lambert's contractors, but the course was large enough, with plenty of natural parkland around it, that it would be simple enough for them to hide out of sight and use binoculars and parabolic microphones, or for Lambert to wear a wire. A marksman fifty metres away wouldn't need a ghillie suit to be invisible to Victor's gaze, although he did not imagine Lambert had gone to such lengths.

And if there were any such watchers behind binoculars he was sure these would not include the young couple from the champagne bar. He wondered if they were still in Lambert's employ at all.

'If you didn't go to the right school and you haven't got a family crest dating back a few centuries,' Lambert explained, setting back his hips to drive, 'you better know how to play golf. Because if you weren't born one of the elite then you need to learn how to play their games.' He pointed to Victor. 'And you know what's even more important than knowing how to play?'

'I'm glad to have absolutely no idea.'

'Knowing how to lose,' he said with a nod of pride and turned the pointing finger into a pinching gesture with a tiny gap of air between that finger and thumb. 'Knowing how to lose by this much. It's all about maintaining the status quo, about reassuring them that they are indeed better than the likes of you and me. That's why I'm here even when there are no deals to make, even though walking around a lawn in these ridiculous clothes ezes my bis- cuits off when I could still be bed. So when the time comes and I'm playing with some pasty, highborn, inbred baronet Sir Silverspoon OBE IV, I can lose by the teeny, tiniest margin and make him feel as though he still rightfully rules the world.'

'Fascinating.'

There was just enough sarcasm for Lambert to smile in response. 'And given you're not one of the aforementioned inbreds I guess there's no need to further dance around the issue. So, you're coming to work for me?'

'I'm curious why you want to hire me at all. You think I'm talented, and whilst my ego doesn't need the validation, I appreciate the compliment. I'm not delusional enough to think I'm the only talented professional out there. I've crossed paths with enough of them to know I'm not unique.'

'Things go wrong in this business. A lot of the time, in fact. You know it and I know it. When it's inevitable, I prefer as little mess left behind as possible. Not every cause of such mess is kind enough to let us know about it before everyone else does. In today's world it gets harder and harder to clean it up without leaving a trail of dirty footprints back to the firm's front door.'

'Now I understand,' Victor said. 'If I'm the mess that's left behind then given my rare anonymity, as you put it, I'm easier to clean up.'

Lambert turned down the corners of his mouth while he shrugged with his hands. 'There's work that is just too delicate to entrust to someone with a family, with a birth certificate. I knew you would understand it's nothing personal.'

'I have thick skin,' Victor said.

'These clubs cost more than my first car,' he told Victor. 'And that's accounting for inflation. Which is not a boast,' Lambert was quick to add. 'I'm just highlighting how ridiculously expensive this sport is to play.'

'Game,' Victor said.

Lambert tipped the visor of his cap in acknowledgement. Without his suit to slim him down, Lambert looked bulkier. Both strong and carrying too much weight. The polo shirt sleeves were tight around his arms and shoulders. The body warmer swelled out around his waist. When he looked down to take his shot, his neck bulged into a double chin.

'That's about as much as I can stomach for one morning,' Lambert said, wiping clean and drying the golf ball before putting it away in a pocket of his stand bag.

He retracted the bag's legs and made sure everything was secure and in place before heaving it up over his shoulder.

He said, 'Let's finish this conversation in the clubhouse at the bar.' He showed a wry smile. 'Which is always my favourite part of the game.' As they walked towards the grand building in the distance, he said, 'They also happen to have a golf museum. The curator will be delighted to point out everything you don't know about handicaps and fairways. I can introduce you if you like.'

'I would not like.'

Lambert chuckled. Then, as they walked, his demeanour shifted. 'I heard a rumour.'

'Do tell.'

'A certain Russian mafia boss was killed a couple of nights ago. Here. In London. Word on the street is there's a hitter out there that's been giving a lot of people a case of the willies.'

Victor raised an eyebrow.

'Yeah, I agree it's a silly expression, but this hitter is making some scary people scared.'

'They call him the Boatman,' Victor said. 'Pray you never have the pleasure.'

'You know,' Lambert began. 'If you've found yourself in a spot of bother with the Russians then I can help out, especially if that's what's preventing you from joining my firm. Can get you out of the country on a Lear from a private airfield where they don't ask questions. No one has to know. Certainly not anyone connected to the Bratva.'

'Even if we say you're right, I've only just paid off one debt. I'm not keen to take on another in the immediate aftermath.'

'Where's the debt? I'm talking about a favour.'

'Since when was a favour ever truly freely given?'

'Who said anything about free? I'm saying if you need a favour, I'm here. And some day when I need a favour, you'll be there. It's the way the world has always worked and there's absolutely nothing wrong with it.'

'I appreciate the offer,' Victor said. 'But you shouldn't believe everything you hear.'

'Then why are you still in town at all? We could have met on the Rock or anywhere else. If your previous boss is deceased, what's keeping you here?'

'Because you're right: someone killed him. The Brotherhood think that someone is me. At least, they will if I don't find out who did, and soon.'

'Risky strategy,' Lambert mused. 'Relying on the patience of the Russian mafia, I mean.'

'Riskier to leave.'

The other man nodded. 'You run, you look guilty. You stay, they might not like what you find. Which is quite the pickle you've got yourself into. Anything I can do to assist?'

'I have two questions that would be helpful of you to answer.'

'Hit me.'

'Do you know anything about something called The Nightingale Foundation? They're a charity, although I'm not quite sure what they do beyond grand slogans. Borisyuk was a patron of theirs almost from the start.'

'Can't say I do,' Lambert answered. 'You're thinking it's a front for . . . ?'

'Something's off about the organisation. I just don't know what yet.'

'I'll ask around, see what I can find. And the second question?'

'You can tell me if your firm was behind his murder,' Victor said, blunt and direct. 'The assassin was a professional, and given your history of working with different factions of the Bratva, it would make sense if he was one of yours.'

Lambert's head rotated from left to right as if realising for the first time they were now the only two people within sight.

He said, 'I have—'

'I know,' Victor interrupted. 'You have contractors observing us from the undergrowth like you had that young couple at the nearby table in the champagne bar. Had I decided to kill you midway through your oysters they wouldn't have been able to stop me starting from three metres away.' He paused. 'So, tell me how useful those contractors behind binoculars are to you now from fifty?'

Swallowing, Lambert said, 'Is that why we're here now, so you can put a bullet in my head instead of a ball in a hole?'

'I note you're not protesting your innocence.'

'I had nothing to do with it,' he said. 'But I think you know that already otherwise this conversation would have taken a very different path.'

'I never said you did. I asked about your firm, your contractors.'

'First thing I did when I heard Borisyuk was murdered was check our fingerprints were clear of it. Had one of my guys been hired as the triggerman I would have been straight on the phone to you to beg for absolution.'

'Okay,' Victor said, and began heading towards the clubhouse. 'That's all I needed to know.'

After a moment, Lambert caught him up.

'I'm glad you waited until I was done before dropping that on me,' he breathed. 'Otherwise, you'd have really put me off my swing. But now I've managed to soothe your suspicions, I would like to know whether we're celebrating the start of a beautiful friendship or if this is your roundabout way of declining my offer. If it's the latter then you can tell it to me straight. I'm a big lad, there's no need to let me down gently.' He paused, trying and failing to read anything in Victor's expression. 'So,' Lambert began, 'are we taking that Lear or not?'

Victor told him, 'While Borisyuk's murderer is still out there, I'm going nowhere.'

FIFTY

Leaving Lambert, Victor headed to the only place on Borisyuk's itinerary he had not yet visited: the Fool's Arms. The exterior was decorated with potted evergreens on the pavements and many window boxes of bristly shrubs. Beneath its colourful sign, a Victorian-style lantern glowed with a welcoming orange light. Huddled outside, a few people smoked or vaped.

When Zakharova answered, he said, 'Tell me about your lunch the day he died.'

'You want to know what we ate? If Maxim was poisoned in a pub by two bullets that found his heart later that night?'

'Very funny,' he said without inflection. 'Did he converse with anyone besides yourself and his bodyguard? Did anyone pay him more attention than they should have done?'

'No and no. What did you find out at the mixer?'

'That philanthropy is the rich man's Prozac.'

'Excuse me?'

'Did anyone else in the Brotherhood know about the mixer? Could anyone else have been a patron?'

'Again, no and no. At least, as far as I'm aware.'

'Does the name Shivika Chandi mean anything to you?' There was a pause, so Victor said, 'Yet another "no"?'

'I'm afraid so.'

'You've been a great help,' he told her, then hung up.

Inside, the pub had a real fire burning away, surrounded by the bare bricks of the chimney. A man wearing cargo shorts, despite the season, warmed himself before it while his Labrador did its best to ignite its upturned belly. With a quick glance, Victor counted nine people – six men, three women – excluding the female bartender. She wore a colourful headscarf, a gele, that for a second reminded him of operations in Nigeria and Sierra Leone back when he had worn a uniform and gone by the name of one of his old crew of street thieves, the only one who had been old enough to sign up. No one could have known in advance he was about to step through the door, so the trio of guys together who looked like they could handle themselves only counted as a threat if he spilled their pints.

The pub was quiet at this hour, after lunch and before the close of the working day. A couple of old guys were nursing dark pints of stout. The group of three who looked like they could handle themselves threw darts against a board on the far wall.

When he asked for a coffee, the lone woman serving behind the bar apologised that she could only give him black. The refrigerator had broken down so there was no milk. Fine by him.

She was tall. In elevated sandals she was as tall as him. In heels, she would be taller.

'Beautiful gele,' he said.

Her smile was even brighter than the scarf. 'From my mother. She doesn't want me to forget where she comes from.'

'Is John here?'

The smile faded a little. 'Who's asking?'

'Ritchie,' Victor answered. 'He doesn't know me.'

'Then I'm sorry to say he won't get to know you today because he's away on business. He'll be back tomorrow if that helps?'

'Then I'll catch him then,' he said. 'I don't suppose you were working here at lunchtime two days ago?'

'Not my shift.' She shook her head. 'How come?'

'Doesn't matter,' he answered, thanked her for the coffee, and went to take a seat.

The wall opposite the bar was lined with wooden booths, each with a low dark-stained table and benches covered by thin cushioning. The walls of the booths doubled as backing to the benches. A stained-glass window looked out from each booth onto the street beyond. The yellow and orange of the stained glass gave the grey street its only colour.

Victor ignored the booths. They offered a considerable degree of privacy but hugely restricted lines of sight. Given the choice, he would rather his enemies see him and he see them than both operate blind.

He unnerved one of the old guys by sitting at the table next to his own. The two tables shared a strip of cushioned seating against the wall to one side of the bar so the old guy gave Victor a confused, scared glance and shuffled away to create more space between them.

He wore a black leather jacket and a flat cap. Lank grey hair extended from beneath the cap down to his shoulders, where the unwashed strands, dense with oil and dirt, coiled motionless.

When he shuffled, he sent a waft of body odour in Victor's direction.

The woman in the gele behind the bar glanced in his direction a few times, which he dismissed as innocent interest or boredom. No way any professional could have known into which establishment he would walk and have time to replace the regular employee. But given King John was a criminal, she could think him to be police. In his suit, he might be mistaken for a detective.

Two of the guys who had been vaping outside came into the pub one after the other, seemingly together until they veered off to separate tables, one to sit by himself with a half-finished pint of lager to watch football highlights playing on a nearby screen, and the second to join the man in cargo shorts by the fire.

Those that were here before him, Victor paid no heed. Those who entered afterwards, he evaluated on the same criteria he used on a daily basis anywhere in the world. No one stood out to him as anything greater than a possible threat, and of those few that did meet his criteria, they did not stay long enough to become actual threats.

Perhaps he was wrong, he thought. Maybe just an error in his threat radar or him picking up the telltale signs of a professional's presence, only a professional with no interest in him.

He asked the old guy, 'Are you here every day?'

Bushy eyebrows pinched together as the old guy's eyes narrowed. 'What's that supposed to mean?'

'No judgement,' Victor said, then: 'I'm wondering if you

saw a group of three people have lunch here a couple of days ago? Two men and a woman. Smartly dressed, but they wouldn't have seemed like typical city types. One of the men was short and old, the other a big guy, much younger.'

'Russians?'

'That's them.'

'What about them?'

'Did they meet anyone else? Did anyone seem to pay them any undue attention?'

'Like you are now?'

Victor nodded. 'Yes, I suppose so.'

'Can't say I noticed. Why?'

'One of them lost a pen. I'm trying to locate it.'

The old guy chuckled. 'Is that the best you can do?'

'Not even close,' Victor answered. 'But I figured you'd see through any lie so I may as well have a little fun with it.'

The old guy shook his head and sipped his pint.

'Was anyone else here at that time who is here now? Stranger or regular.'

'Nope.'

'What about the barmaid?'

'She wasn't here either,' the old guy nearby said. 'And her name is Ify.'

'Good to know.'

'She's single too.'

Victor nodded. 'I'll make a note of that.'

'But if you mess her around you'll have to answer to me.'

Rising from his seat, he said, 'Then consider me appropriately warned.'

Stepping out of the pub, Victor saw that the third man who had been smoking when he had arrived was still there.

He had another cigarette in hand. Three recent stubs lay within close proximity. He glanced Victor's way with an expression of recognition and understanding.

'Stood you up, did she?'

A reasonable question on the surface given Victor had acted as such inside. The smoker could have seen him through a window or when the door opened as people came and went.

'It appears so.'

The smoker shook his head in solidarity. 'How is that still a thing in the era of mobile phones?'

'Maybe she didn't have signal,' he replied, figuring the smoker for thirty-five and a solid ninety kilograms. Right-handed. Stable stance.

'Couldn't have stepped outside or joined the Wi-Fi?'

A cigarette in hand gave a reason for him to be outside. It also made him appear less threatening since that hand appeared occupied. To an amateur, at least.

'She might have run out of battery.'

The smoker shrugged. 'Shame no one takes the time to learn anyone's number any more.'

'But hard to find a payphone these days,' Victor said with genuine lamentation, seeing the man's other hand was red in the chill air despite the availability of pockets.

'I was thinking more that if she knew your number she could have texted from a friend's phone.'

Victor nodded, mentally noting that a civilian in such a situation would indeed turn to a friend or colleague before seeking out a payphone – an assassin's preferred method of telephone communication.

The talkative smoker made sure to turn his head when he

exhaled, to send the smoke away from Victor. The breeze blew a little back nonetheless and he found he had to resist the compulsion to ask for a one and feel a little genuine happiness again.

The smoker wore faded jeans, thick-soled tan safety boots and a dense chequered overshirt that was zipped up to the neck. They were not the kind of clothes Victor would elect to wear while working, which also meant he would never wear such an outfit since what he wore as professional attire was what he also considered tactically shrewd when trying to stay alive. Not all professionals thought like him, however. Many operated in ways he thought of as unforgivable incompetence. Which, of course, he was both grateful for and glad to exploit.

'I take it you're in a similar position,' Victor said.

'Say what?'

Gesturing to the fresh stubs on the ground, Victor said, 'You've been out here a while.'

'Maybe I just like the fresh air.'

The talkative smoker finished with his cigarette and dropped it to the ground where he left it to burn. He didn't tread on it. His hands didn't go into his pockets.

When he neither went into the pub nor went anywhere, Victor said, 'Have a pleasant afternoon,' and walked away himself.

'You too, brother,' the smoker called after a moment.

Victor checked the road for traffic, timing the passing cars so he could cross the road to the other side, wondering if the smoker would follow him. He heard no footsteps over the noise of vehicles and headed to the main intersection less than ten metres away. Victor stopped on the corner and glanced back, expecting the smoker to be inside the pub by now if he was just a civilian curious about him, or walking along the opposite pavement in Victor's blind spot if he was in fact a professional.

Instead, the talkative smoker was still outside the pub, lighting yet another cigarette.

He saw Victor look and raised a hand his way in acknowledgement or farewell.

Victor did not do the same.

FIFTY-ONE

'Shivika Chandi works for a company called Adeptus Global,' Zakharova told him over the phone. 'She's second-generation Indian, family from Mumbai, divorced, two children. Her social media is full of muffins and memes.'

After leaving the Fool's Arms, Victor let the crowds of pedestrians guide him. He liked crowds. Not in the same way he liked trains. There was no fondness for masses of people, only a professional appreciation of the anonymity they provided. He never lowered his guard inside one – vulnerability was directly proportional to perceived safety – and yet he knew whoever was shadowing or converging to murder him had their work cut out.

'And Adeptus Global?'

'Business-to-business middlemen, mostly involved in helping foreign corporations navigate UK legislation,' Zakharova explained. 'She's VP of Euro-Asiatic Development.'

He kept pace with whoever walked in front of him, pausing when they paused, veering off into an adjoining street whenever they did. If they stepped inside a store or crossed the road, he bid them adieu and shadowed the next pedestrian ahead on the pavement. A simple system that ensured his route could not be predicted by anyone observing him.

'She knew Maxim.'

'So did a lot of people. Did you enjoy the food?'

'Excuse me?'

'At the Fool's Arms.'

'I didn't stay that long. King John wasn't there.'

She said, 'And he wasn't there when we had lunch either. What's your point?'

'Keep digging into Chandi.'

Hanging up, he paused near a sculpture rising from the ground on a pedestrianised throughway, letting the consistent movement of the crowds perform his countersurveillance for him. Victor, untouched by the rush, stood out. He had no coffee. He had no guidebook or shopping bag or sandwich. He had no obvious reason to wait by the statue.

A shadow, or shadows, couldn't keep eyes on him for long if they moved to the rhythm of the lunchtime crowd. It would take them away in seconds. They would have to stop too. They would need to single themselves out. Only for a few moments until their professional instincts kicked in and they realised they could tie their shoelaces or stare at a storefront display.

Once, earpieces had been a quick, simple way of identifying potential watchers. No longer. More people had wired or wireless devices than did not. Phones – specifically the lack thereof – had now taken that place. So many people had their heads bowed and their gazes down to their devices that those without marked themselves as noteworthy. And some things never changed. Competent shadows always kept their hands free. They didn't restrict their mobility with shopping bags or backpacks. They didn't wear heels. Bright colours were out. Rising obesity levels in the West helped him out too. As did ageing populations. A modern police force or intelligence agency was not going to fire an employee for being out of shape or over fifty, but they weren't going to put that person on their feet all day either. Private-sector professionals had no rules to follow, no oversight, and yet the trends were the same. As for the Brotherhood, they stood out enough that Victor could pick them out of a crowd without even trying.

Sweeping the crowd, Victor saw no Russian criminals failing to look like they weren't criminals. He saw many pedestrians who were obviously tourists or shoppers or city workers on their lunch hour. Nearby, a toddler, delighted by the simple joy of unassisted steps that did not end with collapse, smiling and laughing as nervous parents flanked her progress, postures stooped, and hands cocked and loaded to shoot into action when balance inevitably became too great a challenge for the little girl. She smiled his way, and though Victor rarely knew genuine mirth enough to smile naturally, it seemed impolite not to do the same in return.

For some reason he couldn't quite understand, he expected to see the talkative smoker in the crowd.

He did not, but in his peripheral vision, Victor saw a different man stop to reach for his phone. It could have rung or vibrated, or he might have remembered he needed to make a certain call that could not wait a second longer. He seemed familiar. Perhaps the average height and common build combined with the uninteresting face made him appear like innumerable other men. Or could Victor have seen him before? Earlier today, whether a few minutes or hours ago, or during one of the preceding days?

The man wore simple, comfortable clothes. Maybe thirty years old. Average height, average weight. The only notable feature was a dark beard.

He saw a woman too who stood out. Unlike the man, who wore casual jeans and hooded sweatshirt, she was dressed in a smart trouser suit beneath a waxed jacket. She seemed the office type, but she was in no lunchtime rush. She dawdled under a shop's awning. Her gaze searched the crowd as though she were waiting for someone. She didn't seem familiar like the man with the phone, although there was something in her body language that felt off to Victor. He sensed too much restrained motion in the way she stood, like she was not so much waiting as expecting to move.

The man brought the phone to his ear to begin a conversation. Victor saw his lips well enough, despite his view being interrupted by the constant flow of people passing between them, to read most of what the man said:

Yeah, it's me ... thanks for calling me back ... I appreciate your time ... No, that's okay ... She's fine. Yeah, much better. Nice of you to ask ...

A plain, innocuous conversation.

Attention back on the woman, Victor saw the reason for the restrained motion in her body language as her face brightened into a huge smile when her lunch date arrived with a bouquet of flowers. A new relationship, Victor reasoned, given her nervous excitement. She rushed to embrace her date and Victor granted them their privacy as they kissed.

A BMW roared by, preceded by a screeching wail and the

pounding bass of what was meant to be music. It rose to a deafening level of decibels as the car neared because if the driver had to suffer through life, then everyone else needed to suffer with him. The noise lingered as the car receded into the distance, the banshee on the stereo refusing to be silenced just as the driver refused to be ignored.

Victor watched the lips of the man on the phone.

I appreciate that, I really do, but you need to understand that's not going to fly ... hold up, no, that's not what I'm saying ...

Still plain. Still innocuous.

Victor could believe that although the man was having a conversation in the midst of a busy crowd of people, neither was he having trouble hearing the caller nor was the caller having trouble hearing him in return. Noise cancelling technology was improving all the time, after all. But there hadn't been so much as a pause while the BMW passed by, let alone acknowledgement of the noise or an apology to the person on the other end of the line.

So, a shadow.

Watching the Fool's Arms or having followed Victor without his knowledge before now. The former was more likely, of course, although Victor was not impossible to shadow. How much the man knew about him and what he was doing was unclear, as was whether the man's orders were limited to purely following him.

Nothing about the man suggested he was Russian. His features were not Slavic. His clothes shared no similarities to the kind of casual wear Bratva heavies favoured. He still might be part of the organisation or affiliated with it. Alternatively, he could be an undercover police or intelligence officer, or a representative of one of the many enemies Victor had made over the years.

Regardless of the man's motives, he was a threat that could not be ignored. And with any threat there were always two ways of handling it.

Fight or flight.

Victor generally preferred the first option.

FIFTY-TWO

King John took his kingship seriously. He had grown fat and lazy on the throne, yes, but he didn't lounge in court while his men set off to battle. Young dealers like Rollup and Fred Head paid their taxes for a reason. King John was a legend. He led from the front. Always had. Especially when an old mate like Maxim had been put in the ground.

Collecting enough shooters for everyone was a challenge, even for a king. Few of even the most dangerous of criminals carried in the UK unless it was absolutely necessary. A lot of the new crowd did and most went to prison long before they ever actually needed to have a shooter.

Given his background in the forces, Terrance did the legwork for the kit, calling in favours, paying over the odds. It was a hassle to get hold of enough firepower but an epic ball-ache to ensure they were clean. No guarantee they weren't going to leave shell casings and bullets all over the place so there could not be a trail leading back to King John's door. Not at this point in his life when he had, despite all odds, never gone down for real time. He considered the year he spent locked up for GBH a minor inconvenience, at most.

As well as the weapons, they needed other equipment if they were going to do this right. King John perused the clothes, the body armour and all the trimmings that completed the look.

'I think this is going to work,' he told Terrance.

'I reckon so.'

'You're a good lad, T,' King John said as he perused the table. 'I don't care what they say.'

Terrance smiled at the pat on the head, then frowned. 'What who says?'

'Everyone.'

King John looked over a few pistols, a couple of shotguns, one of those stubby little shooters that blew their load if you tapped the trigger too hard, and—

'A bloody machine gun.'

'It's a rifle,' Terrance explained.

'Did a time traveller bring it back from the future?'

'German,' Terrance continued. 'G36K with HK33 flash hider.'

'You're just making up words now.'

'It's the business, boss man.'

'And you know how to use it, do you?'

'Course I do. And it pisses over the bloody SA80 they made us use in the Paras.'

Terrance demonstrated, releasing the magazine, inserting it back again, alternating between single shot, burst and automatic, palming the cocking mechanism.

'Stop showing off now.'

He pulled back the bolt to clear the chamber and caught the ejected bullet in his left hand. He gave King John a look of smug satisfaction.

Who said in response, 'I worry about you.'

When the showmen arrived, King John was happy to see familiar faces and happier to see they all still had fingers glittering with gold. You couldn't trust a criminal who didn't have rings on their fingers. If King John didn't see fat sovereign rings glittering then he knew the showman had no credentials. You wore rings so you were always primed for a tussle. Even the most pedantic of the filth had nothing to pinch you with if rings were the extent of your armaments. And though rings were no match for blades or shooters, in a punch-up they turned a super-middle into a heavyweight.

No new faces were allowed on this one. King John only called in showmen with proven track records. Killings were rare these days, so the criminals assembled had been in the game for a combined total of several centuries. Experience was priceless, however. You couldn't trust your life to some baby-faced twenty year old, no matter how much of a hard case he acted. Every line marring the faces of King John's assembled veterans had been etched in with pure steel and will. They wouldn't buckle when things got hairy and they wouldn't flinch when hairy became messy.

'We're going to try and do this carefully,' King John said. 'But we play it by ear. The Russians are saying this character is a proper menace so it's not going to be a case of hanging back and waiting for the best moment. We have to make do with what he gives us because we get one shot at this. If he's in a vehicle then we can try and box him in, one car in front and one behind while the third unloads from alongside if the traffic allows, or if he's on foot then we have more options. We don't want to do this in front of all and sundry so we aim for somewhere quiet. One lad in each car will be connected to a group call with me so if you're in my motor then you do what I say and if you're in one of the others then you follow their lead. They want to question him first, and we've got a nice quiet spot to take him to, but if he doesn't play nice we drop him, okay?'

'Is that it?' one of the showmen sat at a nearby table asked, clocking eyes on Vasili for the first time as he went through printouts of the information the Russians had supplied. 'I thought he was supposed to be massive.'

'This is pathetic,' one of the lads in the back of the function room said, doing the same. 'He looks like a wanker banker. Does he kill people with his calculator?'

'Waste of talent is what this is,' another added.

'You'd rather go after a titan with a Gatling gun?' King John asked, incredulous. 'You get paid the same either way, so what are you moaning about?'

'I'm just saying it as I see it.'

'You know that thing behind your forehead? It's called a brain. It allows you to think about what you say before you say it. And you're also allowed to keep some words in there all for yourself. Clear?'

'No one told me this was supposed to be a wordless gig. If you don't want my opinion why did I get a call in the first place?'

'Stop being so sensitive, you dozy nonce,' King John said. 'Now, just because he's no heavyweight don't mean this is going to be simple. If what the Russians say is accurate, this Vasili has put more bodies in the ground than everyone in this room combined, and then some. We've got the gig because we know these streets better than the Ruskies ever could so if anyone can take him by surprise it's us. I've put the word out to every pimp, dealer, mugger and more so someone is going to get eyes on him sooner or late. Until then, we wait, but you're drinking only pop until this is over. As soon as he's spotted, we roll out, so everyone better be stone cold sober.'

A showman who didn't drink was rarer than a cow that didn't moo, so the grumbles and protests that followed were nothing King John hadn't expected.

'Once we have him,' he said to restore order, 'it's a free bar.'

Smiles all round.

Ify didn't knock on the function room door because expecting Ify to knock first was like expecting a Bengal tiger not to eat you for supper when your head was between its jaws. She was a pure civilian and King John kept it that way on her mum's behalf despite the fact he was positive Ify could have been a real asset to his firm.

The sight of the gnarled showmen and all the guns didn't make her so much as flinch. She took it all in her stride, her platform sandals clonking on the parquet flooring as she made a beeline for King John.

'You had a visitor,' she told him. 'Some bloke named Ritchie.'

So he told her, 'I said I wasn't to be bothered.' He gestured to the weaponry. 'We're working here.'

'Past tense,' she sighed. 'I said you were away.'

'That's what I like about you, Ify. You always do as you're told.'

'Don't try acting the big man in front of all these faces,' she said with a wagging finger. 'I mind the bar and I take requests, not orders. And I do it for Mum, not you. Because she doesn't trust you to look after yourself.'

A couple of the nearest showmen smirked at King John's dressing-down. One further away wagged his finger in imitation of Ify as the others smiled.

'Well, that put me in my place,' he said. 'But why are you telling me about this Ritchie lad? Is he the fuzz?'

'That was my first thought,' she answered. 'Some new CID plod.' She looked around. 'But now I'm thinking he's someone else entirely.'

'Don't keep me in suspense. Gimme what your gut is telling you.'

'Reckon that would be a waste of time,' she said, turning to the closest table and stabbing an index finger onto one of the photographs of Vasili. 'When I'm sure you know a lot more about him than I could ever guess.'

Maybe it was his advancing years, but it took King John a long moment to understand, and when he spoke, the words came out as isolated islands of surprise. 'You're. Having. A. Giraffe.'

Terrance said, 'He was here? Right here? When?'

'Yeah, he was,' she said. 'About twenty minutes ago, looking for his royal highness over there.' When she saw both Terrance and King John about to speak in unison, she cut them off, 'And don't you *dare* tell me I should have told you sooner when you didn't bother to inform me what you reprobates were even up to in the first place.'

Terrance obediently closed his mouth.

'Besides,' she continued, showing King John her beautiful, smug smile, 'I told him you'd be in tomorrow so guess who's coming back then?'

FIFTY-THREE

The first thing Victor did was nothing at all. He continued to wait by the statue. Remaining unseen as a shadow was even more important than keeping the target in sight, so the man on the phone had little choice but to leave the area. There was only so long he could maintain the ruse without giving himself away. Exactly how long the man deemed too long was up in the air for now. If he was part of a team then it would be simple enough for another to take over, and so Victor expected he would go after a few minutes. The longer the man stayed nearby, the greater the chance he was alone.

And if he was in fact alone then he would not give up shadowing Victor until the choice was either abandon the job or give himself away.

Should he be part of a team, Victor figured he would depart within five minutes and let someone else take over. Alone, the man would risk closer to ten before calling it quits.

At almost nine minutes, the man said *seeya*, slipped the phone back into a pocket, and walked away.

Victor waited a few seconds, and followed.

The man's skills at shadowing were better than his aptitude for countersurveillance, Victor soon discovered, having no trouble keeping him in sight while maintaining a tactical distance. Either the man didn't know how to avoid a tail, or he believed there was no need, convinced that Victor had not identified his true nature.

In an ever-shifting mass of people, Victor lost sight of the man several times. Sometimes the pedestrians between them blocked his view as they passed. At other moments it was the target who changed direction or cut in front of other people. These moments were brief, no more than a few seconds at a time, but on occasion Victor had stop and look the other way or hide himself from the intermittent glances over one shoulder the target made. From the basic, obvious movements, this guy was no professional as Victor understood the label. The man's countersurveillance was limited to only basic attempts to spot a tail as he made his way to Liverpool Street station.

Maybe more a soldier than a spy.

Coffee shops and food outlets formed most of the businesses that framed the concourse. He saw a bar, a clothes store and a pharmacy interrupting the monotony. Some had windows or other reflective surfaces, although it was almost certainly too much to expect the man to use them as mirrors to watch his six. Victor kept enough distance to nullify any such attempts by default.

He passed an old man with a drawn and tired face who could not give away the free newspapers he held out to travellers. A relentless public address system spoke of arrivals, departures, delays and 'if you see something, say something ... ' Victor wondered how many people actually did just that as his gaze passed over tired staff manning the ticket barriers, and whether those tired staff could do anything beyond passing on the message to someone else.

Elsewhere, he saw black-clad police officers on patrol in ones and twos. They cradled black MP5 sub-machine guns and paid him no attention as they scanned the crowds for lone men with backpacks and Middle Eastern complexions. They did not look at him twice.

Ahead, he watched the man enter a coffee shop.

Victor slowed to a stop, tilting back his head to look up at departure boards that provided the perfect excuse to linger. There was no convenient cover to hide his presence – that also would not block his own line of sight – but the station was busy enough for him to become lost in the crowd.

Only able to see a portion of the coffee shop's interior, Victor lost sight of the man. He could be meeting someone, prearranged or otherwise, or he could just as easily have wanted a latte.

Or, just maybe, he was informing a teammate or superior what he had observed at the Fool's Arms and reporting in after having to abandon shadowing Victor.

A woman at a nearby barrier waited until she had reached the touchpad before rooting for her credit or travel card, much to the ire of the more efficient commuters behind her forced to slow to a sudden stop.

An attendant at the barrier was quick to open up another gate to let frustrated travellers through before the tuts and eye-rolls became too heated.

A family of tourists went back and forth across the

concourse, the father doing his best to shepherd his unruly teen children while the mother led the way, craning her neck in search of something. Not their platform since her gaze was in the other direction so perhaps she was searching for the facilities or where to buy a healthy snack for her diabetic son. From the sullen children to the red-faced father, tempers were beginning to fray.

He saw them coming. The father, pointing, appeared in Victor's peripheral vision. At first, he thought they had finally located whatever it was they sought, although he realised seconds later he was wrong. The mother was heading his way. She had a nervous smile, trying to appear friendly but failing to hide her anxiety.

She was going to ask him for directions.

With so many busy people on the concourse making their way to their train or heading for the exits the options were limited. Victor seemed like a good option. Stationary, he was not in any kind of hurry. She wasn't going to interrupt someone rushing around.

'Excuse me,' the mother said.

The loud ambient noises of trains, commuters and public address system meant her voice was closer to a yell than a whisper. And was animated too. Waving her hands to get his attention.

'Excuse me,' she said again to him. Then, in response to a question or comment from one of her children, she snapped, '*I'm trying, aren't I?*'

Flashing lights would not have signposted him any better, so he said, '*Je suis désolé mais je ne comprends pas l'anglais.*'

He walked away. His focus split between watching the coffee shop and pretending to examine the departure boards, it took Victor a second too long to realise a police officer was looking his way.

Not one of the black-clad armed cops, at least, but one of the transport police officers present at the station. Victor acted as though he had not noticed, figuring the cop's attention would move elsewhere before too long. He had undeniable instincts since there was no reason to single Victor out. Recognition Victor could have understood. A regular cop might have been on duty in Pimlico the other night, could have seen or heard enough to be on the look-out or been privy to a still from a nearby CCTV camera. This was a transport cop, however. He would not have been involved in the aftermath of Borisyuk's murder or any subsequent investigation. The only thing this police officer recognised about Victor was that he did not belong. Maybe the cop would be unable to articulate why that was, why Victor stood out to him.

The end result was still the same.

The cop walked towards him.

Those first few steps were at a slow, tentative pace, as if he were doubting his actions, doubting himself.

Victor willed him to listen to those doubts.

If anything, they subsided, the cop's pace picking up from shuffle to stride as the confidence in his approach increased.

Leaving the area would only encourage the cop to follow, so Victor stayed still. He had done nothing wrong. At least, he had committed no crime in the few minutes he had been simply waiting on the concourse. However accurate the cop's instincts, there was nothing he could do now. He wasn't going to arrest Victor for standing.

'How are you today?'

A friendly enough question that betrayed none of the suspicion that had brought him over.

Acting as though this was the first time he was aware of the cop's presence, Victor adjusted his feet to face the man.

Up close, he was even younger, his cheeks smooth and red, his eyes without a hint of darkness beneath them or lines at the corners. The same height as Victor, the gear at his waist and bulging from the harness over his shoulder giving him a much wider, bulkier frame. Gel slicked his side-parting down into a glistening dome, solid and immovable.

'I'm very well,' Victor said. 'Yourself?'

'Counting down the seconds until I can get some food.' He smiled. 'I'm ravenous.'

'I imagine your line of work is quite demanding when it comes to calories.'

'I mostly tell drunks it's time to wake up and go home.'

The self-deprecation was a good approach. Less threatening. Victor could imagine it working well at another place in time with someone else. Anyone else.

'Is there something I can help you with?'

He figured it prudent to get to the point. The less time he spent in this cop's company the better it would be for the both of them.

'Oh, I didn't take you for being in a rush.'

The deflection was almost as good as the self-deprecation.

Victor remained silent. The cop had not answered his question and Victor was playing a regular guy and regular guys didn't have to explain themselves for no good reason.

The young police offer seemed to understand the silence. 'We have a lot of thieves operating in and around this station. Pickpockets and such. People have their phones stolen. Wallets too.'

Where crowds gathered, thieves circled. Victor knew this all too well, although that was not the reason for the cop's approach.

'I would hate for you to fall victim to an avoidable crime.'

Had things been different, he might have asked this young man what had made him walk over. How had he known Victor did not fit in here? What was it that gave him away?

But things were not different and he could not ask. Besides, now they had conversed and he had looked him in the eye as they did so, Victor was certain the cop would not be able to explain. He could provide no answer to Victor's question because it had been pure instinct. Something at the primal level had alerted the cop and now they had spoken Victor had given him no justification for that alert.

'Well,' the cop said after a moment of silence, 'you have yourself a pleasant day.'

'You too,' Victor said, and meant it.

The cop wandered back the way he had come, walking at the same tentative pace as that in which he had begun as if that unquantifiable instinct that had brought him over in the first place was now telling him he was wrong to leave.

Then he stopped, and Victor figured he would be maiming the young man within the next few moments without the transport cop even understanding why it was happening.

Only he did not turn around after all. Instead, the cop broke into a sprint, heading in a different direction altogether to chase after a pickpocket who had just stolen a young woman's phone.

At that point, the man with the dark beard left the coffee shop.

He had been inside for only a few minutes from start to finish. Plenty of time in which to get a coffee and yet the man's hands were empty. Similarly, it was enough time in which to use the bathroom, only such establishments would only have facilities for staff, since the station had its own public lavatories.

Which meant the man had entered for a different reason, so Victor watched him exit the station and did not follow. He was more interested in who the man had met than the man himself, who was a watcher at most.

Victor waited to see who left the coffee shop in the next few minutes, examining and analysing them as potential teammates or associates of the watcher. A trio of elderly men with rambling gear were dismissed, as were a teenage couple who left arm in arm.

A man in a suit seemed a potential for a moment, and Victor was debating following him as he weighed up the pros and cons of the suit being a professional, and then he saw there was no need to analyse anyone leaving because he recognised the next person who exited the coffee shop.

Shivika Chandi.

FIFTY-FOUR

Sleek dark hair, parted in the centre, hung down to her shoulders and spooled there against a knitted sweater the colour of milk. Chandi had changed since the mixer in the morning, now wearing loose, high-waisted trousers that flared out below the knees and covered her shoes except for the toes where shiny, red leather caught the light. A modest heel.

She proved harder to follow than had the man. She employed a range of countersurveillance techniques: circuitous route, doubling back, taking three left turns in a row. Victor might have lost her or had no choice but to allow her to notice him had she not walked for only fifteen minutes before reaching her destination.

A man, wearing a bulbous puffa jacket that made him as wide as the pavement, sipped from a tiny plastic bottle of turmeric juice. An inconvenience to pedestrians walking the opposite way but a convenient piece of mobile cover to Victor.

Chandi's destination turned out to be a large building of

steel and glass on a street that was surprisingly quiet for central London. The only traffic he heard was from neighbouring throughways. The kerbs were lined with so many vehicles, however, there was not even a single parking space available. He saw many small vans with signage for catering supplies, plumbing and couriers. Opposite the building, a blackboard sign for a coffee shop advertised beans roasted in-house and signature blends.

In the daylight, one tower of steel and glass looked little different from the next. As the sun set, however, they obtained an individuality by way of the silent movies of the city projected onto their reflective exteriors. On the façade of this building, a helicopter rippled from one window to the next across a backdrop of clouds and taillights.

Broad steps led up from the pavement to a front of house with tall glass windows providing a clear view of the lobby inside, accessible via both revolving doors and a set of electronically opening doors for disabled visitors or people like Victor who chose not to use the revolving entrance. He had to close the distance with Chandi once she had entered or lose sight of her.

By the time he had reached the top of the steps, he saw her at the far end of the lobby, using a pass card to open up one of the turnstiles that blocked access to the elevators and stairs.

There hadn't been anywhere near enough time to register at the reception desk and receive a visitor's card, so Chandi worked here. A tired security guard nodded her way as she passed him without a word.

She had given him her card at the Nightingale Foundation mixer and he was tempted to call her to test how she would react. He decided to reserve that course of action for now and, as soon as Chandi had stepped inside one of the four elevators, Victor entered the building and headed to the reception desk.

Of the two receptionists sitting behind a sweeping desk that curved into the shape of a letter S, a man looked up and smiled.

'How may I be of help to you this afternoon?'

'I was here last week to see Shivika Chandi of Adeptus Global only I left behind my sunglasses. I'm hoping you could provide me with a pass so I can pick them up. She said it was fine to swing by anytime.'

It wasn't always necessary for a disguise or an excuse to be perfect. Few people were truly suspicious by nature and most people didn't like to make a scene. If Victor gave someone a reason to believe him then they usually took it.

The receptionist didn't mention she had just passed through the lobby, so he didn't know her by sight alone. Which made sense. Probably a thousand people walked by him each day.

He reached for a phone. 'Let me give her a call.'

Impossible to know which floor she would step out of the elevator, so Victor could do nothing but hope it wasn't the first and her office was further away than the time it took the receptionist to give up.

'She's not answering,' he said after about twenty seconds.

'I'm not in London again until next month,' Victor added. 'I'd really liked to get my sunglasses. It'll take five minutes.'

He hung up the phone after another eight seconds. 'I'm very sorry but I can't let you in without either permission from Miss Chandi or an appointment on the system.'

'I'd like for you to make an exception in this case. I'll be very grateful.'

The man looked at Victor, trying to make a decision as to whether he could trust him so much as to break policy, to risk getting in trouble. Victor saw the man wasn't going to before he had begun shaking his head.

'Perhaps Miss Chandi can arrange for your glasses to be posted to you?'

When a disguise or excuse failed, when a person either didn't trust him or wouldn't break policy, Victor had the option to drop the disguise that he wore every waking moment he was not fulfilling a contract. In those rare moments, he let the act slip.

Only a little. So that the suspicious person who wanted more than he could give had a hint of the alternative way of doing things. Threatening behaviour could backfire because Victor did everything possible to appear unthreatening. Aggression could encourage aggression. Back someone into a corner and they'd fight because they had no other choice. Victor didn't take that approach. He made no threats and acted with no aggression, and yet he gave the person a glimpse of his true nature. He gave that person a choice: to allow themselves to be deceived or to escalate the situation in a way no civilian would ever want. He preferred not to do this because he didn't want anyone to see even a fraction of his true self unless they would be seeing nothing else ever again. Inevitably, no such civilian could really understand him, but it didn't matter. Their rational, conscious mind interpreted him as just a man in a suit. Well presented without being stylish. Polite yet not charming. Nothing to make them afraid. Their instincts, however, knew better. Stress

323

hormones would elevate their heart rate. They would pale as blood was pulled away from the skin and directed to the vital organs. They would sweat as their internal body temperature rose. They would feel uncomfortable without knowing why, only that Victor was the cause. Almost everyone would take the first opportunity to make that feeling go away. They would capitulate and feel immediate relief as endorphins were released into their brain to encourage them to make such right calls again instead of face avoidable danger. Survival mechanisms at work. They would then find a way to rationalise what had happened and put it down to dehydration or low blood sugar or a poor night's sleep. No one wanted to experience fear unless they were in control of it and so they would convince themselves they had not been afraid in the first place.

It was almost all in the eyes. Victor didn't stare. Staring was a threat. He just didn't blink. He held the guy's gaze and didn't stop. He leaned forward, but very slowly. No sudden movement. A gradual encroachment into the guy's personal space. Victor's face did not change. He maintained a careful, neutral expression. No anger or resentment but no disappointment or defeat either. He was not taking no for an answer. He was waiting for the guy to let him through as though it was inevitable.

'Just five minutes?' the receptionist asked, desperate for the building fear to end.

Victor nodded. 'Just five minutes.'

The guy reached a hand to somewhere Victor could not see, and a red light on one of the turnstile barriers turned bright green.

'Thank you,' Victor said.

'No problem,' the guy replied, a little too hurried and snapping his gaze elsewhere as though something important required his immediate attention.

At the barrier, Victor gave the security guard a polite nod, then tapped a button with a knuckle and the glass turnstile pivoted open.

FIFTY-FIVE

The coffee shop on the opposite side of the street had tall, thin tables and benches instead of chairs. Next to the counter, glass jugs without handles offered water for shot-glass-sized tumblers. The coffee was incredibly hot. He almost burned his lip.

In the far corner, he watched a man wearing a stiff-collared shirt and a racing-green body warmer sat with a laptop. He wore a headset and spoke to someone on the screen with so much volume every patron could hear him as clearly as those sitting right next to him. A couple who made the mistake of sitting down nearby with their coffees and chocolate twists immediately stood up again to find somewhere – anywhere – else to converse.

'He's been like that for almost three hours,' he overheard the barista tell her newly arrived replacement. 'One whole flat white.'

Listening to the specific details of an investment opportunity impossible to ignore, the replacement frowned and said, 'I really hope the Wi-Fi doesn't drop out again.'

The young woman finishing her shift read the tone. 'I have a feeling the router might come unplugged on my way out.'

Even when the call ended, the man with the laptop didn't so much type as stab the keys with needless force, each rapid tap more a thump loud enough to be heard by the entire coffee shop.

On another table, a middle-aged woman stood up too fast and bumped an overhanging tray. The cone-shaped latte glass that stood upon the tray tipped and fell. She was quick to thrust out a hand to intercept, only not quite dextrous enough to catch the glass, instead knocking it further with her hand, guaranteeing the remnants of latte spilled over the widest possible area. The tray rattling and the glass clunking on the table, the long-necked spoon clattering around inside the glass, and the woman's growl of annoyance ensured everyone noticed. With a handful of napkins, she corralled and soaked up the spillage away from the table edge as she muttered apologies to those nearby. Aside from the sudden noises, over as soon as they'd begun, no one else was inconvenienced. It was a strange thing to apologise to those unaffected by one's actions but it was something he observed the British do on a regular basis. He was never quite sure if it was sincere or just habit. Clumsiness seemed to be perhaps the most grievous of social crimes an individual could perform, at least in their own eyes.

He sat by the rear entrance, which led to a terrace. Whenever someone entered, the draft rushing through from the open entrance at the front ruffled his long hair. Now, he wore it loose, unlike when he pretended to be a waiter. Sitting at the front before the plate-glass exterior would have provided him a better view of the street outside and the building opposite, but it would also have given him away. From the back, he could still see the street, albeit interrupted by the other patrons. However, because the office building had steps leading up to the entrance, he had an unimpeded view when Shivika Chandi returned.

Not her real place of business but a cover to help disguise her true profession. He knew what she really did for a living because he knew everything about her.

So, when she entered the office building, he was not surprised. He made a note of the time of her return to add to the other intelligence he had gathered.

He was surprised, however, to see the uninvited guest from this morning's mixer follow Chandi into the same building soon afterwards.

Speaking his native Russian so the other patrons could not eavesdrop, he called Hawk and told him, 'You were right about that hitman ... He's about to work it all out.'

FIFTY-SIX

A job with MI5 wasn't as glamorous as Chandi had once imagined because most spying work, domestic or foreign, was either looking at a screen or it was surveillance. Actual action was as rare as rocking horse dung when not a UC. Even tailing someone – the absolute lowest tier of genuine spy craft – was becoming rarer and rarer. London had more CCTV cameras than just about anywhere this side of China, so putting boots on the ground was mostly unnecessary, with the risk-to-reward ratio not worth the hassle. Running a source could be done from a computer – hell, a phone – and Chandi could hardly remember when she last felt the rush of excitement. Some days she felt more data processor than spook. There was a lot of cross-referencing. A lot of comparing names on databases of various kinds to names on watch lists. Listening to phone calls, reading emails, translating textspeak into the Queen's English. Then reports. So many reports. She would joke that the one skill a career in MI5 had cultivated and enhanced to the highest level was her touch-typing.

If not for the fear of missing some vital piece of information that led to a bomb exploding on Remembrance Sunday or some lunatic running around the Tube with a sword, then she might not feel anything at all. Perhaps that was why the dealings with Lord Milburn was giving her such a buzz. This was more the kind of thing she had fantasised about before becoming a spook: secret liaisons and burner phones. It made her feel alive again in a way she hadn't felt in as long as she could remember. It was a huge risk, obviously, and if she slipped up at all then it would be the end of her career and maybe prison too.

Taking the Tube home, she sat away from the inebriated Londoners splayed on seats while the true drunks didn't trust themselves to get back up again and instead wrapped their limbs around the vertical poles in the centre of the vestibules between doors. She had read that when people threw themselves off the platform in front of Tube trains, the very last thing they ever did was look the driver straight in the eye. She wondered how the drivers were ever the same again.

As befitted a degree-educated, sixteen-year veteran of public service, Chandi lived in a tiny flat in the hairy arsehole of London's East End. Yawning, she fumbled for her keys, knowing she should go straight to bed or she would suffer for it the next day and have to grit her teeth against the inevitable comments. She had a darkness beneath her eyes that made her look perpetually fatigued. Even fully rested after a good eight hours, people who didn't know her better would ask if she was tired, if she had slept well. It was such a polite insult, such a very British way of putting someone down while pretending to show concern. And why was it socially acceptable to draw attention to this feature when that same person with their faux sympathy would never dream of asking an overweight person if they were hungry, if their insulin levels were at pre-diabetic levels?

She had never really learned to cook – no one had ever taught her – and irregular hours meant she could rarely summon the energy to chop and slice, to grill and sauté. The oven door had never needed cleaning because if the ready meal could not be microwaved then Chandi put it back on the shelf in the refrigerated section of the supermarket. Every takeaway and fast-food outlet within half a mile knew her on a first-name basis.

If not for her reliance on ready meals and takeaways, she might not otherwise feel divorced. It was hard to move on when she still saw her ex-husband twice a week to pick up her two young children and take them swimming, to the playground, to the cinema, to the café, or anywhere else that wasn't her one-bed flat. And given she still argued with Brian as much now as she ever did, she preferred to think of them as post-married. He kept the house – which she was happy to agree to for the sake of the twins – and she could not afford anything but a draughty conversion flat in which the washing machine lived in the bathroom. The kitchen was so small if the refrigerator door was open no one could else could step inside the room. Not that this ever came up since as well as the twins and the house, Brian had kept all their friends too.

Her phone kept buzzing with messages from him, keeping her up to date on the latest upcoming school trip and what the twins needed before they left for the weekend. Such messages were laced with passive-aggressive comments about her needing to try harder, to be more involved. In Chandi's opinion, it didn't really matter what you did as a parent as there was a good chance your children would grow up to hate you. If you gave them a respectful amount of space to be their own person, they'd say you paid no attention. If you took an interest, encouraged and supported their whims, they'd turn around and say you smothered them. If you advised them, you were too controlling. If you let them make their own mistakes, you never cared. So, given it was a coin toss at best, Chandi didn't worry too much about her parenting style.

Her takeaway – extra spicy meat feast pizza – arrived by way of a courier on a scooter and Chandi was too busy playing a game on her phone to notice she didn't recognise the courier's voice when she answered the intercom. Given she ordered a pizza at least once a week, Chandi knew all the couriers who delivered for Pizza Heaven. She was too enraptured by the game's carefully designed artificial intelligence algorithms that ensured a constant stream of enemies that had to be defeated, ensuring Chandi's undivided attention at all times if she wanted to gain the experience points and gold coins necessary for her on-screen avatar to advance to the next level so she could then defeat stronger enemies to gain the experience and gold required to advance to the level after that.

She did not notice as she dawdled by her front door, waiting for the courier to climb the stairs to her flat, that the footsteps on the stairs were not those of a young man in trainers working a low-paid job and rushing up those stairs to get this delivery over with as fast as possible so he could get on to the next one.

Chandi only noticed when the hinges of her front door creaked open and she finally looked up from her phone long enough to take the pizza.

If she thought it would make a difference, Chandi would have screamed. But it would make no difference what she did because standing in the hallway was no courier, but the professional assassin she knew only as Cleric.

She retreated with unsteady feet as he stepped into her flat and closed the door behind him.

Getting her second look at him today, Chandi saw a man of maybe thirty-five, maybe older, with a lean face. He wore a suit and might have been a banker or a project manager if not for the absolute lack of humanity in eyes so dark they were almost black. Though tall, he did not seem powerful or intimidating in a physical sense, but Chandi's blood pressure shot up and her heart began beating so hard and so fast she felt dizzy with fear.

She did not so much sit back down as collapse.

'You were married,' he told her. 'You have children.'

'Yes ...' she croaked. 'I do. Why?'

'Where are they?'

'They live with their dad.'

'How modern,' Cleric said. 'Would you like to see them again? Would you like to see your children ever again?'

'Very much so.'

'Then you would do well to bear that in mind when you respond to my subsequent inquiries.'

There was no question to answer, but Chandi replied, 'Yes,' looking down at her trembling hand.

'There's too much cortisol and adrenalin in your blood-stream,' Cleric explained. 'Your mouth is probably feeling like sandpaper right now and your chest is growing increasingly tight, but don't worry. You're not having a heart attack. If you panic, however, you might induce one.'

She swallowed then rubbed her chest with her non-shaking hand. 'That's really not helpful.'

'When you breathe, breathe out slower than when you inhale. It will calm you down. Close your eyes as well, to limit how much information your brain has to process. Picture your children. You can keep your eyes closed the entire time if you like. You don't need to look at me to answer my questions.'

'Are you going to kill me?'

'You want the truth?'

'Yes,' she said. 'I mean, I think I do. I can't stand not knowing.'

'Fifty-fifty right now,' Cleric said. 'The needle can swing either way depending on how this conversation goes.'

'I'll tell you anything you want to know.'

'I believe you,' Cleric said. 'However, that's not the only determining factor. There's another one. When I leave here, I need to know that this conversation of ours will not cause me a problem later on. There's a very simple way to ensure that.'

Taking a breath to steel her nerves, and thinking carefully about his choice of words, she said, 'Whatever you think you know, you don't know half of it.'

'Then enlighten me.'

'The Nightingale Foundation is a cover.'

'I said enlighten me, not tell me what I've already worked out on my own.'

'I don't work for Adeptus Global.'

'If I have to repeat myself again then I'm going to lose my patience.'

'I'm MI5,' she said, speaking fast as she tried to control her fear. 'I can help you.'

'Help me how?'

'You want the truth, right? That's why you're here. You want to know why I was at that mixer, why Maxim Borisyuk was supposed to attend?'

'If you want to keep that needle we talked about in a favourable direction you'll tell me.'

'The mixer, the foundation is a cover.'

'So you could spy on Borisyuk and his organisation?'

'No,' she told him. 'The opposite, in fact. We weren't spying on Borisyuk. He was spying for us.'

FIFTY-SEVEN

Victor listened as Chandi explained. He didn't need to draw
a weapon or threaten her for her to talk. That he was standing in her home was enough to persuade her of the benefits
of cooperation.

'Borisyuk was an asset, a spy for us. I'm his handler. Was,
I mean. That's why I was at the function.'

'A spy in what sense? On his own organisation?'

'On the Russian government, its military, its intelligence
agencies ... He ran in elite circles. Dealt with lots of different people.'

'Then the foundation is not a cover to protect you, but to
protect him.'

'Exactly. I created it from the ground up purely to give him
a squeaky-clean reason to meet somewhere I could control.'

'Why would Borisyuk need an excuse to be anywhere?'
Victor said out loud, though it was almost to himself as he
answered his own question before she could. 'Ah, because
someone suspected him.'

She nodded and he could see her pulse beginning to slow now it seemed he was more interested in gathering information from her than killing her. 'We don't know how they know, but we realised he was being watched. FSB, SVR, GRU ... it's hard to tell.'

'Why meet at all? Why not send information digitally?'

'Because we don't control the internet, because a handover can't be intercepted.'

'I didn't kill him,' he told her. 'Even if it looks like I did.'

'Given I'm still alive, given you're here at all, I'm starting to believe you.'

'If Russian intelligence knew that Borisyuk was spying for you, what would they do?'

'They'd kill him. Or have someone do it for them. But only if they knew for sure. The Kremlin and the Bratva have been on friendly terms for a long time. They wouldn't move against Borisyuk unless they were convinced he was a traitor and I don't understand how they could know that.'

'That Borisyuk was tied to a chair suggests to me Russian intelligence knew he was ferrying information. Why now, though? Why make a move against him at this point, not any other? I gather the information he was bringing you this time was valuable enough to be worth killing him over. What is it?'

'If he told me in advance, then there would be no need to make an exchange, would there? But I suspect it's to do with Russian military build-up. Borisyuk was making an effort to get friendly with Vladimir Kasakov, who has been busy acquiring rare earth metals and components for the Kremlin. They're manufacturing drones faster than they need to ... unless, that is, they're planning on putting them to use in the near future.'

Thinking about Afghanistan, Victor was glad the Kabul cartel had nothing to do with drones. 'Why would Borisyuk have spied for you, for anyone?'

'Because the Bratva have billions of dollars of assets in London and wash tens of billions each year through the banking system here. Borisyuk gave us intel on the lunatics in the Kremlin and we helped keep his money safe.'

'Very egalitarian,' Victor said. 'If the police had found any such information at Borisyuk's townhouse, would you know about it? Or would such a revelation be kept quiet to just a few people?'

'Absolutely I would know about it. I'm advising the task force investigating the murder. Currently, the focus is on you as the shooter and the motive being a mob hit.'

'If the assassin wasn't able to recover the information they'll be looking for it. They'll be trying to retrace Borisyuk's steps.'

'I expect so, why?'

'Because that's what I've been doing and I've already tangled with one of them at the scene of the crime, which means if they didn't know who I am or what I'm doing before, they probably do now. Have any known players landed in the UK recently?'

'The Russians only leave a trail when they want everyone to know they're behind a hit. Because Borisyuk was a traitor, a spy, they'll want to keep it quiet, especially when there's unrecovered intel out there. They can't stand losing face. Which means they're using a team already based here.'

'You sound certain it's a team, not an individual.'

'There are three of them,' she said. 'I only know about two, however. Both British nationals but Alexander Surovkin, the youngest at twenty-five, was born and raised in the Urals.

The other man, Veniam – Ben – Chaban, is an SAS veteran of the Falklands turned mercenary, private spy, and sometimes killer. I think he's in charge given he's more than twice Surovkin's age.'

Recalling his fight with the assassin in Borisyuk's Pimlico townhouse, Victor did not imagine that Chaban matched the physicality of his opponent. If anything, Victor would put that enemy as a younger man, not someone who had fought a war in the early '80s. Which made Surovkin the more likely.

'You didn't say how you know for sure it's them.'

'They've been suspected of espionage in the past and then both were present at the mixer this morning.'

He thought of the waiter with the ponytail and the polite Neanderthal, who must be Surovkin and Chaban respectively. The assassin he fought in the Pimlico townhouse must be someone else. 'The third man?'

'I don't have any intel on them. I just know Chaban and Surovkin work with someone else they refer to as Hawk, which is probably a codename or designation.'

'Or a shortened version of Hawkins, of course.' She nodded in response. 'If they knew Borisyuk was a traitor there's a good chance they know about you too.'

Chandi shrugged. 'Hence why I continued with the charade at the Nightingale Foundation mixer. The news about the murder has been kept out of the media so guests and organisers alike shouldn't have known about it. If I hadn't showed up it would have confirmed any suspicions, assuming I'm not already on their radar.'

He said, 'Why haven't you brought them in?'

'Because the task force doesn't know about them. Only

a few of us at MI5 do. We arrest them and we confirm to Moscow that Borisyuk was indeed spying for us.'

'And why haven't I been arrested yet?'

'The task force haven't cornered you. You've been lucky.'

'I don't believe in luck and that's not answering my question. You met me earlier today. You have someone following me. That I haven't been arrested means you didn't tell the task force you met me at the function. Which also means the man following me earlier is doing so for you directly, not the task force itself.' He paused. 'I want to know what your angle is here. Your first instinct will be to lie, so I do hope for your own sake you have good self-control.'

'When you were in London a few years ago you caused a mess, you ... my boss at the time helped clean it up and I helped him. He was always worried you would show up again and in doing so shine a light on things he would prefer remained in the dark. When I realised it was you who killed Borisyuk ... I mean, when I suspected it was you the task force was looking for, I let Milburn know. After meeting you at that stately home, I kept that to myself. Then, well ... things are getting complicated.'

'Your old boss wants me dead.'

'Your tone suggests you're neither surprised nor upset to learn this.'

'These things happen so often I don't take it personally,' Victor said with a casualness that he saw she almost mistook as humour. 'Is the man following me planning on killing me?'

'I haven't agreed to that course of action,' Chandi explained.

'Yet,' Victor added.

'Yet,' she agreed. 'I told my old boss I'd think about it but the contractor, a man named Mulroy, is putting in the ground work anyway given your ... pedigree.'

'What have you been waiting for? By now I don't take you as any sort of pacifist.'

'I helped clean up Milburn's previous mess to give a boost to my career,' she admitted. 'I'm not so sure doing this would make the same kind of difference.'

'Tell him yes,' Victor said to her surprise. 'Tell him you've thought about it carefully and come to the decision it's the best move for your career. You don't want anyone finding out you helped him back then. I'll take care of the assassin and you tell Milburn he's then lying low overseas. You're going to tell him that you helped dispose of my corpse. Buried, chopped up, dissolved in acid ... you choose something that sounds convincing. If you have a weak stomach then don't try and pretend you took a hacksaw to my ankles or pliers to my teeth.'

'I can,' she said. 'I will. And then what?'

'And then nothing,' Victor answered. 'Every now and again, you'll do me a favour. Maybe I'll call. Maybe I'll show up at your door. If you're useful to me, you stay breathing. Which sounds like a good deal to me. But it might take you some time to realise the same. Once I'm gone, you're going to think you were lucky to survive, and then you're going to convince yourself you survived through your wits, your slick wordplay that had me eating out of the palm of your hand. And then you're going to think about how you can turn this to your advantage, how to bring me in next time I show up and it won't work. Because for every time you see me, there will be a dozen times I've been watching you. And if any of those times I even get an inkling you're not keeping up your end of the deal, I will turn the volume of your television up to maximum so when I set fire to you in your bathtub your neighbours can't hear you screaming.'

Chandi believed him, he saw, but she wasn't done. 'I can be of even more use to you if you let me be.'

'Don't keep me in suspense.'

'The task force is still looking for you. I can steer them elsewhere.'

'You're going to do that anyway,' he told her. 'Because if they catch up with me then they're going to learn all about you and your plans with Milburn. Don't try and pass off your own self-interest as any kind of favour to me.'

'You can't convince me you believe that anyone would take your word over mine,' Chandi replied. 'Whatever you claim about me will be heard through a big, hitman-shaped filter. And even if anyone decides to believe you then that will be the sum total of the impact. Because, as you know, there will be no evidence to support your story. You getting arrested is an inconvenience for me but it's the end of the road for you. You'll never see the free light of day again and you know it.'

Victor remained silent.

'But I can help ensure it never comes to that. You kill me now and the task force will quadruple in size by the morning, and if you manage to get past them and out of the country your face will be on every watch list in the Western world by this time tomorrow. I think you know all that without me saying, but I *have* said it, so you now understand you can't play that threat with me.'

'You're making an awful lot of assumptions about me and my motives.'

'Maybe you care who killed Borisyuk or you don't,' she said. 'In a way it doesn't matter because I know you care about not going down for it. I can help you sleep better at night.'

'In return for what?'

'Luda Zakharova has been uncooperative so far. She's hiding behind an army of solicitors. I'm not able to retrace Borisyuk's steps if I don't know them. But that's what you've been doing, right?'

'I'm still waiting.'

'I've already told you that he would have stashed the intel in some dead drop and then let me know where I could retrieve it.'

'You're saying I know where it is?'

'I'm saying if you've been where he's been then you must have come across it. Obviously, you would not have known about it, but it has to be there, somewhere.'

'How would Borisyuk carry the intel?'

'Micro SD card,' she answered. 'Small enough to hide anywhere.'

'So, I find it and I give it to you? And then what?'

'I'll be a big hero.'

'I meant and then what about me?'

'I know what you meant. You get to walk away from this. You don't go down for Borisyuk's murder. And you can ask for favours now and again.'

'What if I can't find it?'

'Then you take your chances every time you step through passport control.'

After a pause, he said, 'You make a compelling argument.'

'I know what I bring to the table.'

'But you're playing a dangerous game, Ms Chandi,' Victor told her. 'You're playing your old boss, Russian intelligence, the task force, and now you're playing me too. There's a lot that can go wrong.'

'I agree.' She nodded, then smiled. 'It's the most fun I've had in ages.'

FIFTY-EIGHT

January in the UK was no one's idea of a good time. The evening air was cold, made colder by the humidity and the wind that ensured the chill found every piece of exposed skin – and plenty that was covered too. The pavements were more crowded than usual, the savvy Londoners all veering away from the kerb and the real danger of a soaking from a passing black cab or bus as its tyres sent forth of spray of icy water from a puddle-filled pothole.

Even with the heat lamps, no one was stood outside the Fool's Arms tonight. A couple of hours after the end of the working day, the pub was swelling with patrons. The booths all seemed occupied, although he could not see inside them all without making it obvious he was doing just that. It was loud with conversation and laughter, everyone having a good time. On his way to the bar, he overhead a woman talking about a relative who was a surgeon.

'I'm telling you; they need to revoke his licence.'

Victor noted the old guy he had spoken with earlier was

still here, sitting in the same spot, still wearing his black leather jacket and flat cap, a seemingly untouched pint of stout perched on the table before him.

He said, 'Back so soon?' as Victor waited to be served.

'I can't stay away.'

Ify was equally surprised to see him. 'John isn't here until tomorrow.'

'I know,' Victor said, thinking of the Bratva's imminent deadline but mostly of the intel Borisyuk had stashed. 'I'm just here for a drink.'

He asked for a bottle of low-alcohol beer, which was delivered to him with a half-pint glass embossed with the brewer's motif. A little horizontal line ran for a few millimetres above the HALF PINT inscription to prove patrons were getting the full amount for their money. The British were sticklers for accuracy when it came to their beer, he knew.

Taking a seat near to the old guy, he poured from the bottle and took a sip, finding the ale to be quite pleasant. He almost never drank for pleasure outside one of his safe houses and in those rare instances of – not safety, since even a safe house could never be truly safe, so enhanced security only – he chose vodka.

He saw Ify step out from behind the bar and head to a set of stairs that led down, leaving a man with a wallet in his hand waiting to be served. Annoyed, he shook his head and shrugged with his hands at his nearby friends.

'Did you find that missing pen?'

A crisp packet rustled. Someone in one of the closest booths crunched, loud and brazen. The old guy tutted in response and took the first sip of the stout that Victor had seen since arriving. A fruit machine in one corner flashed and trilled as someone won. Coins rattled in the tray.

Victor shook his head. 'I'm pretty sure it's here.'

'What makes you say that?'

'Call it a hunch.'

It made sense to him as a location for a dead drop for something as small as a micro SD card. Borisyuk could have left it in any number of nooks and crannies and it would stay there unseen until someone who knew where to look came to retrieve it.

A man with an open golfing umbrella managed to manoeuvre it through the doorway after a little fuss.

'It won't fold down,' he said as he approached the bar with the open umbrella held high to avoid clipping anyone's head.

Victor wasn't sure if the man was talking to him, Ify or the patronage as a whole.

'I'm going to leave it here next to you,' the man told him after he had a drink in hand. 'That way no one is going to trip over it.'

The man set the open umbrella in a little space between the end of the seating and the bar, leaning it against the wall so it remained in place.

'You don't mind, do you?'

'Not at all,' Victor said, thinking it was no good as an improvised weapon, but it was light and large enough to toss an enemy's way if he needed a quick distraction.

The card could be anywhere, Victor also thought. But Borisyuk had not been alone. Zakharova and his body-guard had eaten with him. He would have to be careful not to arouse suspicion, stashing away the intel in plain sight. Unless ...

'When the Russians ate here,' Victor began, 'did the old man use the lavatory?'

'I was minding my own business, not spying on strangers.'

'You know this place like a lion knows its stretch of the savannah. You don't need to spy on anyone to see what goes on here.'

'The answer is no. The big guy did. Twice.'

Would Borisyuk have trusted the bodyguard with delivering the intel for him? Unlikely. Not with something so secretive, so dangerous.

Ify emerged from the top of the stairs, glancing Victor's way before heading back behind the bar to continue serving.

The old guy sipped some stout then said, 'Are you going to ask me in what booth those three Russians had their lunch?'

'Yes,' Victor said, hiding his surprise. 'But how did you know I was going to ask that?'

'Call it a hunch,' the old guy said with a smirk. 'That and you're not the first person to ask me.'

Again, Victor hid his surprise.

'Who else did?'

The old guy gestured with his chin. 'That far booth over there is where they ate. As for the other person to ask after them, I don't know who he is, but I guess you can ask him yourself.'

Victor waited for more.

The old guy told him, 'He's still sitting in that booth, as far as I can tell.'

FIFTY-NINE

On each wall of the booths hung a pair of brass coat hooks. They had a glassy sheen and Victor saw his own approach as a blurry reflection. He also saw the distorted image of a lone man sitting on one of the padded benches, both palms flat on the tabletop.

The Boatman showed no reaction as Victor took a seat opposite him. If he was surprised, Victor couldn't tell. If he expected this, Victor couldn't tell either.

'I know you didn't kill Borisyuk.'

The Boatman acknowledged the comment with a slow nod. On the table was a bulbous gin glass and Victor wondered if it was there purely to provide an improvised stabbing weapon should the Boatman decided he required one.

'He was assassinated by Russian intelligence agents who found out Borisyuk was spying for MI5.'

'There are three of them,' the Boatman said. 'But they are not Russian intelligence.'

'How do you know?'

349

The Boatman gave him a look as though the answer was obvious. 'They take their orders from Moscow, naturally,' he explained. 'But they are independent contractors.' He paused. 'Like you.'

'You think I'm working with them? That I killed Borisyuk on their behalf?'

'I work only with facts, not speculation.'

'I will soon have proof to show to them.'

'Do you mean this?'

The Boatman moved aside a palm to reveal a tiny black micro SD card on the tabletop.

'Where was it?'

'Stuck on the underside with chewing gum.'

'This is why he was tied to the chair,' Victor explained. 'They wanted to know where he stashed it. Given it's so small he could have done so without Zakharova or the bodyguard noticing, perhaps when they first sat down or as they stood up to leave.'

'The exactitudes are irrelevant.'

Looking at the SD card, Victor asked, 'What are you planning to do with it?'

'Is that your way of asking me to hand it over to you?'

'It would be impolite to simply take it,' Victor answered.

'You told me you were seeking Borisyuk's assassin and who sent him.'

'I did.'

'Have you found them?'

'No,' Victor admitted.

'And yet here you are.'

Referring to the card, Victor said, 'Hopefully that will help.'

'Alternatively, this is why you tied him to the chair and this is why you remained in London. Not to find out who killed him but to finish the job you were hired to complete.'

'If you believed that we wouldn't be having this conversation, would we?'

'I told you before,' the Boatman said. 'It only matters what the leadership believes. I will present my findings and they will decide. I am merely an instrument of fate, not its arbiter. I ferry the dead across the Styx, but I do not decide who waits for me on the shore.'

He stood. The micro SD card remained on the tabletop.

'It's not my mission to retrieve it,' he explained. 'So, I leave it in your hands.'

'Surprisingly kind of you.'

'It is no kindness,' the Boatman said. 'If you are right and they killed Borisyuk for this then they will kill you too.'

'I welcome them to try. In fact, you could help me finish this.'

'Tell me who sent them and for that person I shall reserve a seat on my boat.'

'I don't know who did,' Victor admitted. 'But I'm sure they can tell me.'

'Then you will get your answer very soon,' the Boatman said as he stepped clear of the booth. 'They're waiting for you outside.'

SIXTY

They were easy to spot given Victor had encountered all three of them before now. The waiter with the ponytail wore a baseball cap this time, pulled down low to put his face in shadow, and the hood of his sweatshirt up and over the cap to disguise his long hair. He was the closest, waiting on the opposite side of the street with his hands buried deep into the pockets of his hoodie and huddled against the chill. The hooded sweatshirt was baggy enough to hide a pistol but not anything larger.

Alexander Surovkin according to Chandi.

The firepower could be the polite Neanderthal's role, Victor saw. Ben Chaban was sitting at a nearby bus stop to disguise his height, a knee-length overcoat covering most of his size. A small SMG could be under the garment, although it was more likely to be inside the sports bag he had resting on the bus stop bench alongside him.

Which left the third member of the team. The one they called Hawk.

He took longer to spot. Only when Victor set off along the pavement in the opposite direction to the polite Neanderthal did the third man become apparent. Given the team couldn't know in which way he would walk, it made sense that if the polite Neanderthal was covering one direction, Hawk would be covering the other.

Victor watched as he climbed out of a parked car. The last time Victor had seen the man he had been wearing safety boots, faded jeans and a chequered overshirt. Now, because he was dressed for a confrontation, he wore cargo trousers and lightweight jacket. Walking shoes instead of heavy boots.

The talkative smoker who had been outside the Fool's Arms earlier in the day.

There had been a feeling then Victor had failed to articulate, a tremor on his threat radar he had not understood then but he understood now because he had seen those same walking shoes before when he fought the assassin who had killed Borisyuk.

A stalemate that night.

Now ... Hawk was not alone.

As they wanted the intel, they would not just gun him down on the pavement. They were tasked with saving face, not drawing attention to Moscow's embarrassment with bullets and blood on the streets of London. They would need to get him somewhere quiet so they could ask him the same questions Borisyuk had been asked when he was tied to that chair.

Given they were all now on foot, either they weren't interested in asking him any questions or they had decided bundling Victor into their car wasn't a viable plan given

London's narrow, congested streets. That meant their actual plan must be to shadow him until an opportunity to corner him alone and unobserved presented itself, or to find out where he was heading and take him by surprise while his attention was elsewhere.

In either case, if he found he could not shake them, it gave him the luxury of selecting a favourite location to drop his guise of ignorance. Like them, he would want that somewhere to be quiet and unobserved. That their focus was solely on him revealed they either had no clue about the Boatman or they had already dismissed him as inconsequential to their aims. And they were right.

In the first instance, however, it was always prudent to try to escape. With no firm destination, Victor walked to where the mass of pedestrians was most dense. He had no need to look back to know the Russian assets were following. With three of them, they were not going to lose him in any crowd but the more people around Victor, the less chance they had to make any move.

Ten metres ahead, and maybe fifty from the entrance to the Fool's Arms, a bus stopped and a waiting young woman, dark haired and pale, stood to board with her many bags. She was pregnant. If she wasn't a teenager, she was only just an adult. She had been sat on a bench, playing with her phone in the same way that everyone else but Victor did. Laden with shopping, she tried and failed to make the step from the kerb to get onto the bus. She had to be close to her due date. Victor couldn't imagine her belly could get much bigger without popping. He found pregnant women mysterious, almost otherworldly, because he had never known one to any real degree. He didn't understand children, let alone why anyone would choose to have them. Maybe because he understood how much danger was really out there that he couldn't comprehend willingly putting someone so vulnerable at such considerable risk.

As he reached her, she made eye contact and in that look he felt the plea for assistance.

Walking on, he wasn't sure why, but not helping her felt like the worst thing he had ever done.

Maybe it was the pregnant woman distracting him or his focus otherwise occupied by the three-man team, but Victor did not hear the two black SUVs coming up from behind until they screeched to a stop alongside him.

By that point there was no time to react except to raise his hands when the vehicles screeched to a stop and multiple black-clad armed police officers poured out and surrounded him.

SIXTY-ONE

With many guns pointing his way, Victor did not resist. They disarmed him fast and cuffed him just as fast. Surovkin, Chaban and Hawk watched it happen from a safe distance. Whatever their desire to retrieve the intel from him, they were not going to interfere right now.

Strong hands ushered Victor to the nearest SUV where he was bundled into the back of the vehicle and it pulled away from the kerb moments later.

Not bad, Victor thought. Less than forty seconds from start to finish. Along with his gun, they emptied his pockets, the commander taking everything he had, including the micro SD card.

For an instant, Victor saw two of the Russian assets watching him depart. Surovkin had a phone to his ear and was shouting numbers and letters into it. An empty crisp packet, swept along by the wind, was pinned against the outer side of Chaban's shoe. Hawk was nowhere to be seen, but presumably on the other end of the line, no doubt sprinting back to fetch the car he had been waiting inside. Victor already knew he was younger than Chaban and now he also knew Hawk was the faster and more athletic out of him and Surovkin.

The SUV was quiet. Not silent because there were many sounds: the engine, the exhaust, the rain, passing traffic. But no one spoke. Everyone sat still except the driver who worked the wheel and the gear shift. He was so huge Victor wondered how he had even climbed inside in the first place.

'Aren't you going to call it in?' Victor asked.

No reply. The commander upfront reacted, however, with a slight rotating of his head.

'No radio on the dashboard,' Victor continued. 'Which could be because it's an undercover vehicle.'

The commander said, 'Aren't you a clever boy?'

'You have a radio on your harness, however. Surely the higher-ups need to be informed I'm now in custody.'

'There are no higher-ups,' the commander replied. 'I'm in charge of the operation.'

'What's your rank?' Victor asked.

No answer.

'What about your division of the Met? Flying Squad? SO19? LFT6?'

'You really don't need to know such specifics, okay? Just sit there and enjoy the scenery.'

Outside, the London streets were grey behind a curtain of rain.

Victor said, 'You haven't arrested me yet.'

'National security protocols,' the commander said, swivelling in his seat so he could face Victor. 'Due to your designation as a highly dangerous individual.'

'That's going to cause problems in court if you're detaining me against my will without arresting me first. My barrister will have the whole case thrown out before it even gets to trial. It'll be a scandal. You'll be demoted. You might lose your job.'

'You're overthinking this, mate,' the commander said, a slight smile creeping across his face. 'Besides, we're not currently detaining you.' The smile broadened. 'You're coming with us of your own volition.'

The guy to Victor's right grinned too.

'That won't hold up in court,' Victor told the guy who grinned. 'Are you prepared to lose your job too?'

He did not answer.

'You all must have earned your pensions by now,' Victor said, figuring each man was at least forty. 'If you've botched this arrest and they kick you out then that pension is up in smoke. You need to think about your long-term prospects.'

Still no response.

'If you have to talk,' the commander said. 'Talk to me.'

'Because of the accents?'

The commander, still smiling, hesitated.

'You sound like you were born and raised in this city.' Victor glanced at the others in the vehicle. 'But they don't, do they? That's why no one else has said a single word since you all showed up. Can't hide their Russian accents.'

The commander's smile retreated until his expression was blank and his lips closed tight. 'You're not as clever as you think if you're taking us as Russians.'

Victor thought about this then nodded. Maybe the commander was right and he had missed something here, except:

'There's no such division as LFT6.'

For a moment it seemed as though the commander was going to take a different approach. His mouth opened to respond, perhaps to claim he had felt no need to correct Victor on this error, but instead the smile returned, only this time it was wider in mocking smugness.

'I'll give you full marks for that one, mate. Give yourself a gold star for being such a smarty-pants. Trouble is, being a smarty-pants isn't going to help you now.'

'We'll see.'

Headlights swept over the entrance to the recycling facility, revealing a man holding open the chain-link gate. He wore a long, dark raincoat and a baseball cap pulled down low to shield his face from the downpour. As the SUV pulled onto the site, the man promptly closed the gate behind them. Looking over his shoulder, Victor watched as the man in the long coat secured the gate with a heavy chain and padlock after the second SUV had also passed into the site.

The vehicle rocked and swayed as it traversed uneven ground. Victor heard the tyres splashing through deep puddles, and the pitter-patter of aggregate tossed up against the undercarriage.

No streetlamps here, so it was pitch black outside the swathe of headlights that caught the massive piles of refuse just metres away, rising up like hills and yet invisible in the darkness once the light had passed.

These guys didn't seem like professionals as Victor would define them, but they did everything right. The second vehicle emptied first, and then the guys from inside Victor's SUV exited. Two dragged him out while the rest had their weapons pointed his way.

They gave him no opportunities to exploit so someone had

been well advised. Not Bratva, but they had been told about him by someone.

That person was Andrei Linnekin, who waited inside the main building. He had a phone in one hand that he tapped in a rhymical fashion against his thigh. Maybe in excitement.

'Excellent work, King John,' he said to the commander.

King John nodded. 'Turned out we didn't need to be tooled up at all. This lad's a pussycat.'

'I was distracted,' Victor said. 'And I made it easy for you by turning up at your place of business. Aren't you interested why I was there for the second time?'

'I'm all ears,' King John answered.

Linnekin said, 'What does it matter? He was putting on a performance, a distraction.'

'The deadline isn't up,' Victor told him. 'I still have time.'

'Didn't you hear?' Linnekin asked. 'Time is relative.'

'I know who killed Borisyuk.'

'We all know you killed him so save your lies. You're going to admit what you did.' He held up the phone. 'You're going to tell the rest of the Brotherhood that Zakharova had you murder Maxim so she could take his place.'

'That's not what happened.'

'Are you going to do the honourable thing and confess your sins or will we need to convince you to do so?'

'Another day and I'll be able to prove what did happen.'

'I didn't take you for a coward,' Linnekin replied. 'I didn't think you would try and worm your way out of this.' He thumbed the phone's screen, saying, 'We have him,' when the line connected. 'Yes, Igor, we will wait until you're here. I have a feeling it's going to be a long night and I wouldn't want you to miss out on all the fun.'

SIXTY-TWO

They took him to an empty office overlooking the facility's main sorting operation. There were many huge pieces of machinery and multiple conveyer belts running both horizontally and diagonally across the space, going from one machine to the next. He had seen no workers operating the machinery so he guessed they had been sent home early in readiness, yet the facility was loud as the machines cycled through automatic processes.

Victor was pushed into a chair while the man named King John smiled and chatted with another man in armed police uniform, the driver of the vehicle that had brought Victor here. Linnekin did not follow, either waiting elsewhere for Rakmilevich to arrive or perhaps collecting up tools or instruments to help *convince* Victor to confess.

'This is the second time in as many weeks that I've been in handcuffs,' Victor told them.

'Is that right, Vasili?' King John said. 'Then I hope the last time was of the more fun variety than this.'

Thinking of the contractor's hand split in two, Victor said, 'It was pretty fun.'

'I'm pleased for you, I really am, because this is going to be the literal opposite.'

'Speak for yourself,' the driver joked, although his expression didn't quite match the confidence of his voice. He'd had had to duck and shuffle sideways just to get through the office door.

'I worry about you, Terrance.'

'Maybe you should worry about him,' he said, gesturing to Victor. 'He hasn't even broken out into a sweat so far. What's up with that?'

'I had my perspiration glands removed,' Victor explained. 'To save on showering.'

King John smiled a little. 'If I were you, I'd take this a little more seriously. Do you understand what's going on here?'

'Just because you're going to kill me doesn't mean we can't have a civil conversation first.'

Terrance and King John exchanged looks.

'Are you pulling my leg?' King John asked, eyes widening. 'Who told you that?'

'No one,' Victor answered. 'I find this line of work is far more palatable if you try not to take these less pleasant occurrences personally.'

'I honestly can't tell if he's winding us up right now,' Terrance said to King John.

'I'm serious,' Victor insisted. 'No reason why we can't pass the time with polite discourse.'

Both men burst out laughing.

'Now I know you're a wind-up merchant.' King John shook his head. 'Who the hell says things like *polite discourse*? I bet you'd be a lark to work it. I'm a little melancholy that we will never get to find out.'

'Don't be sad about it,' Victor said. 'You'll be over it before you know.'

'Listen,' King John began. 'Whilst Maxim was a mate, he was still the devil despite the harmless old man persona he perfected. So if someone killed him I have no doubts he deserved it. He's spent thirty years and more deserving it. You're just the showman who gave him his curtail call. Who am I to judge? But I'm not calling the shots. I can't stop things getting messy for you. The next best thing I can do is give you a favour. Last request sort of thing. If I can accommodate, sure. When the time comes, when you've given them what they want, what's it going to be? How do you want to go?'

'Forty years from now,' Victor answered. 'Peacefully in my sleep.'

Laughing once more, King John said, 'Ah, that's a problem because I simply cannot accommodate that.'

'Why not? You don't have to do anything. I'll take care of the details.'

'I've been around the block quite a bit, I've been in this situation many times, and I've never, ever, known anyone to be so calm about their rapidly approaching demise, let alone crack so many jokes about it.'

'I saw a fortune teller,' Victor explained. 'She told me exactly how I was going to die. I'm sorry to break it to you but this isn't it.'

Serious once more, King John said, 'Do yourself a favour and tell them the truth. We'll all have a better night of it that way. Don't do the dumb thing and drag it out for ego.'

'I didn't kill Maxim Borisyuk,' Victor began. 'Contractors working on behalf of the Kremlin did.'

'*Sure,*' came the reply, the word drawn out in sarcasm. 'The hitman is innocent.'

'I really don't like that word,' Victor said, then, 'The memory card you took from my pocket can prove it. You have it on you now. Going through with this isn't going to change what really happened and also means I won't accept any apologies when you realise the truth.'

King John began to smile as if Victor was again joking. The smile reached the halfway point, King John's lips opening enough to show his teeth before it retreated as his face grew grave. He realised the sincerity in Victor's words, impossible as they were given his circumstances.

He was about to question this contradiction when Terrance nudged him and said, 'Can I have a word?'

King John allowed himself to be guided a little further away for privacy. With the constant background rumble of machinery in the background, it was impossible for Victor to hear what was said.

When you said messy, he read on Terrance's lips, *you're not being serious, are you? We're not really going caveman on this fella, are we?*

King John replied, *That's up to the Russian. We're playing second fiddle on this one. If he says play, we play.*

Terrance frowned. *You didn't tell me anything about that when we agreed to do this.*

Don't be soft, big man. You've buried enough bodies.

Killing someone and torturing them are two different things.

I get you, King John told him. *If it comes to it, just take a step back, yeah? I'll use the pliers. You think of your wife, of your boys. You're doing this for them, okay? Your hands get dirty so theirs don't have to, remember? Now, get your game face on, there's a good lad.*

Terrance nodded, but he didn't seem convinced. King John gave him a supportive slam on the arm.

'Everything okay?' Victor asked when they returned their attention to him.

'Peachy,' King John said.

'You believe in that kind of stuff?' Terrance asked. 'Fate? Destiny?'

'He was pulling your leg about the fortune teller,' King John said, then to Victor, 'Weren't you?'

'Well, you haven't killed me yet, have you?'

'All in good time,' King John answered on Terrance's behalf.

'A few years back,' Victor began, touching his abdomen. 'I was cut here. I was cut other places too.' He used his chin to gesture towards his left forearm. 'A knife went all the way through here but it's the cut to my stomach that I really remember. That's when I realised the man with the knife was better than me. Faster. Stronger. More stamina. I was unarmed, sure, but had I too had a knife it would have just taken longer to reach the inevitable conclusion, which was him winning. And yet here I am anyway. He won and it's me who is alive today. I'm alive because the point at which he beat me, the point at which he won, I wasn't dead. He celebrated – just the hint of a smile, the first emotion he had displayed – before I was dead. That's why I'm here now. Because until my heart has stopped and no neurons are firing in my brain and I'm cold on a slab, I'm not done. So, just like him, you're going to die too.

Because just like him you're already celebrating a victory. You too are overlooking the only thing that matters. Not these handcuffs, not that gun in your hand. Would you like to know what that is?'

'Sure,' King John answered with an indignant sigh. 'What is this one thing I'm missing?'

'I'm not dead yet.'

'I don't think that was the truth bomb you wanted it to be,' he said after a moment. 'You're only alive because I'm keeping you alive until the Russian says otherwise.'

'He's making a mistake,' Victor told him. 'I told you who killed Borisyuk.'

'And I told you I don't really care.'

'Those assets were following me when you guys arrived. They saw you take me away. That's why you should care,' Victor explained. 'Because they're coming here. These are serious operators, not just gangsters. They want that memory card you have. And to get to it, to get to what they want, they're not going to be as personable as I am now.'

King John tapped the pocket on his harness in which he had placed the micro SD card. 'This little thing? Does it have the winning lottery numbers on it? I have plenty of guys here keeping a lookout so don't worry your pretty little head about anything else except what's about to happen to you if you don't confess.'

Terrance stiffened.

Victor said, 'When your guys stop answering their phones, you'll know I'm right.'

King John and Terrance exchanged looks and Terrance said, 'Maybe we should ... ?'

'I'll do the rounds, just in case,' King John said as he

approached the door. 'You watch him until I'm back, okay? You do not take your eyes off him for a second.'

'Of course,' Terrance told him. 'But don't sweat it, boss man. This one is going to be a good boy.' He closed his hand into a huge fist, 'Aren't you, Vasili?'

'I'll be on my very best behaviour,' Victor assured.

SIXTY-THREE

After King John had left the office, Terrance took a seat on another chair, sitting opposite Victor. Enormous, Terrance could not get comfortable on the regular-sized chair and constantly fidgeted and shifted his considerable weight in a vain attempt to relax. He fidgeted with his watch strap too, pushing and pulling at it as though it had just this moment become too tight around his wrist. The shifting movements in the chair became more frequent. The fidgeting with the watch became more agitated.

Maybe just a restless soul unable to relax, except the huge masseter muscles in Terrance's jaw were flexed, pushing taut the skin of his jaw and making his wide skull even wider. On the surface, a sign of aggression. The rest of Terrance's facial muscles told another story. He was stressed, not aggressive.

Victor saw that Terrance was gearing up to say something, something that he was thinking long and hard about. Something that he had thought about a lot before. He wanted Victor's take on those thoughts, so he valued Victor's opinion – the opinion of a man he didn't know.

Although he knew one thing about him for sure.

'No,' Victor said. 'I don't enjoy it.'

'What?' Terrance asked, fingers falling away from the watch strap. 'Don't enjoy what?'

'Killing,' Victor answered. 'That's what you really want to ask me about, isn't it?'

Terrance, surprised and uncomfortable, adjusted the way he sat, sitting straighter and leaning back on his chair. He didn't realise it, but it was an unconscious reaction to create distance because he was scared at a primal level. Not of Victor, of course. Terrance was scared of what he felt.

'Whatever,' he said, forcing an indifferent look onto his face. 'I don't care what you enjoy or don't enjoy.'

'But you care what you enjoy.'

Not a question, because Victor understood Terrance in a way that Terrance failed to understand himself.

'You think you should enjoy it,' Victor continued. 'You'll do what your boss tells you to do, but you don't like killing and you think it makes you weak that torture makes you feel queasy.'

'I'm not weak,' Terrance was quick to say.

'I didn't say you are. I said you think you are.'

Terrance saw this as an insult and stood up from the chair. 'Don't tell me what I think.'

'Your call,' Victor said.

Terrance interpreted Victor's response as conceding. As Terrance was aggressive because he was defensive, concession was the same as weakness. He was emboldened, his previous apprehension giving way to dominance, and rose from the chair so he could loom over Victor.

'I didn't ask for your opinion,' Terrance said.

Victor shrugged. 'You were going to, so I just expedited the conversation.'

'You are really starting to get on my nerves.'

'And there I was thinking I was being merciful.'

Another step closer. 'Merciful?'

Victor nodded. 'I could see you were anxious so I decided to spare you the trauma of working up the courage to speak to me.'

Terrance's face was flushed with rushing blood and his eyes were wide. 'You're saying I was scared? Of you?'

'No,' Victor explained. 'You weren't scared of me, you were scared of what you were feeling. And considering your watch is a fake, I doubted the strap could take much more abuse.'

Terrance glanced down at his left wrist and to the leather watch strap. A little of the stitching was frayed from his picking at it. 'It's not a fake. It's an anniversary present.'

Victor raised an eyebrow.

'You're really starting to piss me off,' Terrance said.

Probably not the best moment to request he didn't curse, Victor thought.

Terrance edged closer, still aggressive, still powerful, but he stopped just outside of arm's reach. He wasn't committing himself just yet. His orders were to watch Victor, not hurt him.

'Listen, mate. You don't get to tell me what to do and you don't get to tell me what I'm feeling and you certainly don't get to believe you know me.'

'I may not know you, but I know you worry that you don't like killing and that makes you feel weak. I also know you have a temper and can't take others thinking you are weak without overcompensating. I know you have a wife and I know you trust her and will defend her honour without question. And I also know that, despite all of this, you aren't confident to follow through on that defence of her honour without your boss's permission,' Victor said. 'So no, I don't believe I know you, but I know everything I need to know about you and it took me less than sixty seconds to do so.'

Terrance wasn't sure what to say, although his mouth was open ready to speak. No words passed his lips, which then closed as he clenched his teeth. He looked away, only for a moment, although it was long enough for Victor to understand exactly what was coming.

Fast, Terrance lurched forward, enraged, temper overriding King John's orders.

He had stayed out of arm's reach for a reason but had failed to realise that put him within leg's reach.

Victor, still in the chair with his hands bound, kicked a heel into Terrance's lead shin the instant he made his move.

The jolt of impact on his load-bearing leg took Terrance's stability out from under him.

He doubled over, straight at Victor – who was out of the chair in an instant – both hands snatching Terrance's leading forearm in a vice-like grip, trapping the limb between them so it could not block the headbutt Victor launched up at Terrance's unprotected chin. His free arm was flailing for balance as the top of Victor's skull found its target.

A man mountain, Terrance stayed standing, but he was temporarily dazed, and that was more than enough time for Victor to use his momentum to drive Terrance back until his unstable feet could no longer secure his balance and he tumbled to the floor.

His resilience was as impressive as his size, and despite the air rushing from his lungs as his shoulder blades struck the carpet, Terrance wasn't done.

With the use of Victor's hands impeded by the handcuffs, Terrance's resilience might have been enough, except the big man wasn't used to such aggressiveness. He had never been in this situation before and mistakenly rolled over so he could push himself back to his feet.

In doing so, he exposed his neck.

Victor, who never let an advantage go to waste, hooked his bound wrists over Terrance's head and used the handcuffs to strangle him to death.

SIXTY-FOUR

The handcuffs prevented Victor from being able to apply a proper choke to cut off the blood supply to Terrence's brain, so he had to focus on the windpipe, on preventing the big man breathing in precious oxygen and expelling carbon dioxide. Most people could go without doing so for a couple of minutes before they weakened enough for it to be a foregone conclusion. Terrance had no kind of exceptional cardiovascular fitness, but his size and strength fighting back meant Victor could not maintain constant pressure on the oesophagus and he lasted closer to four.

By the time Terrance stopped moving, Victor had finally broken into the sweat Terrance had expected to see earlier.

Handcuffs could not be popped open in the same way as cable ties but Victor knew every conceivable way of escaping them, although he didn't need to improvise a pick or a shim because Terrance had the key on his person.

Free of the handcuffs, Victor took Terrance's G36 from where he had left it by the door and a spare magazine from his harness. The Kevlar vest that formed part of Terrance's police uniform was far too large to properly fit Victor so he left it on the corpse.

The lack of suppressor on the rifle would have been a problem if not for the incessant ambient noise of the facility. That should disguise a few of Victor's initial gunshots.

He tested the theory as soon as he exited the office and stepped into the adjoining hallway. One of King John's guys was approaching.

A headshot dropped him before he understood what was happening.

At the end of the hallway the noise of the facility increased as Victor neared a metal staircase that led down into the primary sorting floor. He killed the next guy as easily as the first, taking him by surprise as he toyed with his phone at the head of the steps.

Whether they heard the gunshots or glimpsed their team-mate tumbling down the stairs, Victor could not know, but he was down the stairs himself before bullets began coming his way.

Taking cover behind a sorting machine, he took a moment to consider the facility space, identifying positions of cover and concealment and areas to avoid. The many machines, conveyer belts, pillars and storage all offered numerous defensive and offensive advantages for his enemies as much as they did for him. King John's guys were no trained and cohesive military unit, but if they spread out to take advantage of their numerical superiority, he doubted they could do so while covering one another. That would give him the opportunity to pick them off one at a time, using the space's many line-of-sight blocking features to ambush individuals when they were most vulnerable. If they opted to stick together – safety in numbers – then that gave him more time and space to outmanoeuvre them.

They did the hard work for him.

Despite their numbers, they were amateurs, not professionals. Put on the back foot with Victor attacking them, they panicked. No one could understand the intensity of a life-and-death struggle without experiencing it, and the incredible lethality of modern firearms meant that a firefight could easily overwhelm even the most stable of minds. More often than not, training was forgotten, discipline abandoned, and skill became irrelevant. Instinct took over as the brain failed to cope with an overload of stimuli and flood of stress hormones. Decision-making became non-existent until fear could be conquered, and so only the most macro of signals could be heeded, only the most immediate of danger was noticed. What might happen in a few moments' time was irrelevant because this very second needed to be survived.

A firefight was the pinnacle of stress. Waiting to be in one, however, came a close second. As he killed those closest to him the others could not see him, but they could hear the shooting growing louder and louder. Each time there was a lull in the firing they hoped that was the end of it, that hope being dashed when the roar of exploding gunpowder began anew.

Human nature was hard to overcome. It took regimented training that had been perfected over generations to get soldiers to behave tactically under fire and not simply hit the deck and hope for the best.

King John's guys had not been trained.

When Victor's bullets came their way, they took cover.

They backed away from open spaces and ducked behind machinery.

Yet they stayed in place.

They gave away their positions with their own fire, so Victor knew exactly where to find them. When he attacked from their flank, he shot three in the back.

He withdrew before the others could adapt, and when they did adapt, they did so from the perceived safety they felt in their positions.

They adapted by facing the way from which he had attacked.

So, his next assault was from his original direction, again taking them from behind.

He only killed one more before the remaining two gave up, calling out from their hiding places that they wanted no further part of this.

He had them throw out their weapons before ordering them to show themselves. One was bleeding from a wound to his shoulder. Victor wasn't sure if the cause was a ricocheted round or shrapnel from damaged machinery.

When he could see their weapons on the floor and their hands in the air, he shot them both.

The way they shook and whimpered were clear signs they were no longer threats, but it was just too much effort to secure them so they could not warn anyone else, and scare them enough to ensure they never revealed anything about him that could cause a problem later. Besides, Victor preferred to keep things tidy and organised where possible. Five dead with two disabled, including one wounded, was messy, it was disorganised.

Seven dead had a much neater ring to it.

The G36 clicked dry.

Victor had used the spare magazine, so switched his grip on the weapon, taking the barrel housing in both hands and holding the gun close to his chest, with the stock high and ready to swing into ...

King John himself, rounding machinery in an effort to take Victor by surprise.

He swung low in case King John was fast to react and ducked a headshot.

He was fast. He did duck.

The stock hit him in the chest, clanging on the ceramic plate protecting his heart. The plate, the Kevlar, absorbed some of the energy, but plenty travelled through to the torso beyond.

Enough to make King John stagger and almost crumple. He stayed on his feet, however, bringing his own weapon up in an instinctive defensive reaction to protect his most vulnerable areas.

Victor had expected this.

His follow-up attack went low, hitting the closest knee with a downward sweeping strike.

King John's police tactical gear included toughened polymer knee guards. But they were designed to make kneeling more comfortable, they were not armour.

Victor took his leg out from under him and he went down.

Another swing of the rifle as a club knocked the gun from his enemy's hand as he tried to align the muzzle.

He jerked his head to one side to avoid the stabbing thrust Victor aimed for his face, drawing a combat knife from a thigh sheath at the time same time.

He slashed the front of Victor's leading leg before he could withdraw it, opening a cut across his shin.

There was a hot sting of intense pain, but Victor didn't react because it could only be a superficial wound. No arteries crossed the shin bone.

He retreated to avoid more quick attacks from the knife, and King John exploited that moment to slither away and get to his feet from a safe distance.

He grimaced as he rose and shifted his weight from the knee Victor had struck. King John stood so that leg was behind him, out of reach of future strikes.

Sensible on one hand, but on the other his only good leg was forward and exposed without the stability necessary to move it out of harm's way.

Victor switched grip again so he held the heavier end, leaving the lighter muzzle to attack, and more importantly to defend. The rifle provided him with a reach advantage but the knife was much faster. If King John could get inside Victor's reach, he would be defenceless.

So Victor threw the G36, hard. Fast.

With the wounded knee, King John couldn't get out of the way quick enough and the spinning rifle clipped him on the side of the head as he tried.

Painful, but not serious, doing little more than splitting his scalp and knocking him off balance.

But his balance was compromised already and he took a couple of seconds to recover and right himself.

Two seconds was more than enough time for Victor to close the distance to where a dead guy's pistol lay and scoop it up.

'You win,' King John said, almost shouting to be heard over the sound of the sorting machines. He tossed the knife away.

'Where's Linnekin?'

'He ran as soon as the shooting started.'

'You should have done the same.'

'I don't leave my lads behind, no way. Never.'

'I respect that,' Victor said.

With hums and whirs the sorting machines quietened and the overhead fluorescent lights flickered off, plunging them into darkness.

That darkness lasted only a few seconds before emergency lights came on, bathing the facility in a weak glow of red.

King John hadn't moved. 'The Russian agents?'

Victor nodded.

'What do we do?'

'First, I need that SD card back,' Victor said, then shot him twice in the face.

SIXTY-FIVE

In the weak red light, the shadows cast by the machinery were black and impenetrable. Without the background roar of those machines in action, the facility was silent. Victor heard his footsteps, his breathing and little else. He moved with caution, staying close to the sorting machines, pivoting out to check the angles, the lines of sight, identifying the most tactical routes of approach, the best positions of cover and concealment.

With only three of them, the numerical advantage was not overwhelming on its own. But they weren't like King John's guys. These were professionals. Victor had already tangled with Hawk and that single assassin caused enough problems on his own. Three of the same at the same time was not going to end well.

They had made a significant error in shutting down the power to the facility and turning a well-lit area into semi-darkness. They must have anticipated going against King John's guys, using the lack of visibility to nullify those numbers. Now, however, they had nullified their own.

A mistake they would soon realise.

If they stuck together, they could cover one another, but the flip side was Victor would just withdraw. They wouldn't want to risk that and waste this opportunity to complete their mission, so Victor pictured them entering from different points to simultaneously surround him and cut off any escape routes.

The polite Neanderthal, Chaban, came out of the darkness in a sudden blur of movement that transformed into bright, blinding flashes of light as his shots came Victor's way.

He dropped low behind the cover of the nearby machinery. Bullets pinged from metal. Sparks flared in the darkness.

As soon as there was a lull in the shooting, Victor popped out of cover – from a different part this time – snapping his gun in line to where Chaban had appeared.

Nothing.

Like Victor, his enemy had ducked out of sight. No doubt reloading his magazine while Victor wasted seconds peering at shadows in an attempt to identify one that did not belong among the others.

'*We just want the intel*,' Chaban called from the safety of cover. 'You can walk away from here if you play nicely.'

Victor withdrew behind the machinery just as fast as he had appeared, knowing his enemy would not be reloading from a stationary position, and would be in motion, moving to a different position, in search of a better angle.

Victor had to do the same – to remain stationary in a firefight meant failing to remain alive – only his options were limited. The machinery meant solid, impenetrable cover. No matter how many rounds came his way, none would make it through so much steel. Yet it was no tank. The dense steel could only protect him from so many angles, so many attacking positions. When the other two converged on him, it was over.

'If you don't answer then there's only one way this goes.'

Victor called back, 'Tell me who gave you the order and I'll make it quick.'

Despite his words, he had to move. Every moment he stayed put meant more time for his enemies to reach him.

If he left the shielding of the machinery, however, there was a couple of seconds' worth of open ground before he'd reach anything that would stop a bullet.

Two seconds was not a lot of time to acquire a fast-moving target but it was plenty of time for a nine mil to find his spine should Chaban or one of the others already be aiming in his direction, waiting for him to appear.

No option had an inarguable advantage over the other, so he remained in his position. Had their roles been reversed, he would expect a competent opponent to understand the vulnerability of his position, of inaction, and thus expect him to move. That meant Victor's enemy would try to keep eyes on target while he moved to a more advantageous position. He would anticipate Victor dashing to the closest piece of available cover.

Which would be the conveyer belt to Victor's left.

A quick calculation told him the route Chaban had to take if he wanted to maintain line of sight on Victor's current position behind the machinery and the conveyer belt that would be the closest, best choice of cover to head to, and most importantly, the space between the two.

So, he popped out to the right – a swift, lateral movement – exposing himself for a split second. Not long enough for anyone to draw a bead on him. Not long enough for him to identify his target in the dim light.

He shot anyway.

A slim chance of landing a bullet anywhere close to on target but a decent chance of that bullet striking close enough to cause a reaction. Incoming fire was impossible to ignore. No one could concentrate fully on lining up a perfect shot with rounds snapping and whizzing nearby.

Ducking back behind the machinery, he waited three seconds – about the right amount of time for someone to draw in a deep breath to steel their nerves – and popped out again in the same way. Fast. Withdrawing just as fast. Shooting off another round. This time a bullet came back his way.

It struck the ground a little behind and to his right, telling him Chaban was as good as expected and that he was at elevation.

No more time to evaluate further because Victor scrambled to his left to pop out of cover at exactly three seconds after his last shot.

He swung his arms to the right, aiming up, catching sight of Chaban aiming down to where Victor had previously emerged an instant before the man realised his mistake.

Both shots of Victor's double-tap hit their mark, the head, but higher than he'd aimed because the man was desperately trying to drop down into cover, the first bullet hitting just above the ear, the second blowing off the top of the skull in a haze of glistening pink.

Victor then twisted around the corner of the machinery, a fast, long side-step so as he turned into the open space he also dropped into a low squat, reducing the size of the target he presented while simultaneously providing a visual distraction for an approaching ambusher expecting the sudden appearance of a full-height enemy.

Rushing closer, the waiter with the ponytail – Surovkin – took a split second to adjust his aim. Which was far too long.

Because Victor was low to the ground and his target further away than he expected, Victor's first two shots hit low, to the abdomen, not killing Surovkin but taking him from his feet.

He dropped his weapon as he fell, writhing and squirming on the floor.

Rising back up, Victor saw the blood glistening in the red light and pooling beneath Surovkin so he knew he had hit an artery. The younger man was quick to apply pressure on the wound. He might survive several minutes like that – plenty of time to interrogate him – except Victor saw the darkness shift in his peripheral vision, to his left, so snapped off a shot underneath his armpit as he darted forward.

The bullets sent his way missed their mark by millimetres, ripping the fabric of his suit jacket along his shoulder blades.

No need to look to know his snapshot was similarly off its mark because more incoming rounds followed the first volley, chasing him as he powered away, too fast a target for the shooter to track.

He dropped into a roll as he neared the cover of a conveyor belt, absorbing most of the energy that would otherwise have stripped skin from his hands and knees had he thrown himself down to the rough concrete.

The roll almost meant the instant he came out of it he sprang up beyond the wall to return fire, sending a trio of bullets at the man named Hawk, now visible enough in the dim lighting for Victor to see the outline of the talkative smoker with a sub-machine gun in hand.

The three rounds struck the metal shelving unit that Hawk, having anticipated the play, was rushing behind. Sparks flashed, bright and yellow, further illuminating Victor's enemy, if only for an instant.

Hawk went low, out of sight behind boxes stacked tight on the lower shelves. Even odds they would stop bullets or let them pass through, which was not good enough for Victor to risk precious ammunition on, so, instead, he dashed to the next defensible position, both to improve his chances of lining up a shot and to force his attacker to constantly change his approach. No one position was without its disadvantages. The more time spent in one place gave the enemy more time to identify those disadvantages and exploit them.

Hawk knew this too because when Victor had reached the cover of more boxes, which gave him a route to a line of sight along the other side of the shelving unit, the bullets that came his way originated from elsewhere.

With more ammunition to play with, Hawk was content to shoot at the boxes themselves. None came through. Only the reverberations reached Victor's back.

Sharp clanging sounds told him metal tooling was stored in the boxes. Over the roar of the sub-machine gun fire, Hawk would not have heard the same.

Despite the impenetrable cover, Victor's problems were only paused, not solved. Even way back on his first tour, being surrounded by dense walls of sandbags had felt intrinsically wrong to him, despite assurances the bunker was safe. Safe from small arms fire, yes, but not from the RPG the insurgents brought along that night when the next sentries were posted inside.

He leaned out, pivoting from his hips so his head and

arms poked into the open space and little else. Shots came his way before he could identify the position of the attacker. The resulting muzzle flashes, however, did that for him.

He waited for the shooting to halt then leaned out again, pivoting in the same way but from a squatting position this time.

The muzzle flashed from the same place, the bullets zipping over his head. He squeezed the gun's trigger three times, but Hawk was already ducking clear.

Exchanging fire in this way built a certain, inarguable narrative. Victor continued telling the story: appearing out of cover in darting motions, loosing off snapshots, ducking back, doing the same from a different position, using a different angle.

The longer he told the story, the more his enemy would believe it. The back-and-forth rhythm of their exchanges of fire; his strong defensive position; and most importantly the varied way he appeared out of that cover. As the seconds ticked on, Hawk's stress levels would decrease. He would become comfortable – as comfortable as was possible – in the gunfight.

He would try to anticipate from which area of cover Victor would appear; he would attempt to get off his own shot faster, more accurately – that would be his sole focus.

He wouldn't notice how the gaps between Victor's brief appearances were growing longer, from a second in between, to a few, to several. Hawk wouldn't know Victor was about to burst out of that cover an instant after ducking back into it, exploiting the narrative he had built that told his enemy there was a respite, a safe handful of seconds to regroup, to reload, to ready himself.

But the assassin he had duelled to a standstill in Borisyuk's townhouse had built a narrative of his own, and Victor, to his shame, had been so focused on telling his own story he had failed to understand he had believed the one told to him.

As he ducked back into cover, switched positions to the far side, and leapt out to take his enemy by surprise, he found himself face to face with Hawk, who had been doing the exact same thing.

SIXTY-SIX

The only upside was Hawk was as surprised as him, so that as they collided with each other, there was no chance for him to loose off a burst of sub-machine gun fire into Victor's chest.

They recovered at the same time, attacking and defending as the other did the same.

With his shorter gun, Victor had the advantage, which his enemy knew too, dropping the sub-machine gun to free up his hands to deflect the pistol before Victor could put a bullet into his throat.

The gun went off with the impact, then a second time as the assassin looped Victor's arm and spun him around while trying to prise it free.

He gave up that idea with the first elbow Victor whipped against the back of his skull, aiming for the vulnerable brainstem and hitting a little above with the instability of their mutual stances; turning and staggering, pushed and pulled, neither notably stronger or sufficiently more skilled to end the stalemate.

Hawk threw his whole body backwards before Victor could land a second elbow, the sudden and explosive force driving him back, further diminishing his chances of securing a footing until he crashed into the nearest wall of machinery.

The impact knocked the wind from Victor's lungs, reducing the strength of his hold on the pistol enough for Hawk to palm-heel it from his grip.

With the gun no longer demanding his focus, Hawk was free to realign his efforts, throwing elbows of his own before Victor could reinflate his lungs. He brought his free arm across to defend his ribs as his attacker had intended, giving him the opportunity free of attacks to release Victor's trapped arm, re-establish his hold, and throw him over his shoulder and onto the ground.

'I don't care about any intel,' Hawk told him. 'I do my job for *this*.'

For the second time in moments, Victor was breathless, but not witless, performing a quick lateral roll to avoid the heel stomps aimed at his head.

Flipping back to his feet, Victor blocked the punches and elbow strikes but knees made him double over. Then, as he rose back up, an arm wrapped around his throat. Before the pressure could be fully applied, he turned in to the choke to flare out and tense the thick sternocleidomastoid muscle of the side of his neck while at the same time dropping his chin. This combination meant the choking arm could not make full contact and pinch shut his carotids any more than it could flatten his oesophagus.

'So, I'm glad you didn't run, I'm glad we get to do this a second time,' Hawk said. 'Because you're good. I'll give you that.'

Temporary measures, however, because Hawk had him pulled tight against his chest and had a hand pushing at the back of his skull, multiplying the force he had to resist by a staggering degree. The assassin had all the positioning and leverage, and so had all the control.

Victor was not escaping this choke.

He had to convince his enemy to release him.

The elbows he threw had little effect, Hawk in constant backward motion denying Victor any purchase and preventing him generating any real power.

'But you were lucky the cops showed up when they did back in Pimlico.'

The whole time, the force on Victor's neck was relentless. His skull felt as if it was ready to burst with the pressure being applied.

'This might be your job,' Hawk whispered. 'But it's my passion.'

Unable to gain the secure footing necessary to enable an achievable counteroffensive, Victor lifted both feet from the floor as he gripped the choking arm in both hands so he was hanging from his own neck. In doing so, he forced Hawk to hold all of his weight, which might have been possible had he been braced and ready for it. Instead, he was bending over applying the choke, his centre of gravity compromised and in backward motion.

He tipped forwards, unable to support Victor's weight, who dropped his feet down so the soles of his shoes hit the floor; his attacker then doubled over his back, unwilling to compromise on his chokehold even when it put him so far off balance there was no way he could recover it without first letting go of Victor.

'Just give it up,' the assassin said. 'You're embarrassing yourself now.'

Hawk, on top of him, still choking him, didn't doubt the superiority of his position until Victor began to push through his feet and started to rise. Only when Hawk's own feet began to lift from the floor did he understand the precariousness of the situation.

Every muscle in Victor's lower body burned with the strain of lifting over twice his body weight all the way from the floor to full height, Hawk stubbornly hanging on to the choke as his feet dangled beneath him. Mere millimetres away since they were of comparable stature, though only Victor had leverage now.

He used it to catapult the assassin over one shoulder and send him slamming down into the floor.

Still he refused to release his choke and so Victor was catapulting himself too, but he landed second, and on top of Hawk, who both took the brunt of the impact while cushioning Victor from it.

Backwards headbutts stunned and winded the assassin before he could process what was happening, crushing the nose, breaking the jaw, shattering teeth, splitting the tongue.

Only when Hawk's throat was filling up with the resulting blood loss did he release his hold. He could not, however, do anything to prevent himself drowning in that deluge.

Rolling away, Victor used the time it took to catch his breath to watch the man die.

'Passion kills,' Victor told him.

SIXTY-SEVEN

Before dawn the streets were black and empty. With the city still asleep, no sound went unheard. Every footstep was a collision of sole on asphalt. Every passing vehicle a hurricane of exhaust. Hard to remain unnoticed at this hour. Easier to watch out for shadows, however.

At this hour, the roads were quiet. The only vehicles using them were rubbish-collecting trucks and kerb sweepers. The single other pedestrian had the crumpled suit and mussed hair of someone who had been out all night and would be in a serious amount of trouble when he finally stumbled through the front door. In his own dishevelled suit, Victor was mistaken as a fellow reveller.

'Good night?' the man asked as they near one another.

'Energetic,' Victor admitted.

'See you in the next life,' the man called after they passed.

In the railway station concourses, not even the coffee kiosks had yet opened. A woman in a high-vis vest strained and sweated as she pushed a laden cleaning trolley.

As the sun began to appear on the horizon, the façades of the tall buildings became irregular chequerboards of light and dark windows. Even as daylight brightened the sky, the city remained dark under clouds of flat grey. Colours beneath were desaturated. Shadows reduced to ghostly blurs.

He remained mobile throughout the morning, catching buses, taking taxis, walking. Once the shops opened, he bought new clothes, ditching his old ones in several rubbish bins. During rush hour, he kept on the move, knowing he disappeared into the crowds. There was a water-like quality to the crowds of commuters as they flowed and washed through the streets, always in motion as they followed the path of least resistance. If the crowd was water, then Victor was the oil that streamed inside of it but as a separate, distinct entity that shared similar characteristics but could never be fully part of the whole. Few people ever noticed him. His muted attire attracted no attention. Neither did his movements. Alone, he could melt into the background, as good as invisible.

At lunchtime, he found an eatery in Canary Wharf and sent the details to Chandi as he perused the menu. Victor rarely ordered what he had the appetite for, preferring to eat dishes that did not necessitate the use of both a knife and fork at the same time. He never liked having both hands occupied, although a steak knife did make for a good stabbing weapon in a pinch. Victor was so used to eating alone he found it uncomfortable to eat in another's presence beyond the simple vulnerability dining entailed. He was no monk, so occasionally he ate with company if he deemed there was no possible deception at work, but he could never fully enjoy those experiences.

Given he never booked a table in advance, it could be problematic dining alone. Many establishments did not want to give up a table to a single diner so he always asked for a table for two. That he did not eat his meals at typical times meant there was often no need for such a deception. On occasion, if he needed to refuel when an eatery was busier than expected, to mitigate the loss of revenue to the restaurant and reduction in gratuity to the waiting staff, he would order far more food than he would ever eat: always hors d'oeuvres, starter, main, plenty of sides, dessert and coffee. He would assure the concerned server that it was all indeed delicious despite leaving so much on the plates. Not the most tactically shrewd move given it made him more memorable, but since he would take this position only when a restaurant was busy and therefore less chance of being remembered, he considered the risk balanced.

'I wasn't sure I'd see you again,' Shivika Chandi said as he met her nearby at the Tube station. 'You look tired.'

'Let's skip the small talk this time,' he told her.

'You found it then.'

He produced the micro SD card. 'I give this to you and the task force leaves me alone?'

'That's the deal.'

He tossed it her way and she caught it in one palm without breaking eye contact.

She called out to him, but he wasn't listening.

Instead, as he walked away, he saw the same table and the same chair outside of the same bar where he had once waited for – what should he call her? – an associate. He had watched Rebecca as she had watched him, thinking she did so without his knowledge. What had she said to him when he asked her why she had done so?

Something about him being an asshole.

Despite the crude language, as fair a critique then as it was now.

TWO WEEKS LATER

SIXTY-EIGHT

Killing people for money was not a reliable way to make a living, which was why Fionn Mulroy still had a day job. Murdering the occasional person and being paid for the deed meant he could afford to travel all over the world and do so in style. Sometimes colleagues would see his social media posts from Goa or Saint Lucia and wonder how he could afford such extravagances. He would laugh off such comments, deflecting with replies such as 'you only live once' and 'you can't take it with you'.

Of course, everything was accounted for on paper if the almighty taxman ever came knocking. It would appear he flew economy and stayed in modest hotels on such excursions, when in reality he had a bank account in the Cayman Islands that HMRC would never know about, and it was with the funds from this secret account that he paid for the business class seats and the five-star resorts.

Mulroy never travelled when moonlighting – too many

risks and complications – and so most of the jobs he took meant a domestic target or a visitor from overseas.

His current mark was the latter.

Already paid in full, Mulroy had done extensive preparatory work given this mark was a killer himself. Mulroy enjoyed that part of the process far more than the execution itself. In the prep he had the opportunity to fantasise, to run through the many potential variables, to feel smug when he found weaknesses to exploit, and powerful in knowing they would never see him coming until it was too late.

The exotic holidays were nice, but it was that feeling of power that kept his CV out there for potential customers to find.

He had no middleman, no agent to leech off his talents. He dealt with customers directly and he kept the entire fee as a result. Maybe he had fewer jobs that way and perhaps an agent might have more weight behind their attempts to haggle up the fee. So what? He didn't want to be overworked. He wanted to pick and choose when he moonlighted, not have it decided for him. He wanted to take his time and do a few jobs perfectly than several sub optimally.

He used a new, clean phone for every job and disposed of it the moment the contract had been fulfilled.

It only chimed for one reason: the customer, who was a woman named Chandi.

When he received the message to tell Mulroy he had the go ahead, he got his first rush of excitement that rippled through his body like a narcotic wave. When another message arrived confirming the time and place, that wave was so intense he felt lightheaded.

He kissed his wife and his little girl goodbye before

stepping out the front door with his overnight bag. His day job meant that sometimes he had to work away from home so his moonlighting went unnoticed.

He had a lockup he paid for in cash where he kept fresh clothes, an unregistered car, surveillance equipment, tactical gear, and a range of weapons.

This contract had a few stipulations as to how it was to be carried out and so he selected what he needed and packed it into the car.

He knew various places in the city where he could stay for cash with no CCTV cameras to capture his face, so he booked a flat he had used before that was located near the target's location and checked in.

The elderly host remembered him from a couple of years before, which wasn't ideal, although not an issue that would derail his current job. He would just make sure not to come back again unless the hit made the news. Then it would be prudent to kill her, of course.

He only felt powerful when he was paid, so murdering her would provide no satisfaction. But given her age it would be ridiculously easy, so he could experiment with methodology. He had a carbon fibre recurve crossbow he had picked up on a whim at an outdoor lifestyle fair that had never been used on anything other than hay bale targets and he was keen to find an excuse to give it a proper test.

As she handed over the keys, she asked him if everything was okay because he looked a little tired.

He felt fresh and energetic, so was insulted. He smiled with tight lips and assured her he was absolutely fine.

By the time he had unpacked his things, he was enraged. Checking himself in the mirror before taking a shower, he decided her insult sealed the deal. Whether the hit made the news or not, the crossbow would be Christened before the week was out.

Towelling his hair, he entered the flat's lounge to begin his final preparations and found his mark waiting for him, an FN Five-seveN in hand.

Mulroy froze.

'Never take showers,' the mark told him.

SIXTY-NINE

A far younger man, Sergei had that youthful verve impossible
to fake. He had ambition, drive, both seemingly in endless
supply. He would still be working at a laptop when Vladimir
Kasakov bid him goodnight and back at the computer long
before his employer roused in the morning. He went wherever Kasakov went, so he had a wing in all his estates around
the country. Izolda liked him better than she had ever liked
any of his previous aides and Sergei could put Illarion into
hysterics with his energetic slapstick routines.

Kasakov made sure to maintain a professional distance
himself, however.

Working with friends was not a mistake he ever intended
to make again.

It had been deeply saddening to choke his business partner
and boyhood friend to death. Izolda still asked after Tomasz
now and again. Kasakov had told her there had been a falling
out with the Kremlin and his friend had needed to go away.

He's living in Argentina these days, I think. At this point,

I'm not sure he would come back even if we could repair relations with the government.

Thus, he never shared a drink with Sergei. He never invited him to eat dinner with the family, although Izolda would take him to breakfast every so often. The occasional yoga class. Horseback riding on the beach now and again. A champagne picnic or two.

'The Kremlin have called.'

'Is this about the drones?'

Although domestically manufactured, many of the components came from elsewhere and were notoriously difficult to source. The Chinese had swallowed up almost all the mining rights to rare earth metals and America did everything possible to stop Russia reverse-engineering technology, so Kasakov's network did what the Kremlin alone could not.

'Because,' he continued, 'everyone's going to know about the secret build-up if they keep ordering more and more components that aren't used in anything else. We cannot make such trails disappear, however much they're willing to pay us to do so.'

'But there is something else I feel we should discuss first,' Sergei said in a tone Kasakov couldn't read. 'Something more time sensitive.'

'Do I need to sit down for this?'

'No, no,' Sergei answered, stepping closer. 'When was the last time you saw Maxim Borisyuk?'

'Who knows? At some function or other a couple of weeks before he died, I suppose. Which reminds me, make a note that I need to have a very delicate conversation with his successor.' He thought about Izolda's increasing pressure to take Illarion to Disneyland. 'I'd rather keep the details to myself for now, but please make sure he knows it's really important to me that we talk as soon as a new leader has been decided on. Please notify me as soon as his replacement has been named because I will need to have the same conversation with him as I intended to have with Maxim. Which will require some groundwork first. Some topics cannot be broached with pure strangers.'

'Why don't we start that groundwork beforehand?'

'I'm not following.'

'The Brotherhood has a lot of ties in a lot of useful places, does it not?'

'What are you getting at exactly?'

'Obviously, the Kremlin is never going to tolerate you arming their enemies, but better relations with the Brotherhood might give us some room in which to manoeuvre. They are, after all, as widespread in Ukraine as they are here. I appreciate it's a delicate subject for you to stay neutral on the annexation efforts. I feel that perhaps with the Brotherhood's supply channels, we could slip under Moscow's watchful gaze.'

'I was friendly enough with Borisyuk and I would never have even contemplated bringing up such an idea with him.'

Sergei gave an understanding nod. 'Which is why it would be beneficial to be friendlier with his successor.'

'You provide the answer without the equation.'

'Borisyuk was head of the organisation since before I was born. He was going to be in charge for another twenty years as far as anyone knew.'

'I'm still waiting.'

'No one is prepared for this,' Sergei explained. 'No one

is going to have an inarguable claim to the top seat at that table. It could take a long time until a worthy successor can be decided upon. Luda Zakharova is back in Moscow and is currently in charge, and though I don't know how long she will be, I know several other important individuals of the Brotherhood joined her in London while she was still there, to discuss the succession.'

'They will begin fighting over Borisyuk's seat at the table before too long. And even should they manage to keep from attacking one another out of greed, paranoia will tell them if they don't strike first they leave themselves vulnerable to he who does.'

'I agree there might be bloodshed among the contenders.'

'There will be,' Kasakov said. 'No maybes. There will be a lot of bloodshed.'

Another understanding nod. 'Therefore, should we lend support to a prominent candidate I could imagine that being the difference in such an – for want of a better word – election.'

'And such a candidate would be eternally grateful.'

Sergei did everything in his power to hide some of the smugness from his face.

'Very good,' Kasakov said, thinking out loud. 'Let us discuss and decide who shall soon be in our debt.'

SEVENTY

'A beautiful home, Vasili, is it not?'

'More like a fortress.'

Zakharova chuckled. 'I have filled it with soldiers for the time being. They are necessary if distracting from the otherwise tasteful ambience.'

The dacha lay just outside Moscow, in Rublevka. Hidden behind tall walls and surrounded by three acres of land, the house dated back to the eighteenth century. There was so much gold and marble inside it was almost a palace.

'Sensible,' Victor said. He glanced around the drawing room. 'You seem to have settled in easily enough.'

'One of our companies owns the property,' Zakharova explained. 'Maxim was a mere tenant. Come sit down and let us discuss your future in the Brotherhood.'

Leather creaked as they both sat on opposite sides of the large, dark-stained desk.

Zakharova said in response, 'I shall have them replaced by the time you come a second time. Some proper mesh chairs, not these relics Maxim chose to torture himself upon.'

'I like them,' Victor said, using a thumb to run across the shiny surface of one of the arms. 'Not everything in this world needs to be in its most optimum form.'

'I'm afraid I don't share that sentiment. All life is progress or it is nothing at all. To stand – or in this case, sit – idle is to admit defeat. It is to give up the battle and to die.'

'As long as I have breath, I'll fight.'

'This is exactly why we will get along going forward despite my initial reservations about Maxim bringing you into our world,' the Russian said, nodding. 'I'll never admit defeat because I'll never accept I've lost, only that I have not won yet. I trust you got out of the UK without too much trouble?'

'I had some help. I may stay away for a while.'

'Linnekin passes on his apologies, as does Rakmilevich. Forgive me,' she added, changing the subject, 'I have not yet thanked you for all you did in London hunting down Maxim's murderer. It is a shame, however, we will likely never know who gave the order.'

'I'm sure you have a good idea.'

'It's true I know some people in the intelligence services, but that doesn't mean I could guess who ordered that team to go after Maxim.'

'That's not exactly what I meant,' Victor said.

'Explain.'

'It took a long time to follow the financial trail back to you, but thankfully I had Ritchie Forrester to help me do it. You were withholding funds that the property development needed. Without the funds, the project would go bankrupt, so Maxim and the Brotherhood would lose their money. If that happened, the hierarchy would make him stand down or remove him, leaving the seat free for you.'

Zakharova was silent.

'But he was about to find out about your investments, was he not? If that happened, not only would you never get to be in charge but you probably wouldn't have survived. So, you gave Maxim up to Russian intelligence to take care of the problem for you. The only thing I can't work out is how you discovered he was selling secrets in the first place.'

For a moment, she looked away and it seemed she might deny everything he had said. Then she met his gaze once more and smiled.

'I discovered nothing,' she admitted. 'Maxim kept no secrets from me. And whether Maxim or the Brotherhood lost money on property is irrelevant, certainly no one would dare even try removing him over it. Our personal financial matters are just that. The reason I betrayed him to Moscow, however, is you. His fondness for a killer, an outsider, made him look weak. It was only a matter of time until someone else moved against him. Better it was me so I could control what came next. And though I did not expect to reveal this to you so soon, the timing is less important than what we must do to secure our positions. The leadership still lacks unity. I would like you to help me remove remaining dissent.'

'I'll pass.'

'It was not a request, Vasili,' Zakharova said in a displeased tone. 'Don't let your loyalty to a dead man override your sense of self-preservation.' She gestured to her desk and to where she held an upturned palm hovering just below the underneath of the desktop. 'I merely have to tap this button and my men will be flooding in through that door before you've even taken a step towards it.'

Victor remained silent.

'In truth, I am as surprised as I am disappointed in this development. I thought you would know when you were given a good deal. I thought you would understand when you had no choice. Surely, whatever the anger boiling inside you, you understood the final walk you were taking in coming here. Or perhaps that was not your original intention, and you have truly lost control of your senses?'

'I'm not sure I ever had any to begin with.'

'It's good you've kept your sense of humour in the absence of all others. But please, humour me now and tell me what you were thinking?'

'Killing you was always my intention in coming here.'

'Then it amazes me you ever rose so far in your chosen profession.' Zakharova shook her head as she spoke. 'Because even a fool would know coming here alone was suicide.'

'I agree.'

'Had you not wasted so much time with idle chat you would have had a better chance.'

'Not idle.'

Zakharova didn't seem to hear. She was enjoying herself. 'Perhaps you might even have succeeded before my men arrived had you not told me of your intentions.'

'That's what I've been trying to avoid.'

The Russian heard that. She did not understand, however, and in that confusion, she lost her mirth. She stared at Victor in an attempt to unravel the mystery without admitting the growing sense of unease within.

Victor stared back.

With a sudden jerking motion, Zakharova pushed the panic button beneath the desk, immediately retreating a step as though Victor was about to launch himself at her.

Victor did not move.

'My guards will be here in seconds.'

Unmoving, Victor asked, 'How many?'

Zakharova gave no answer. She took another step backwards.

'Five seconds?' Victor asked. 'Ten?'

Zakharova took yet another step backwards.

'Shall we count them and see?'

The Russian had run out of space. Behind her was the grand window. She pressed her shoulder blades against it as though she might melt through the glass to the other side.

'I'd say we're past ten already,' Victor suggested, still in the exact same spot. He looked over his shoulder at the closed door to the drawing room. 'I don't hear anyone, do you?'

His continued passivity gave the Russian a new sense of confidence, or perhaps the unwavering calm unnerved her into action, and she darted forward to push the panic button a second time. And a third time. A fourth.

Victor watched as Zakharova grabbed the phone from the desk, stabbing at buttons and despairing when no answers came.

'Maybe they're busy?'

Zakharova stared at him in growing disbelief, turned and peered through the window to where the front of the dacha was visible, where guards patrolled.

No guards.

The silence that followed lasted only a moment until a soft

sound reached them. A thud. Then another. Then more, in rapid, rhythmic succession.

Thud-thud, thud-thud.

They grew louder, nearer. Other sounds adding to the arrangement. Clattering. Running.

Screaming.

Zakharova rushed to the door of the drawing room, pulling it open to reveal one of her guards rushing to her aid.

Only the man was walking backwards along the hallway, his hands up, his head shaking, face etched with terror, not even noticing Zakharova was standing adjacent to him.

'*Pozhaluysta*,' the man yelled.

Please.

Thud-thud.

Blood sprayed onto Zakharova's face as the sentry was shot twice in the head. Blinded, Zakharova staggered away, swiping at her face, horrified, terrified. She stumbled into an armchair, lost her footing, and fell to the floor.

As she cleared her vision, a blurry silhouette appeared in the open doorway.

Blinking, the silhouette came into focus.

'*You*,' Zakharova gasped.

She scrambled further away as the Boatman stepped into the room. He wore black tactical clothing, his belt and harness bristling with weapons and ammunition. He released the magazine from his Vector sub-machine gun, slipped it into a pouch, and withdrew and inserted a fresh one so fast it seemed like a magician's sleight-of-hand trick.

Victor handed the Boatman a glass of vodka and they raised their glasses.

'Wh ... what is this?' Zakharova croaked.

The vodka downed, the Boatman said to Victor, 'There are more guards. Some have fled. Others are regrouping, for when you are done here.'

Victor nodded as he returned the glasses to the trolley. The Boatman drew an FN Five-seveN from his harness and passed it to Victor. Spare magazines followed.

Zakharova could do little except watch.

After releasing the safety, Victor shot the woman three times in the head.

'I'm done.'

'Then,' the Boatman said as he made for the exit, 'let us finish what we have started.'

SEVENTY-ONE

The airfield was just outside of Zarzis, Tunisia. It lay at the end of a long dirt road that connected to the winding, dusty highway that stretched all the way south to Ben Gardane. Nearby Djerba-Zarzis International Airport handled most of the inbound flights from across the Mediterranean. A major port city, Zarzis lay on the coast in the south-east of the country. Once a part of the Roman Empire, it had existed for centuries. In comparison, the airfield had been there less than a decade. Officially, the airfield did not exist. It had no sign. It appeared on no map. The only people allowed through the gate were the man who owned it and those who worked for him. Of which, none were locals. Only employees with no ties to the area could work at the airfield, for security reasons. Near to the border with Libya, the airfield existed only to serve the mercenary endeavours of Marcus Lambert.

Once, it had been the starting point for a group of hard-ened private military contractors flying to the UK for a job that would kill them all. Tonight, it was the end point for a man travelling from Russia.

At this time of year, the temperature plummeted with sundown, the winds blowing from the sea fierce and chill. As he descended the steps, cold air ruffled his hair and seeped beneath his collar.

The setting sun flared on the horizon, sending blazing red and orange light into a dusty sky. Lambert stood alone on the tarmac, the coastal breeze pushing his linen shirt tight across him. Wraparound sunglasses shielded his eyes from the glare as well as the dust. He wore a baseball cap pulled tilted low so only a little of his face remained without disguise. In London, he had been clean-shaven. Now, outside Zarzis, his jaw and upper lip were black with stubble and his cheeks were hazy.

Victor reached the tarmac alert despite the fatigue he felt from two days without sleep. Lambert was sluggish even when rested, which was a good sign.

He smiled as Victor neared. 'The food here is like a fat man's flytrap. There's no escape.' He patted his abdomen. 'Ridiculously Moorish.'

'Clever,' Victor said.

Lambert offered a big hand and Victor shook it.

As he held his hand, the little affection in his expression disappeared as he wrenched Lambert close – sudden, brutal – and the Brit had no time in which to resist. He floundered for an instant before Victor had spun him around and snaked a forearm before his throat. A former military man, once a soldier, Lambert had grown fat and slow in the private sector. Maybe once he would have been able to put up a fight, but that fight had long retreated from within.

With strength and mass on his side, he put up a decent job of resisting until Victor kicked him in the back of one knee and he collapsed down, only prevented from hitting the ground by the arm around his neck.

'You thought you could lure me here to a quiet death in the middle of nowhere?'

Lambert had no answer. No air could reach his lungs to be expelled back through his vocal cords.

'Let me guess,' Victor went on as he continued to apply pressure. 'There's a team of your best guys somewhere nearby and you were going to drive me straight to them. You did the right thing by meeting me alone, but if you think that's enough to fool me then I can only assume you got to where you are in life more by tenacity than tactics.'

Victor walked backwards as he choked Lambert, preventing the man from finding any kind of purchase with his boots so there could be no release from the crushing force against his windpipe.

'I'll do you a single kindness,' Victor said. 'I'll break your neck to end your suffering if you tell me who paid your firm to do this, or if the entire elaborate act was merely to even the score. When I ease the hold on your throat, you'll have just enough time to gasp and tell me what I want to know and it'll be over in an instant. Use those few seconds unwisely and give me nothing and I'll ensure these last few minutes of your life are the purest form of agony of which this is merely a taste.' He paused. 'Are you ready?'

Lambert, of course, could not answer. Both hands were gripping Victor's forearm in a vain attempt to loosen the hold.

When he eased the pressure closing Lambert's windpipe

he did so just enough to allow the man to suck in a desperate breath of air.

'*No one*,' Lambert gasped in a thin, croaking voice as loud as he could muster. 'There's no team … I swear. I swear. Don't kill me, please don't—'

Victor released him and Lambert fell straight to his hands and knees, coughing and vomiting onto the ground.

'I had to be sure.'

He handed Lambert a handkerchief so he could clean himself up.

'You bastard,' he wheezed. 'You son of a b—'

'No swearing, no blasphemy,' Victor said. 'If we are to work together those are my conditions and they are non-negotiable.'

He held out a hand. Lambert stared at it for a long moment – the pain still pulsating from the previous time he had taken Victor's hand – before gripping it with his own.

Victor pulled him back to his feet.

With a finger, Victor brushed his own cheek. 'You missed a spot.'

Lambert narrowed his eyes as he wiped his face. 'So, you trust me, finally? Now you've half choked me to death, that is.'

'Let's not get carried away.' Victor raised an eyebrow. 'And you were nowhere near halfway.'

'I even got you a bigger suite than my own. This is the thanks I get.'

'You'll sleep better now we've been through this,' Victor explained. 'When you wake up in the middle of the night, you'll know for certain that little sound that roused you is not me coming to take you far beyond halfway.'

'If I'm not bounding with energy in the morning, I want my money back.'

'No refunds.'

'Okay,' he said with a resigned sigh. Then, 'I heard the Russians call you Vasili. Should I do the same?'

'They named me Vasili a long time ago,' Victor explained. 'If you call me the same, I won't answer.'

'Then what is your name?'

'I have too many to count. Only a taxi driver in New York knows the truth and he has absolutely no idea how much power he has over me. Like the Russians, you may also call me something you choose to.'

'Then,' Lambert said in a slow, thoughtful way, 'let me think. They used to call this place Gergis a long time ago, but that doesn't quite roll off the tongue, does it? I heard that's from Biblical times when Jews settled here in the time of . . . *Joshua*. I like the sound of—'

'I'm usually easy-going with these things,' Victor said, interrupting. 'But I'm going to pooh-pooh that one if it's all the same.'

'I can live with that,' Lambert said before stabbing the air with a finger. 'This area was once an important part of a certain famous empire.'

'I see,' Victor said. 'I like it.'

'Walk with me.' Lambert gestured, leading him from the runway to where his Toyota Land Cruiser was parked. 'I appreciate you coming straight here, by the way. I know this is not the most typical way you would begin a new business relationship.'

'And I appreciate the transport, both out of London and out of Moscow. The guns too, of course, were most useful.'

418

'No problem,' Lambert said. 'Happy to help. And, naturally, I'm delighted you've finally decided to join the Premier League.'

'Then why don't you tell me who I'm playing next?'

With Tripoli only a four-hour drive along the coast, Victor had a pretty good idea why Lambert had brought him here.

'Well, I figured you'd want a few days to unwind by the pool first before we put you back out there.' Lambert paused as he opened up the Land Cruiser and looked into the distance, where lights from the coastal resorts turned the blackening sky a yellow-grey. 'But, if you're already happy to lace-up, *Roman*, then I'd be delighted to tell you all about your first match.'

ACKNOWLEDGEMENTS

As always, I can't do this alone so I say a sincere thank you to everyone who has helped with the completion of this novel. In particular, my agent, James Wills, not only provides an excellent sounding board for my thoughts, ideas, and rants, but offers astute advice and insight, fantastic Hollywood-level motivational speeches, and the occasional kick up the backside in a manner that would make a drill sergeant proud. My editor, Ed Wood, never misses when it comes to his feedback on my early drafts and everything I write is better for his invaluable contribution. The people behind the scenes at Watson, Little have my continued gratitude for the essential work they do, in particular Helena Mayberry and Rachel Richardson. Similarly, thank you to all the people who do amazing things at my publisher, Sphere, especially Jon Appleton. And lastly, thank you so much to my many readers around the world whose messages of support, encouragement and appreciation make this job so very worthwhile.

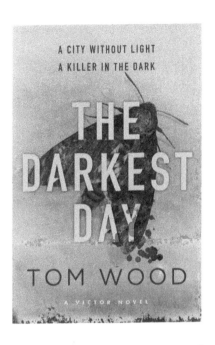

A CITY WITHOUT LIGHT
A KILLER IN THE DARK

THE DARKEST DAY

TOM WOOD

A VICTOR NOVEL

He is darkness. She wants him dead.
In a city starved of light, she might just succeed.

She moves like a shadow; she kills silently: Raven.
This elegant assassin has been on the run for years.
This time though, she has picked the wrong target.

The hitman known only as 'Victor' is as paranoid as
he is merciless, and is no stranger to being hunted.
He tracks his would-be killer across the globe, aiming
not only to neutralise the threat, but to discover who
wants him dead. The trail leads to New York . . .

And then the lights go out.

Over twelve hours of unremitting darkness, Manhattan
dissolves into chaos. Amid looting, conspiracy and
blackout, Victor and Raven play a vicious game of
cat and mouse that the city will never forget.

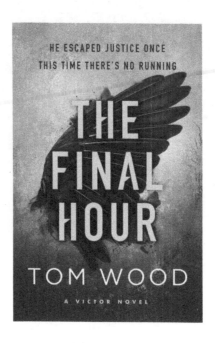

HE ESCAPED JUSTICE ONCE
THIS TIME THERE'S NO RUNNING

THE FINAL HOUR

TOM WOOD

A VICTOR NOVEL

Former CIA agent Antonio Alvarez has been
tracking a vicious murderer for years, a nameless
hitman responsible for numerous homicides.

Once, the Agency deflected him away from
his search, but now promotion has given
him a second chance to right the past.

Only problem is, the killer has vanished.

Thousands of miles away, the professional known as
Victor has stopped working – recently he began to care;
he made mistakes. But there's another assassin, Raven,
who needs his help – and she is hard to refuse . . .

DISCOVER THE MAN
BEHIND THE ACTION
TOM WOOD

© Charlie Hopkinson